The Chislehurst Murders

Francis Szeben

Hawkwood & Lane

The Chislehurst Murders

Second Edition, 2015

Published Worldwide by Hawkwood & Lane,
Chislehurst, England

Cover: Petts Wood Obelisk

The Cunningham Files:

The Chislehurst Murders
The Chislehurst Connection
The Chislehurst Avengers

Contents:

Thursday, 2 August 2012

Chapter 1

Confidence is always a useful characteristic, overconfidence usually a foolish one. In truth, Ian Green had been more foolish than useful throughout his twenty-seven undistinguished and profitless years. Only now, in his final moments, would his expendability be of any functional value.

Of course, his foolish overconfidence failed to provide him with any useful intuition, any serviceable forewarning of imminent danger. On the contrary, as surprising as the invitation to meet had been, he still turned up. Turned up alone and on time, and without having told any of his few friends - let alone his bullying, self-important and always angry father - where he was going or who he was meeting.

And once met, a somewhat weak and half-hearted handshake exchanged, he amiably chatted away about nothing at all as they walked from the car park, around the back of some shops and down a comfortingly respectable street of good quality houses.

He was just starting to wonder where they were going - as they walked up a narrow path after taking a short tunnel into an area of woodland - when he sensed something small and cold touch the back of his neck. He wondered and sensed no more.

Chapter 2

"Well, as always, I'll want to triple-check and faff about just to show what an important chap I am," Ron Patterson, the widely regarded best pathologist in south London joshed in his lilting west-Country way. "But I'd say this guy was shot around 8am, give or take half-an-hour."

"Typical," DS Gerard McAvoy smiled towards the brightly and dedicatedly attentive Trainee Detective Constable Martha Cunningham. "Another so-called expert wasting us hard-pressed-coppers' time."

"Yes, well, you know how it is," Ron smiled with teasingly false sincerity. "Start acting like all this stuff is easy and they'll replace me with some school-leaver with half a pass in double-science. Or whatever it is they take these days."

"Triple science," Martha spoke.

"What?" Ron asked.

"I think they call it triple-science."

"Oh well, in that case I take it all back. Best I resign before I'm pushed."

"Sounds like a plan," Gerard agreed. "But if you could just knock up something that looks a bit like a report first, that might be of some small help."

"Yeah, yeah, whatever," Ron replied disinterestedly while starting to walk away. "There is just one thing," he said, stopping to look again at the body. "Doesn't it look to you as though this body has been dragged *out* of that undergrowth? Kind of dragged back towards the path?"

"Eh, yeah, I guess," Gerard accepted a little uncertainly.

"Don't you think that odd? I mean, it seems unlikely he was shot in there."

"True. So what does that mean?"

"Haven't a clue!" Ron smiled. "And unlike you bright young things, I'm not supposed to do any of that intuition stuff. But it might just be worth ..." he mused, before continuing purposefully: "Look, I know you're going to be under instant pressure so I really don't want to waste your time. But it might just be worth bagging some cuttings from the stuff here, as well as some of the soil and leaves on the path and also from beneath those trees over there," he requested, nodding towards two large plane trees just to the side of the bramble bush in which the victim lay.

"OK Doc," Gerard accepted, his faith in the man just about topping his feeling that there was nothing very suspicious about the victim's actual death at all. Shot in the back of the head and dragged into the bushes. What's to fathom!? Who he was and who couldn't stand him, they were the things to focus on now. Not how many and which genus of thorn he'd got stuck in his arse.

"So what do we do now?" Martha asked as the still thoughtful pathologist walked away. With unblinking eyes she stared at the little crater of matted hair, dark blood and bone splinters. The entry wound seemed to suggest, they had all agreed, that the shot had been fired upwards from behind. So what was the significance of that, she wondered.

"D'you think whoever shot him was a bit short?"

"Sorry, what?" Gerard replied, his careful and methodical mind still listing ideas to answer Martha's first question.

"The bullet went up, so Dr Patterson said. So does that mean whoever shot him was a bit of a, you-know, midget?" she giggled, somewhat inappropriately given the circumstances.

"Well, that's one possibility," Gerard agreed benevolently while reaching behind Martha, his fingers making a mock gun. "But I would have thought it's more likely the killer just did this: bang," he grinned as his fingertip touched the back of her neck.

"Oh yeah, I guess," she accepted, without being totally sure whether she'd been dim. Or even whether Gerard was teasing her because he thought she was.

"Mind you," he continued. "If that's how it was, then they knew each other. Well, they usually do anyway, but to get away with a shot from behind like that the killer has to feel the Vic isn't going to smell a rat and knock them aside ...

Let's see if we can work out what happened beforehand," he suggested.

For the next hour or so Gerard and Martha walked around the woods and the streets nearby, trading thoughts and ideas on what could, and could not, have happened. Actually, despite identifying a few options they never did come up with any 'could nots', mostly because every time they got close Martha came up with a 'yeah, but what if?'

All of which made Gerard more and more certain that Trainee Detective Constable Martha Cunningham was worth giving time to. The girl had an interesting, if slightly ditzy and off-the-wall, way of looking at things. Not a talent senior brass always warmed to, but vital for those at the nuts and bolts end of an investigation, if only because most of them - maybe even him included - weren't especially good when faced with nuts and bolts that resolutely refused to fit neatly together.

It helped that she was nice to look at, even if the modern copper had to deny ever knowing such thoughts could exist in the hearts of men. All big dark eyes, unruly wavy hair, pale skin, delicate features and a coy smile never too far from her pouting red lips.

Of course, she was also far too posh and educated to see him as her cup of Earl Grey. Well, so he assumed without letting it bother his ego too much. When all's said and done - his full eighteen months in CID had taught him - it is best not to get too entwined in colleagues' lives. Not least as the only thing you ever have in common is low-life and the crappy things they get up to.

"OK, so what d'you think?" Gerard asked as they sat down at a rather large table by the window in a largely empty Costa Coffee, on a parade of shops half a mile or so from the crime scene.

"Honest?" Martha smiled, her lips speckled with chocolate dust from her cappuccino.

"Of course, we're a team," Gerard suggested.

"Yeah, well, I hope you're good at all this because I really don't have a clue," she giggled nervously.

This was only her fourth day as a TDC. The first had been spent following their boss, DI Charlton, around. Learning next to nothing. The second had been devoted to reading through some old case notes the DI had said, rather unconvincingly, she thought Martha might find interesting. She hadn't.

On the third, with the DI in Court, she had followed Gerard around a selection of old warehouses, apparently in search of evidence or information about smuggling. They didn't find any, but at least she found the Sergeant a good deal more friendly than the rather bossy Inspector.

And now, after nearly two hours spent focused on what seemed a somewhat incongruous crime - a not especially prosperous looking guy shot just off a leafy, well-to-do street - she was wondering whether she'd ever have anything useful to contribute. All she'd manage to do so far was ask lots of questions.

"OK," Gerard smiled, rather liking the idea of being the leader for a change. No doubt all that would end shortly - a murder was bound to get the DI out of Court duties asap. "Well," he continued, opening up his rather prissy, loose-leaf filofax-whatnot. "Let's just go with the idea the victim knew his killer ..."

"Because of the back-of-the-head hole thing?"

"Exactly that. Not a foolproof piece of evidence, but the idea of fore-knowledge is credible enough. So, next question?"

"Why there?"

"Right again," Gerard smiled, almost but not quite managing to avoid sounding patronising. "I mean, on the one hand it is out-of the-way ..."

"Is it?" Martha asked. "We saw people ..."

"That is true ..." Gerard agreed, struggling to get his thoughts into the right order. "What I'm saying, I think!" he smiled self-deprecatingly. "Is it feels like a more out-of-the-way kind of place to shoot someone than say here," he offered, waving his hand towards the steady flow of people outside, walking to and from various shops. "But at the same time, you have to get there ..."

"And the guy didn't really look like a woods walker," Martha pondered.

"No, exactly," Gerard smiled proudly. "That's the point, so why would he go there ..."

"But I thought ..." she began. "I mean, we were assuming he knew and trusted the killer?"

"Yeah, but where did they meet? How did they get from wherever that was to those woods? And why didn't he think that odd?"

"I don't know," Martha apologised, feeling suddenly inadequate, the confusion of the evidence and ideas whirring in her head.

"Me neither," Gerard smiled. "So, let's just think about the how. How did the dead guy get there?"

"Well," she thought while breaking a little amaretto biscuit in half. "He didn't have any keys on him ..."

"No, good point," Gerard offered, freeing a separate sheet which he labelled TTD.

"It was?" Martha replied, crumbs of biscuit falling from her surprised smile.

"Yeah, keys could have been taken by the killer. So, we need a check of all the cars in that road ..."

"Birchwood?"

"That's the one!" Gerard smiled. "If both parties drove there, which is logical enough, then they'd have parked as close to the tunnel as they could. If they did there should be one car left over."

"Oh yeah," Martha agreed without any conviction. "And if they didn't both drive, or at least, didn't both drive there?"

"OK, go on: options."

"Er, right. Victim drives, killer doesn't. Killer leaves in the victim's car."

"That's one," Gerard nodded, writing the thoughts down in a neat hand on yet another fresh sheet.

"Or the killer brought him here in his car."

"If they knew each other, that's a definite possibility ..."

"Or maybe the victim didn't drive ..." Martha pondered while gazing out the window.

"So how'd he get here?"

"There?" Martha suggested, pointing across the square to Petts Wood railway station.

"Yeah, now that is a more interesting possibility," Gerard nodded. "Also, I'm pretty sure that over the other side of the station there are a few bus routes," he added, now writing thoughts on all three sheets in quick succession.

"Why is that more interesting?" Martha asked.

"Because it's something other people might remember. Two people in a car won't get remembered that easily. On the other hand, two people walking down that road ..."

"Birchwood," Martha smiled, having found a role.

"Birchwood, Birchwood," Gerard repeated, trying to make the name stick. "So, two people walking along Birchwood Road towards the tunnel ..."

"If they walked from here," she interrupted, her mind calculating. "That's getting on for ten minutes. So what's that, maybe a hundred, hundred and twenty houses?"

"Something of that sort, but I wasn't thinking so much about people in houses seeing them, as other people on the street. At around eight in the morning everyone walks *to* the station. Two people walking the wrong way in commuter-land might get noticed."

"So doesn't that rather work against the theory they walked?" Martha asked. "Obviously that wouldn't have been anything for the victim to think about. But the killer?"

"Well that is true. If the killer's smart they would have thought quite a bit about how to get to the place they'd picked without attracting too much attention," Gerard agreed.

"And if we find a car then we'll not need to worry about the other options. Even so, I think it would be worth asking around. If someone saw something, great. If not, we focus more on the next idea."

"OK," Martha pondered thoughtfully.

"But the more you think about," he continued. "I mean, this is still all conjecture, but the more you look at it the more logic suggests the victim couldn't have been exactly fearful. He didn't expect trouble, let alone getting shot. Yet the killer had obviously planned it quite careful. No-way could it have been a spur-of-the-moment thing ..."

"No?" Martha asked without intending a challenge.

"Well, no," Gerard replied a little defensively. "Why, d'you think it does?"

"Me?" she replied wide-eyed. "I'm the new girl and like I said, I haven't really got a clue. I was just checking, that's all," she babbled fearing she'd upset him.

"Actually, you've done just as much as me here," Gerard smiled. "And even if you didn't realise it, you're right: we have to be careful not to leap on ideas that might end up distracting us from what really happened. So, like you said earlier, the Vic doesn't look like a woods-walker, meaning he's out-of-place in the spot he's killed in ..."

"But we don't know that wasn't true for the killer as well, do we?"

"No, we don't," he agreed. "But I think that is my point. If this was a spur of the moment, unplanned killing, it really is hard to explain why it took place in those woods. I mean, spur of the moment just happens wherever the 'moment' spurs ..."

"Eh, what?" Martha asked, pulling a confused face.

"Sorry, got a bit obscure there!" Gerard laughed. "It seems to me that a spur of the moment killing happens as the result of an argument, or something like that. But if that is right then where it happens is kind of down to chance. It happens where the argument happens ..."

"So that's not quite a question of chance, is it?" Martha thought out loud. "I mean, it can only happen in the kind of place the two parties are likely to go, independently of each other ...?"

"Yes, that is it!" Gerard agreed a little excitedly. "That is the point. If the victim had been wearing a pair of walking shoes we would have to say one option was that he was in the woods with one or more others. Then it all went off and bang. But like you said, our Vic here simply does not look like he was expecting to end up in the woods."

"So are we ruling out spur of the moment?"

"Well, we're thinking it's unlikely," he suggested. "So, if we continue to think the victim knew the killer and, for whatever reason, trusted them enough to walk down into that tunnel ... There's still another question ..."

"Why not shoot him down there?"

"Exactly," Gerard beamed. "And the most obvious answer is that the killer knew where the tunnel led. Knew places where he could get the job done without being seen."

"In other words," Martha nodded, impressed. "The killer knew the spot. So," she continued more quizzically. "Does that suggest he might have taken care not to look out of place? Might have been dressed more like the other woods-walkers? He could have made his escape through the woods if so ..."

"Possibly it does," Gerard pondered. "Although I suppose there is another possibility: the killer didn't look out-of-place because they don't just know this area, they are from it."

"Do killers normally kill on their own doorstep?" Martha asked.

"I'm not sure there is a 'normally' to all this," he thought out loud. "But I take the point - being known must increase the chances of other people remembering you being around ... The more probable scenario is that the killer knows this area well enough to see it as a good enough place to do what he wants to do ..."

"Well enough to dress so they don't stick out like a sore thumb?"

"Does all seem plausible," Gerard nodded. "Remind me, who found the body?"

"Er," Martha mumbled, flicking through her bog-standard-issue pad. "Mrs Helen, no Halina Dearmer. Oh yeah, that's right. She actually lives in Birchwood Road."

"Walking her dog, right?"

"Yes."

"How many dog walkers did you see while we were in the woods?"

"D'you mean the actual number?"

"No," Gerard smiled. "A lot will do! I think this is far too speculative even for me, but one way the killer would have avoided looking out of place would have been to walk a dog, don't you think?"

"Yeah, I guess. So does that mean it's worth us just asking people who they saw, kind of general like? If only so we can get a feel for the kind of people who would naturally have been around at the time?"

"I rather think it does," Gerard agreed, taking a long sip of his no longer scalding hot coffee. "And we should do some of that now. But I think we'll need to come back tomorrow as well. Which means manpower. Which means talking to Jeffrey."

Chapter 3

Gerard McAvoy was many things, not least amongst them a generally optimistic kind of a guy. He was also dedicated and methodical, always finding the time to think through how best to make something work. So he'd given all the time it took Martha to drive them back to Bromley Central Police Station to planning how best to put the case to Chief Superintendent Jeffrey. And what with bridge works, a lorry breakdown and the afternoon school run, those four miles offered up the best part of thirty minutes.

For his part, Borough-Commander Tom Jeffrey was occasionally able to convince himself that he was the right man in the right job; though in truth, a lot less regularly than his 'people' tended to assume. He was far too vain, in a dim rather than preening way, to recognise that his obsession with being seen to do things the right way had become a comfort blanket. A convenient cover to hide the worrying thought that doing things the right way wasn't always the same as doing the right things at the right time.

An ability to speak the new language of 'community engagement', 'policing-by-consent', 'good liaisons gather good intelligence', and so on had got him up the greasy pole. And to be fair to the man, he was scrupulously honest and personally committed to redressing the damage left over from the days when the Met was at best limited in its vision, at worst corrupt and racist in its operations. But his inability to judge the difference between politically acceptable activity and action which might actually catch a crook or two was, well, a limitation at best; a total liability at worst.

Without doubt, not being anything like as bad as those that went before had been a genuine virtue back in those dark days when the Neanderthal paucity of the Met's gene pool became public knowledge. Any smart organisation with such dirt beneath its carpets would have felt justified trusting an inadequate but honest toiler like Tom Jeffrey - until they could recruit some people with real talent. But, once that moment had arrived a smart organisation would have looked its chap in the eyes, pinned a medal to his chest, slipped a sensibly enhanced pension into his pocket and led him out the door with a friendly hand placed firmly on his back.

Sadly, for all that the modern Metropolitan Police Service might now be pretty smart on the recruitment side, its institutional instincts remained stolidly cautious. Given a choice between people under thirty-five with genuine flair, purpose and originality, some kindly dolt decided that dear old Tom deserved one more promotion, lifting him now to something around four steps above his competence horizon.

And so, Chief Superintendent Jeffrey arrived to command the large and, he had assumed, backwater borough of Bromley. For a couple of months his delusions of importance allowed him to conclude - from the various 'performance charts', 'exception reports', and 'status surveys' he insisted upon - that while his people were young and enthusiastic, they needed the steadying hand of an experienced captain to guide them.

Then, little by little - through a politely-framed challenge here, a comparison with practice in other boroughs there and a growing pattern of him being told of decisions rather than asked for them - he started to get the disagreeable feeling that rather too many of his young and enthusiastic people were a good deal sharper and subtler than he was comfortable with.

More and more often he found that, in contrast to all his previous experience, his extended homilies about reform and modernisation actually drew suggestions for change. And then that his always balanced responses about needing evolution not revolution got greeted with wry smiles and much behind-hands whispering. It was all becoming most troublesome.

"Sergeant, I do understand your enthusiasm. We need that in the Modern Police Service ..." One of the Chief Superintendent's infuriating habits was a grandiloquent way of talking in proper nouns.

"But we must never forget that the public are our masters in all that we do. It is their expectations that count ..." A second was a random and usually quite fallacious claim to possession of unique insight into the wants and not-wants of the law-abiding majority.

"And I rather think they would like you to work just a little more with what you have, before we drag other of Our People away from Making London Safer for Londoners, where Londoners right now includes a rather large number of those we might otherwise think of as non-Londoners, as you of course know," he smiled, proud of his way with words.

"Yes Sir," Gerard nodded, his body rigid, his concentration all going into the related challenges of trying to offer solely logical reasoning while controlling the nerves he always had in the presence of senior brass. Notwithstanding the common view of this particular specimen of the species. "But with respect ..."

Tom could not help but flinch when he heard that phrase, suspecting, even when not justified in doing so, that it lied.

"... we're not really talking about either / or here. We have spent time today talking to people in the area. Trying to find out if anyone saw the deceased or, indeed, anything else that might be significant. So far we've come up with nothing."

"Yes, but you've still got the pathologist's report to come and SOCO have only given you their first observations. So you see Sergeant ..."

"Hello Sir, sorry I'm late," spoke the confident voice in the confident possession of Detective Inspector Rosemarie Charlton as she calmly closed the door behind herself and walked over to the Chief Superintendent's desk, dragging a chair behind her. "McAvoy, Cunningham," she nodded to her little team.

"Ma'am," the little team replied in perfect harmony.

"Rosie," Tom smiled, just a trace of supplication in his eyes. Just like many faux-modern men, he always tried too hard to pretend he was comfortable amongst clever and determined women. With the result that more often than not he resembled a hapless child hoping his nanny will convince his mother that the broken vase wasn't really his fault.

"Sir," the DI smiled back. "So, I've picked up the gist from Superintendent Mitchell, but perhaps you'd be so good as to let my Sergeant bring me right up to speed."

For a fleeting nanosecond poor Tom thought he'd heard a question mark. Well, maybe he did, but it was instantly obvious that what he thought was not uppermost in Gerard's mind.

With his confidence buoyed, as often it was, by Rosie's presence, Gerard ran quickly through why - in addition to following the traditional line of identifying the victim and then any likely enemies, etc. - it seemed possible that the killer himself could have been seen. Yet not seen, because far from looking out of place he was very much of the place.

Of course, he went on - recognising the telling objection Jeffrey hadn't offered, but which he knew his boss would - a lot of vague information about, in effect, a lot of innocent people who just happened to be around at the time of a murder could end up being more distracting than useful. But this murder had to have been planned. It seemed too implausible to think it was a crime of passion that couldn't wait for a better time or location.

Meaning the killer must know the area and have believed they could easily blend into it. Meaning, there was a possibility that the killer was - or was once - local. They could even be out and about doing whatever tomorrow. And in answer to Rosie's question about what he thought was the most likely 'out and about thing' someone could do to blend in, Gerard replied: dog walking.

"So are you saying you want to flood the area with uniform to stop dog walkers Sergeant?" Chief Superintendent Jeffrey asked with uncomprehending incredulity.

"And others Sir. We need to see if any commuters walking to the station saw anything ..."

"I'm sure they'll be only too pleased to miss their trains for that," Tom butted in sarcastically, regretting his gracelessness instantly.

"Of course, so it'll be a case of walking with them, showing them the victim's picture. Did you see this man? Did you see anything else ...?"

"Sir," Rosie began with calm and calming assurance. "As with all delicate investigations, we need to think a moment about what the public would expect. They, as you often and rightly say, are our masters ..."

Martha coughed rather shrilly into her hand to cover an uncontrollable gasp of mirth.

"... and I rather think they would like to see us there with them. Making them feel safe. They must know by now that *something* has happened, so they would surely think it odd if we were not around, asking questions, gathering information. So long as we don't massively inconvenience them, they'll be happy to help. If only to keep their very respectable area just that. Or put another way," Rosie suggested more darkly. "If we don't show a few determined faces tomorrow we're not really going to have very much to show the press, are we?"

"Oh Lord, have they been on already, I didn't think we'd ..."

"No, no press release yet. I believe Superintendent Mitchell is thinking of something low-key with the locals tomorrow afternoon. But as you know from all your years of experience Sir ..."

Martha's second bout of coughing was now echoed by Gerard's.

"... bad news has a habit of travelling around regardless. Often as not twisting itself into confusing little spirals which end up spinning our Fear of Crime stats into a bit of a tizzy."

"Yes, they're not good this month," the Borough-Commander nodded, feeling momentarily comfortable in a piece of process he actually understood. A comfort he rarely found in the messy business of investigating crime.

"So, I would think we'll need a dozen uniform ..."

"Ten, for four hours."

"OK Sir, ten it is. I'll sort that with Superintendent Mitchell. And I thought I might borrow the other two TDCs ..."

"Is DCI Harris around?"

"I wouldn't have thought so, Sir. It's a bit after five now."

"OK," Tom sighed wearily. "You can sort that with him in the morning."

"Happy to do that, Sir," Rosie smiled. "Although it'll have to be after-the-fact, won't it. We will want to get there for 7am. Quick briefing and start ..."

"Oh yes, of course, eh ... I'll have a word with Bert when he gets in then. OK, well ... Well done Rosie, it's good we've sorted this out. Got our strategy and plan in place," the Chief Superintendent smiled, for a moment looking as though he truly had convinced himself he'd played the star leadership role (again) until Martha's third bout of curiously unnatural coughing interrupted his self-assurance.

Chapter 4

It was a little after 9pm when Martha got home, her mind abuzz after the most interesting and rewarding day at work she'd ever known. She felt a curious mixture of exhilaration and tiredness. As she took a quick shower and readied herself for bed, she replayed excerpts from the investigation. Then, sat down with a glass of milk and a few oatmeal biscuits, she took out her notepad and tried to make her own summary.

No sooner had she started than she resolved to copy Gerard and get herself some kind of loose-leaf notebook. His ability to organise information into different lists was, she had quickly realised, truly impressive. He might look a bit dim, she giggled ungenerously, but there was no doubting his eye for detail.

Then again, all of that would have been as nothing but for the DI. The speed with which she had drawn stuff together had been impressive. Immediately after the meeting with the Chief Superintendent, the three of them had sat down for no more than ten minutes to review what had been done and what needed to be done before the morning. Following which: the DI went off to organise the manpower, transport and other stuff they would need the following day; Gerard went down to see if the Scene of Crime guys had anything more to offer; while she was sent off to sweet-talk the pathologist.

A couple of minutes before 7pm they sat down again in the DI's office - with a pot of freshly brewed coffee and a large bar of Fruit'n'Nut - and went piece by piece through what they knew and what they thought.

With little hesitation, the DI accepted that the most plausible background to the murder was: a) that the victim knew and felt no reason to fear his killer; and b) that the killer knew the killing ground reasonably well. In fact, she no sooner accepted those arguments than assumed them for her own. So, tomorrow, she'd said, we need to get in there and get to know that ground as well as him.

They were then interested in the preliminary findings Ron Patterson had shared with Martha. The victim was, according to the pathologist, not exactly in the peak of physical condition. He had poor skin, nails, teeth and gums, all suggesting a poor diet. Plus traces of cannabis and amphetamines in his blood. Beside cannabis, his teeth and the stains on his fingers suggested he was a heavy smoker. Yet neither cigarettes nor a lighter nor matches had been found on or near him.

Nor did he carry any identifying evidence. In fact, all he had on him was a £10 note and £5.37 in change, all in one pocket of his jeans. Plus, a somewhat battered mobile phone with a new and unused pay-as-you-go SIM card. No contacts, calls or texts were stored in the phone or on the card.

On top of which, Patterson was now even more convinced that the body had been moved. There was plenty of earth and leaf-mulch in his hair and around the wound, but the blood beneath was already dried, suggesting he might have been dragged a little way, feet first, a good two hours at least after being shot.

Why questions also had to be attached to the victim's small collection of possessions. The DI and Gerard both felt it was highly likely - to the point of certainty - that some of the guy's stuff had been taken. So why not all of it? The answer to that had seemed obvious to Martha: to slow us down. But why, Rosie had shot back.

Gerard had said that the SOCO guys had found two distinct sets of prints on the phone, but none at all on the card. Those prints had been fed into the police database, but the DI felt sure neither would have belonged to the killer. If they were careful enough to insert a new SIM without prints they were hardly likely to make a mistake with the phone.

But why bother with a new card, Martha had asked. No card or a new card, they were both as obvious as each other. That is a fair question, Rosie had accepted (a little patronisingly, Martha had thought); in fact, why leave the phone at all?

After a short break, during which the DI managed to find yet another bar of chocolate, Whole Nut this time, to go with another pot of really good coffee (the lady had style, Martha smiled) they had speculated on the key question: motive.

They had all agreed that money was unlikely. Sure, if the guy had been carrying £15,015.37 then leaving a few quid might have been easy enough. But there was nothing in Patterson's summary of the victim's health to suggest he was at all well-to-do. Something to do with drugs was a possibility. Perhaps he'd fallen into too much debt, but the area wasn't at all known for dealing. So why there?

They bounced that underlying question around and around: why did the victim go to those woods? Whatever the specifics of any eventual answer, they concluded it had to be because the killer invited him: nothing else could make sense.

Which pretty much brought them full-circle. Someone wanted the guy dead (obviously) and yet seemed trusted enough to get him to a somewhat out-of-the way spot that he knew - but in all likelihood, the victim didn't - to do it. And it seemed clear enough that the killer had intended for the body to be found. Regardless of whether they had moved it, the plain fact was no attempt had been made to hide it, let alone bury it.

That, the DI had suggested, pointed against a drug-related killing. Evidently, those came in two types. Killings that were meant as some kind of warning were always committed where those supposed to get it would see it. Those that were just the disposal of unwanted baggage, however, rarely left a trace, let alone a body.

Yet, one thought lingered for Martha, one she'd not found the right moment to share with either the DI or Gerard. Surely, by leaving the body to be found the killer was making a statement, leaving a message of sorts. But, apart from poor Halina Dearmer, the only people who were going to get it were them, the police. Did that mean anything?

Friday, 3 August 2012

Chapter 5

"Morning Macca. And a fine one it is too."

"Well I'll be," Gerard smiled, stretching himself as he got out of his car, "Mitch must think this is serious if he's made you get out of bed this early."

"Thought I'd just make sure that boss of yours doesn't snaffle any more of my good young PCs!"

When Gerard had been a young PC, Sergeant Keith 'Wilco' Wilkins had been his Skipper. And a fairer bloke it was hard to imagine. He looked - and for that matter, acted - much older than his forty-something years. But that was perhaps the inevitable result of living in a small house with five ever-demanding daughters. Gerard had met Mrs Wilkins a couple of times and she, just like her husband, seemed to be unfailingly happy, helpful and busy.

That said, for all that the Sergeant always seemed to be on the side of his PCs - certainly in front of brass - if you fouled up you knew about it. You knew about it in none-uncertain yet cleverly optimistic terms. The man's favourite coda to any telling off was always: right, so you won't do that again will you!

No doubt some had. Indeed, one of Gerard's little cohort had been shown the door labelled 'Suitable for Further Training' after less than a fortnight. But, that seemed to be Wilco's true and uncanny talent: he could tell who would make it and who had no chance within an hour. Rumours were that he'd mellowed over time. That back in the day an hour was all you got, with those he considered useless on the train back to Hendon by minute the sixty-first. Now, the kinder - 'investing in our people' - Met liked him to spin things out for a while longer. But no-one ever doubted his judgement.

All that said, he was a sensitive old soul. And increasingly so about his age. Mostly because, Gerard had spotted a while back, the bloke really had no idea what he'd do with himself once his thirty-five years were up, which would probably coincide with the last of his girls leaving home. He'd been what he wanted to be - a good and always busy husband, father and Sergeant - for so long, he couldn't really imagine how he and Mrs W would fill their time on their own.

"You've heard she's taken Hartley and Kandola then," Gerard nodded, taking the Sergeant's outstretched hand as they met by the large and somewhat overly-obtrusive white van with its cargo of fresh-faced, but not exactly bushy-tailed, young coppers.

"Of course," the Sergeant smiled. "Not that I blame her at all. She's alright, your boss, in my view. Picks good people and lets them get on with the job ..."

"Absolutely right on first part Skip!" Gerard agreed proudly.

"Hmm, what could I have been thinking?" Wilco mused wryly, continuing. "They'll do OK though, Hartley and Kandola. She'll never be as clever as Cunningham, but if it's action you want, she's your girl ... although she doesn't always stop to think first!" he confided. "But then the boy's not bad for that. Well, some of the time anyway, other times he looks lost in some faraway world of his own. But he's got a good, logical brain. Reminds me a bit of you actually," he smiled. "Well, you'll be the judge now, but I do think it would be good if you could spare him a little time. He's also handy with all that computer gobbledegook ..."

"Computer gobbledegook," Gerard repeated. "And they say the old don't move with the times!"

"Remind me, Detective Sergeant," Wilco teased while simultaneously staring daggers at two young PCs fooling around as they got out of the van. "How did we manage to recover that long and detailed report on the lead thefts?"

"I spent a weekend typing it up again," a duly embarrassed Gerard grinned.

"Hey Sarge," one of the young PCs interrupted.

"Detective Sergeant to you Fletcher," Wilco snapped with a kindly bark.

"Oh yeah, sorry Skip," the clearly not in the least troubled PC Terry Fletcher replied before continuing. "Scalesy here reckons you're a bit of a Bradley Wiggins, Detective Sarge. That true?"

"Which bit?" Gerard laughed.

"No, straight-up," the other insisted. "The other Sunday you went flying past me up that hill outside of Downe. Man that kills me."

"Yeah, well, you should have seen me after," Gerard smiled. "Still, he's the man, don't you think. I'm glad he won."

"Yeah, and that Hoy dude did it again. Looks like we're the world beaters on bikes ..." the smiley, good-looking and effortlessly charming PC Charlie Scales added.

"But that's what the papers are all saying," Fletcher interrupted. "They says we's only good at the sitting down stuff, bikes and boats."

"I thought we won something at shooting?" Wilco pondered.

"Yeah, but that's worse. They lie down for that!" Gerard laughed. "Anyway, doesn't all the running stuff start this weekend?"

"Any hopes in that?" Wilco asked.

"Not sure really, not exactly my thing. Can't say I'm expecting much, what d'you say Scalesy?"

"Well, there's that Jess babe. Man, she looks hot ..."

"She may look hot, Constable," Sergeant Wilkins smiled indulgently. "But the question is, can she bloody well run?"

"Nah, probably not," Charlie smiled back. "Probably not. My guess is the Chinese and the Yanks will walk off with everything."

"Walking, well now that sounds a bit English," Wilco suggested. "We must surely have someone in that?"

"Yeah, probably," Fletcher agreed without any enthusiasm, before adding with genuine admiration. "I tell you who is gonna win, that Usain guy. Shit, he's unbeatable."

"Make you right there," Gerard agreed.

"Hey up, smarten up lads," Wilco suddenly boomed to his little force, and a fair number of sleeping neighbours no doubt. "The boss has arrived."

With minimum fuss, Rosie and Sergeant Wilkins worked out a basic allocation of the team.

PC Fletcher, of whom the Sergeant clearly had a high regard (but one he deliberately chose not to let the young PC get too cocksure about) would lead the two local PCSOs - Holmes and McMorgan - up to the railway station. Talking to as many people as possible, but walking with them rather than stopping them. Anyone who had made the same walk the day before was to be asked whether they had seen anyone who looked lost, out of place or noteworthy in any other way. Maybe with a 'perhaps walking in the wrong direction, that kind of thing' prod where it seemed appropriate. They were left to use their own judgement and instinct in deciding whether any of those they spoke to might be worth talking to again. If not, no contact details were to be taken.

Sergeant Wilkins and the two additional TDCs Rosie had taken on - Jo Hartley and Gurmel Kandola - were to go door-to-door in the road by the tunnel entrance.

The remaining five uniform - PCs Collins, Connelly, Johnson and Scales plus PCSO Gascoigne - were to wander the woods asking similar questions to Fletcher's little team.

With that organised Rosie, Gerard and Martha went to look around the area.

Chapter 6

"OK," Rosie said. "Tell me what we think we know."

"Well," Gerard began, pointing along the still roped off path. "We know the victim was found there."

"Who found him?"

"A lady called," Gerard answered slowly while flicking through his notes. "Halina Dearmer, at 12.30pm. She lives in this road here," he added, pointing airily across the railway.

"Birchwood," Martha put in helpfully.

"Yes, Birchwood," Gerard nodded gratefully.

"Right, so Mrs Dearmer *says* she found the victim there."

"Sorry, yes," Gerard agreed a little sheepishly.

"Just a small pointer for you Martha," Rosie smiled with a rather unbecoming sense of her own wisdom. "It's important we're always clear about the difference between things we definitely know ourselves to be fact, and those 'facts' we're inclined to accept because we've no reason to doubt their source. Do you see that?"

"Yes ma'am," Martha nodded without any great enthusiasm.

"Right, Gerard, you were saying."

"Yes, well actually ma'am, I think it would be good at this point to consider what Patterson told Martha."

"Oh yeah, well," Martha began hesitantly while her eyes roved rapidly over the area in front of them. "Ah, yes, now I get it," she continued more certainly. "So, you see that big clump of brambles at the top where the path splits in two. What Dr Patterson has suggested is the victim seems to have been dragged *out* of them, and sometime after death at that. It doesn't look that far though to where Mrs Dearmer *says* she found him," she concluded, copying the DI's pedantry.

"Right, OK ..." Rosie replied, her eyes scanning the area frame by frame. "So all logic says, if they came in through the tunnel - which we don't actually know as a 'fact' - then they must have walked up that path," she considered while looking at the wider area. "Unless," she pondered, looking now up a much broader track that seemed to divide the woodland in two. "You two walked around here yesterday, didn't you? Presumably, if you walk up there you reach a point where you can then come back down towards the bramble bush?"

"Eh, yes, I think so," Martha replied, adding rather unthinkingly. "Why?"

"Why?" Rosie barked. "Because we're trying to look at every angle and from here the idea that our victim, however dim he might have been, would have gone up this path, stopped and turned left to face a bramble bush just so as not to inconvenience his killer does not feel that compelling!"

"Yes, sorry," Martha replied like a scolded child.

"It's OK, I'm sorry," Rosie apologised ruefully. "But you better get used to the fact that murder cases cause tension and tension makes people snappy," she predicted. "I'm not saying it's impossible that they did just come through the tunnel, take the first path they found, being this one," she accepted, waving her arm once more towards the roped off area. "And bang ... eh, so to speak," she laughed. "But let's just check another idea."

Together, the three of them walked up the wide track which, in truth, neither Gerard nor Martha especially remembered from the day before. They found, barely twenty metres up, a narrow path which, just as Rosie had guessed, ran round in a short loop to the little junction of paths by the apparently pivotal bramble bush.

"Well, for all that we're still guessing," Gerard observed. "This feels more likely. If they came this way they would be walking down hill by the time they approached the bush. The killer hangs back a pace saying something like 'left', the Vic goes to turn back down the path, gets shot and falls nice and neatly into the undergrowth ..."

"Yeah," Rosie began uncertainly.

"What's wrong now?" Gerard asked, a little tired of the exhausting focus on something which was beginning to seem irrelevant.

"We were struggling last night to think of a reason why even a super-dumb guy would follow someone into these woods in the first place and now I've gone and suggested he took the full tour ..."

"Sex?" Martha suggested.

"Sex," Rosie repeated with unintended and unnoticed - by her - relish. "We didn't think of that yesterday, did we?"

Speak for yourself Gerard smirked to himself. "No ma'am."

"Worth asking the local PCSOs - who are they, by the way?"

"Mary Holmes and Tyler McMorgan," Martha said. "You sent them up to the station with Fletcher."

"Did I? Gosh, that was almost sensible," Rosie smiled. "I mean, at least they won't get lost. Anyway, ask them later if this area's known for cottaging. Somehow I doubt it, but it's worth checking. Right, so, where does this path lead to?" she asked, pointing up a track that seemed to run parallel with the railway.

"Can't say I know," Gerard apologised.

"Sorry, me neither," Martha added pensively. "Eh ma'am," she continued hesitantly, a haughty look of well-bred displeasure pursing her lips. "Cottaging, I mean, it's ..."

"Homosexual sex Martha, it happens," Rosie smiled breezily.

"Sorry, I get that much," Martha snapped. "Well, I think I do," she added, blushing uncomfortably. "Isn't it, you know, messy? Doesn't it leave traces, evidence ..."

"Of course, why didn't I think of that," Rosie accepted. "Ask Patterson to look for ..." she began, stopping halfway. "Yeah, just ask him to look. Right, let's see where this leads."

The three of them walked down a gently sloping track, in parts still muddy from all the June and July rain, talking over once again the various thoughts they had about a possible motive. Finding themselves increasingly troubled by the idea it was somehow a murder designed to get their attention.

"Well I'll be," Gerard mumbled, as they suddenly found themselves at the bottom of a set of steps up to a footbridge across the railway lines, the entirety of which was caged in with heavy-duty wire mesh.

"Ask Holmes and Morgan ..."

"McMorgan ma'am," Martha corrected.

"Really? Odd name," the DI thought. "Anyway, ask them. Find out why this bridge is like this," she ordered, adding to Martha's lengthening to do list.

"Suicides, I guess," Gerard offered.

"Probably, but as with so many other things, it's worth at least asking to see if there are any facts worth knowing about the place. It seems ... well odd, frankly," Rosie continued. "Although I can't imagine how this could relate to our case ..."

"No ma'am," Gerard agreed. "Unless the victim came here first intending to jump, had to give that up but then got lucky ..."

"Brilliant!" Rosie laughed. "So, the victim was a manic depressive, couldn't ring Samaritans, couldn't find a bridge to jump off, but did manage to bump into someone with a gun and time on their hands ... What did SOCOs say about the bullet, by the way?" she added with renewed seriousness.

"Well, nothing really," Gerard explained. "I mean, they said something like it seemed a bit unusual, but I'm not sure they weren't covering up for forgetting to collect it from Patterson. Still, we should get their report later this morning."

"Right, so where are we?" Rosie asked after the three of them had crossed the bridge and wandered down a narrow alley into yet another road of genteel suburban villas.

"Sorry ma'am, haven't a clue," Martha confessed. "But I guess if we keep the railway on our left we'll get back to the cars?"

"So the railway obviously runs behind these houses," Rosie thought out loud as they wandered along. "Meaning their gardens run down to it, but the only crossing points are the tunnel - if ever we find that again," she smiled wryly at Martha. "And the bridge we've just come over ..."

"Seems that way," Gerard agreed. "And then there's a path that leads the other way from the tunnel, up to the main road ..."

"Which is?"

"Chislehurst Road, but that is currently blocked because of repairs to the bridge ..."

"Another bridge?"

"A road bridge ma'am. The road should run between Chislehurst and Orpington, but right now it is shut," he explained.

"Completely? Could no-one get into the woods from there?" Rosie asked.

"Er, well maybe that's another for Sherlock and McMorgan ..."

"Sherlock?"

"Holmes, ma'am."

"Oh right, too funny," Rosie tutted.

"Where was I? Oh yeah," Gerard smiled. "We'll check ma'am. I know the road, I mean I've driven it before. Mostly, it runs through these woods, but there are a few houses near the bridge and ..." Gerard paused, thinking. "Actually, I would guess it is much easier to park there right now seeing as nothing can pass through. Park up there, walk in ..." he pondered out loud.

"Or out," Rosie added.

"Yeah, we didn't really have that thought yesterday," Gerard continued a little contritely. "Because it just seemed too far from there down to the tunnel, but that's no reason for thinking the killer wouldn't have left that way ..."

"Same for all these other paths though," Rosie pondered. "I don't see any reason right now to change our assumption that the killer led the victim into the woods through the tunnel, it seems to make most sense. Well, at least until we find out who the victim actually is ..."

"How's that going to help?" Martha asked.

"Well it may not," Rosie smiled. "But it's worth hoping that once we know who he was, we will also identify a reason why he might have wanted to come to this little bit of suburbia. On the other hand, if we find out he owned a car and it's parked by Gerard's broken bridge, well then we'll re-think ... aha, at last," she sang as they saw Sergeant Wilkins, Jo Hartley and Gurmel Kandola some fifty metres ahead. "What do you know, friends. Oh, one more thing Martha," she added. "We'll need a map of the area, could you sort that out for us please."

Chapter 7

The screaming echoed up from the tunnel as Rosie, Gerard and Martha reached the police van. On instinct, Gerard began running. Sprinting down into the woods and up the wide path ahead, called ineluctably by the never-ending and ear-piercing wailing.

"Oh Christ, oh Jesus fucking Christ," Rosie gasped on reaching the scene.

"Oh shit," Martha and Jo sighed sadly.

To one side a young, red-faced PCSO sat leaning against a large granite obelisk, crying while a slightly older PC did her best to comfort her, despite being quite visibly affected also. PCs Collins and Connelly knelt either side of the body with Gerard crouching down, horror and despair filling his eyes as he stared blankly at the blood oozing from the ugly wound to the top of PC Charlie Scales' head.

"Oh fuck no," an out-of-breath Sergeant Wilkins rasped on reaching the scene. "When, what, how-the-fuck how?"

Gurmel just stood and stared, his eyes unblinking, his face expressionless with shock.

"Gascoigne found him Sir," Connelly said, nodding towards the still inconsolable young PCSO.

"Martha," Rosie ordered in an icily calm voice. "Please ring the Borough Commander's secretary and tell her to tell him what's happened; and that I'll ring him shortly. Then ring SOCOs and get them down asap. Say I'd really appreciate it if Richard can come himself. Then ring Patterson. Thank you." Fully confident of her young TDC's competence, Rosie placed a consoling pat on Wilco's arm as they stepped across to the sobbing PCSO.

"Hi, I'm Rosie," the DI smiled thinly with disarming grace and compassion. "Everything about this is awful. But it really is important that you try to tell me right now exactly what you saw and what you heard."

"Yes ma'am," the tearful, shaking girl - barely twenty at most - said with all the poise she could muster. "Charlie ..."

she sobbed. "I mean ..." she continued, as if in a daze of incomprehension. "We'd only been talking a few minutes before," she sighed, her red eyes gazing up into Rosie's still, empathetic face. "Then I went down there, talking to this old guy with his black dog and then ..."

"Keep going Gascoigne," Sergeant Wilkins whispered.

"Yes Sir. I didn't hear anything. I mean no shot or any shouting or running or ..." the girl burst into tears again, pressing her now swollen face into the shoulder of the slightly older woman holding her, who Rosie recognised as PC Erica Johnson.

"I think I got here pretty quick, ma'am," the ashen-faced Erica insisted. "I was up this path here," she continued, pointing with one hand to a wide track that seemed to run into a fairly dark and dense part of the woodland, while gently stroking the neck of her distraught colleague with the other. "But I'd not been gone long. Like Gloria said, we'd only just left here ..."

"We'd been wondering what this thing is," PC Connelly put in, pointing to the granite obelisk. "The old guy with the black dog, a collie I think it was. He told us all about it. Seemed worried we were going to take it down or something ..."

"So," Rosie nodded encouragingly, looking back and forth into the eyes of each of the young officers now. "You were here with PC ..."

"Scales ma'am," Sergeant Wilkins whispered unobtrusively in Rosie's ear.

"PC Scales," Rosie continued without missing a beat. "You were all here for a little bit before, what, taking a path each?" she asked, her eyes now quickly scanning the area, her mind instantly calculating the awful potential of an apparently open and welcoming clearing with its curious granite centrepiece.

"Yes ma'am," Erica confirmed.

"But before you did that, you met who, the man with the black collie. Anyone else?"

"Well, we must have seen, I don't know," Collins considered. "Half a dozen people just in those few minutes ..."

"All dog walkers?"

"Yeah," Collins nodded.

"No," Johnson contradicted, as if sure she'd remembered something important. "No, there was that weird looking guy ..."

"Oh yeah, no dog," Collins recalled.

"And not having a dog stands out?" Rosie asked.

"Well, yes," Collins and Connelly agreed in unison.

"I didn't see another," Connelly added.

"OK. So, the weird guy. What was weird about him, apart from having no dog?"

"Well, I'm not sure really," Erica replied unhelpfully. "I suppose he was just a jogger, he didn't come that close so I couldn't really see what he looked like but ... Well, that was the thing that was weird, I suppose. It's a warmish morning, but it's quite shady in here ..."

"Yeah, and he was wearing sunglasses and a hoodie!" Connelly completed. "Weird!"

"Which way did he go?" Rosie asked.

"Er, I'm not sure really," Collins thought. "Down there, I think," he suggested, pointing none-too confidently to a path Rosie felt quite probably led to the caged-in bridge over the railway.

"Yeah, I think so too," Johnson added with no more certainty.

"So who took that path?" Gerard asked from his position still kneeling by Scales' body.

"Charlie, Sir," Collins and Connelly replied sombrely.

"Shit, shouldn't we?" Collins asked sharply, jumping up as if ready to give chase.

"Wait Constable," Rosie ordered. "Three things: first, remember that at this moment in time it could have been anyone we've seen or not seen around here, agreed?"

"Yes ma'am."

"Second, TDC Cunningham will want a list from you asap of everyone you saw. Descriptions, names, dog names even and third ..."

"Yes ma'am?"

"Be careful. Stay in touch. No heroics."

With a final: "Yes ma'am," the two PCs turned and sprinted up the path.

Calmly, Rosie turned her attention back to the still sobbing Gascoigne. "Now, PCSO Gascoigne, Gloria ..." she smiled sweetly. "Let's just check a final few facts please. So, I think you were saying you were the last to leave P ..." she stopped herself, grimacing with shared sorrow as she continued. "Charlie. You were the last to leave Charlie, is that right?"

"Yes ma'am, I mean we spilt up. I took my path, he took ..." a renewed burst of crying filled the air as Gloria looked hopefully along the track Collins and Connelly had just sprinted up.

"Yes, yes I know," Rosie continued softly while giving the girl's hand a gentle squeeze. "And it could be that the guy without the dog is important. But tell me, after you and Charlie parted, did you see or hear anything to suggest he'd met someone. Followed someone. Anything?"

"No ma'am, sorry."

"It's OK," Rosie nodded kindly. "And what about you Erica, who did you see?"

"Hmm," she thought, concentration not coming easy. "Well, I passed a guy with a small white dog, like in the Cesar adverts. He was walking down towards here, said he hadn't been in the woods yesterday. Then there were three women I saw, but didn't speak to. They were a way further up the path. Two were going one way with a pair of large, beige dogs, labradors I think. They stopped a moment to talk to this other woman who had a shaggy-looking dog on a lead. She was heading back towards the railway I guess. They seemed to know each other, women and dogs."

"OK, and that was it?"

"Yes, I think so."

"Alright, thank you," Rosie smiled, patting Erica's shoulder comfortingly.

"Ma'am, there was one other," Gloria began. "I spoke to this very pretty girl with a really cute little brown dog ..."

"She was walking where?"

"Eh, not totally sure. I kind of almost bumped into her as I started to walk back down."

"Gloria, why did you decide to come back so soon?" Sergeant Wilkins asked.

"I ..." Gloria started before beginning to sob once more. "I was just gonna see how Charlie was doing ..." she managed to say before burying her face into Erica's shoulder.

"They were, you know ..." Erica nodded sideways towards her distraught colleague while looking intently yet sadly into Rosie's eyes.

"Ah," Rosie nodded, understanding instantly. "OK Gloria, listen. That has all been really, really helpful," she smiled while noticing Martha rejoining them. "Will you just wait here for a moment please, I just need to sort a couple of things then we'll see about getting you home, don't you think Sergeant?"

"Yes ma'am, of course," Sergeant Wilkins agreed with alacrity.

"Well?" Rosie asked Martha as they, with Gerard and Wilco, walked a few paces away from the scene.

"SOCOs and Dr Patterson are on their way ..."

"Richard?"

"Yes, Mr Bartholomew is coming. He'll probably be first, he was on his way in ..."

"And Jeffrey?"

"Not sure, I left the message. Didn't hear again."

"OK, I'll ring him in a moment. Seen any of the others?" Rosie asked before, as if on cue, seeing an obviously whacked Collins and Connelly walking up the main path from the tunnel with PC Fletcher, PCSOs Holmes and McMorgan following a few paces behind. Their sombre faces said they knew.

"Terry Fletcher and Scales were very close, ma'am," Wilco noted.

"Thank you Sergeant," Rosie smiled. "And by the way, did you know about Scales and Gascoigne?"

"No. Well not as anything official. Then again, we always try not to get ahead with that sort of thing. Once it's official they have to be kept apart ... Yeah, well, guess that's not such a silly idea," he accepted, looking back to the still inconsolable Gloria.

"Sorry ma'am, no trace," Collins spoke with clear regret.

"Don't be, Constable," Rosie insisted. "You tried. And from now till it's done, we'll all try. We'll chase every lead ... Terry," she all-but whispered now on catching Fletcher's sad gaze. "I am so very sorry. Please," she smiled comfortingly while stepping aside. "You'll want to see your friend. And perhaps have a word with Gloria."

"Thank you ma'am," Terry Fletcher replied, all the fun-loving optimism of thirty minutes earlier now erased from his eyes.

"Sergeant," Rosie began, her attention now focused on the sad and enquiring eyes of PCSOs Holmes and McMorgan. "Would you be so good as to explain ..." she asked, her resolve suddenly gone.

"Of course ma'am," Wilco nodded with instant understanding.

"So, what do we think?" Rosie asked once alone with Gerard and Martha.

"Well apart from being a hideous fucking mess," Gerard replied, his thoughtfulness making his words sound almost philosophical. "I think it's connected ..."

"Me too," Martha put in instantly, confidently.

"Why?"

"It's why we were brought here," Gerard suggested.

"That's my idea too," Martha agreed. "You know, yesterday, when you two were talking about some murders being meant as messages, I couldn't help thinking: so who's this aimed at ..."

"And?" Rosie asked.

"Us. The killer obviously wanted the victim dead. By why here, where's the benefit in that? The only answer that makes sense is to get lots of us here today ..."

"So you think the killer is some kind of cop-hater?"

"I don't know that," Martha replied confidently. "I mean, we cannot know that, can we? Not yet," she suggested. "All I'm saying is, Charlie wouldn't be dead but for yesterday's killing."

"I agree with Martha," Gerard put in. "Of course, if we're right, the question now is why ... why him?"

"Yes," Rosie nodded pensively. "And the worry is where that question might lead."

"Sorry ma'am?" Gerard asked, confused.

"Well, if the killer was after Charlie, then there has to be a reason. And if we work at it long enough, we should find it. In a past arrest or whatever ..."

"But if it was random ..." Martha gasped, as if appalled by her own thoughts.

"Exactly," Rosie agreed reluctantly.

"Yes, well," Gerard nodded slowly, thoughtfully. "But yesterday's killing, that can't have been random. No way. We need to find out who that victim was ..."

"Indeed," Rosie acknowledged. "Right, look I'm going to have to talk to Jeffrey. While I'm doing that I think you two could usefully complete a quick de-brief of the whole team. Involve Hartley and Kandola, we need to get them fully engaged now. I want a summary of the people seen, identifying details, etc. Best to get that before memories start to go fuzzy."

Chapter 8

"Yes Sir, a totally awful situation," Rosie acknowledged.

"I've spoken to the Assistant-Commissioner Ops ..."

"Good. It would really help if the Yard could take control of the media side of things ..."

"Detective Inspector," Chief Superintendent Jeffrey snapped nervously. "The AC-Ops and I think we need more than just a bloody press officer ..."

"Sorry Sir?"

"Detective ..." Tom began sharply before shifting into his more creepy, oleaginous empathy voice. "Rosie, this is gun crime. Probably organised. Possibly black on black ..."

"What!" Rosie gasped. "What are you talking about?"

"PC Scales was black, wasn't he?"

"Yes, and?"

"So it could be racist, or some gang thing, or ... Well, like I said, I've spoken to AC-Ops and he's now talking to Trident ..."

"Trident!" Rosie near-on screamed. "Sir, we have absolutely no reason whatsoever to think Scales was murdered because he was black ..."

"And therefore no reason to believe he wasn't," the pompous Borough-Commander replied, using his favourite and infuriating 'well, if you cannot disprove a negative' style of warped logic. "Now, you need to stop, think and act sensibly here DI Charlton. You're young and keen and that's great. But this is a major crime and I don't have to tell you there's an Olympics on ..."

"What's that got to do with it?" Rosie rasped, additionally bridled now by Jeffrey's needless and tactless reference to her age, a numerical fact about which she was, in truth, becoming increasingly paradoxical: irritated whenever forced to admit her twenties were fading in the rearview mirror of life; infuriated when anyone treated her like she was still in her teens.

"Everything Rosie. Every-Bloody-Thing. Everything! We won't just have the press crawling all over this, the Mayor will want briefing, Number 10 as well ... probably that Coe character too. The Commissioner's got manpower probs left, right and centre so we need this cleared up and we need it cleared up today ..."

"What!" a now completely exasperated Rosie cried. "This is a murder investigation Sir, not a hundred metre dash. We're gathering all the evidence we can from the scene, collating what we saw and next we'll try to find any members of the public who might have seen ..."

"You're still out in those woods!" Tom cried with genuine incredulity. "How do you know the bloody killer isn't still there?"

"That's the fucking point, Sir," Rosie replied sharply. "If he's still here we'd rather like to catch him before he kills someone else!"

"How do you know it's the same killer?"

"Well obviously I cannot know that for certain," Rosie continued with the same pent-up edge in her voice. "But first impressions suggest a very similar calibre weapon and whilst we can't be sure until the bullets have been matched, the odds on the two murders not being connected are surely very slim ..."

"Well I wouldn't know ..."

"No Sir, you wouldn't," Rosie snapped, the many past jibes she'd heard about Jeffrey's total failure during a year in CID adding additional fuel to her frustration over the man's seeming lack of support or empathy for the investigation at hand. "What we need to do right now, Sir, is collect any and every scrap that might help us identify who was in these woods with us today. We saw a lot of people, one of them was the killer ..."

"DI Charlton ..."

"... obviously, the chances of success with that aren't great. But we'll give it a go for an hour or so. Then we'll piece together who saw what, by which time we should be able to compare provisional findings from SOCO and the pathologist ..."

"Rosie," Tom tried again.

"... maybe we'll get an ID on yesterday's victim. Then it's hard detective work, trying to find connections, hypothesise motives, test them, all while pulling in all the public intelligence we can get. So, the Yard's going to handle some press stuff. Yes?"

"TSG will be here in an hour."

"TSG?" Rosie mumbled uncertainly, as if trying to remember the details of a faded dream.

"The Tactical Support Group, they're only based in Lewisham ..."

"I know who they are," Rosie rasped on realising she wasn't leaving a misty reverie but living a real-life nightmare. "What the fuck do they know about ..."

"AC-Ops thought ..." Tom began, hurriedly shifting his focus. "AC-Ops and I thought, what with all the attention and pressure we'll get we need ... Well, we need manpower, Rosie. There will be a dozen of them."

"A dozen!" Rosie exclaimed. "To do what exactly? Sir!"

"Why that's for you to decide," the Borough-Commander offered, trying to pass his personal panic off as an act of largesse. "They're coming to help us Rosie ..."

"Are they now. And their experience with murder ... No, let's make that serial murder. Their experience with that is what?"

"Rosie, I fear you're in danger of letting yourself down here," Tom replied condescendingly. "Now, I need to ring PC Scales' family, not exactly a fun job. Meanwhile, you need to be back here for half ten to meet Inspector O'Neill from TSG."

"Yes Sir," Rosie sighed, "I know him."

Chapter 9

"Ma'am?" Gerard smiled uncertainly as the DI returned to the crowd still gathered around the granite obelisk.

"Probably best not to ask, Gerard," Rosie replied, her lips still thin and pursed.

"Guessed so. Wilco got a call from Superintendent Mitchell ..."

"Already?" Rosie replied, deflated. "So, I guess they're back to base?"

"Er, well," Sergeant Wilkins smiled on joining them. "It really wasn't a great line. I think what the Super meant was ..."

"Sergeant," Rosie insisted concernedly. "I don't want you ..."

"Ma'am," Wilco interrupted. "Neither Mike nor I are quite as dumb as we look ..."

"Mmm, well I wouldn't quite go that far ..." Gerard put in, with just the right touch of levity, receiving an un-Sergeant-like elbow in the ribs for his trouble.

"We'll put in another hour or so, see if we can learn anything," Wilco suggested. "But perhaps you could ..." he continued in something barely above a whisper. "Gascoigne and Fletcher ..."

"Yes, of course, I'll take them back," Rosie smiled, warmed by the feeling of herself as some kind of protected niece, Sergeant Wilkins as a favourite uncle. Looking to Gerard she asked: "Have you got all you need?"

"Ah, well," he began, his eyebrows arched ruefully. "Not exactly a detailed set of notes ..."

"Sorry ma'am," Wilco apologised. "Piss-poor to tell the truth, but who could have known ..."

"Well, to be fair Sarge," Gerard continued. "Young Holmes has got us something." Turning to Rosie he explained: "One person she spoke to mentioned seeing a guy who sounds, superficially at least, like yesterday's Vic. It was a little before eight and he was standing outside a shop ..."

"Which wasn't going to open for another hour ..." Rosie thought.

"Exactly. And he was smoking."

"But we didn't find cigarettes or a lighter ..."

"No ma'am," Gerard agreed. "I thought I'd go up there and have a wander round, might be nothing ..."

"OK," Rosie nodded. "And other than that?"

"Nothing much. The guys in here saw just over a dozen people walking dogs of various sorts, plus 'weird guy' of course. Kandola's drawn up a list. He's quite organised ma'am, with notes and things ..."

"Well coming from you, that is praise," Rosie smiled. "Ah," she continued, her attention drawn down the main track. "Here's Richard ..."

"Right, well I'll get on ma'am," Wilco suggested. "I'll leave Gascoigne and Fletcher then?"

"Of course," Rosie nodded. "And Keith ... thanks."

Rosie and Gerard watched in silence as the Sergeant walked across to have a quiet, comforting word with Terry Fletcher and Gloria Gascoigne. The two of them still looked so lost, almost disbelieving in their shared grief. As Wilco moved away, calling his remaining uniform team together, Martha and Jo stepped over to talk to their distraught colleagues, shielding them with intuitive compassion from the two SOCO officers now kneeling down beside Charlie Scales' body.

"Hello Richard," Rosie sighed sadly as the wan, floppy-haired and somewhat shy leader of the borough's Scene of Crime Team reached them.

"Yes," Richard Bartholomew nodded, following the DI's gaze over to the slow, almost noiseless yet achingly depressing unzipping of a fresh, opaque plastic, body bag. "Not nice."

"No, indeed," Rosie smiled thinly. "But look, I'm very grateful to you for coming personally ..."

"Not at all, of course not," Richard replied with his habitual air of apology before starting towards Scales' body. "This is just too horrible."

"Yes, totally," Rosie agreed, hesitating a moment before following him and Gerard. "Look," she continued, "I don't have much time myself. Gerard will be around, but I have to get back ... Chief Superintendent Jeffrey," she rasped, her disrespect for their mutual boss undisguised.

"I don't doubt," Richard replied sympathetically, the three of them now looking down on the dead PC.

"So, obviously," she mumbled, her stomach churning uncomfortably as she watched the body bag being readied. "We're interested in any evidence connecting this to yesterday's ..."

"Of course, of course," Richard nodded, kneeling down with his team to take a close look at the ugly exit wound on the top of the young officer's head. "Hmm, going to be hard to find ..."

"Yes, well ..." Rosie snapped sharply.

"He means the bullet ma'am," Gerard put in quickly.

"What?" Rosie asked, her mind only now registering a further unwelcome detail. "Oh god."

"It passed through, I assumed you'd ..."

"No, no, sorry, I ..." Rosie gulped, the emotion of the moment suddenly choking her words.

"But we'll work with Patterson," Richard continued. "I know he'll only be a few minutes. My instant first thought is the chances of it being a similar weapon are very high," he offered. "And I'm sorry we haven't got you a specific identification from yesterday ... Bit sluggish on our part getting the bullet from the Doc," he admitted openly.

"OK," Rosie nodded.

"What I can tell you," Richard went on while carefully lifting Charlie Scales' lifeless head to view the hole at the top of the neck. "Very similar," he mused, now working with his colleagues to line up the bag. "Yesterday's bullet is common enough, 9x19mm Parabellum and ... I take it no shot was heard," he asked, looking quickly up to Gerard before examining Charlie's neck once again.

"No."

"Guessed not. Silencer, just like yesterday," Richard concluded. "Shot from very close range if not actually touching, but no powder you see ... Now," he continued, sitting back on his heels to look at both Rosie and Gerard. "The key thing about yesterday's bullet is the markings. They suggest an unusual gun. Well, unusual inasmuch as none of us know what it is!" he smiled sheepishly before leaning forward again to help roll the prone body onto its side while his colleagues slipped the bag underneath. "So," he explained, wiping his hands down his white suit as he stood. "I had it couriered down to Maidstone. They've a couple of specialists there, good people. We should have an answer this afternoon."

"OK, thanks," Rosie nodded, turning away quickly, the sound of the zipper making her feel sick.

"Shall I carry on here ma'am," Gerard suggested sympathetically.

"Yes, please," Rosie nodded before adding: "Oh, Richard, would you have time to look again at yesterday's scene. There's a chance the body might have been covered over and then moved ..."

"Why yes, of course, we should have ..." Richard accepted. "Yes, so you want to know if there's evidence of cuttings, that sort of thing ..."

"Exactly," Rosie replied, her confidence restored by the reminder that - Jeffrey apart - she did have some excellent, committed and intelligent colleagues to draw on. "OK," she resolved while looking again at the still inconsolable Gascoigne and Fletcher. "I'll take them back with Martha."

Chapter 10

"Detective Inspector Charlton," spoke the hard, northern Irish accent in the possession of a hard, unsmiling Ulsterman who, more chauvinistically than chivalrously, raised himself from his chair to stand fully twelve inches taller than the hardly diminutive Rosie.

"Inspector O'Neill," Rosie nodded without breaking her purposeful stride towards the one vacant chair in the room, smiling warmly towards Superintendent Mitchell, her one friend (she hoped) present.

"Ah, so you know each other, splendid," an over anxious Chief Superintendent Jeffrey beamed, blissfully (or perhaps dishonestly) missing the tension that suddenly filled the space between the two Inspectors.

"Same intake at Hendon Sir," an obsequiously correct O'Neill barked.

"Excellent. And Sergeant Nancy?" the Borough-Commander asked, smiling somewhat pleadingly towards Rosie, like a baby looking in its mother's eyes for an explanation of wind-pains.

"No, don't think so," Rosie replied, quickly looking up and down at the slightly plump if also fairly attractive woman sat next to O'Neill, her fixed smile and over-starched uniform matching her boss' inch for inch.

"Zeta Nancy," the woman explained.

"Of course," Rosie smiled insincerely, her mind trying to guess, to the day, how long this woman with a back-to-front name had been sleeping with O'Neill.

"OK," Tom began. "Well, first off Inspector we are very grateful to you for coming down here to help us."

"That's what we're for," O'Neill smiled. "When the going gets tough ..." he added creepily.

"Yes, quite," Tom smiled to cover his incomprehension. "So, perhaps best if I let Rosie provide you with a quick summary of what we have."

In less than five minutes, Rosie did as she was asked, with all the enthusiasm of a hydrophobic entering a swimming baths.

"So, no suspects, no real witnesses, two dead bodies," O'Neill summarised, with deliberate curtness.

"That's about it," Rosie agreed neutrally, determined not to let someone she could not help but dislike rile her.

Indeed, quite the contrary. She had always found Billy O'Neill too ... Well, too much not to her taste. At Hendon, he had been a star to the tutors, a bit of a hero to the shallower of the boys and a pain to any woman with an IQ higher than a goldfish. Shame was, their intake had included half-a-dozen goldfish-lite women, each one of which thought they were getting exclusive extra-curricula attention. That really was the problem with Billy O'Neill: he used people as much as they let him.

For all that, Rosie had no doubt he was good at his job. Although they had never been in the same part of the Met at the same time, she knew well enough that he could no more get a leadership post in the TSG without due merit than she could have got her DI.

So, whilst there was time for either of them to change, Rosie felt reasonably sure that they were unlikely to find themselves in direct competition for at least ten years. He clearly wanted an operations career, she investigations.

Even so, she knew he was every bit as fiercely ambitious as she was. Meaning, one day, she would have to find a way of tarnishing his brand.

But all that Machiavellian stuff could wait for another day. For the next few days she needed to make sure O'Neill, Nancy and the rest stayed exactly where she wanted them.

"Yes, well, but we're looking at various ideas, options, strategies ..." Tom blathered defensively.

"Indeed we are," Superintendent Mitchell agreed, taking over effortlessly as though he had read Rosie's mind. "So, all of that part is in good hands, led by DI Charlton. What we're so obviously lacking though, Inspector O'Neill," he smiled as if truly impressed by the presence of a rising star. "Is the insight the locals could offer."

"Go on," O'Neill ordered more than asked.

"Well, whilst those woods are quite large, with paths criss-crossing in all directions, you have to go down - or park in - one of only three roads to get in there ..."

"So you're thinking ..." O'Neill began, worrying he was being set-up for something lacking the glamour he believed was the Tactical Support Group's right.

"Exactly," Mike smiled triumphantly. "We're not that flush with manpower right now, but we could maybe add half-a-dozen, possibly ten at a stretch to your ...?"

"Dozen," Sergeant Nancy put in with naïve enthusiasm.

"Perfect," Mike beamed. "I would think, assuming we can get this underway right now, twenty officers could complete door-to-doors on every house near those woods. Too rarely do we get the chance to complete such detailed police work so we really are so grateful ..." he grinned dishonestly while sneaking a sly wink to Rosie. "So very grateful you are here to help us."

"Yes, eh ... indeed," an uncertain if not totally bemused Chief Superintendent Jeffrey mumbled. "So, that is the sort of thing you were expecting to take on?" he asked of O'Neill, some slow-to-function instinct inside his dull mind momentarily troubled by the fixed and not wholly friendly stare with which the TSG Inspector now held his Superintendent.

"Of course!" Mike answered before O'Neill had the chance. "With TSG help we can do some thorough, professional and modern, work."

"Oh right," Tom smiled, any nagging doubts easily outweighed by the comfort of such important words as 'thorough', 'professional' and 'modern'.

"And while we're knocking on doors," an obviously irritated O'Neill barked. "What will DI Charlton be doing?"

"Leading the CID investigation," Mike smiled.

"Indeed," Rosie accepted. "Now, for the moment, we obviously have to keep both possibilities open: that the murders are connected; or that they are not ..."

"Surely all that matters is the dead officer?" O'Neill insisted.

"Well actually, no Billy," she replied, using O'Neill's first name with patronising patience. "You see, for all that we have to keep both ideas in mind, without the first murder there would have been no opportunity for the second ..."

"No, but even so ..."

"Please don't misunderstand me Billy," Rosie chided. "Charlie Scales was a very special colleague. His family and friends expect us to find whoever killed him. And we will. I have no doubt that, with your help, we will turn up some important leads ... so long as we stay focused. What we cannot do is allow ourselves to get misdirected by grief. We just don't know whether today's killer was on some kind of cop-hating mission or after Charlie personally ..." she accepted regretfully, pausing for a moment to let the memory of the zipped-up body bag pass from her mind.

"So ..." O'Neill began after a respectful moment.

"So we need to work that out, Billy, of course we do. But let's be clear. To take Charlie the killer had to get us all into those woods today. That means he's either also responsible for yesterday's killing; or he knows who was. So, our first focus is to find out who yesterday's victim was and who wanted him dead."

"So, clear on that?" Mike asked.

"Yes, OK, fair enough," O'Neill accepted.

Chapter 11

As Rosie walked through the CID open-plan, her mind momentarily weary of everything - of Jeffrey; of O'Neill; of death; of the unremitting glumness of police life - she all-but bumped into an obviously animated and exhilarated Martha.

"We've got an ID, ma'am," Martha gasped, her words tumbling out. "Prints match one Ian Henry Green, aged 27, dob 7 April 1985," she continued, reading from a crumpled piece of paper. "Last known address in Penge. Released from Brixton last week after serving nine months of eighteen for handling smuggled goods. Also got previous for drug dealing and theft."

"So, it could have been a drugs meet?" Rosie pondered without breaking her now newly purposeful stride.

"It could, but why Charlie as well?" Martha asked.

"That is going to be your task Martha," Rosie ordered breezily. "It's a long-shot obviously, but I want you to get all the info you can on this Green and see if there's any chance at all that he and Scales crossed paths. Any word from Gerard?"

"He's on his way in ma'am. I don't think they've got anything new ..."

"No, no," Rosie replied without thinking. "Look, as soon as he gets back, I want the four of you in my office. We need to get a plan together ... Martha," she continued, more reflectively and in an almost inaudible whisper. "No, look. Pop in a moment ..."

Closing the door of her office carefully, Rosie continued the question that had been in her mind since Jeffrey put it there. "Look, I dismissed this as soon as I heard it, but the Borough-Commander's first reaction was to think Scales was killed simply because he was a black copper. That occur to you?"

"Yes ma'am," Martha replied without hesitation.

"Really?" Rosie asked. "But why? I mean we had Gurmel, that PCSO, McMorgan and ... how would you describe Gascoigne?"

"Gurmel and Tyler weren't in the woods ma'am ..."

"Oh no ..."

"And Gloria? Well, in there she wouldn't have looked very black. But Charlie ... well yeah, obviously."

"You know, it just never entered my head ..."

"Well, I don't want to believe it ma'am," Martha went on. "Who would. And if we find a connection to this Green ..."

"And if we don't?" Rosie asked. "You see it now, don't you? I accepted the idea that yesterday's murder of Green was designed to get a lot of us in those woods so quickly, I forgot to ask why? To do what?" she continued sadly. "But, if now we assume it was to kill a copper, then why not think it was more specific than that? Pretty good chance that in a van load of police at least one of us will be black or asian ..."

"Oh dear ..." Martha sighed.

"I know, this is not a nice job Martha. No point pretending otherwise. In fact, sometimes it can be a simply horrible job."

"Yes ma'am," a sad Martha agreed, reaching for the door handle. "I'll bring Gerard and the others in as soon as."

"I'll make the coffee," Rosie nodded.

During the fifteen minutes or so it took for Gerard, Martha, Jo and Gurmel to get there, Rosie spent most of her time just gazing sadly out of her office window. In a way, she wished she'd matched O'Neill's raw anger at the death of a fellow officer. Not for anyone else's benefit, not to prove she cared. Just to get the hurt out.

Then again, maybe she couldn't have done that for one simple and guilt-inducing reason: for all that it was possible to convince herself they were dealing with a cynical killer who had taken out a piece of low-life by the name of Ian Henry Green solely to get a flood of police into some kind of trap, the bottom-line was she had been the too-sure-of-herself dumb Detective Inspector that fell for it.

"Ma'am, OK?" Gerard asked, putting his head around the door.

"Yes, of course, please," Rosie smiled thinly while unnecessarily re-arranging the empty cups on her desk one final time. She didn't feel like pouring, didn't much feel like doing anything. Not least because screaming past any self-pity in her head was the acceptance that one task had to be completed sooner than later, and that she would have to do it. "Turn up anything?" she asked of Gerard a nanosecond before he put a shortbread between his teeth.

"Uh-huh," Gerard mumbled while pouring himself a coffee, handing the pot on to Jo before taking the unbitten biscuit out of his mouth. "Not a great deal, in truth, ma'am. SOCOs did look again at the first scene ..."

"Cuttings?"

"Well, could be ..." he began sceptically. "Siân Roberts, who I do think is quite good, she took a quick look and said straight off there was enough to suggest those bushes had been cut, not just torn. So that could fit with a theory of the body being covered a while before then being moved ..."

"Or?" Rosie asked.

"Well, I suppose this doesn't rule out the theory as such ... But to be honest, when I looked around it seemed like the whole area had probably had some work done recently. Then again, I suppose a local could have known that ..."

"Does this really matter?" Martha asked. "Apart from anything else, doesn't it seem a little unlikely that the killer went armed not just with a pistol, but a pair of secateurs too!"

"I don't know, I mean, if they planned it all ..." Jo pondered.

"Oh, I'm sure they planned it," Martha agreed. "I just think we might be getting too nerdy about pruning. If they did play around with the body then surely the more likely evidence would be scratches?"

"That is what I was going to say," Gerard nodded.

"So what you thinking," Jo puzzled. "We should have asked SOCO to look for blood traces?"

"Well, not really," Gerard smiled benevolently. "I mean, I suppose there could be some, but finding them ... No, like Martha, I was just thinking that our killer may well have scratched themselves getting the body in or out of those bushes ..."

"Torn clothing, is that worth looking for?" Rosie pondered.

"Maybe ..." he nodded. "As I said, Siân had only managed a quick look. She said she'd go back later. I'm sure if something like that is there, she'll find it."

"I agree. I think we have a good SOCO team."

"I wonder where he went through Green's pockets?" Martha pondered.

"I suppose that does depend on precisely where the body fell," Rosie thought.

"Yeah, well that, but also when. I mean, I suppose the killer could have waited till they pulled the body out ..."

"No, no that wouldn't make sense," Gerard suggested. "The killer clearly took that stuff - well, the SIM card definitely - to make sure there was no connection back to him ..."

"Oh I agree with that," Martha nodded. "But that doesn't say they did it first off. They could have left the body, then realised some time later that a phone could be a problem and so gone back ..."

"Actually ..." Gerard began thoughtfully. "That is true. In fact, we may be overcomplicating this whole thing anyway. Like you said, it really doesn't matter why the killer went back, only that they did. And, in doing that, they risked being seen a second time ..."

"For which," Rosie nodded. "They needed a good reason. Yes, that's all helpful. OK, anything else?"

"Nothing re: the identification by the shop, assuming it's even that," Gerard said. "But possibly something in the car park just along from there ... Gurmel," he smiled across to their new colleague.

"Maybe nothing ma'am, but there were two cars that looked to have been parked a while. Lots of lime sap ..."

"Lime sap?" Jo asked, pulling a face.

"From trees," Gurmel explained with just a little too much seriousness. "So, I figured they'd perhaps been there since at least yesterday morning ... I've asked for checks ..."

"Good," Rosie smiled while inwardly giggling at Gurmel's obvious love of precision: 'lime sap', not just 'stuff off trees'! "And seeing as we have a name," she continued. "Who knows, we may get a direct link. What did you make of the spot the killer chose for ... for PC Scales," she asked, finding strength in formality.

"At first," Jo began. "I thought it odd. I mean, there were all those narrow, twisty paths the killer could have chosen, so why there, in so open a place ...?"

"I wondered the same," Rosie agreed. "But then I got focused on the fact that five paths in equals a choice of five out ..."

"Yeah, agree that," Jo went on confidently. "But you know, for a while earlier we - Gurmel and me - we were kind of standing around not really knowing what use we could be ..."

"But of course ..." Rosie started.

"No, that's not my point," Jo breezed on dismissively. "The thing is, we were perhaps the only ones not looking down on the ground ..."

"We didn't see anyone," Gurmel finished.

"Sorry?" Rosie asked.

"It may be nothing, just a coincidence," Jo continued. "And I heard what the others said about people they had met. But during the ten minutes or so we were standing around we did not see a single other person."

"Which doesn't mean it's always that unpopular," Rosie thought. "I mean, maybe some people changed route on seeing or hearing all of us but ... but local knowledge could tell you, what? That you won't look out of place stopping there for a moment, maybe reading that stone thing. That you've got plenty of ways out. And that every now and then, you won't see another soul ... hmm."

"Yeah, well," Martha put in. "I get all of that. But isn't the key thing for us 'opportunity'? Our killer may be local and patient, but surely he wouldn't just hang around hoping for the chance coincidence of a single copper on his own and no-one else in sight?"

"Just got lucky," Jo suggested a little defensively.

"Nah, he made at least some of his own luck," Martha held. "Must have. I buy all the stuff about that place perhaps being counter-logically quiet now and then. But there had to be something else that got Charlie there and off-guard, something in addition ...?"

"For all that I worry we might make the whole thing sound like a kid's story, I guess I have to agree with a possibility Gerard is no doubt about to suggest," Rosie smiled.

"I had no intention of mentioning dogs again," Gerard smiled back.

"No, well ... the fact seems to be that, apart from 'weird guy', everyone seen had a dog. I would not be in the least surprised if that was true of everyone we didn't see as well. No idea where that gets us mind," she grimaced.

"Yesterday's victim," Martha put in. "There can't have been a dog at that killing ..."

"Why not? If we think today's ..." Jo asked.

"All the evidence we have for yesterday suggests the victim knew the killer and was somehow or other lured to his death. Dog just doesn't fit. What's it going to do while the killer's emptying pockets, removing the SIM-card, etc.?"

"That does sound right," Gerard mused. "Apart from anything else, a dog would likely as not try and lick the Vic back to life!"

"Hold on," Rosie cried. "So are you now off the dog walker idea?"

"For Green? Yes, I think it's less likely. But today ..." Gerard began.

"Yeah, me too," Martha agreed. "The need for some kind of diversion to attract Charlie's attention, that does feel ... well, probable."

"All of which would mean the one person we don't suspect is the one we chased after!" Rosie smiled. "OK, we need to crack on with a few things. First off, there is one crap job that needs doing ..."

"OK ma'am," a hung-dog Gerard began.

"And I'm doing it," Rosie smiled. "Martha, like we said a few minutes back, I want you to dig out files on everything PC Scales has been involved with in the last year or so and see if you can spot any possible connection to Green. Gurmel, I want you to work alongside Martha, digging out everything there is to know about Green. Gerard, there's another potentially unpleasant side to this: could the killer have picked on Charlie because ..."

"He was black? Yeah, we've all wondered that," Gerard acknowledged.

"OK. Get on the Yard and get what you can on any nasty, racist groups and stuff with any link to Petts Wood."

"OK."

"And Jo ..."

"Yes ma'am?"

"I would like you to come with me."

"OK," Jo accepted, her voice betraying her intuitive fear of a harrowing experience.

Chapter 12

The news, when it came, could not have been more of a shock. The hour or so Rosie and Jo had spent with Charlie Scales' mother and his two younger sisters - Marjoria and Geri - had been simply horrible. If they had never met Charlie, had never known him for the bright, kind and charming guy he was, they would have been able to guess all that and more after just a minute with his family.

Even in her grief, Lorrietta Scales was dignified and considerate, worried as much for all Charlie's friends in the Force as she was for herself. Proudly, she spoke of a boy who had never needed to be told how to separate right from wrong. Never needed to be asked to do things around the house, look after his sisters, put effort into his school work, believe in God. From the age of nine, when Mr Scales senior was tragically 'taken by the Lord for a higher purpose', Charlie had just been the 'man' - even when standing barely four foot, six - around the house.

And the house bore testimony to all that and much more. The walls were covered with pictures of Charlie doing this, Marjoria that and Geri something else. And in every single photograph the young Scaleses looked joyful and at one with the world.

There had, of course, been tears - and little stories about falling out of trees, being scared of cats, not liking fruit. And then there had been the open acknowledgement that some of his school friends had seen him as an Uncle Tom for joining the police. 'Some folk spends too long thinking about being black, too little on being good folk', the thoughtfully philosophical Lorrietta had observed while accepting, painfully but necessarily, Rosie's careful questions about possible motives away from police work for her son's killing.

But for all that she acknowledged there remained some in her community who actually wanted to stop black boys joining the police, she then gently dismissed its relevance: she could think of nothing Charlie had done that had ever caused anyone else real upset.

And so, humbled and slightly embarrassed by the list of ten of Charlie's friends they had collected for further enquiries, Rosie and Jo had slumped into the car and sighed. Indeed, Rosie was still in mid-sigh when her phone rang. She probably would have ignored it but for GERARD flashing insistently on the screen.

"Yes Gerard," she said resignedly.

"There's been another, ma'am. In Chislehurst."

"Another?" a momentarily uncomprehending Rosie replied. "Another what ..." she asked disinterestedly before adding a sharp: "Oh god."

"Don't have much detail, but TSG are there. Actually, they were there already ..."

"Sorry, what d'you mean?"

"Someone called Gallini was shot on his doorstep with some TSG guys halfway up the street. It's called Manor Park, all very des-res evidently."

"Are you there?"

"No, we're in Petts Wood, just on our way. It's only five minutes, I think."

"OK, get there. I've no idea how long we'll be, half hour at least. Rush hour's just starting. Ring me as soon as you learn anything. I take it SOCOs are on their way?"

"Yes, the Super's got things going ma'am."

Chapter 13

For all their irritatingly well-pressed correctness - to say nothing of the fact they also seemed to have the best vans, best radios and even the trendiest notebooks - Inspector O'Neill's TSG were serious and highly efficient police officers. Of that, Superintendent Mitchell had never been in any doubt. As a result, he'd offered O'Neill command of a good group of PCs and PCSOs before being asked. O'Neill had deployed sixteen officers in four Sergeant-led teams, taking care to mix'n'match TSG and local. Two - those led by Bromley's own Sergeant Wilkins and TSG's Sergeant Nancy - had been at either end of Manor Park when the shot was heard.

That was the first curiosity about the murder of Stefan Gallini, a swiss banker who had lived in just about the largest house in the über-expensive little enclave of Manor Park for four trouble-free years. Why, why, why, Gerard had asked himself as soon as he got the first report from the still starched but no longer calm Zeta Nancy.

Option 1 was obviously that what they had on their hands now had no connection whatsoever to the two murders in the woods.

Yet the woods were right there, a huge brooding presence behind the large, gated houses. Indeed, it had been from them that Sergeant Wilkins had led his team. Having completed door-to-doors with those living in Chislehurst Road, they had taken a broad track up through the woods, more in hope than knowledge, suddenly finding themselves walking up the side of one of Mr Gallini's near-neighbours - assuming anyone actually calls another a 'neighbour' when separated by several acres of walled-in garden.

More even than that, as Tyler McMorgan - who had been in Sergeant Nancy's team - knew and pointed out instantly, there was another narrow path back into those woods running alongside Gallini's wall. Meaning a killer with local knowledge would probably have laughed to themselves at the sheer evil poetry of it all. As two teams of the Met's finest ran full-pelt towards the sound of death, he just disappeared from between them, a will'o the wisp, a phantom.

All of which supported Option 2. That Gallini had been the main target all along, the last in a planned sequence. Meaning, the killings of Ian Green and Charlie Scales had just been cynical diversions. Cold-bloodied acts designed to leave the police bumbling around like Keystone Cops, while the killer strolled calmly through the chaos. Maybe that was the sub-plot: an intention to make the police look foolish.

But then, as he watched Jo drive up to the gates, Gerard realised there was an Option 3. What if Gallini was but another plot device in some cruel, senseless drama. Were they now just waiting for the fourth?

Slipping beneath the blue and white tape held up by PCSO McMorgan, Rosie and Jo left the small crowd of seemingly terrified yet mesmerised local residents - or more likely, their servants - and walked through a wide open gate into what might as well have been another world.

Hurst Hall was an imposing, if somewhat ugly, neo-Gothic thing that made her think of Jane Eyre or Wuthering Heights, one of those anyway. What it lacked in charm it more than made up for in grandeur. All around it, like oases, well-tended lawns swept out towards well-stocked flower beds, while in the middle of the driveway - right in front of the main door, of course - there was the obligatory pond and fountain.

"This is a serious looking place," Rosie observed on meeting Gerard and Gurmel.

"No question," Gerard agreed. "Worth millions. No idea how many, but plenty."

"So what do you have so far?"

"Well, there is a reasonable amount of useful evidence this time. We've already got some foot-prints, a shell-casing and a possible description, albeit rather vague. The TSG guys are going up and down the road now talking to anyone and everyone ..."

"They offered?"

"Superintendent Mitchell spoke to O'Neill, I believe."

"And ... did I just see Jeffrey's car?" Rosie asked a little despondently.

"Eh, yeah," Gerard replied sheepishly. "I borrowed it, nothing else left in the pool you see ..."

"Excellent!" a relieved Rosie beamed. "I couldn't bear having him bumbling around."

"Yes, well Martha says he's been doing plenty of that at the station ... Oh, hold on," Gerard apologised as his phone rang with an incongruously cheery tune. "It's Martha again," he explained before turning to walk, for no good reason other than habit.

With little obvious enthusiasm, Rosie walked around the fountain - past a couple of clue-hunting SOCOs she did not recognise - and up the pale-grey granite steps, to the chequerboard black and white marble terrace beneath an overly-ornate porch. White tape marked around where Gallini's body had been found. "Constable," she eventually smiled at the tall, young, gingered-hair officer standing stock-still just by the doorway.

"Ma'am."

"I'm Detective Inspector Charlton."

"Scott ma'am, TSG," the all-but statuesque young guy responded, proudly.

"Not exactly turning out to be much fun, this case," she smiled, her lightness a deliberate counterpoint to the obvious horror of the situation.

"No ma'am," Scott replied. "You guessing this is all related?"

"Well, yeah," Rosie smiled self-deprecatingly. "Guessing is about all we are doing. Were you amongst those who found him?"

"Yes ma'am. Four or five of us ran in here, but ..."

"You didn't see anyone leave?"

"No, but I heard ..."

"Yes, my Sergeant tells me the killer may have been seen ... How'd they get in?"

"Gate was open when we arrived ma'am."

"Mmm, that sounds odd," Rosie began, taking another look around the place. "Jo," she called down. "Go and ask PCSO McMorgan to join me, will you." Turning back to Scott she continued. "So, what else?"

"The family had gone out, some school thing. Left the chap on his own. Seems he opened the door and ..."

"They back, the family?"

"Yes ma'am, came back about ten minutes ago. Inspector O'Neill and Sergeant Nancy led them inside somewhere. Family Liaison are on their way ..."

"That's good," Rosie smiled. "I must thank the Inspector ... And the family is?"

"Wife, quite young, lot younger than the Vic ... than Mr Gallini ..."

"Don't worry, Vic is OK," Rosie offered reassuringly. "Wife and ...?"

"Two youngish children and a Housekeeper. She was with them ..."

"No-one else?" Rosie asked, a little surprised.

"As far as I know ma'am. It is a big place though ..."

"My thought too," Rosie agreed.

"Ma'am," McMorgan asked while taking the steps.

"Ah, yes," Rosie began. "Constable Scott says that when he got here the gates were already open. That unusual?"

"Er, yes ..." McMorgan started. "And the Constable is right, I was just behind ... But now you say it, yeah, we did all just run in. Never even thought about it ... Yes," he added more formally. "It is normal for the gates all along here to be closed."

"So why were these not I wonder?" Rosie muttered, noting a rather animated Gerard running towards them with an equally excited Gurmel flagging along behind. "Well?" she asked as her Sergeant bounded up the steps.

"Look over there," Gerard all-but ordered, pointing to a collection of what looked like gardeners' sheds beneath a clump of plane trees.

"At what?" Rosie replied.

"The skip ... Oh, no, you can't quite see it from here. There's a builder's skip, ma'am, with a sign propped up against it. It says: Green & Sons ..."

"And?"

"... Gerry Green ..."

"Gerry Green?" Rosie repeated.

"He's not something to do with ..." Jo began.

"It seems he is," Gerard nodded. "He's Ian Green's father," he added for an apparently dumb-struck Rosie.

"Go on," Rosie encouraged.

"OK, well short story is, Superintendent Mitchell made the first connection, telling Martha he thought Ian Green might be the son of a local villain. So, Martha checks it out and ... well this is almost unbelievable," Gerard offered a little breathlessly. "This Gerry Green owns a building firm, they've been working here ..."

"Here? You mean right here?"

"Yes ma'am, exactly. Right here. Until about ten days ago, that is. Then there was a row. Green, Gerry that is, threatened Mr Gallini's secretary. A Mr Battersby ..."

"The secretary's a man?" Rosie asked with politically-incorrect incredulity.

"Seems so," Gerard replied. "So, Green threatens him. Actually went to hit him with a piece of wood, but stopped himself. Walked off the job and left all this rubbish. More round the back. There's also some damage, evidently ..."

"To the gates?" Rosie asked quickly.

"Er, not sure. Martha's checking what she can ..."

"Has she spoken to this Mr Battersby?"

"No, he's in Switzerland ..."

"Why?"

"Gallini, he's Swiss. Owns a bank with offices in ..." Gerard paused uncertainly. "Zurich, I think Martha said. Anyway, that's where this Mr Battersby is. Over there doing something or other, but before he went there was a complaint. Martha's dug out the papers ..."

"Not Scales?"

"No ma'am, that would be too much of a coincidence for anyone. No, it was Erica Johnson, you met her early ..."

"I remember."

"She and PCSO Holmes. DI Russell then took it and issued Green with a Formal Caution."

"OK, we need to get back to the station. I'm not sure what this adds up to yet," Rosie thought. "But it must mean something. Jo, Gurmel," she looked across to her two too-raw TDCs with all the confidence-boosting trust she could fake: "I'd like you to stay here for another hour or so. I want to know as-soon-as if TSG turn up anything. Also, I don't think we'd do any good trying to talk to the family. But assuming Family Liaison take them away, take a good look, see what you think. Does the wife look properly upset? ... can't rule out something domestic even when everything points at something quite different."

Chapter 14

"Woo-Hoo," Gerard cooed in admiration as he followed Rosie into her office.

On a large pin-board, resting a little unsteadily on one of the chairs, was a map of the area immediately around the woods - Hawkwood, to give them their proper name. Three large yellow tacks marked the location of the murders of Ian Green, Charlie Scales and Stefan Gallini. Next to the map stood an easel with an A1 pad already divided into three sections. The name Gerry Green was circled in Gallini's third of the pad, connected by a thick line up to Ian Green. A few blue and orange post-it notes were scattered across the different sections.

"Hiya," an almost supernaturally calm Martha said as she walked into the room, a mess of different bits of paper in one hand, an odd collection of pens and markers in the other. "Right, got lots here ..." she smiled, pushing the door closed with an elbow before walking confidently across the room.

"Martha, I take it ..." Rosie began, nodding towards the board and A1 pad.

"You said get a map, ma'am," a suddenly disconcerted Martha said.

"I did, and I am very grateful ..."

"Got the easel from the training room. I doubt it'll be missed ..." she said with an easy confidence, seemingly made all the more trustable by her cut-glass accent.

"Yeah, I doubt that too," Rosie smiled. "Well, look, you've obviously been busy. Tell me what you think I should know."

"OK," Martha began, carefully setting out across the DI's desk her apparently random collection of notes. "First, DI Russell had already done some checking on Gerry Green. He did time in the late 70s for drug smuggling. Then a five stretch a couple of years later for GBH section 20, connected to a robbery evidently. But the more interesting thing is the Yard believe he was part of the crowd that shifted the Brinks Mat gold."

"You say DI Russell ..."

"He was very helpful ma'am. He'd already spoken to Serious Crimes, but I rang them again to see if there was any more. Basically, No! Meaning either: there isn't; or they're just not saying. Makes little difference really ..."

"I guess that's true," Rosie nodded while actually still absorbing the sense of Martha's point.

"But whilst it doesn't sound like he got a great deal from it, the suspicion is Green's business was set-up with a Brinks payout ..."

"So what, the business is some kind of front?" Gerard asked.

"No, don't think so ..." Martha replied, shuffling her papers. "It looks legit," she continued, glancing down at some notes. "I looked on the Companies House site - accounts surrendered on time. Turnover around £750,000 a year. No obvious funniness ..."

"Gerard said it's called Green & *Sons*," Rosie recalled.

"Yes ma'am, but Ian Henry doesn't seem to be one of them. There are four Directors, all Greens: Gerry, Patricia, Michael and David ..."

"And your guess is?"

"Well, I couldn't find anything else on them. But one thing I did notice: Gerry Green is sixty-two, Ian was twenty-seven, that's quite a gap ..."

"And?"

"And the dates kind of suggest he may have been something of a post-prison mistake: Green was released in July 1984, Ian pops out April 1985 ..."

"Yeah, well ..." Rosie smiled. "Remind me what we have on Ian Green?"

"Been out only a week after doing nine months of eighteen for smuggling cigarettes ..."

"Cigarettes, not drugs?" Gerard clarified.

"That's what the record says," Martha confirmed, dragging out yet another set of notes. "I wondered whether there might be some kind of continuation from the father, but he looks very small time ... and dim, frankly. He's been caught dealing or thieving over a hundred times. Done six different stretches, first one aged sixteen. At that time his address matches the Registered Address of Green & Sons ..."

"Eh?" Gerard asked.

"I'm guessing that it's just their home address, sounds like it: 7 Hill Crest. It's over in Bexley."

"But what you're saying," Rosie put in. "Is that since then, he's never given that address?"

"No ma'am. There are about twenty-five different addresses recorded on the system. Seems he bounces around but never anywhere that near to Bexley. Apart from Penge, we've addresses in Peckham, Norwood, Forest Hill, Catford ... it goes on, but the general theme seems to be: poor ..."

"Yeah, I get the point. So whilst we need to dig deeper ... Actually, we really ought to speak to Mr Green senior, nice and friendly. He has lost a son after all ..."

"Fair enough," Gerard agreed. "But the link with Gallini, Brinks Mat gold, Swiss bank ..."

"Oh yes," Martha burst excitedly. "That's the hottest thing," she breezed while shuffling through her notes. "Right, so I thought, why not ask if anything was known about Gallini ..."

"You thought of that?" Rosie asked, impressed.

"Yeah," a slightly offended Martha replied. "So I rang DI Russell's contact in Serious Crimes. He couldn't find much, but did have one note suggesting Gallini's bank - it's called Rütger's, by the way, based in Zurich. Anyway, DCS Benson ..."

"Sorry," Rosie interrupted, "DCS ..."

"Benson ma'am. He's the guy I rang in Serious Crimes ..."

"You rang a DCS in Serious Crimes, just like that?" Rosie asked, wide-eyed with a mixture of disbelief and admiration at her TDC's obvious disinclination towards the usual grade-conscious timidity of most young officers.

"Yeah, well DI Russell said ..."

"No worries, carry on."

"So DCS Benson had a note saying the City Police have an on-going interest in Rütger's alleged involvement in some rather complicated currency exchanges ..."

"Is that smart talk for money laundering?" Rosie asked.

"As I understand it ..." Martha smiled.

"So, you're putting this together and, what, thinking maybe there's more to why Green was working at Gallini's ... hot money or something ...?" Rosie wondered, a hint of exasperation building in her voice at the thought her TDC was getting carried away.

"Oh no ma'am," Martha replied simply. "Couldn't really make that fit with what we know so far, could we. But I did ring the City Police ..."

"Go on," Rosie smiled, newly indulgent and forgiving.

"DCS Benson suggested I try a Superintendent John Carney, but turns out he's on holiday ..."

"Not Switzerland," Rosie laughed.

"No, Scotland, so his Sergeant told me," Martha answered with mirthless directness. "Madeline Terry, very nice and all that, but either she knew nothing or was saying nothing. Superintendent Carney's back on Monday."

"OK, but ..." Rosie asked uncertainly. "Why are we bothering with this? Did DCS Benson say something else?"

"Gold ma'am. Seems there is also a belief that Rütger's move gold," Martha replied matter-of-factly.

"Wow, so that really would be one serious link," Gerard gasped. "How long has Gallini been over here?"

"Don't know," Martha said a little defeatedly.

"No, me neither. Though something I picked up earlier made me think not that long, just a few years."

"But I think the bank has had an office in London for quite some time," Martha suggested, rushing through her pile of notes. "Nah," she muttered, finding nothing. "Maybe I just thought that because of the way DCS Benson suggested the interest in Rütger's wasn't exactly new."

"OK," Rosie said, trying to gain some control over the threads. "We've got some possible pointers here as to why Gallini might have attracted criminal attention. But we can't get more on that until Superintendent Carney gets back from up north ..."

"I did also try to get someone called Imogen Wilson, she's some kind of Director at the Financial Services Authority ..."

"DCS Benson again?" Rosie asked quizzically.

"Well he was trying to help ma'am," Martha replied sharply. "He thought she might know something but ..."

"Also on holiday?"

"No idea. All I got was an ansaphone. My guess was she'd just gone home."

"Terrific!" Rosie grimaced. "We're going to struggle to get more on this before Monday ..."

"When do you plan on talking to Mrs Gallini?" Gerard asked.

"Well, I was going to check with Family Liaison later," Rosie began. "But really, I doubt they'll advise talking to Mrs Gallini tonight ..."

"No, of course not. But when we do, we could ask her for a contact within the bank. Say we need to ..."

"Yes," Rosie nodded. "In fact, it would look odd, I should think, if we didn't say we needed to look for a motive connected to her husband's business ..."

"So you think that is it now?" Gerard asked.

"I don't know Gerard, I really just don't know," Rosie answered sadly, tiredly. "But you have to say this: it's much easier imagining motives for the murder of a rich and possibly somewhat shady foreign banker than poor Charlie ..."

"I agree," Gerard nodded. "By the way, I did check with the Communities Team at the Yard. Absolutely nothing on any organised racists in and around Petts Wood. Plenty in Penge where Green junior lived. Lots more over in Eltham and Woolwich of course. But nothing obvious where we're looking ..."

"No, I didn't think so. Never say never, but I really did not get any vibe suggesting Charlie was killed because he was black. Just because ..."

"He was a copper," Martha completed the thought.

"I fear so," Rosie acknowledged. "Actually, Martha, I think you got the scent of this first. If Ian Green was killed to get lots of police down to those woods then Charlie was killed to get us all in an almighty tizz. Then, while we're all faffing around the real target gets hit ..."

"Forgot to say ma'am," Martha replied while obviously thinking of something else. "One of those two cars Gurmel asked for checks on: no tax, no insurance. It is registered to a Peter Lupton, same address as Ian Green ..."

"Has anyone gone to it?"

"Not yet ma'am. They're all a bit ..."

"No, I realise that," Rosie apologised. "Look," she began business-like before pausing to ask: "Sorry, anything more?"

"Dr Patterson says no obvious sign Green had had sex - or anything close - for a while ..."

"Mmm, so what was he expecting to get?" Gerard pondered.

"Could still be that. Just hadn't got to the right spot yet, something like that?" Martha suggested.

"Suppose so ..."

"I know we think he was ..." Gerard started, stopping midway to complete a deep swallow. "I know it seems Charlie was killed almost at random, but anything from his family?"

"Well apart from being just about the nicest people you could hope for, no, not really. A bit about some of the less sympathetic people of Catford not much liking black policemen. But nothing concrete to go on. His mum's given me a list of friends to talk to if I want more, but to be honest I'm not sure I do," Rosie smiled thinly. "OK, look, what's the time ... quarter past six. We expecting Jo and Gurmel back?"

"I'm sure of it," Gerard nodded. "You want me to ring?"

"Yeah. Let's take a break. I'll talk to Family Liaison. You get the other two back and let's meet again in thirty minutes. We need a plan for tomorrow ..."

"Might want to make that forty-five ma'am," Martha suggested, some instinct having made her turn to look through the frosted glass wall to see the shambling gait of Chief Superintendent Jeffrey approaching.

"Oh terrific!" Rosie snarled as the door opened.

Chapter 15

"Sir," Rosie said a little pensively as Tom stood waiting for Gerard and Martha to leave, closing the door slowly behind them.

"Rosie," he smiled nervously while walking across to the map, the three large yellow tacks momentarily consuming his gaze. "Terrible, terrible business," he opined meaninglessly.

"Yes, of course," Rosie replied, watching now as the Borough-Commander stared blankly at the almost empty A1 pad.

"Not got much to go on ..." he thought out loud while turning, with clear reluctance, to face his obviously weary DI.

"Well, not enough ..." Rosie began. "But we do have an interest in this Gerry Green," she offered, pointing vaguely towards the note on the pad.

"Really?" Tom asked, obviously knowing nothing of the development. "Has ... have you talked about all this ..." he continued, waving a hand in a circle that broadly traced around the yellow pins on the map. "With DCI Harris?"

"I don't think I've seen DCI Harris all week, Sir," Rosie replied a little sharply.

"What? Oh, right, yes, well ..." Tom blathered. "I'm not sure whether Bert's ..."

"But don't worry Sir ..."

"Don't worry!" he suddenly burst.

"I meant, Sir," Rosie continued, even more sharply. "Don't imagine we're not working this through. Superintendent Mitchell has been excellent. TSG likewise. DI Russell has also been very helpful. We're starting to get intelligence on the first victim, Ian Green. And we've also got a possible link between Gallini and Green's father. TDC Cunningham spoke to ..."

"DCS Benson ..." Tom put in, carefully sitting himself in one of the chairs opposite Rosie.

"How?"

"AC-Ops ..."

"But ... why?" Rosie asked, her instincts unable to conceive of anything but negative reasons for Jeffrey being told Martha had been on to a senior Yard detective.

"Rosie," Tom began, trying as hard as he knew how to appear both empathetic and wise. "This has become a very, very big deal for the Commissioner, for the Mayor ..."

"Yes Sir, I can understand that. That's why ..."

"So the situation has to be ... managed," Tom explained, with an unintentional suggestion of management in a very Machiavellian sense.

"What does that mean?" Rosie replied.

"It means ... It means the media, the press, they have to be told something. Have to be helped to believe everything is under control ..."

"It is under control," Rosie barked.

"Is it, is it really?" Tom replied sharply, instantly regretting his tactlessness. "Look Rosie, I told you earlier this could get political. The death of this banker, this Gallianni ..."

"Gallini," Rosie corrected angrily.

"Whatever," Tom sighed, waving a hand as if to dismiss trifles like accuracy and fact. "The press have to be given something. AC-Ops has spoken to this DCS Benson and, as I understand it, they do not want any of this Green stuff getting around ..."

"So they think it's a potentially serious link then ..."

"Yes, I think they do. That's why ..." he paused, his hand visibly shaking, his throat dry.

"What, Sir?" Rosie asked with barely concealed insolence now.

"DCS Benson is joining us. From tomorrow. You will ..."

"What!" Rosie all-but screamed. "I will what?"

"He will ... I mean you and he will ..."

"Are you telling me he's coming here to take over?"

"Yes," Tom confessed with child-like despair.

"Why, I mean, how the fuck ... How fucking dare you?" Rosie suddenly burst, months of frustration and disrespect pouring out in one less-than penetrating question.

"What!" Tom replied, momentarily finding the character to act like a powerful and competent leader. "What do you think you're saying, DI Charlton? Let me tell you this ..."

"Save it," Rosie ordered. "I'm not in the least interested in whatever drivel you want to share. Go tell this DCS Benson that I'll be here at 7am and I expect him to be also ..."

"What?" Tom replied uncertainly. "I can't ..."

"Then find someone who can," Rosie shouted back. "I'll sort this case. With or without DCS Benson this case gets solved. Then I'll find a way out of this borough. Till then, stay out of my fucking way. Now, get out ..."

"Wh-what?" he mumbled.

"I said, Sir," Rosie all-but spat. "You've done what you've done. Fine. I'll work with this DCS - who actually sounds, from what TDC Cunningham tells me, like he at least knows what he's doing. So, I'll work with him, get the case closed and then get as far away from you as I can. Clear? Now go."

As an obviously defeated and slightly desolate Tom stood, turned and walked towards the door, Rosie realised what she'd said. Her bottom lip started to tremble, her heart race, her hands shake.

His movements seemed reduced to slow-motion, each step taking an age. She felt certain that he would turn around any moment and suspend her with immediate effect. Her career, if not over then certainly placed in the coldest of storage. And for how long? She'd have to leave the Force. No way could she bear five years on Traffic trying to rehabilitate herself. Fuck, fuck, fuck, she chided herself as she waited for the inevitable.

Yet it didn't come. Without looking back, Tom gently opened the door and slipped out, closing it with equal gentleness behind him.

As if in shock, Rosie stared over to the map and pad. For all that she felt massively let down by the apparent lack of faith in her ability, her intelligence could not help but recognise the political logic of appointing a senior Yard detective to lead what would now be a highly scrutinised investigation.

Two tiny tears rolled from the corner of her left eye as she began to regret losing her temper. She'd been in the Force for twelve years, joining after a year spent at Uni realising that the idea of her as a teacher just did not fit. It had taken her four years to make Sergeant, five DI. In her little plan of ambition she would make DCI in another year, max. All she needed to do was approach every new challenge with logic, calm and determination, and the results would follow. And results equalled success, successes equalled a career.

Now, in one moment of rage, she had let herself down.

Chapter 16

"What?" Rosie asked sadly on hearing a gentle tap on the door.

"Hi," Superintendent Mitchell smiled, closing the door behind himself.

"Oh, it's you," Rosie replied tensely, subtly wiping the tears away.

"Thought we might just sort out a plan for tomorrow," he continued.

"Well, we've got this ..."

"I know," Mike smiled, holding a hand up to stop Rosie's flow. "And of course, an old foot-slogger like me couldn't possibly understand the mysteries of high-brow detective work. But the Chief Superintendent's off this weekend, so operations are all down to me ..."

"Jeffrey's off?"

"Some family thing, I think. Anyway, let's get to the point. I've told O'Neill to be here with his team for 8am ..."

"They finished?"

"Yes, I've just stood them down. Got our people guarding this Hurst Hall overnight. The Gallinis are in a hotel up the road. So, we're calm for now. But obviously, we need to get out and about tomorrow. So, what do you want?" he asked, his smile and open-armed gesture putting Rosie totally at ease once more.

"Er, well, it's all about Manor Park now I suppose ..." Rosie began.

"So you want more door-to-doors?"

"Yeah ... but maybe first off we need to collate what we've got so far ..."

"Right. Well look. I can see this O'Neill is a bit of a prick," Mike noted. "But I hear he's an efficient one. So, once we're all clear about what we already know, I'm going to let him be in charge of ops at the scene. Organising more knocking on doors. Showing photos of this Ian Green. All of that OK?"

"Yes, sure," Rosie beamed. "Great ..."

"And the woods?"

"To be honest, I'm not sure there's much more there. I mean, for all that is where two killings happened, the killer had to get in and out of there ..."

"I agree," Mike nodded. "Right, about this car ..."

"Oh yeah, shit ..."

"I've sent a truck, it'll be in the garage tonight. You'll want SOCOs to examine it in the morning."

"Yes, of course," a now awed Rosie agreed.

"Do you want me to send a couple of uniform round to see the registered owner or you going to do that?"

"Yeah, uniform would be good ... Hold on, no," Rosie decided, changing her mind. "No, we better take that. We'll get this DCS up to speed and then split up. We need to talk to the lady that found Ian Green, then this Peter Lupton, then Mrs Gallini and then ..." she thought out loud. "Then, depending on what more we can get out of the City Police and FSA, this Gerry Green ..."

"Yeah, be careful there though Rosie ..."

"Why, sorry, what d'you mean ..."

"Just that, be careful. I was too young to really understand it all at the time. I was at Greenwich and we weren't that involved. But I've always thought there must have been something seriously funny about the way that Brinks Mat thing was handled ..."

"Funny as in ..."

"Exactly," Mike grimaced with a knowing nod. "So, this Benson may be brilliant for all I know. I've never heard of him, which at least means I've never heard anything bad. But just trust your own judgement Rosie. Don't let anyone - and I mean anyone - lead you towards conclusions or ideas that feel wrong. Any of that and you talk to me."

"OK boss," Rosie smiled. "So how do I know I can trust you," she smiled.

"Use your judgement," Mike smiled back.

"Fair enough," Rosie giggled, suddenly thinking that actually, she'd been totally right to lose it with Jeffrey. He was a man totally over-promoted and out of his depth. By contrast, Superintendent Mitchell was under-stated and too easily under-estimated. Maybe, she wondered, this case would change all that.

"But there is one last thing re: Green," he suggested.

"Really, what's that?"

"Someone needs to tell the family."

"Oh yes. God, how stupid of me ..."

"DI Russell lives over that way and ... Well, seeing as he has recently met Gerry Green, I thought I'd ask him to go round. That OK with you?"

"That would be so helpful Sir, thank you."

"Pleasure Rosie, a pleasure ... And anything else you need, come to me," Mike insisted, standing to leave.

Chapter 17

As Superintendent Mitchell closed the door, Rosie picked up the phone and dialled the extension for Family Liaison. The change in ring-tone told her she was being patched through to a mobile.

"Reeves," a gentle voice answered.

"Oh Hi," Rosie began, suddenly concerned that she might have rung at the wrong time. "This is DI Charlton, Rosie ..."

"Hello Detective Inspector," the soothing voice replied. "How can I help?"

"I was ... I wanted to check on the Gallinis ..."

"We've got them safe for tonight. Very shocked, frightened, disturbed ... All the things you would expect."

"Yes, of course ..."

"And we've got a message through to the Swiss Police. They will visit the family, there are some much older children evidently."

"Oh," Rosie replied without thinking.

"Yes," the voice continued. "They're from Herr Gallini's first marriage ..."

"Herr?"

"Yes ma'am, despite the name the Gallinis are German-speaking Swiss. Although in my experience, there's rarely a language the Swiss cannot speak. Like the Dutch ..." Reeves began to babble.

"Yes, quite so," Rosie interrupted. "So ... sorry, have we met?"

"Yes ma'am, once or twice. When I was a PCSO. Stella Reeves?"

"Oh yes," Rosie agreed, recalling an older - for a new recruit - mousey-looking woman. "So, how long have you been ..."

"Family Liaison? Nearly two years ma'am. Suits me quite well, I think."

"Good, I can imagine that Stella. Look, the real point for me is I would like - I mean I really need - to talk to Mrs Gallini. Do you think that would be OK in the morning?"

"Well, it's going to be difficult whenever ..."

"I know that," Rosie interrupted more sharply than she intended.

"Which was my point ma'am," Stella replied firmly. "So, if no time is a good time, then tomorrow morning is no worse than any other."

"Yes, of course, thank you," Rosie acknowledged and apologised in one less than confident sentence. "There's also a Housekeeper?"

"Yes ma'am. And her husband, he does the driving, gardening and odd jobs. Mr and Mrs Cassidy."

"And they are?"

"They went home ma'am. Insisted on it. They live in a cottage in the grounds, Mrs Gallini said ..."

"Yes, OK," Rosie replied while thinking. "We have so little to go on with all this it's hard to know who, if anyone, could still be at risk ..." she thought out loud. "But there's a guard on the gate ..." she continued, stopping as she remembered that there had been two teams of uniform at either end of Manor Park when Stefan Gallini was shot.

"Do you have a time, ma'am?" Stella asked.

"What?"

"If you have a time, ma'am, I'll ring that through. My colleague, Tilly Cowdrey, is at the Hotel now. I'll tell her. I'll be back there from seven in the morning myself ..."

"Of course," Rosie replied, acknowledging the sense and thoughtfulness in Stella's subtly crafted half-question / half-instruction. "Do you think the family will want to go back to Hurst Hall tomorrow?"

"I wouldn't have thought so, ma'am. And I think we'd try to dissuade them for another day or two anyway ..."

"I see. OK, can we say 11am then. That will give them time to take breakfast, maybe take a walk or something ... is there," Rosie suddenly thought. "Is there a nanny?"

"No ma'am. Not that we've heard of, anyway. Mrs Gallini is quite young, so maybe she's happy ..." Stella began before changing tack. "I got the impression Mrs Cassidy kind of takes on the Granny-role though ..."

"You think all seemed, you know, like happy families?"

"Yes, I do think that ma'am. I mean, hard to tell in the circumstances, but the grief was unquestionably real and painful. Mrs Gallini does look a little, how to say this ... Well, she looks like the young wife of an older man."

"Now what does that mean Stella?" Rosie laughed gently.

"Well, it's only a quick impression, but like I said, she seems very young. Can't be over thirty. And she's a long way from home. I think she said they're all from Zurich ..."

"Yes, I think we heard that too."

"Yeah, so maybe it's unfair to judge. But she did seem to hold on to Mrs Cassidy like a girl holding onto her mother. And the way she talked about her husband, it was almost like you might hear ..."

"Someone talking about their father?"

"Yeah, that's kind of it. Like I say, I do think the family is strong. But I could imagine Mrs Gallini might feel a bit friendless now and then, you know, in a girly sense. Maybe living with three people who are all as old as her own parents explains why she wouldn't want a nanny ..."

"Yeah, could do," Rosie pondered. "But of course, for all we know she could have plenty of friends amongst the other local mums. Weren't they at some school thing?"

"Yes ma'am."

"And the school is?"

"Scadbury College. Small independent school not very far from Manor Park ..."

"We'll need to talk to ... hold on," Rosie realised. "It's holiday time!?"

"Yes, but evidently they run various things through the holidays for the younger children. This was a sports thing, I believe."

"So there will be someone at the school we can talk to on Monday?"

"I guess so. I don't really know the school ma'am," Stella explained. "Just where it is and what Mrs Gallini and Mrs Cassidy said earlier ..."

"Yes, of course," Rosie acknowledged. "And it may not matter one jot," she accepted. "Look, thank you Stella, you've been a great help ..."

"Really?"

"Yes, truly. And if anything else about the family pops into your head, we can talk about that in the morning. See you at eleven."

As she put the phone down Rosie began to see even more clearly than before that the odd murder out was that of Charlie Scales. Whilst she knew well enough that the challenge right now was to avoid closing down any idea or option, it seemed most likely that the explanation for Gallini's death lay somewhere in his business-life, clean or crooked. The existence of a wider family in Zurich could be of interest. They might at least offer an explanation as to why Gallini had come to England. But for all that she wanted to keep all options open, such evidence as they had gave no suspicion at all that this was some kind of domestic.

But what about Ian Green? If he really was the useless and maybe even embarrassing runt of an otherwise well-functioning - if criminal - family, might he have been killed simply as an irritant? The evidence for him definitely suggested he knew his killer. But could anyone be so stupid as to kill their own son and then, twenty-four hours later, someone they'd recently had a very public row with?

Chapter 18

"Ma'am?" Gerard asked, popping his head around the door.

"Yes, please," Rosie smiled. "Come in."

She watched her newly expanded team enter, wondering mischievously how they would cope with the fact she now only had three available chairs. Confidently, Gerard sat in the middle seat, followed by Jo who - with equal confidence - took the chair to Gerard's right. She liked Jo, she was nothing like as obviously clever and insightful as Martha, but there was something both charmingly simple and resolutely determined about her.

Gurmel, bless him, was soon in a dither. His natural politeness and innate sense of asian chivalry meant he really wanted to stand. Yet Martha had already disdained the remaining chair and walked purposefully over to the map and pad, a thick marker-pen already in her hand.

"Would you like," the super-diffident young guy asked.

"Of course not," the independent, slightly annoyed Martha replied.

"I'll get another chair for tomorrow," Rosie smiled. "But I don't plan on keeping you long," she continued, nodding for Gurmel to sit. "We've had a long day and we will have another tomorrow ..."

"Tomorrow," a wide-eyed and somewhat supplicant Gurmel put in.

"Yes Gurmel, tomorrow," Rosie smiled with a hint of menace. "Why?"

"It's just that I ... er, well ..."

"They have to find out sooner or later," Gerard offered.

"Sorry," a now puzzled Gurmel replied.

"Family, friends. They have to find out sooner or later what this job is like. That's just how it is. Get used to it."

"Yes, OK. Right, yes ..." a still uncertain Gurmel mumbled.

"So, sorted?" Rosie smiled.

"Yes, OK," Gurmel smiled shyly in reply.

"Good. Right, a few things. First off, tomorrow morning, we're getting more help ..."

"Really?" a slightly surprised Gerard queried.

"Martha's new best friend DCS Benson will be here at seven ..."

"Him, wow ... er, why?" Martha asked.

"Well, for a number of reasons," Rosie replied with a hint of bitterness. "The only one of which we need to focus on, though, is this stuff to do with the bank, Rütger's ... er," she hesitated, looking to Gerard.

"Yes ma'am, shared that."

"Good," Rosie smiled to Jo and Gurmel in quick turn. "There's obvious interest in that. So, tomorrow, here's the plan to start. I'll meet and greet our new DCS, make him coffee, that kind of little-girl-out-of-her-depth kind of thing ..."

"Not that you're bitter," Jo smiled empathetically.

"Moi!" Rosie smiled, adding: "In all seriousness, I don't want to suggest he's in any way an issue. The issue is politicians fretting about their precious Olympics!"

"Oh yeah, I think we may have won something," Gerard suggested.

"Fabulous," a resolutely non-sporty Martha smiled dismissively.

"So," Rosie continued. "I'll meet the guy. If you could be here for seven-thirty ..."

"Wonderful," Gerard yawned.

"Could make it 7am if you want ..."

"No, no. Seven-thirty's good," Gerard smiled.

"Fine. We'll take him through what we've got ..." Rosie began before looking across to Martha's map and pad. "Yeah, well, might not take long! Anyway, we'll do that, then join part of the uniform briefing ..."

"TSG back tomorrow?" Martha asked.

"Yes, the Super has sorted that. Actually, he'll be in charge the weekend ..."

"Jeffrey off?" a slightly incredulous Gerard asked.

"Seems so," Rosie could not help but smile. "So, we'll need to agree a few priorities with the DCS. But really, I'm thinking we still have far too little from the people in Birchwood ... And now, of course, this Manor Park."

"For all that I think that is right," Gerard began thoughtfully. "It's hard to see a serious lead coming from all that ..."

"I don't disagree," Rosie nodded. "But having plenty of uniform around is probably a good thing in itself. While they're doing that, I've a few things for us. First, we'll need to go through more systematically what we've got from SOCOs and Patterson. That's a large part of such evidence as we have and we need to be more on top of it. Gurmel ..."

"Er, yes ma'am?"

"Sergeant Wilkins tells me you not only have a good, logical brain, but you are good at creating summaries, spreadsheets, those sorts of thing?"

"That was nice of him," the ever polite young TDC replied.

"Listen, for all that the Sergeant is a good guy, don't ever think he's just being nice," Gerard advised. "If he thinks you're useless, he'll tell you!"

"So, there you have it," Rosie smiled. "A voice of experience!"

"Yeah," Gerard laughed. "Guess I could have put that better!"

"Anyway," Rosie continued, looking back to Gurmel. "I shall look to you to work on that. Next, we need to carry on digging into Ian Green's past and his father's, and any links to Charlie Scales. I'm going to ask you two, Jo and Martha, to be our lead on that. You can decide how to divide the work between you ..."

"And Gallini ma'am," a slightly put-out Martha asked, thinking her earlier initiative was being forgotten.

"He, I rather think, is going to be the key focus for the whole investigation," Rosie opined. "Sure, we all want to know why Charlie and this Ian Green were killed, but the answer I suspect will lie with Gallini ..."

"So who ..." Martha began.

"All of us," Rosie smiled. "We'll have to split our time, but my feeling is eventually we are going to find something in someone's past that connects ..."

"Ma'am, supposing there isn't any connection ..." Jo asked.

"Well, in the case of Green's father and Gallini we know there is," Rosie replied. "You know, one weird idea did pop into my head earlier. What if Gallini had Green junior killed, because of this dispute thing. Then Green senior reacts ..."

"Changes the dynamic from our earlier thought of Ian being nothing but a disappointment ..." Martha pondered.

"Agreed," Rosie nodded. "And I do think the disappointment theory is the stronger of the two, not that either is that compelling. Anyway, we'll no doubt keep coming back to all that. But, for tomorrow, besides more digging we'll need to start talking to people: Mrs Dearmer; Mrs Gallini, her Housekeeper and the Chauffeur, a Mr and Mrs Cassidy I'm told; possibly Green senior; probably this Peter Lupton ..."

"Sorry, who he?" Jo asked.

"Owner of one of the car's Gurmel traced," Gerard explained. "Lives at the same address as Ian Henry ..."

"How about the other car?" Gurmel asked.

"That is a good question," Rosie acknowledged. "Probably too late now, but chase that in the morning, would you."

"Yes ma'am."

"Right, so tomorrow is another day," Rosie smiled. "So, let's all try and get some rest to be ready for it."

Chapter 19

As she closed the door to her flat Martha wondered if she had the energy to walk all the way down the hallway to the kitchen. First on the left was her bedroom, and for all that the bed would still be unmade from the morning, she knew that in her present state of physical and mental exhaustion she would fall asleep as soon as she lay down on anything. A bed of nails made red-hot by glowing charcoal layered beneath would spirit her into the arms of Morpheus in no time.

But she had just enough wit to recognise that the mild pulsing in her forehead would develop into a full-blown migraine come the morning if she didn't drink some milk and eat something sweet.

On auto-pilot, she turned on the radio after flicking on the lights. A cheery - to the point of spaced-out - voice filled the room, talking quickly and energetically of a day of wondrous success. Two women called Katherine Grainger and Anna Watkins (Martha had never heard of them) had evidently won gold in a boat of some kind. Four guys - Burke, Clancy, Thomas and someone else (sounded like a firm of accountants, Martha thought) - had done the same on bikes. Rebecca Adlington (who Martha had heard of) had got a bronze. Some girl called Karina something-or-other had done the same in Judo (Judo? Martha puzzled). While Victoria Pendleton (being the second person Martha had at least heard of) had got a gold as well. In total, the breathlessly euphoric voice sang, *we* now had 8 golds, 6 silvers and 8 bronzes with 'more surely to follow' when 'our Jess and Mo' hit the track ...

Martha was about to switch the thing off when the announcer's voice suddenly dropped three octaves in search of seriousness. 'Meanwhile, police in south London are investigating the unexpected death of a prominent City banker.'

Unexpected? Martha all-but laughed, who would 'expect' to open the door and get shot through the forehead?

She stopped listening to the remaining news - something about France followed by something about some C-list celebrity - to the point that she was surprised the thing was still on as she finished a first glass of ice-cold milk. Refilling her glass while munching an oat cake, she pressed her elbow down on the large on/off button, welcoming the peace in which to think. With just the sound of her teeth crunching through sweet, crispy biscuit, she let her mind drift for a moment.

Why, she started to focus, was it all suddenly just about Gallini? Is he really the key? Wasn't it still relevant to look deeper at Ian Green? He may have meant little, but everything says he knew the killer. More than that, the killer must have seen the problem that posed. Why else take the guys stuff and fiddle with his mobile? Find his killer and we find the killer of all three.

Then she remembered Rosie's apparently off-the-wall question: what if Gallini had Green junior killed and Green senior found out? That meant more than one killer, so who for Green? The Butler! she giggled. Or rather, the chauffeur ... Funny, she thought, no-one seems to have wondered where he was?

But none of that helped at all with Charlie's death. Why on earth would anyone really want all that police activity around on the day they planned on killing Gallini? Everything so far pointed to the killer knowing, somehow or other, that the man would be on his own during the afternoon and that the gates to his house were broken. That pointed to Green senior, no question. Yet he didn't sound stupid enough to want an audience!

Or could it just be that the killer was being over-clever. Calculating that the presence of police up and down the road would lessen any worry about opening the door?

Actually, Martha pondered while taking another long drink of cool milk, that's not such a silly thought. Maybe that was the whole point of Charlie's killing? An act so extreme it paradoxically made people feel safer because their area was awash with police.

Saturday, 4 August 2012

Chapter 20

It was a little before 7am when Rosie turned into the service road leading to the large Waitrose, and then immediately right into the narrow slipway down to the Police Station car park. Waiting at the bottom was a greeny-blue Japanese hatchback of some kind. Can't be, she thought to herself, stopping short of the little card-reading machine and getting out of her car.

"Can I help?" she asked, walking around the back of her car while looking, as friendly as she could muster that time in the morning, at the calm but unsmiling guy looking back.

"Front desk said wait here," the guy replied. "Guess I forgot to ask what for!"

"Eh, yeah," a slightly uncertain Rosie replied. "Sorry, you're not by any chance ..."

"Jeremy Benson," the guy smiled at last. "So, are you by any chance ..."

"Rosie Charlton?"

"Yes," Jeremy smiled more widely.

"No, sorry," Rosie teased. "Never heard of her. Guess the desk will let you in when they're good and ready," she suggested, making as if to turn without offering any conviction in the idea.

"OK, no probs," Jeremy accepted.

"Alright, look," Rosie relented, turning back to face the most senior officer she had ever dared joke around with. "Follow me and we'll see what we can do."

Having made more serious introductions in the car park, Rosie led DCS Benson upstairs to meet the Duty Desk-Sergeant and collect a temporary pass. Then up to the almost deserted CID wing on the second floor. Almost deserted save for Jo and Martha, both with their eyes glued to screens, pens scribbling on pads.

"Ladies," Rosie acknowledged on her way to her room.

"Ma'am," Jo and Martha replied without losing focus on their work.

"Your people?" Jeremy asked as Rosie closed the door.

"Two of them, TDCs but I've high hopes ... Of course, you've already spoken to Martha."

"Ah yes," Jeremy smiled, "TDC Cunningham, is that ...?"

Rosie nodded proudly while filling her cafetière with something richly aromatic.

"Well, she was certainly, how to put it, persuasive ...!"

"You mean wouldn't let you brush her off with: well now, this is all very sensitive ..."

"Exactly that," Jeremy laughed. "But she was charming, if a little posh?"

"Yes, she is," Rosie nodded, pushing a cup of coffee across to DCS Benson. "Both," she added, trying judge, evaluate, weigh-up this presumably very well-thought of senior officer.

And first impressions were a little confusing. The car - obviously not Met issue - was understated yet clean (how many DCS' have time to wash their cars?) and fitted with a very dinky-looking child-seat in the back (so he's left a wife and kid car-less!?).

He wasn't especially tall, maybe 5'9", but stocky. Looked like he'd probably been good to have around in those early PC days. His accent - and his ways for that matter - were very London. Not like some EastEnders' caricature, just so of the city.

More cuttingly, Rosie considered, he didn't seem to fit the University-educated model of most of the younger senior people she'd met at the Yard. Yet he did look young for a DCS, maybe early forties. So, either he was a favourite of the new Commissioner, or he must have pulled off some seriously impressive results as a DI / DCI. Or both, she supposed.

As they talked briefly through the few facts they had, Rosie began to wonder more and more what DCS Benson's unique selling point really was. He nodded at appropriate points, smiled encouraging, looked like he was taking everything in easily enough - well, there wasn't much to take in of course - but he didn't actually question any of Rosie's assumptions or calculations.

Next, with the whole team present (Gurmel having snaffled two extra chairs) he was really quite charming, deliberately playing down his rank and purpose, insisting they all call him Jeremy; and so on. Once or twice, Rosie felt she saw hints of interest in both Jo and Martha that might be a tad unprofessional ... But then she saw the moment differently and felt a little ashamed for being so ungenerous. He was no Billy O'Neill. And nor was he a Chief Superintendent Jeffrey. For all that he didn't come over like an intellectual, there were no reasons at all for thinking that DCS Jeremy Benson was anything but one very smart cookie. The question was - Rosie thought - when's he going to start making sure everyone knows it?

Then he did something that surprised Rosie even more. It was with some hesitation - trepidation, indeed (that she did a poor job of disguising) - that she turned to the immediate tasks as she saw them. The elephant in the room, for her, had been a fear that the DCS would insist on leading all the major interviews. And yet - maybe sensing such a sensitivity, maybe because he'd never dreamed of doing such a thing - Jeremy suggested he might most usefully stay back and work with Gurmel on collating the latest from SOCOs and the pathologist. For a moment Rosie truly didn't know what to say. Her mind was awash with negativity: he obviously thinks I'm not on top of the evidence, she chided herself.

Then she heard him add: "And Mrs Gallini has a right to expect a visit from the investigation's lead detective ..."

And so it was agreed that Gerard and Martha would head off to Penge to visit Ian Green's address and find, if they could, this Peter Lupton; while Rosie and Jo would visit Mrs Dearmer and then make the eleven o'clock appointment with Mrs Gallini. Depending on their success or otherwise, Gerard and Martha would visit the Cassidys. If not, Rosie and Jo would do that also. They would then meet again early afternoon to cross-check and, hopefully, reflect on anything the uniform teams turned up.

Rosie, Gerard and Jeremy then put in fifteen minutes with the uniform briefing. Again, Jeremy was charming and friendly, warmly shaking hands with both Superintendent Mitchell and Inspector O'Neill while taking care to insist he was down to help, not take over - he was sure Inspectors Charlton and O'Neill were more than capable of getting the job done.

Amongst all this cheery glad-handing, Rosie noted the scepticism and occasional disbelief lingering in Mike Mitchell's eyes. He smiled whenever the DCS said the right thing, supported smilingly his easily dispersed praise and confidence, acknowledged genuinely his concern to avoid destabilising things. Yet for all that, Rosie sensed, the Superintendent remained unsure of their guest. Suspicious even.

And if Mike was suspicious, then she needed to be also. Or at least, be mindful not to allow the guy's apparent humility and generosity to blind her to the fact that his presence was due to either or both: a lack of trust amongst the Force's most senior people (and/or their political masters); and, the hint that there could be a connection to an infamous crime that remained suspiciously unsolved.

Chapter 21

Inevitably, Gerard and Martha chatted to no real conclusion about DCS Jeremy Benson, arriving at the run down 1960s estate almost without realising it.

"Been here before?" Gerard asked.

"Never," Martha replied, looking around the area somewhat quizzically. "It kind of ..." she continued, trying to make some sense of the story of the four low-rise blocks arranged around a scruffy square: part-concrete, part-scrub, part rubbish-tip. "Well, it doesn't look that bad. I mean, the Marsfield it is not."

"No, not so wild. But trust me, it's still grim. Mostly addicts, inadequates and hookers ... was once better, but all the families moved out years ago. I doubt there's anyone here with what you'd understand as a job. Shame, but I guess places like this serve a social purpose ..."

"Which is?" Martha asked.

"Saves everyone else the bother of knowing stuff they'd rather not," Gerard smiled. "Now, which block is it?"

"Mark," Rosie replied. "They all named after Apostles or something?"

"Yep, clue's in the name," Gerard nodded with a hint of sarcasm. "The Apostles' Estate!"

"Ah," Martha giggled.

"Now," Gerard mused, scanning the blocks for any sign of movement behind the windows. "That one," he continued, pointing towards an entrance with one still intact door, the other smashed and hanging off its hinges. "You see anyone around, any movement?"

"None," Martha replied. "Why, you worried ..."

"What ... oh no," Gerard laughed. "I mean, we need to be sensible, but there's no history of this place housing serious villains. They usually want somewhere that doesn't stink of piss, sex and weed. No, I was thinking, while we're here we might as well watch to see if anyone does a runner ..."

"Lupton?"

"Or anyone. Everyone's got something to hide ..."

"So, thinking about Green, there's likely to be plenty of dealing here?"

"Yeah, low level ... Uniform come round now and then and we raid occasionally, but obviously the real interest is who brings the stuff in. Bigger problem, at least as far as the posher houses up the road are concerned, is guy's cruising around at night looking for a ... yeah, well," Gerard stopped himself as they entered the lobby.

"Aw god," Martha groaned as the stench hit them.

"Yeah, well," Gerard grimaced. "As I was saying ... Right, my guess is number 11 will be on the top floor and frankly, even if there was a lift I wouldn't use it ..."

"Mr Lupton?" Gerard asked of the pale-faced, sleepy-eyed, half-dressed, skinny guy.

"No," came the reply, half muffled by the closing door.

"Then get him," Gerard barked, kicking the door fully open.

"Who the fuck ..." the skinny guy started, trying to look tough.

"Police," Martha smiled sweetly, holding her Warrant Card with a casual elegance that seemed to all-but mesmerise the once angry-man.

"OK, what do you want?"

"Like I told you," Gerard smiled. "Peter Lupton."

"Th-that's m-me ..." the guy replied, sensing - wrongly - a gathering menace behind Gerard's smile.

"But ... well now I'm confused," Gerard grinned, casting a momentarily perplexed glance to Martha before staring back into the guy's troubled face. "Just now you said you weren't?"

"I was ... look, what do you want?"

"ID first," Gerard ordered. "No, first, make that an invitation to come in ... Thank you," he grinned without waiting for an answer. "Then ... we'll talk ..."

"But I ..."

"About your car," Gerard added, looking back over his shoulder while walking down the unlit and obviously unloved hallway.

Martha closed the door behind them and gagged momentarily on the stale stench of sweet smoke and poor food. The place was a dirty tip, probably hadn't been cleaned in ten years. The carpet - such as it was - was almost black with dirt, the walls a shitty-shade of beige, the ceiling a yellow-shade of white ... possibly. To the right was a room containing an unmade bed and a mess of junk, clothes and boxes. To the left a bathroom so disgusting Martha pulled its door to with her sleeve. A little further down was a kitchen even more disgusting, not least for the absence of a door to hide it away. At the end of the hallway a room maybe twelve feet square boasted two filthy sofas and an equally horrid chair, a broken table and a cardboard box supporting a small, old-fashioned portable television.

"Right," Gerard began, choosing to stand as Lupton slumped down defeatedly in the chair. "So you are Peter Lupton?"

"Yeah."

"Date of birth?"

"Eh," the now resignedly timid guy began, his dim face suggesting an inner-struggle with the intricacies of the question. "10th of October."

Gerard looked across to Martha who checked her notes before nodding.

"How long have you lived here?"

"Eh," Lupton began in his now common way. "Some years ..."

"OK, let me just check, you last left prison in ..."

"February 2009," Martha confirmed.

"February 2009," Gerard repeated. "A little over three years ago. Did you live here before you went inside?"

"No."

"So you've lived here three and a bit years," Gerard smiled.

"I guess."

"You guess," Gerard continued sarcastically. "And Ian Green, how long's he lived here?"

"Ian, he don't, I mean, he was ..."

"Does Ian Green live here?" Gerard asked more sharply.

"No, not really, he's ..."

"Yes, I know, he's been in prison," Gerard continued somewhat exasperated. "But before he went inside, did he live here?"

"Yes."

"And since he's been out of prison?"

"He stayed a couple of nights ..."

"And then went off in your car?"

"Well, yeah, but that's because ..." Lupton stopped, as if realising he was about to say something he perhaps would be better off not saying.

"Go on, that was because of what ... You owed him?"

"Well, kind of ..."

"Look," Gerard said with sudden sharpness, tiring of Lupton's dimness. "We really don't give a damn what you sold of his, or whatever it was you did. We just want to get a couple of things straight. You own a Citroën, registration ..." he began, looking across to Martha.

"R529XWR."

"Well?"

"Yeah. Well kind of ... I mean, really the car belong to Flipz ..."

"Sorry, who is Flipz?"

"He's," a suddenly very scared looking Lupton began. "He's like this person and he's like ..."

"Mr Lupton," Gerard barked. "Right now I'm not interested in Mr Flipz other than this: are you telling me this car, this ..."

"Citroën zx Temptation," Martha said, enjoying the teasing ridiculousness of the car's name.

"This Citroën zx Temptation used to belong to someone else?"

"Yeah, that's what I'm saying," a relieved Lupton agreed.

"But then it became yours ..."

"I guess."

"Well I think you can do more than just guess," Gerard smiled, this time with a hint of menace. "I think, seeing as it's your name on the fucking record, you might as well just say Yes!"

"OK, yes, yes ... but ..."

"But what, you've got no tax, got no insurance. Indeed, you don't appear to have a licence, as far as we can tell ..."

"How'd you ..."

"We're police, shit-head," Gerard replied harshly. "So, Ian Green stayed here for, what did you say, a few days?"

"Yeah, about ..."

"And then he went off in your car. You let him?"

"Yeah, like I said, I ..."

"You did. Where was he going?"

"I don't know," Lupton replied with believable speed.

"You sure?" Gerard asked, deliberately playing up the menace now.

"Yeah, he just said he was going out. Wouldn't be back 'cos he had to go and see someone the next day ..."

"Hold on," Gerard interrupted. "When did he go out, not Thursday morning?"

"No, like I told you, he went out Tuesday. Tuesday night ..."

"Tuesday? How can you be so sure?" Gerard asked while trying to weigh the relevance of the possibility there might be upwards of thirty-six hours unaccounted for in Green's movements.

"Flipz comes for his money on Tuesdays. Ian didn't want to see him ..."

"Flipz comes for the rent?" Gerard asked. "So this place belongs to Mr Flipz?"

"Yeah."

"And tell me this Peter," Gerard continued with disarming charm, smiling as he took a step towards the guy. "What does rent mean?"

"Money," Lupton replied with matter-of-fact stupidity.

"Money," Gerard smiled. "Are we talking about money you draw from that Trust Fund your rich uncle set up for you ..."

"What?" a truly puzzled Lupton replied.

"No, thought not. So let's try another guess ... How about this: Flipz supplies, you sell. He comes round once a week for the money and you get to keep, what, 25%"

"Fifteen," super-stupid Lupton replied.

"15% ... right," Gerard sighed while looking back at Martha who just shrugged her shoulders. "So why didn't Ian want to meet Flipz?"

"He owe Flipz, from before like ..."

"Before he went inside? But that was for something to do with cigarettes, wasn't it?"

"I don't know."

"You don't know," Gerard sneered with renewed hostility, delivered now from barely two feet away from a visibly trembling Lupton. "Why don't I believe you?"

"I ... I don't know ..."

"Look, grow the fuck up Peter," Gerard barked. "Do you honestly think I'm here because of you. Do you serious think Detective Cunningham and I would risk catching some god-awful disease in this dump over you? We're not interested in you," he continued. "We are interested in Green. Now, you haven't seen him since Tuesday whenever. Do you know why?"

"He hasn't come back ..."

"Yeah, well," Gerard laughed, rolling his eyes to an equally amused Martha. "That's a fact, but not a reason. What we want to know is whether Mr Flipz could have been that reason?"

"Sorry?"

"Flipz, fucking Flipz," Gerard shouted. "Do you think he would harm Ian if he found him. Teach him a lesson, that sort of thing?"

"Well, yeah, course ..."

"How much of a lesson?"

"Well, bad like," Lupton replied, shaking. "You know, bad like ..."

"Bad as in kick the shit out of him ... or worse?"

"Yeah, just the shit," Lupton suggested, sadly if somewhat ambiguously.

"OK. Where does Flipz live?"

"I don't know."

"No, I don't suppose you know his address. But where abouts: Crystal Palace, Norwood, Croydon ..."

"Nah, don't think so, I think ..."

"Is he black?"

"No."

"Oh, right," a slightly puzzled Gerard acknowledged. "Unusual sounding tag for a white guy, isn't it?"

"No," an equally puzzled Lupton replied. "Crisz is black."

"Whose Crisz?"

"Flipz' friend."

"Know where he lives?"

"Nah. Nice car though."

"What car?"

"Crisz. Got a BMW ..."

"You don't say," Gerard laughed.

"Well cool ..."

"So Crisz and Flipz are a team, same car and all that?"

"Sometimes, but not on Tuesdays," Lupton smiled, thinking he was being praised for helpfulness.

"So what does that mean?" a now exasperated Gerard asked.

"Tuesdays Flipz just comes alone."

"Car?"

"BMW."

"Right," Gerard smiled. "So they both have BMWs?"

"Yeah, Flipz's is red, Crisz's is black."

"Right, OK," Gerard sighed. "So, let's just check this one last time. Ian stayed here for a few days after getting out, but didn't want to be around when Flipz came by. So he slipped out on Tuesday and you haven't seen or heard from him since?"

"That's right."

"You worried about him?"

"Nah, Ian's alright. He knows when to stay out the way."

"Does he," Gerard smiled thinly. "Does he now. But if, let's say, he did run into Flipz, you reckon he'd take a beating. That's all?"

"Yeah."

"And Crisz, what would he do?"

"Nothing. He ain't got no issues with Ian."

"OK. Thanks," Gerard smiled. "We'll be getting along then."

"You know where Ian is?" Peter suddenly asked, a little sad-eyed.

"Er ..." Gerard began, weighing whether it might be a kindness to lie, at least for now. "Right now, no I don't," he replied with technical accuracy.

As they headed back towards the car, across the scruffy, crap-filled square, Gerard asked: "Well?"

"Well what?" Martha replied a little clipped. "What do I think about you lying? Or what do I think about who you lied to?"

"Let's start with the second," a sheepish Gerard suggested.

"OK. Dimmer than anyone I've previously met, but probably telling the truth."

"Yeah, I thought that too," Gerard nodded. "Well, actually, not the dim part. Trust me, you'll meet worse! But yeah, telling the truth. So, we need to get some local intelligence on who Flipz and Crisz might be. Doesn't sound totally promising, but we have to check to see if they could kill ..."

"And the lying part?" Martha asked.

"No need, I can guess," Gerard accepted with good grace.

Chapter 22

Rosie got out of the car and had a good look around. It took her a few seconds to work out that the row of large, detached houses they had pulled up outside backed onto the railway line. Only when she spotted the narrow alley ahead and to the right, did she realise this was the same row of rather attractive, detached, Tudor-Bethan villas they had passed the day before after crossing the suicide-proof bridge. So this is where Mrs Dearmer lives, she thought, nearer the bridge than the tunnel. Did that mean anything?

"Hello, Mrs Dearmer?" Jo asked of the small, well-dressed, middle-aged woman who answered the door.

"Yes?"

"We're from Bromley CID, Detective Hartley and Detective Inspector Charlton. May we come in for a moment?"

"Yes, I suppose," the woman replied a little hesitantly.

As she followed Mrs Dearmer into the large hallway, Rosie felt herself being surprised by a clear and elegant sense of good-taste filling the space. The nostalgia-evoking style of the outside carried on inside. At the end of the hall, a wide staircase ran up towards a large window with a very attractive stained-glass image of a peacock diffusing the light into delicate blues and greens. The walls were partly wood-panelled, part painted bright white.

That, no doubt, was just how the house had been built. But the things Mrs Dearmer had added spoke of independence and affluence. An elegant, blonde wood table ran along one wall, contrasting beautifully with the dark-wood panelling. On it stood a multi-coloured vase, perhaps ten inches tall. A much larger version of the vase stood on the floor, against the opposite wall. This one filled with half a dozen huge, swirling peacock feathers. Then, beneath the arch formed as the staircase turned back on itself, there stood a wide, multi-coloured plastic chair that looked exactly like something Rosie had seen in a glossy magazine when last having her hair cut. Something, she recalled, staggeringly expensive.

Following the woman through the wide, double-doored opening into a lounge that ran from front to back down one side of the house, Rosie was struck once again by the obvious care - and money - that had gone into finding the right combination of sofas, side tables, rugs, glassware and paintings. And all of it modern; not ultra modern in any kind of kitsch way, just elegant, simple and well-made.

Accepting the invitation to sit Rosie looked Mrs Dearmer up and down. Her clothes, like her house, looked expensive, well-chosen and stylish. A simple navy skirt, a twin-set in silver-grey, a thin row of pearls, an expensive looking watch.

"I'm sorry to have to take up your time," Rosie began, watching Mrs Dearmer sit in the sofa opposite, folding her hands demurely in her lap. "I appreciate you had quite an unpleasant experience on Thursday ..."

"It wasn't nice, that is true," the lady replied in a polite if slightly clipped way.

"No, of course not," Rosie smiled as empathetically as she could. "Obviously, we are doing all we can to find out what happened ..."

"And since I believe?"

"Yes, indeed," Rosie nodded. "I ... can I just ask one question about 'since', as it were. I believe you have a dog ..."

"Yes, Roger."

"Roger, nice," Rosie said for no good reason. "Do you take Roger into the woods every day?"

"Yes, pretty much every day," Mrs Dearmer said, her voice gentle yet precise.

"I see, so yesterday ..."

"Yesterday, yes."

"At what time?"

"Usual time, I always go at noon. We have lunch when we get back."

"We?"

"Roger and I."

"Of course," Rosie smiled. "So yesterday, you didn't see any of what happened?"

"No, but also, I am thinking I didn't go to same place."

"Sorry?"

"Each day I try to take different walk. On Thursday I was going to go up the central paths when ..."

"Yes, of course, like I said, horrible experience for you. We are truly very grateful you took the trouble to ring in ..."

"What else could one do?" Mrs Dearmer asked, as if genuinely shocked by a suggestion she might have walked on past.

"Of course," Rosie repeated. "But yesterday?"

"Yesterday, I took bridge, went down to river and back. Was not great choice. Roger got very muddy."

Rosie smiled on imagining the elegant Mrs Dearmer having to scrub some playfully filthy mutt. "I see. We're interested in a much earlier time. I don't know whether you might perhaps have seen, from your window ..."

"Seen what?"

"Would have been shortly after 8 o'clock, a man ... Jo," Rosie prompted.

"We don't have a great description ..." Jo began.

Please don't say weird guy, Rosie thought.

"... white, slim, around five foot nine, wearing dark trousers, possibly jogging bottoms and a dark top. Could have had the hood up ..."

"See anyone looking like that go past shortly after eight yesterday morning, Mrs Dearmer? Probably coming from the bridge direction ..." Rosie asked.

"No," Mrs Dearmer replied simply.

"OK," Rosie continued slowly, not sure where to go next. "Can we just come back to Thursday. I've been to the scene.

As I understand it you were, what, walking up the path just to the left from the tunnel and you saw ..."

"Yes."

"What did you think?" Rosie asked without being sure why.

"I thought perhaps man had fallen. Had heart attack or something. But when I got closer I saw ..." Mrs Dearmer's voice petered out.

"Yes, I know, awful for you," Rosie smiled reassuringly. "Who else did you see, just in those first few moments. Who did you see?"

"See?" Mrs Dearmer began, thinking. "Well, I think I saw the man with the West Highland Terrier. I often see him going up towards the main road ..."

"West Highland Terrier?" Rosie pondered.

"Small white dog, ma'am," Jo explained helpfully. "Really cute. There's one in that Cesar advert ..."

"Oh yes," Rosie nodded, vaguely recalling being told something like that before.

"They look very similar," Mrs Dearmer put in.

"What do?" Rosie asked, confused.

"Westies and Cairns."

"Right, OK," Rosie said slowly while wondering what had happened to the conversation.

"Is that what Roger is?" Jo asked.

"Yes." Mrs Dearmer replied proudly if unspecific.

"Cairn ..."

"Brindle."

"Er, sorry Mrs Dearmer," Rosie smiled pleadingly. "So Roger is a ..."

"Brindle Cairn. Looks like a West Highland Terrier, but brown."

"I see. I'm pleased we got that straight. Anyone else?"

"On Thursday?"

"Yes," Rosie replied, her patience waning.

"Well, yes. After I called police I sat on bench waiting. Lots of people walked past ..."

"All dog walkers?"

"Yes, of course," Mrs Dearmer replied, as though the question was amongst the most stupid she'd ever heard.

"Can I ask," Rosie continued. "Do you recall seeing anyone there without a dog?"

"No."

"Do you ever? I mean, in the woods, are there people walking without dogs?"

"At weekends, yes. Sometimes a lot, families, groups ... But during the week, no, not really."

"I see," Rosie nodded. "Well," she continued, thinking there was something else she should ask but unable to decide quite what it was. "Best we leave you now," she smiled, standing. "But I'll just leave you this," she said, placing a card on the wood and glass table next to Mrs Dearmer's sofa. "Please ring me if you want to know anything or if anything else pops into your head."

"Ah, here is Roger," Mrs Dearmer sang as a small bundle of curly brown fur with an excitedly wagging tail met them in the hall.

"Aw," Jo sighed, all gooey and smitten, leaning down to stroke the dog's head.

"Yeah, nice," Rosie agreed without meaning it. She'd never much liked dogs. "Tell me," she looked to Mrs Dearmer. "I guess you probably all recognise each other by your dogs?"

"In woods? Yes, I think that is true," Mrs Dearmer laughed.

"So, lots of different types of dog?"

"Yes, lots. Some people have same dog. Lots of labradors for some reason ..."

"How about West Highland Terriers?" Rosie asked suddenly, remembering something Gloria Gascoigne had said.

"No, I think I only see one," Mrs Dearmer replied, her interest more focused on the attention Jo was paying her dog.

"I bet there's not another Roger either," Jo smiled, tickling the now even more excited dog beneath his chin.

"No, not Brindle," Mrs Dearmer confirmed proudly. "Lady I see has a Wheaten ..."

"Really," Jo nodded absently, her attention taken fully by Roger. "You a good boy?"

"Yes, well," a mildly embarrassed Rosie began. "We'll leave you now Mrs Dearmer ..."

As they got back in the car Jo's phone rang. "Hartley. Yes Gurmel? It's Gurmel," she explained unnecessarily for her watching and listening boss.

"Really," Rosie laughed.

"Yes ... right ... really, how's that ... mmm ... No!" Jo suddenly exclaimed, her voice rising an octave. "Ma'am," she said, her hand over the mouthpiece. "They've got an ID for that other car ..."

"Other car?"

"Yes, you remember Gurmel had suspicions about two cars ..."

"Oh yeah, and?"

"Belongs to a Ryan Christopher Kenny, address on the Marsfield Estate ..."

"Hmm," Rosie sighed, rolling her eyes.

"Yeah, but there's more. They checked his history, we know him. And while it's yonks ago, looks like he was in Feltham with Ian Green; 2001."

"Really? That sounds too much like a coincidence," Rosie thought. "What's the time?" she asked rhetorically while looking at her watch. "Just after ten, we couldn't get there

and back to Mrs Gallini for 11am. Tell him to ring Gerard.
Get him and Martha down there, see what's what ..."

Chapter 23

For all that the Apostles' Estate was sad and somewhat depressing, the Marsfield was simply horrible and almost beyond belief. It was built in the same brutalist style as the soulless blocks one might expect to see in documentaries about poverty in eastern European slums, or alienation in American ghettos. It was the kind of place that literally sucked the hope out of anyone who visited it - so god alone knew what it did to those forced to live there.

One of the more recent sadnesses about the place lay in the fact that it had - largely because no-one who knew it would accept living there - become home to a mixed-up cocktail of the recently arrived: migrants awaiting clearance, refugees awaiting processing, Albanians, Bulgarians and Croats waiting for a change to some EU-directive or other. Having suffered whatever they had endured in search of a better life, they had ended up worse off than even their nightmares could have dreamed.

The lobby to the sixteen storey, dirty-grey concrete tower named, for no obvious reason, Mallard was, in a curious contrast to Mark of Penge, fairly clean. Certainly, there was no obvious filth. The lift also seemed clean enough and working, but Gerard's innate scepticism insisted they walk the six flights to Flat 31. The windowless corridor was less welcoming. Just a single light managed to stay flickeringly awake, and that down the far end.

"OK, we take this carefully," Gerard suggested while looking around for something to prop open the door to the stairwell, which did at least enjoy some natural light from a long slit of frosted and wired glass running up the outside of the block. "Fuck it," he concluded, finding nothing of use and so resorting to flipping out several sheets from his neatly ordered notepad, folding them over and over till they were thick enough to use as a wedge. "Right, onwards," he smiled.

The girl who answered could have been seventeen, but certainly no older. That wasn't to say she looked either blooming or pretty. More that her pale skin, emaciated body and spaced-out eyes still bore a fleeting memory of juvenilia that in all probability would be gone in another year, maybe less.

"What," the girl tried to sneer, but only succeeded in slurring.

"Police," Martha replied, wafting her Warrant Card without any expectation of the girl actually being able to focus on it.

"Ryan Kenny at home?" Gerard asked.

"Who?"

"Ryan Christopher Kenny, this is his flat."

"Is it?" the girl asked dumbly.

"Who the fuck are you," asked the much older, unattractive but at least less stoned woman who suddenly appeared from behind the door.

"Police," Gerard snapped back. "And who the fuck are you?"

"What's it to you?"

"Look, this isn't a fucking game. We're the police. We're looking for Ryan Kenny. If we don't find him, we're gonna nick you instead. OK? So I'll ask again. Who the fuck are you? And where the fuck is Ryan Fucking Kenny?" Gerard shouted with intentional malice.

"Don't know him," the older woman snarled back.

"You know what, I don't believe you. Now, invite us in ..."

"No ..."

"Thanks," Gerard replied, pushing the door fully open and stepping in quickly to see if anyone else was behind it. They weren't. "Now," he said slowly, gazing down the long hallway that ran parallel to the outer corridor, a series of rooms opening down the righthand side. "Why don't you walk down there," he ordered, pointing to a room - he guessed to be the lounge - at the far end of the hallway. "Nice and slowly while we just check where Ryan is ..."

"I told you, ain't no Ryan here," the older woman snarled while doing exactly as she was told.

Closing the front-door quietly, Martha watched as Gerard followed the two women down to the first door.

"Bathroom," Gerard called back. "Empty." The girl was by now nearly at the end of the hallway. "Stop there," he ordered, making the poor thing turn with a jump, her startled face looking sad and anxious.

"Just wait there a moment," Martha said, feeling some inner need to make the experience as unthreatening as possible.

The girl said nothing. Indeed, it wasn't absolutely obvious whether she had even really registered the sense or tone of Martha's words. She just stared back, her dark, deep-set eyes looking haunted, her pale face looking gaunt, her skinny body looking angular and ill-at-ease in a thin dress that was at least one size too big, possibly two. Martha wondered whether it actually belonged to the older woman.

"Kitchen," Gerard called while looking through the next opening. "Also empty ... hold on," he ordered of the older woman as they reached the third door. "Let's take a look in here ... you first."

Martha waited by the doorway as Gerard followed the woman into a rather large bedroom. While the bed was unmade and the plain white furniture cheap, she could not help but contrast the general feel of this place with Lupton's hovel on the supposedly less-ghettoised Apostles' Estate. Maybe it was a woman's touch - not that the woman now standing sullenly watching as Gerard checked under the bed and in each of the two wardrobes - looked like she spent too much time thinking about appearances.

Her age was hard to guess. Her face - and just about everything about the way she looked and held herself - said drinker. And probably since she was the girl's age, or younger. Her skin was yellowed, her lips pale and pursed, her eyes bloodshot and barely half-open, her neck thin and scrawny, her shoulders slumped, her breasts obviously sagging beneath a plain white t-shirt that fell maybe three inches down thighs whose only colour lay in a pair of unsightly bruises and a prominent mauve vein. Her hands trembled slightly as she tried to tuck an unwashed streak of mousey-brown hair behind one ear.

But for all that the place carried the same sweet fragrance of weed - mixed with the strong scent of cheap gin - it seemed reasonably clean, cared for even.

"OK, next," Gerard said breezily while striding back out into the hallway. "And this is?" he asked of the woman while looking into a small, empty room, permanent shadows on the walls and grooves in the cheap carpet telling of at least some past purpose.

"Empty, no use," the woman replied with a mixture of sarcasm and fractured grammar.

"You got too much space, right?" Gerard nodded while walking into the room as if expecting the space to talk for itself. "OK, on ..."

As Gerard walked back into the hall the shy, wordless girl caught Martha's eye with an uncertain gaze. "Yes, in there now," Martha smiled, following both women and Gerard into a surprisingly large and bright room. To the far side an oblong window ran almost the full width of the wall.

"And she is?" Gerard asked, pointing to a girl - probably younger than the first - lying totally zonked-out in a corner.

"A friend," the older woman replied, but without quite so much confidence or challenge as before.

The air in the room was even sweeter and more stale. Two bottles of Tesco gin stood on the table, one empty the other halfway there. Besides them, scattered with no obvious pattern, were two packets of Silver Kings, a cigarette roller and giant papers, a see-through plastic bag containing maybe a couple of ounces, three tumblers, two ashtrays and two lighters.

Two faux-leather sofas in a kind of faded green formed an L-shape around the table, one of which bore an odd assortment of clothes. The windows were curtain-less - perhaps not a necessity six floors up with a view out to the

North Downs some ten miles south. A selection of candles (unlit) and incense-burners (one lighted, two not) stood on the windowsill.

And that was it. No television, no photos, no ornaments. Nothing really to confirm that the place - though clean - was truly a home.

"A friend," Gerard repeated, looking around, tying to work out the story. "OK, so where is Ryan Kenny?" he asked sharply, taking an intimidating step towards the older women.

Pleadingly, the still wordless girl stared to Martha while pressing herself up close to the woman.

"I told you. Don't fucking know him!" the woman shouted.

"And I told you," Gerard shouted more loudly. "I don't fucking believe you! Now, here's what's going to happen," he continued more reasonably while walking across the room to look closely at the girl lying in the corner. "What she had?"

"What you mean?"

"What has she had?" Gerard barked. "Gin, blaze, what else?"

"Nothing else," the woman replied sharply (honestly even, Martha thought).

"So, she's passed out on gin and a few puffs of weed, yeah?"

"Yes," the woman replied precisely.

"And she's what, fourteen?"

"About," the woman replied less convincingly, a protective arm now holding the older girl, who looked like she was starting to cry.

"OK," Gerard began, coldly. "You tell me in the next five seconds where Ryan Kenny is, or I'm arresting you for brothel keeping ..."

"What! What the fuck you talking ..."

"And seeing as you've already told me this one," Gerard sneered, pointing down to the half naked girl on the floor.

"Isn't even fourteen, that will come with a charge of assisting the rape of a minor. What's the tariff for that?" he asked of Martha.

"Sixteen, minimum," Martha extemporised cruelly.

"Sixteen years, minimum," Gerard repeated slowly while walking back from the window, his stare burning into the startled eyes of the girl now clinging to the older woman. "And what about you, how old are you?"

"Sixteen," the girl replied, her fear sobering her up rapidly.

"Sixteen! Such symmetry ..."

"Eh?"

"You been in prison before. Those old dykes in Holloway will just love you ..."

"No!" The girl started to sob, burying her face in the older woman's shoulder.

"Alright, alright, alright," the older woman shouted.

"Alright what?" Gerard snarled, softening slightly to ask: "You got a name by the way?"

"Maureen Freeman."

"You known to us Maureen Freeman?"

"I guess."

"What for? Drink, drugs, whoring ..."

"Yeah, I guess," the woman replied sadly.

"OK," Gerard replied, somewhat chastened by the woman's meek surrender. "Look, sit down," he ordered, turning away to gather his thoughts, his eyes focusing sadly on the tiny girl in the corner, still oblivious to everything.

"So why," Martha asked, sitting herself on the curved arm of the sofa Maureen and the older girl sat in. "Why don't you want to tell us where Ryan is?"

"He don't live here," Maureen replied, her eyes staring at Martha with a look that could only be disbelief.

"Well, we guessed that," Martha smiled. "But that wasn't what I asked. I asked why you don't want to tell us where he does live?"

"Because ..."

"Listen," Martha continued, her voice calm, charming and calming. "In a moment, my colleague is going to ask you again where we can find Ryan Kenny. If you don't answer, then we will arrest you, and her ..." she smiled hurtfully while nodding to the girl shaking and sobbing gently next to Maureen. "And have her put in care," she smiled even more cruelly while waving a hand vaguely towards the corner.

"Why them?"

"Why not? They're here, you're not helping us, they get to suffer. What d'you expect us to do?"

"They suffered enough."

"OK, then tell us what we want to know and maybe we'll leave you in peace," Martha suggested tantalisingly, while inwardly wondering whether they really could or should do that.

"Who are they by the way?" Gerard asked, connecting naturally with Martha's obvious concern.

"Sisters."

"OK, sisters. Who are the parents?"

"Mary."

"Just Mary?"

"Yeah, well - No. Mary Lee, lives over in Tarn."

"That the next block?" Gerard asked.

"One after."

"Right, but ..." Gerard began without being sure quite what to ask.

"So what, you're looking after them?" Martha asked, while unable to stop herself looking unfavourably at the mess of drink and drugs on the table, and then to the simple mess that was the younger sister.

"Kind of ..."

"Yeah, well I was going to say kind of," Martha agreed disapprovingly. "Let me ask a different question. Does Mary know they're here?"

"Yeah, no ... maybe ..."

"Well which is it?" Gerard snapped. "I mean, where does she think they are?"

"Mary don't know. She don't know fuck all most of the time ..."

"And you do?"

"Look, I'm not good, I know that. I fucking know that better than anyone. But Mary ... you wouldn't understand, you won't understand," Maureen sighed dispiritedly.

"Maureen," Martha began, an idea suddenly connecting the disparate concerns growing confusedly weary of each other in the room. "Has this got something to do with Ryan. I mean, is Mary ..."

"Like I told you," Maureen sighed sadly, her voice barely a whisper now, "Mary's not well ..."

"What she on?" Gerard asked matter-of-factly.

"Drink, crack, dolphins, vallies. I dunno ..." Maureen relied sadly.

"So you've taken the girls in?" Martha asked, nodding to them one after the other.

"Yeah, this is Candy ..."

"Oh No!" Gerard sighed.

"And that's Jade."

"And they're both drunk and stoned," Martha commented sharply.

"Yeah, most of the time," Maureen accepted.

"And Mary?" Gerard asked.

"All of the time."

"And what's all that got to do with Ryan Kenny?" Gerard asked.

"He ... he ..."

"He what, supplies her?"

"Yeah," Maureen accepted quickly.

"And what else?"

"What you think?" Maureen snapped, a spark of anger firing her eyes for a moment.

"Right, so he supplies her, she whores for him," Gerard summarised. "That your story too?"

"No! I don't have anything to do with him, he's ... he's ..."

"So who supplies you?" Gerard asked out of habit.

"Mikey. He's OK. Don't want much ..."

"Don't want much?" Martha asked, her eyes narrowed into quizzical stare.

"He brings someone now and then, that's all. Not often ..."

"But you think Mary ..." Gerard began. "You think Ryan expects more from Mary?"

"Yeah, of course. That's all expensive shit she's on all the time," Maureen replied, as if the trade were obvious.

"Yeah, so to get the girls away from all that, you're letting them stay here?"

"Yeah, that's kind of it," Maureen all-but whispered.

"Well, is that it?" Martha asked, sensing something else.

"Yeah, like I said. Yeah," Maureen tried to insist.

"Why's that room empty?" Gerard asked, pointing through the wall.

"Sold the stuff."

"But why?" Martha asked. "I mean, wouldn't it be better ... now you've got ..."

"I needed the money, needed to ..." Maureen began, stopping in mid-thought. "Look, I'm trying for them, they're not bad girls. I'm trying. I've given them the bed. I've paid ..."

"Hold on," Gerard ordered. "Let me guess, you owed Ryan money?"

"Yes," Maureen confessed in an energy-drained whisper.

"So he used to supply you and ... whatever," Gerard sighed, a mixture of exasperation and disapproval echoing in his voice.

"Look," Maureen snapped. "Yes. OK. O-Fucking-K. I did used to take stuff from him, but he's ... you don't know what he's like, he's ... He's a cunt, that's what he is," she all-but spat while hugging Candy close. "But I won't have him near me no more, nor them ... Mikey paid him so I let him take the furniture, wasn't much ..."

"What he want it for?" Martha asked.

"He got flats too," Maureen explained, as if it was obvious.

"So that's it," Gerard checked. "That room's not used for anything else?"

"No, no, I promise," Maureen insisted. "I ... I sleep in here, the girls have the bed."

"And how long ..." Gerard began, looking back towards Jade, noting sadly how the riding-up of her grubby vest had revealed a rash of unsightly red blotches on her concave stomach. "How long they been here Maureen?"

"A few weeks."

"You think they're getting better, you think they're better off?" Gerard asked, not meaning to sound judgemental or accusing.

"Of course they're fucking better off out of there ..."

"Out of where?" Martha asked, "Mary's place? Why, does Ryan ..."

"Of course he goes there, it's his place. I told you ... I told you ..." Maureen sighed, a few sobs muffling her words now.

"Hold on," Gerard said. "Can I just get one thing clear. Are you telling us that Ryan lives with Mary?"

"What? No, of course not!" Maureen all-but laughed.

"OK. So why doesn't she get rid of him, like you did. Maybe get this Mikey to ..."

"Mikey don't have nothing to do with Tarn. He's got here, Ryan's got there ..."

"So that's what, that's the local deal is it?"

"Yeah, it is now. Has been for a few months," Maureen confirmed.

"I see. So who's got Kingfisher?" Gerard asked of the middle block.

"Rumanians," came the implausibly obvious answer.

"Of course," Gerard laughed despondently.

"OK," Martha began gently. "So Ryan lives over there, somewhere in Tarn?"

"Yeah, yeah. As far as I know he does, he's got ..."

"He's got a few flats, yeah I get that much," Martha nodded. "But not with Mary?"

"No."

"So what number does Mary live at?"

"I told you, he ain't there ..."

"You did say that," Martha smiled. "And I'm believing you. But if you can't tell us which flat he's actually in, you might at least tell us where he isn't. Save us bothering Mary unnecessarily."

"Eh?" Maureen replied, struggling to cope with Martha's obvious, but far too logical argument.

"Just fucking tell us the number," Gerard growled.

"Fourteen."

"Thank you. Oh, and one more thing. What does he look like?"

"Er, about your height," Maureen suggested. "But slimmer ..."

Martha grinned at her colleague, amused, her head mockingly held to one side.

"... dark hair, dark eyes ..."

"White?"

"Yeah, white ..."

"Anything obvious, scars, tattoos?"

"Er, yeah, got a knife scar to his face," Maureen said while tracing a finger down her own right cheek. "And that funny writing stuff up one arm ..."

"Like Beckham," Gerard laughed.

"Yeah, I guess," Maureen agreed uncertainly.

"OK, Maureen, OK," Gerard smiled. "Look, thanks, OK? Stay there, we'll let ourselves out."

Chapter 24

Martha and Gerard said nothing, not a single word, as they retraced their way along the poorly-lit corridor and back out into the relative bright of the stairwell. They said nothing as Gerard paused to gather the torn and dirtied sheets from his notepad. And continued in stoical silence as they went deliberately, one step after another, down towards the ground.

They stepped out into the humid drizzle that had suddenly fallen around the cold and unlovely trilogy of concrete towers. Mallard, Kingfisher and Tarn. Named by an unremembered Council official who, no doubt sincerely, believed he was giving a naturalistic identity to a new and optimistic reserve. One designed to give flight to all those dreams and talents the poor are apocryphally blessed with.

Named in vain. Named only to stand as piss-taking monuments to civic conceit. The Marsfield Estate was no Champs de Mars, no Elysium, no Campus Martius.

But of course, it wasn't the official's fault any more than it was the fault of the builders who put the towers up. Or even of the steel and concrete that kept them standing against wind, rain and the disapproval of those who would never have to live there.

People have to be responsible for their own actions ... and inactions.

"Over there," Gerard suggested, pointing to a battered wall surrounding a collection of large bins on wheels.

He watched as Martha walked to the bins, letting the gin bottle empty on the ground behind her. With some difficulty she pushed the heavy plastic lid up far enough to throw the bottle in before letting the contents of the plastic bag scatter into the foul darkness.

"Well, what did you think?" Gerard asked of the obviously thoughtful - to the point of distraction - Martha.

"I ... I'm ... those girls," Martha mumbled. "I think I believe her. I mean, I want to believe her ... But ..."

"We can go back. We can call Social Services and go back," Gerard noted without enthusiasm.

"I guess ... but would they really do any better? Won't they just try and put them back with the mother and then ..."

"I think we go and see this Mary," Gerard answered decisively.

"I agree," Martha smiled. "In any case, that's part of looking for Kenny."

"Exactly," Gerard nodded, stepping purposefully towards the far tower.

A small group of young, leather-jacketed eastern European men watched them from the lobby of Kingfisher as they walked past. Gerard's phone rang.

"McAvoy."

"Gerard, Jeremy here."

"Jer ... yes Sir," Gerard replied with Pavlovian correctness.

"Have you found Kenny?"

"Not yet. Doesn't live at the address we have, but we're told he may be in one of the other towers ..."

"You think that good intel?" Jeremy asked, sounding more like the pompous and self-important DCS Gerard had expected.

"It's all we have Sir," Gerard replied. "The address we had is old. Woman in the flat now says Tarn, that's all ..."

"You believe her?"

"On balance, Yes. I searched the flat ..."

"She let you in?"

"Yeah ..."

"OK, sorry. Look, there's something new. There was a tag on Kenny's record ..."

"A tag?"

"Sex Offender ..."

"Oh!?"

"The record shows he was arrested a little over three years ago for statutory rape ..."

"Oh god ..." Gerard gasped, looking quickly over his shoulder in the vague location of Maureen Freeman's flat.

"Yes, but there's more. One of the arresting officers was PC Scales."

"Fuck, No! ... But how come Kenny's not ..."

"Girl wouldn't testify. He got off. Happened twice before ... But obviously, right now, the link to Scales ..."

"Yes, of course, but look Sir," Gerard said urgently. "The address we're going to now, in Tarn ..."

"I think you should wait for the van."

"You're sending uniform?"

"Of course. Ten, including two armed."

"OK, right."

"We have to assume he's armed."

"Yes, sure," a slightly disconcerted Gerard answered. "But the address we have now. There used to be two young girls living there, but they're now with ... They're with the woman in Kenny's old place."

"Jesus Christ," DCS Benson exclaimed, his cool momentarily gone. "You think she's keeping them for him?"

"No. No, I honestly don't. I think she's keeping them *from* him."

"OK," Benson replied. "Look, I'm told we'll be about fifteen minutes. Be careful out there."

"Yes Sir ... you're coming yourself?"

"Of course."

"And the DI?"

"I've sent a message. I believe she's with Mrs Gallini. I'm sure she'll join us straight after."

Chapter 25

As she walked up the long gravel path - framed by ornate walls, the perfectly spaced pillars of which were topped with large, flower-full vases - Rosie felt decidedly ill-at-ease. Partly, of course, that was simply because meeting people who had just lost someone in tragic or unexpected circumstances was always difficult, often harrowing. But it was also because she really did not have much to say or ask of Mrs Gallini. For all that logic suggested Gallini's murder was some kind of key to understanding the killings of Ian Green and Charlie Scales, when it came to understanding why someone wanted to kill Herr Gallini there were only two questions to be asked of his wife. Did you do it? If not, do you know who did?

Rosie really did not feel like asking the first, while her instincts - based, of course, on nothing but the little Stella Reeves had been able to share - were that a young, second wife would not know much at all about any dark corners to her husband's business life.

The Hotel was several grades above anything Family Liaison would normally use. A Regency mansion, built for the son of a Kentish farmer who made a fortune from African mines while earning a highly dubious reputation through association with the circle around the dissolute young Prince George. The place had then known highs, lows and lowers, before being reinvented as a school for the sons of the newly-rich middle classes then colonising the once rural village of Bromley.

When, in the 1980s, the school, now co-ed, moved to a brand-new campus of fit-for-purpose buildings on a site a mile or so down the road, a local consortium bought the old house and invested far more than they had intended rediscovering and restoring all those intricately elegant rococo features. It then reopened as an expensive - and so, exclusive - Hotel and Conference Centre.

The grounds, Rosie noted, looked lush and very, very well kept. Lawns of a uniform shade of green wrapped around various islands of bushes, flowers, trees and the occasional sunken, walled garden. To the righthand side of the entrance ran a wide terrace, set with a collection of tables, chairs and umbrellas. Rosie was thinking that maybe they could sit there to interview Mrs Gallini, that the open-space and calming feel of the whole setting would make the experience just a tad less tense for them all. Then the drizzle began.

Stella Reeves met them in the wide, high-ceilinged Reception that had obviously once been the very grand and stylised Hall to the old house. Whilst the black and white marble floor and grey marble columns were plain enough, the red and gold chinoiserie pattern on the walls seemed to make the whole space glow warmly.

"The family are in the library, just down there," Stella smiled while pointing down a corridor off to the left.

"The family?" Rosie asked.

"Yes, er ..." Stella continued a little hesitantly. "Mrs Gallini wants to meet you first with her children ..."

"Oh," Rosie sighed.

"But she does understand that you will also want to speak to her alone," Stella reassured. "Perhaps, if you could just say a few things to them all, then I'll take the children for a walk. They are very, very nice ... Although I'm not sure they really understand."

"What, you don't think she's properly explained ..." Jo began.

"I don't think so, No," Stella nodded a little sadly. "I'm not sure Mrs Gallini herself has quite ..." she let the thought tail off, replacing it with the more upbeat: "Mrs Cassidy came earlier, that seemed to perk them all up for a while."

"And what is she like, Mrs Cassidy?" Rosie asked.

"Lovely," Stella smiled. "About five foot nothing, podgy, more Irish than a bag full of clover and more energy than a bag full of monkeys ..." she smiled.

"And how old did you say she is?" Rosie asked, not sure whether they had discussed that before.

"Hard to say, late fifties probably," Stella offered. "But she could be older ..."

"And her husband?"

"Haven't actually seen him ma'am ..."

"Oh really, but I thought ...?"

"I think Tilly may have," Stella thought. "He was out yesterday, as I understand it. Just came by here later to pick up Mrs C. Guess she must have rung him or something ..."

"So, how did she get here earlier?"

"I believe she walked, ma'am. Like I said, a bundle of get-up-and-go ..."

"Isn't that quite a walk?" Jo asked, trying to work out the route.

"No, I don't believe it is really. The grounds here connect to Jubilee Park from which there's a bridge over into Hawkwood ..."

"She walked through those woods?" a suddenly incredulous Rosie exclaimed.

"So she said. I doubt it had even occurred to her not to."

"Well, well, redoubtable indeed," Rosie smiled. "OK, let's get to it."

Marianna Gaultier Gallini, as she introduced herself, was, despite the obvious tension and anxiety in her manner and movement, a stunningly beautiful woman. Tall, maybe an inch short of six foot, blonde, slim, blue-eyed and elegant, she looked like the kind of model one would expect to see in advertisements for first-class travel, exclusive jewellery and expensive perfume. Even her hands were beautiful: small, with slim, graceful fingers that Rosie shook with the greatest of care for fear of damaging them.

The children, Petra and Michael, were also most clearly their mother's creation and concern. Thankfully, the trial of judging what to say and, more crucially, what not to say to the attentive, polite but clearly somewhat uncertain girl and boy did not last long. After Rosie and Jo had introduced themselves - as nothing more than Rosie and Jo, friends of

Stella - Mrs Gallini smiled, encouragingly yet nervously to the super-attentive Stella, who with no fuss or drama gently tempted the children away.

"Thank you for coming to see me," the poised, pensive woman began with disarming grace. Now alone, sat perfectly still in a dark blue skirt and grey blouse, she looked almost school-girlishly young. An impression made all the sadder by the sweet but heavily accented tone of her voice, which betrayed the fact that she was also a long way from home.

"Mrs Gallini," Rosie smiled. "Believe me, we know this is an awful experience for you ... and your children."

"Yes, of course. Thank you."

"And we are deeply sorry for your loss."

"Thank you," the woman repeated, the nervous knitting of her fingers revealing the sorrow inside.

"And if we could, we would just leave you and your family ..." Rosie assured. "But, given the circumstances, we have to ask you a few questions, to see ..."

"Yes of course, I understand," Mrs Gallini suggested unconvincingly.

"OK," Rosie began, taking a deep breath for courage. "Can I ask first, how much do you know about your husband's business?"

"I used to work there," Mrs Gallini replied in a way that could almost have been taken for an assertion of complete and total understanding of everything Rütger's of Zurich had ever touched.

"Really?"

"Yes, that ... Well, I suppose it is obvious that is where I met Stefan," Mrs Gallini smiled softly.

"Can I ask how long ago that was?" Rosie asked, sensing a relatively gentle way of collecting some family background.

"Well, I joined the bank straight from school. My father knew one of the Directors, so that helped ..."

"One of the Directors. Not Herr Gallini?"

"Oh no, not Stefan himself. Stefan was ... Well, Zurich is a small place compared to London. But just about everyone is in a bank, which sort of makes it big," Mrs Gallini smiled with intentional if inscrutable meaning. "So, people like Stefan ... You knew of them. You did not actually know them."

"I see," Rosie lied. "So, you are from Zurich yourself Mrs Gallini?"

"Yes. And please, call me Marianna. It will make this ... Make this a little less formal, I think."

"OK, of course, thank you," Rosie smiled appreciatively. "I, er ..." she hesitated. "Well, I suppose I asked where you are from because your names, they sound ..." she continued while almost thinking out loud.

"Ah yes, of course, I understand," Marianna acknowledged as though this was a perennial problem for people in her situation. "Switzerland is a funny country. The people they all like to think they have lived where they live for hundreds of years, that their families were like the founders of whatever town or Canton they are in," she smiled indulgently. "But, like you can see - or guess - names can be deceiving. My family has a French name, Stefan's an Italian one. Yet both families have lived in Zurich, speaking German as their main language, for as long as anyone knows."

"I see," Rosie nodded, worrying she was beginning to sound shallowly repetitive. "Like the tennis guy, Fed..."

"Exactly so," Marianna laughed. "Roger Federer," she pronounced in a phoney-thick French accent. "Is German-Swiss, but from Basle."

"Is Basle a nice place?" Rosie asked for absolutely no reason save that it stopped her asking something more difficult.

"Very," Marianna nodded. "It is right on the Rhine. Has a wonderful old quarter ... But it is a university town," she smiled. "So there, they make only students. In Zurich we make only money!"

"I see," Rosie said for a third time, blushing inwardly at her lack of linguistic variation. "Can I ask now, your husband's business, the bank ... Can you think of anything, anything at all ..."

"This question I thought you would ask," Marianna accepted seriously, the importance of it temporarily wrecking her previous command of English grammar. "The honest answer is I just do not know. I really cannot imagine that there could be anything to explain ..." her voice trembled and then died beneath a couple of deep, gulping sobs.

Rosie and Jo sat silently, patiently watching, waiting. In a way, the fact that Marianna's control ran out at the very moment she, to her word, had expected to have to consider awkward things seemed to back up Stella Reeves' view. For all the obvious distances that must have yawned between her and her husband, there was a connection between them that seemed too deep to be faked. And so, too strong to have dissolved recently into bitterness and murder.

"I'm sorry," Marianna tried to smile.

"No need Marianna. It's OK," Rosie insisted, leaning forward to rest her hand on the back of the woman's for a moment. "This is all dreadfully difficult ..."

"Yes, but you must ask, I know. So last night I spoke to Roberto ... You are laughing, I think," Marianna grinned sweetly. "At the Italian name? He is Stefan's eldest son."

"No, well I wasn't," Rosie smiled. "Although I probably am now!" she giggled.

"Yes, well he - when you meet him you will see this too - he does look Italian. Which is perhaps not so surprising. Stefan's first wife was from Lugano in Ticino ..."

"Sorry, where's that?"

"Ticino is the Italian-speaking part of Switzerland, to the south. And Lugano is a beautiful town right at the head of a lake. That is where Marlissa was from ... and where she died," Marianna added sadly.

"How did she die?" Rosie asked.

"Car crash. In the mountains. It was ... well obviously, it must have been very difficult for her children," Marianna said, her gaze suddenly lost in the far distance as the cruel symmetry of her and the older Gallinis life-experience came into view.

"Did you know her?"

"Not at all. Like I said before, people like Stefan and Marlissa were people you saw in the papers. Attending something or opening something else."

"I know this is going to sound, I don't know, maybe a little thoughtless ..." Rosie started.

"Please," Marianna encouraged.

"Well, I asked about your husband's business affairs earlier. But were there, I mean, could there have been rivalries between different families in Zurich? Who is the most important, who does the most charity work ..."

"Inspector," Marianna interrupted a little sharply. "Switzerland is not America. We do not get jealous about each other. We are proud of what we are and what we do ..."

"Of course, of course," Rosie apologised, allowing a few moments silence before continuing. "You said you spoke to Roberto ..."

"Yes," Marianna nodded, just a little of the patience and grace having disappeared from her eyes. "He said that perhaps it would be best if he spoke to you, he runs things in Zurich now ..."

"OK, so ..." Rosie began.

"So, perhaps you will come back tomorrow," Marianna said as a statement, not a question.

"Oh, right, I see ..."

"He and Mr Battersby are flying over tonight."

Chapter 26

"Who is it?"

"Police."

"What now?" Maureen asked while opening the door with submissive resignation.

"Where are the girls?" Gerard asked stepping into the hallway.

"I've put them to bed," Maureen explained, nodding down to the now closed third door.

The woman had changed. She still looked worn out, anxious and ever-so slightly out of it, but she had obviously made an effort. Her hair was clipped back tidily and she'd put on some eye-shadow and lipstick. Put it on somewhat imprecisely, but even so, the effect was to soften the sallowness of her complexion. And the simplicity of a pair of plain, slightly faded cheap jeans and equally cheap jumper in a kind of petrol blue worked for her. She didn't look sophisticated or elegant, but she did look as though she'd tried.

"OK," Gerard smiled as kindly as he knew how. "Let's go down there."

Closing the front door quietly, Martha followed Gerard and Maureen down to the lounge. Gone was the pile of clothes on the second sofa. Gone too the empty gin bottle, the tumblers, the roller and the papers. Even the scent in the room had become less sweet, more aromatic thanks to a perfumed candle burning in one of the (now clean) ashtrays.

Maureen's nervousness had not changed. Sitting in exactly the same spot as earlier, she reached for a packet of cigarettes, pulling one out with shaking fingers. Lighting it with a trembling hand. Drawing hard between thin, tense lips.

"Maureen," Gerard began, his voice quiet and betraying his own tensions. "The girls, did he ... Do you think he's been ... raping them?"

Maureen stared back with eyes that seemed, somehow, both shocked and intrigued by the question. "H-how ... I mean, why didn't you ...?"

"We've only just found out," Martha explained, sitting herself next to the seemingly stunned woman. "Found out that he's done it before. We need ..."

The combination of Maureen's staring, unblinking eyes and the tear trickling down one side of her misshapen nose dried Martha's throat.

"We want to know whether he's done that to them. If that is why you've taken them in."

"Candy ..." Maureen began before taking another long, deep drag on her cigarette.

"So you think he's been raping her?" Gerard pressed.

"No," Maureen sighed, breathing out used smoke. "No, I'm not sure about Candy ..."

"She never said?" Martha asked.

"No, but then Jade never said nothing either ..." Maureen sobbed. "Not until a couple of days ago ..."

"But you guessed?" Martha prompted.

Maureen nodded, wiping away a tear while taking another deep drag on her cigarette, stubbing it out urgently before reaching again for the packet.

"Do you think Mary knew?"

"Maybe, I don't know, maybe ..."

"Fucking hell ..." Gerard despaired.

"Mary she's ..." Maureen began while trying to light another cigarette. "She's not well. I mean, it's not just the drugs, she's slow like ... simple ... not really, not really well," the woman concluded sadly.

Gerard walked slowly over to the window and gazed out to the rolling, tree-rich hills in the distance. For no obvious reason he wondered whether girls like Candy and Jade ever got to visit such places, ever got to see a world that was not full of concrete and anger and hopelessness. "So you know he's done this before," he stated more than asked on turning back to look at Maureen.

"He ... he's ... you don't know what he's like ..."

"What the fuck does that mean?" Gerard asked angrily. "He rapes young girls but deep down he's really a great guy?"

"No, of course not," Maureen shouted back. "He's not a nice guy. He's never been a nice guy. He's fucking horrible. He's ..."

"Violent, intimidating, you're scared of him?" Martha suggested.

"Of course I'm fucking scared of him," Maureen gasped. "He's ... sometimes he comes over all nice and concerned and wanting to do things for you. And then ..."

"Yes?"

"I don't know," the woman sighed. "He's just evil. He can be nice and then he just turns, flips and fuck ..."

"What did you say?" Gerard asked.

"What did I say?" Maureen asked, confused.

"You said he flips ..."

"Yeah, goes like crazy ..."

"People say that about him?" Gerard asked. "Say things like, I dunno, call him 'the man that flips'?"

"Maybe, I don't know," Maureen replied blankly.

Martha looked back to Gerard for a moment, waiting to see whether he wanted to press the link again. Seeing him shake his head she asked: "He ever rape you Maureen?"

"Me?" she laughed, taking a long pull on her cigarette before stubbing it out. "How can anyone rape someone like me?" she sighed dismissively.

"Did he?" Martha pressed.

"I dunno, probably, maybe. Who gives a shit ..."

"Maureen," Gerard began, gentle once again. "We do. We do because we now know, Detective Cunningham and I, we now know that three times other police have failed to get him for this. Not once, not twice, three times he's been arrested for raping young girls. Three times he's got off ..."

"Yeah, well," Maureen accepted.

"And he gets off because no-one will go to Court against him. And I'm not even going to ask you whether you think Jade will ..."

"No, she's not. She just need to get well ..."

"Maureen," Martha smiled, touching the woman's arm with a kindly, settling delicacy. "We guessed that. But you could ..."

"Who would believe a slag like me?"

"We do," Gerard smiled. "Look, I don't know for sure what we can do, but I'm gonna ask for you Maureen. I'm gonna ask and see whether we can maybe get you and the girls moved somewhere, somewhere different," he suggested, his gaze again drawn to the innocence of the green nature shimmering in distance beneath a now hazy sun. "I'm going to try," he insisted, his eyes now drifting round to the corner of Tarn just visible past Kingfisher. "Someone has to stop him."

Chapter 27

The strength of the sun was making the wet tarmac steam now, drawing the drizzle of ten minutes ago back up to the wispy clouds hovering above. The warmth had also brought the Rumanians - assuming that was where they all really were from - out onto the walkway of rotten concrete and broken slabs that connected Kingfisher with the small hillock that rose between it and Mallard.

As they got nearer, Gerard and Martha saw what really interested the small group of identically dressed, identical looking, identically smoking men: a large white police van parking up outside Tarn. The same sight intrigued a small gang of boys - not one of whom could have been more than ten - sat on their now stalled bikes watching what for them was probably a welcome and amusing distraction from the boredom and monotony of riding round and round the same desolate tracks.

"Macca, Cunningham," Collins and Connelly nodded in unison.

"Guys," Gerard smiled back, noting the seriousness in the two young PCs eyes. An anxiety even, mixed with a clear sense of mission. "We got a number?"

"Not exactly, but we have a lead to follow up. Might help us narrow the search."

"But we think this is the cunt," Steve Collins more stated than asked, before taking a heavy drag on a cigarette.

"Sorry Martha," John Connelly apologised for his partner.

"No worries," Martha smiled a little condescendingly while watching Inspector O'Neill striding with great self-importance towards DCS Benson, who had just got out of the rather unlovely pool car Gurmel always seemed to pick.

"Yeah, sorry Martha," Steve whispered with child-like contrition

"What you make of him?" John asked.

"Who, Just-Call-Me-Jeremy? Not sure," she mused.

"Guess we're about to find out," Gerard suggested, seeing the DCS and Inspector heading their way, with Gurmel an afterthought in their wake.

"Martha, Gerard," Jeremy smiled confidently.

"Sir, Inspector," Gerard replied.

"Jeremy," Martha smiled with just a hint of a giggle before also acknowledging O'Neill.

"OK Gerard," Jeremy began. "So what's the plan?"

"Er, well 'plan' might be pushing things a bit far," Gerard replied a little sheepishly. "Not least, as we cannot be sure he's actually in the block right now ..."

"So why are we here?" O'Neill asked in a harsh growl that seemed to echo from somewhere deep in his body.

"Because what we do believe," Gerard began, just a little defensively. "Is that Kenny has a strong interest in this block. That he's got whores in some flats and probably dealers in others ..."

"How many flats?" Jeremy asked.

"You mean does he run, Sir. Or in the block?"

"Well, both I guess," Jeremy laughed.

"Yeah, well," Gerard smiled. "On the second, 70-odd, I think. Could be 80. As for how many Kenny's got and could be holed up in, don't know. Sorry."

"OK," Jeremy accepted, turning to O'Neill. "So what would be your advice, Inspector. Just go door-to-door. Or might we be better advised to sit it out for a while?"

"Sitting it out never works," Billy suggested. "In the end, we just get bored and go in anyway."

"Yeah, I guess," Jeremy thought. "Did I mention the car's gone?" he asked of Gerard.

"Er, No. You mean from the car park, obviously."

"Yeah, sent a truck earlier. No sign."

"Well, it might be worth taking a quick look around to see if it's here. Wouldn't necessarily prove anything either way ..."

"So why do it?" Billy asked sharply.

"Because it's always better to know things than not to," Jeremy replied philosophically. "And it's not unreasonable to assume that if the car is nearby and we spook him, he'll head for it. Now," he continued while looking around at the assembly of officers hanging in twos and threes by the van. "I think we've got the local PCSOs ...?"

"Daintith and Dakin," Gurmel put in.

"That's right," Jeremy smiled. "Sound a bit TV, don't they ... they here?"

"Yes Sir."

"OK, well perhaps you and they can make a quick search for us, Gurmel. If it's here, it won't be far away. So," Jeremy continued, turning back to Gerard and Martha. "Inspector O'Neill says no point in waiting, let's just get in and see what happens. What do you say?"

"No," Martha smiled while Gerard pondered the right word to start with. "There's one lead we want to try first. Might get us nowhere, but ..."

"What is it?" Jeremy asked.

"Her name is Mary Lee," Gerard answered. "We believe she whores for her supply. We also suspect she'll be pretty much out of it," he smiled sadly. "But it won't take long to go and see. At least we have a number and it'll be on the second or third floor ..."

"Presumably, he keeps all his whores near the ground," Jeremy thought out loud while staring up the full height of the block. Then, resolved he turned to O'Neill. "Right Inspector, we need to get organised. You've two armed officers, right?"

"Yes Sir. Arthurs and Jones ..."

"Good, experienced? Not trigger happy?" Jeremy asked quickly.

"They are good, Sir. I vouch for them," Inspector O'Neill said with some touchingly obvious pride.

"OK, so we're going to recce this ... What number did you say, Gerard?"

"Fourteen."

"Yes. Can't be sure whether he'll know. Can't be sure whether he's watching us as we speak," Jeremy pondered. "Come to think of it, we've been a bit lax in not wondering whether he's got a rifle ..."

"Fuck," Billy gasped, his eyes roving quickly across the lifeless windows.

"Yeah, well. Guess he'd have shot us already if he did," Jeremy laughed with just a hint of nerves. "But we obviously need to take care with all this. What I'd like Inspector, for now, is for you and your TSG team to secure things down here, keeping one armed. I'll lead back-up for Gerard and Martha ..."

"OK," O'Neill accepted, his face again betraying a feeling of slight hurt for not being picked for the glory roles. "We got a description?"

"White, five feet ten, slim ..." Martha recounted, while smiling inside at the effortless, drama-free way Jeremy had assumed command. "Dark hair, dark eyes, scar to right cheek, some hieroglyphic tattoo thing to one arm."

"Right," Jeremy began. "We need vests, whistles ... ah, Gurmel," he noticed in mid-flow.

"Car is here," Gurmel confirmed. "Parked in front of a garage round the back."

"Well, well, well," Jeremy smiled. "Guess we'll give that a search later. OK, get yourself a vest," he ordered before looking past Gurmel to the two young and somewhat apprehensive-looking PCSOs. "And you two - you know these blocks?"

"A bit, don't really come out here much though," the tall, freckle-faced guy replied.

"Why not?" O'Neill asked gruffly while buckling his vest. "Too scary?"

"Well ..." the PCSO began.

"Mmm," Jeremy pondered, while looking around the bleak estate stuck up on a hill nearer the M25 than anything that might pass for civic society. "I share your worry Inspector: a little too far out of the way, too full of hookers, junkies and immigrants. Just too unimportant ... You got a name, young man?" he asked a little sharply.

"Harry Daintith."

"OK PCSO Harry Daintith, get a vest and a radio. You can come with me. And you?" Jeremy asked of the other young officer.

"Amanda Dakin," came the rather timid reply.

"You too, get a vest and a radio and stay close to Inspector O'Neill here. You and Daintith have got important work to do keeping us all in touch. OK?"

As Gerard and Martha neared flat 14 they noticed that the door was slightly ajar. Flanked by John Connelly and an ultra-serious looking TSG officer - who apart from introducing herself as Billie Arthurs, had said nothing - Gerard gently pushed the door open.

Instantly Arthurs jumped in, her gun pointing straight ahead, held firmly in both hands. "Clear," she said.

Stepping into a hallway almost identical to Maureen's, Gerard called: "Police."

There was no reply.

Slowly, Gerard and Billie Arthurs walked down the corridor while Martha and John stood guard at the doorway.

"Empty," Billie said of the first and second rooms.

"Whayawan," asked the young woman who suddenly appeared, fearless and dark eyed from the third room just before Billie and Gerard reached it.

"Police," Gerard repeated quietly, stepping in front of Billie who pointed her gun to the floor while taking two steps back.

"I heard," the woman replied in the curious accent that was part EastEnders, part country burr.

"Now I'm going to guess," Gerard smiled unthreateningly while looking closely at the woman. "That you are not Mary Lee."

"Prize man," she replied, her dark eyes still staring with unblinking unfriendliness.

"Right," Gerard half laughed. "Look," he continued. "We're not here to arrest Mary or anything like that ..."

"So what's she for?" she asked, pointing to Billie.

"She ..." Gerard began before looking back over his shoulder, nodding to send Billie back to the doorway and for Martha to join him. "Look," Gerard tried again. "We aren't after Mary for anything. We just think she might know ..."

"Know what, you seen her?" the woman interrupted with a look of utter contempt burning in her eyes.

"Is she here then?" Martha asked gently.

"Of course, where else she gonna go," she replied, looking hard and curiously uncertain at Martha.

"So, perhaps we could just see her for a moment ..."

"You wanna see her ... and then what? What good you gonna do?"

"Let us talk to her first, then we'll see ..." Martha suggested.

Which seemed enough. Without another word the woman stood aside.

The bedroom was almost identical to Maureen's. The same size with the same kind of cheap furniture and poor quality carpet. The light breaking between the otherwise drawn curtains seemed to struggle to cut through the air, a stale and unpleasant mix of acrid smoke, sweat and iodine.

Yet even in the gloom the discoloured and misshaped face of the woman sat up in the bed could not be missed.

"Is that Mary?" Martha asked.

"Uh-huh," the young woman replied while swallowing the hint of a sob.

"Kenny?" Gerard asked while stepping closer to the half-asleep Mary.

"Who else?"

"When?" Martha asked while watching Gerard slowly, quietly, concernedly walking round to the far side of the bed.

"This time? A few days back."

"This time?" Martha pressed. "There have been others?"

"Of course," the young woman spat bitterly.

"But ... why?" Martha asked, sounding stupid.

"Why?" the woman laughed. "P-lease!"

"I mean," Martha insisted. "You're saying this time a few days back. But before that ..." she stumbled uncertainly before asking: "Is this to do with Candy and Jade going?"

"How did you know that?" the woman asked, genuinely surprised.

"Look," Martha replied, serious and impatient. "We're trying, OK. We're trying to catch him. So ... so we've learned some things, but we don't know where he is. Do you know where we'll find him?" she demanded, urgent and animated now.

"I ..." the woman half said, half sighed.

"Look," Martha said more calmly. "We don't understand everything, not yet. But we know enough to know we've got to get him. But without help ... Well, without some help we'll probably fail just like you expect."

"Yeah," the woman agreed, laughing dismissively while staring hard at Martha. "How old are you?"

"Me?" Martha replied, slightly taken aback. "Twenty-three. You?"

"Same. Ain't that funny," the woman laughed.

"Is it, why?" Martha asked.

"Let me guess. You grew up in a nice house. Went to a nice school. Got nice friends, nice family. So when you come out to a shit hole like this you just feel 'oh so sorry' ..." the woman sneered while trying to sound like her idea of posh.

"No, I don't feel sorry. I feel angry," Martha snapped back. "And you know what makes me angry the most? Not the fact that there are nasty people like Ryan Kenny in this world. Nah, what makes me angry to the point of despair isn't the existence of the likes of him. It's the fact that you and people like you won't do fuck-all to help us put him inside."

"What?"

"You heard. You want to know how many times we've arrested him for raping young girls? Three. Why's he still here, smashing up women like her?" Martha snarled rhetorically, pointing across to Mary by whom Gerard was now sitting. "Because no-one has the courage ... No-one cares enough to stand up and tell a Court what he's done. So don't you dare laugh at me for feeling something ..." she rasped, pointing an angry finger now at the startled young woman in front of her. "At least I'm trying. What are you doing?"

The young woman stood dumb-struck and open-mouthed for a moment, her eyes staring in unblinking amazement. "You got a name?"

"Martha Cunningham. You?"

"Kylie Smith."

"You live here, in this block?"

"Yeah, down the corridor, number seventeen."

"Ryan Kenny run you too?"

"Uh-huh," Kylie nodded with obvious sadness.

Martha stayed silent a moment, just looking at Kylie. For all the insolent fury that obviously simmered inside her, she was almost pretty. Sure, her bleached-blonde hair, shiny green eye make-up and thick, dark red lipstick made her look both older and tougher. But there was still something impudently girlish about her. About her slim body. About the playfully bright shoes she wore with her faded jeans. About the jumble of bracelets and chains around one wrist. About the delicacy of her pale arms barely a shade darker than her plain white t-shirt.

"You always lived round here?"

"More or less. Me mum and dad were travellers, but mostly I grew up in Swanley. Moved in here with a guy, didn't work out. You can guess the rest."

"OK," Martha smiled sweetly. "So, which flat we going to find him in?"

"This time of day," Kylie began. "Almost certain to still be in thirty-three."

"That where he lives?"

"As far as I know."

"And who we going to find there with him?"

"Not sure, maybe some girls ..."

"What I mean is, are we going to run into any serious support?"

"Nah, I doubt it. Might be one or two but with her outside," Kylie smiled. "You'll be fine. Bullets don't ask questions, right?" she laughed.

"Er, yeah, I guess," Martha smiled, wondering whether that was a quote from some rap song or something. "You taking care of her then?" she asked, turning back to face the bed to see Mary trying hard to say something to Gerard.

"Best I can, but she's in pain. She don't say, but she is."

"We'll get her an ambulance. Get her to a hospital for a while ..."

"No!"

"Why ever not?"

"Ryan, he'll ..."

"Kylie, we're going to get him, right now. So forget all that crap. She needs proper care, we'll make sure she gets it."

"OK," Kylie replied, unconvinced, uncertain.

"And later, if we need your help - as a witness or something - you gonna give it?"

"I dunno ..."

"Yeah, well like I said earlier, the likes of Ryan Kenny can only do harm if no-one tries to stop them. I'm coming back in a few days Kylie Smith," Martha promised. "To find out whether you're going to try."

"Martha," Gerard whispered as they walked back along the corridor to rejoin their colleagues now grouped on the landing by the stairwell. "Well done."

"Thanks," she smiled.

Chapter 28

The picture that greeted Jo and Rosie as they drove up towards Tarn was, mercifully, nothing like they had feared. More village fête, in fact, than crime scene. On a small patch of grass, three shirt-sleeved officers were playing football with a scruffy gang of boys, using bikes for goalposts.

Elsewhere, beneath a now bright and benign sun: Gerard and Billy O'Neill were laughing with a couple of SOCOs making their way into the block; DCS Benson was engaged in some odd looking play-acting with Gurmel and a young officer neither of them recognised; Martha, Sergeant Nancy and a couple of paramedics were showing great concern for a woman in a wheelchair waiting by a garish green and yellow ambulance; while just the other side of the empty police van a group of officers, still in protective vests, stood chatting to the driver of the Borough's only secure wagon.

The capture and arrest of Ryan Kenny had, in the end - and somewhat against expectations - been fairly drama free. Understandably - if just a little over-intently - DCS Benson had spent five minutes or so agreeing with O'Neill, in the minutest detail, the placement of all ten uniform and four CID. For an awkward moment Martha had thought she caught a hint of him wanting to keep her from the front. Maybe he had, but when it was settled the initial plan was to repeat the formation as it had approached Mary Lee's flat.

Number 33 was, they had guessed from their experience of Mallard, on the sixth floor. The layout of this floor was, however, slightly different to the others: the door to flat 33 was right at the far end of the corridor looking back, as it were, towards the stairwell. The DCS' cautious instincts had found this troubling. Having first asked why Kenny would deliberately choose a flat so far from the only exit, his ultra-careful reasoning then saw a different problem.

To get to thirty-three they would have to walk some fifteen meters down a narrow - but for once, brightly lit - corridor. That equalled a long period of exposure. So, two heavy, unwieldy shields were called for. Connelly and Collins worked the shields with Billie Arthurs tucked in tight between them. Gerard, carrying the team's other accessory - a heavy rubber ram - and Martha walked safely behind. Blocking the exit were the DCS, Gurmel and young Harry Daintith.

After three rounds of heavy rapping on the door - backed-up by loud and clear calls of Police - the ram went through. As if they had trained together for years rather than only just met, John and Billie jumped in protected by a single shield. Calling out every other step they had slipped deeper into the flat with Gerard tucked in behind.

Stop right there! Jeremy's voice had boomed. Spinning round, Martha had seen a slim but powerful looking guy bursting out of number 34 and running quickly towards the trio of Jeremy, Gurmel and Harry. He was perhaps no more than three feet away when Gurmel calmly took half a turn sideways and threw the runner around his body and onto his back. As the guy went to get up, Harry Daintith grabbed an arm and, twisting it sharply, turned him over to lie face-first and screaming beneath a rather large boot planted firmly between his shoulder blades.

On the way down Martha had listened in confusion to a whole new language of dans and wazas. The hierarchies in judo, she had previous thought, ended with black. Not a bit of it. Evidently, Harry's 'go-dan' trumped Gurmel's 'yon-dan', meaning he was now working towards gaining a red-and-white belt. 'Roku-dan', Gurmel had gasped with wide-eyed respect, even though young Harry had already waxed lyrical about the perfection of Gurmel's 'hane-goshi' - which seemed to be the name for some kind of throw - that had left him with the easiest 'aikido'?

Whatever, Martha had concluded wordlessly.

As the wagon pulled away, with Kenny handcuffed and chained inside, the truck arrived. After offering a few instructions backed-up by much arm-waving, Gurmel, Jeremy and the young unnamed officer followed it on foot, disappearing down a ramp to the side of the block.

As they parked in a gap, a little way past the ambulance, Rosie noticed a group of stocky, dark-haired young men watching the action from a walkway outside an almost identically awful concrete block.

"Who do you think they are?" she asked Jo as they both got out the car.

"I dunno. Poles, Bulgarians maybe?"

"Oh right," Rosie replied blankly.

"Ma'am," Gerard beamed.

"DI Charlton," Billy breezed.

"Gentlemen," Rosie smiled back. "I'm guessing you got him."

"Indeed we did," Billy nodded enthusiastically. "Indeed we did."

"With top thanks to Gurmel and Harry Daintith, local PCSO," Gerard explained.

"OK, how's that?"

"Judo, evidently," Gerard smiled. "Kenny made a run for it - but ran into two guys who look like they should be in the Olympics to me."

"Well, lucky for us they were here by the sounds of it. So, what have we found by way of evidence?"

"SOCOs made a quick sweep," Gerard began. "No gun, but enough drugs to secure a custodial."

"Well, that's a start ..."

"OK, I'll leave you two to catch up," Billy offered. "Time to get my lot away, I think."

"Right, yeah ... and Ins ..." Rosie began before tutoring herself into a more friendly gesture. "Billy ... thanks."

"No problem."

"OK," Rosie said turning back to Gerard. "You were saying."

"Yeah, so, drugs and a stack of cash and just possibly counts of GBH and statutory rape ..."

"Really?"

"Not sure how much you picked up about this Kenny, ma'am ..."

"First, all we got was a possible link to Ian Green. Then, when we got back to the car, Jo had another message saying you were all coming out here because Scales might have known him. Or known of him?"

"Right, OK," Gerard began. "So, a few years back Charlie used to be PCSO down here. He and a guy who I think is over at Croydon now - Pike, Andy Pike - they arrested Kenny for rape of a minor, 2009 ..."

"So that gives us a double connection ..."

"It does ma'am."

"What happened to the rape case?"

"Fell. Couldn't get witnesses to testify. Seems that was the third time such a case had failed ..."

"Intimidation?"

"Well, you have to assume so," Gerard nodded. "Like I was saying, we think we've also got the possibility here of another statutory rape case. A thirteen year old called Jade Lee. That was her mother you saw going off in the ambulance, beaten up by Kenny. So, like I said, it's possible ..."

"But you're not sure either will see it through?"

"No ma'am. They might and I think it would be worth the effort. But this is a tough place to live ..."

"I don't doubt," Rosie nodded, looking around. "OK," she pondered. "So what link do you see between this Kenny and Stefan Gallini?"

"Truth ma'am?" Gerard grimaced a little resignedly. "We've yet to find one."

Chapter 29

"Interview commencing at 16:07, Saturday, 4 August 2012. Present Detective Inspector Charlton and Detective Sergeant McAvoy. Your full name please," Gerard asked formally.

"Ryan Christopher Kenny."

"And your address and date of birth."

"33 Tarn, Marsfield. 27 November 1984."

"Thank you. And having understood your rights you have elected not to call for a solicitor to be present at this time, is that correct?"

"Yeah, yeah."

"OK, so you were arrested at 11:58 this morning on suspicion of possession of Class A and Class C drugs with the intention to supply," Gerard continued. "A subsequent search of flat 33 Tarn and the adjoining flat, number 34, found: 6 kilos of a substance thought to be marijuana; 300 grams of a substance thought to be cocaine; 200 grams of a substance thought to be crack cocaine; and two bags weighing a total of 100 grams containing a selection of pills thought to be hallucinogens. Do you admit possession?"

"Nah, you planted all that shit."

"I see. So you deny bringing those substances into 33 Tarn. So what do you want us to do, keep them all?"

"Yeah, keep it. Do what the fuck you like with it. It's yours."

"OK. And the £55,276 found in various denominations of used notes. You're happy for us to do what we like with that as well are you?"

"Smart cunt," Kenny hissed.

"Sorry, I'm not sure we quite caught that on tape. You want to repeat it?"

"Look, why don't you just fuck off," Kenny sneered.

"Because that's not how this works," Gerard smiled. "Now, in a moment we are going to charge you with possession with the intention to supply. You will ask for bail, we'll refuse ..."

"Why, just for that?"

"Actually, No. Not just for that," Gerard replied. "We are also going to charge you with causing grievous bodily harm to Miss Mary Lee of ..."

"That slag," Kenny laughed dismissively.

"So you know her?"

"What? Yeah, of course. I seen her around the place."

"How about her children, Candy and Jade?"

"What about them?"

"When did you last see them?"

"I ... I dunno, recently, not long ..." a now more puzzled, more uncertain Kenny replied. "Why you asking about them?"

"I'll come back to that," Gerard smiled dismissively while slowly opening the manila folder neatly positioned between him and Rosie. "Now," he continued while looking down at the top page. "Tell me about Millicent Ferguson."

"Who the fuck is Millicent Ferguson?"

"She's the thirteen year old you raped on the afternoon of 6 June, 2009. In a house in Chelsfield Lane ..."

"Who says?"

"She said."

"When?"

"The next day. You were then arrested, at 10:09 on 8 June for her rape. You remember that?"

"She made it up. Her and that silly little slag friend of hers. You all sussed that, you just wanted to piss me around for a day."

"Did she make it up Mr Kenny?" Rosie asked.

"What? Yeah, like I told you ..."

"That's not what you said at the time. At the time you told us you had never met her ... And I don't see any reference here," Rosie said, looking down at the folder. "To any silly friend?"

"Look, I don't know what you're doing with this shit. That's like three years ago ..."

"So what?"

"So what?" Kenny shouted back, but in a voice that sounded more pensive than angry. "So what is nothing happened, OK? Nothing happened 'cos I didn't do nothing."

"Do you remember the officers who arrested you?" Gerard asked calmly.

"What? I dunno. Yeah, pair of schwartzers I think. So what?"

"You got issues with black people Mr Kenny?"

"What? What you mean 'issues' ..." Kenny replied, lisping the word to make it sound fay and childish. "I ain't got no issues. I just don't need them fucking with my space."

"I see," Gerard replied neutrally. "One of those officers was PC Scales, you remember that name?"

"Yeah, maybe, I think," Kenny replied.

"You think," Gerard repeated.

"Mr Kenny," Rosie began, pulling a stapled collection of papers from the file. "You were in Feltham Young Offenders Institution from March 2001 until January 2002 ..."

"And?"

"Tell me about Ian Henry Green."

"What is with all these fucking names. Who's he?"

"He was in Feltham for some of that time."

"Was he," Kenny laughed. "So were a couple of hundred other kids. You gonna ask me about all of them too, one after the other?"

"No, just him."

"Well, I don't remember him. Why should I?"

"Thought you would have had some things in common," Rosie suggested. "You were both in for petty thieving. Both came from the same parts - he lived in Bexley, you lived in North Cray at the time ..."

"Yeah well, maybe I did talk to him," Kenny accepted. "Fuck all else to do in there. But like I said, I don't remember that name."

"You don't," Rosie smiled while turning a couple of pages over. "So how about in Brixton. You were there in 2007 and guess what ..."

"He was there too," Kenny smiled mockingly. "You ever been in there? The only people you get to talk to are screws and those on your square, maybe twenty guys at most. I don't remember no Ian Fucking Henry Green being amongst them. Now look, what's this all about?"

"Maybe you knew him under a different name," Gerard suggested. "Like Ginger or H or something. Some people prefer nicknames, don't they ..."

"Yeah, I guess."

"How about you? What do you have people call you? I heard it was Flipz. That right, people call you Flipz?"

"Do what? What I want with some schwartzer tag?"

"Where were you yesterday around 8am?" Rosie asked.

"Asleep, why?"

"Who you got who can back up that story?"

"Who can what? ... Look, what the fuck is this all about?"

"Answer the question," Gerard snapped. "Tell us where and who with."

"What? At the flat. On my own. Why?"

"Yesterday, Mr Kenny," Rosie said, speaking slowly and softy. "At a little after 8am, PC Scales was shot. In the woods between Chislehurst and Petts Wood ..."

Ryan Kenny stared back at her, unblinking, his mouth open in a surprised oval. "Hold on ..."

"He was there with a number of other officers investigating the murder, on Thursday, of Ian Henry Green ... in those same woods."

"No, no. No fucking way ..."

"While your car was parked just around the corner ..."

"No, no you're not ..." Kenny insisted, his eyes now showing genuine signs of worry.

"So, I'm going to ask you again. Who have you got who will say you were asleep in your flat at 8am yesterday morning?"

"I told you ..." Kenny sighed, fear now darkening his eyes.

"You said no-one," Rosie smiled. "So, how about Thursday morning. Anyone going to back-up whatever story you want to tell us about then?"

"Right, that's it. I'm not saying any more, get my solicitor," Kenny insisted, his insolence and incredulity now replaced by an experienced instinct for self-preservation.

"Of course. We'll suspend this interview now and reconvene some time tomorrow ..."

"Tomorrow?"

"You got a prior appointment?" Gerard asked.

"So what happens now?"

"You get to enjoy our food and hospitality," Gerard smiled. "OK?"

"No, it's not fucking OK. I've got a shit-load of shit to sort out ..."

"No, not any more," Gerard smiled. "Like we've already told you, we're going to charge you right now with possession ..."

"Yeah, yeah, yeah ..."

"... and GBH. Before we start again tomorrow I also expect to charge you with the statutory rape of Jade Lee ..."

"She'll never ..."

"You know what, this time, I think you're wrong," Gerard grinned with faked confidence. "Then, once we've got that little lot neatly documented, to your solicitor's professional satisfaction," he continued mockingly. "We'll talk again about those issues you had with PC Scales and Ian Green. Interview suspended."

Sunday, 5 August 2012

Chapter 30

Martha woke at 7am feeling just a little unsettled. She had slept like the proverbial log for a full eleven hours, having got home exhausted: too tired to eat or think. Now, as she stretched her still sleepy body - her still drowsy eyes drifting slowly around her cosy bedroom - her still weary brain started to think and fret. For all that she longed for another hour's rest - another hour of blissful relief from all the threads and ideas and stresses that had been spinning in her head for more than two days - she knew she wouldn't get back to sleep now. Her mind was already making lists, rearranging pieces, forming new questions.

She treated herself instead to an extra-long shower, washing her thick, wavy hair with a new shampoo she'd been recommended. It smelt of apples and honey and lathered up like foam. Having dried herself she used up a small bottle of body milk that had come free with a food magazine she'd picked up last time she went shopping. An odd combination, she'd thought at the time, but the stuff was wonderfully creamy and fragrant. Scented like vanilla and lavender.

Wrapped up in a warm towelling robe, she flicked on the radio while sorting herself breakfast. Today's presenter was super-hyper, more euphoric still than the energetic if slightly incredulous voice of Friday night. Maybe it was a Sunday morning thing, Martha pondered as the voice rose and rose, detailing with increasing jubilation - and an irritating addiction to the word amazing - the super-ness of Super-Saturday. Super-Saturday, it seemed, had trumped all the nation's previous moments of momentous sporting history.

The details seemed to be, as far as Martha could be bothered to focus, that several amazing people (all of them ours) had so bravely and amazingly been better at something than other people (all of them very much not ours). So, the country was - apparently - gripped by celebratory love for the amazing Jess and Greg and Mo, as well as the equally amazing ...

She switched the radio off as she settled on the high stool to eat her cereal, a vague recollection at the back of her head of cheering and horn-honking during the night. Staring thoughtfully out the window, the only sound in the room now that of her crunching through a mouthful of honey-nut flakes, she finally let herself answer the question she'd been avoiding since she woke. No, she did not believe Ryan Kenny was a killer. An arrogant, violent and horrible little shit, Yes. No question whatsoever. But he wasn't who they'd set out to find.

She felt sure enough of this simply on the back of the interview. Watching through the glass with Jeremy, Jo and Gurmel she had noticed - and she thought they had also - that Kenny never seemed in the least troubled by questions about Green or Charlie until murder was mentioned. Surely, she had reasoned, if it had been him he would have been far more careful with those questions. More than that, for all that he was a shit he clearly wasn't dim. If it had been him he would surely have prepared a far more convincing story placing himself - to say nothing of his car - nowhere near either killing.

Then there was the absence of evidence. Jeremy and Gerard had been as one in saying the fact they hadn't found a gun proved nothing. It could have been dumped after the Gallini murder. Or could be stored in another flat (or garage, the one they had suspected turning out to be unlocked and empty). And it was true they had not found anything to confirm how many flats Kenny did have control over.

Against that, she calculated, if he was the kind of guy who would use a gun then he would have had one in his flat. Numbers 33 and 34 clearly were his base. SOCOs had found more than enough drugs and money to secure something like a five year conviction. They had found all that, but no weapon of any kind. She had come back to this point a couple of times during the long and thorough debrief the team held after the interview.

The one odd fact that paradoxically seemed to undermine her scepticism about the absence of a gun, was the very specific make and model the Specialist Firearms Unit in Maidstone had identified. The weapon that had fired the bullets that killed Ian Green and Stefan Gallini was a SIG P210. Evidently, this produced a unique set of grooves on the bullet, grooves found on the bullets extracted from Green and Gallini. Whilst the bullet that had passed through Charlie hadn't been found there was no sense in thinking it would be different.

SIGs were Swiss and evidently rather common there, being the weapon of choice for the army. All of which as good as convinced Jeremy, Gerard and Rosie that Gallini had always been the main target and that the reason lay somewhere in his business dealings back home. Following that logic, they held, if Ryan Kenny was the killer then whoever put him on the job supplied and then reclaimed the gun. To round the theory off, they argued that Kenny had either been given licence to sort out a couple of bits of private business first, or had just taken it.

So Martha had stopped challenging and got on with posting all the various facts they'd collected and ideas they'd thought of onto the A1 pad. But all those facts, half-facts, ideas and half-baked theories just seem to cast more doubt on Kenny having any connection to or interest in Green. Indeed, they as good as showed he had no interests outside the Marsfield Estate, let alone as far away as Penge.

Meaning that, for all he could have had some long held grudge for the Millicent Ferguson arrest, the idea he made a patsy out of Green to set up the killing of Charlie sounded … well, silly. Silly, because the killing of Green did not guarantee Charlie Scales would be amongst the team that turned up the next day (or even the other officer, this Andy Pike, who one might assume Kenny did not know was now at Croydon). Sillier still, because it would surely be a lot less hassle just to go and find Charlie and shoot him in an alley somewhere?

Of course, it was one thing to think they hadn't yet got the right guy, quite another to identify pointers in the evidence that would lead them to him. There was - she thought as she poured out a large mug of rich, black coffee - one obvious line they needed to go back to. All along they'd agreed the evidence suggested Green knew his killer. However boring it might be, someone ought to go through all the information they could find on him, looking for possible links, enemies, bits of unfinished business, etc.. She resolved to offer to do this, assuming no-one else would, and as part of the task to see if there was any local intelligence on Flipz and Crisz.

Looking more immediately to the people they had already met, she had found it odd that neither Rosie nor Jeremy seemed especially interested in the whereabouts of the so far unmet Mr Cassidy. Jo had mentioned this, receiving no more than a 'yeah, we probably ought to talk to the Cassidys' by way of a reply.

However, a different missing man now popped into her head: was there a Mr Dearmer?

Right from the start, Rosie had cautioned against assuming that what a witness told them was the absolute truth. By Jo's account, Mrs Dearmer was as charming as she was petite. But something else Jo had said had left Martha thinking. In talking about the interview they'd had with Mrs Gallini, Jo had mentioned in passing how mixed up the people, names and languages in Switzerland seemed to be. Evidently, Mr Gallini's first wife had been from the Italian-speaking part, whilst he, despite the name, came from a German-speaking area.

All of that was nothing in itself, but then later, when talking about Mrs Dearmer, Jo had said she too seemed to have a slight accent which she reckoned was probably French. Martha had meant to make the connection with languages not always matching the name at the time, then the thought slipped away. Now though, she was thinking: what if Mrs Dearmer was French-speaking Swiss married now - or once - to someone from a German-speaking city, such as Zurich?

Chapter 31

They met in Rosie's room at 9am. Their host had found a second large cafetière so they were not going to run out of good coffee, while the ever-surprising Jeremy had turned up with a bag full of rock cakes he'd made (he said) last night ... what kind of DCS makes rocks cakes?

So, they were there and ready, yet somehow not quite ready. Initially, the chat was about the Olympics, with everyone but Martha seemingly desperate to exchange pieces of sporting trivia while wallowing in patriotic pride. Then, the unspoken determination not to talk about Kenny started to become a little surreal. According to Jo, there had been some report or other about unusual storms appearing on the surface of the sun. I thought you weren't supposed to look directly at the sun, Gerard had said, sparking a bit of recall about the two-coloured glasses everyone had tried to find a few years back to watch an eclipse. That done, the conversation went back to the sun with Gurmel saying that he'd read (although he didn't say where) that some cult or other believed these solar storms proved the world was going to end on December 21, 2012.

"Be good if we could solve this case beforehand then," a bored Martha had suggested.

"Yes, well ..." a momentarily sheepish Rosie had replied.

"I was just saying ..." Martha smiled, trying to make light of her previous comment.

"No, no. You're right," Rosie accepted. "OK, so, let's recap where we've got to ..." she waffled.

"You know what," Jeremy put in gently. But no matter his friendliness, his rank quietened the room. "Why don't we just ask ourselves this: do we think we've got the right man?"

Whilst everyone stared dutifully and attentively back, no one spoke.

"Gerard?" Jeremy prompted.

"Well, er, um ... I'm not sure."

"OK, who's next, Gurmel?"

"I'm not sure either."

"Me neither," Jo put in before being asked.

In answer to Jeremy's enquiring eyes Martha replied: "Well I am sure ..." leaving a pause which drew all five pairs of eyes to her. "It wasn't Kenny. He's a shit. We should get him for everything we can. But he's not the killer."

"You seem very certain," Jeremy commented thoughtfully.

"I am. Do you want me to say why?"

"Rosie?" Jeremy asked.

"Well, I would probably have fudged it and said not sure too," she smiled. "So yeah, I think we have to hear Martha's reasoning."

"OK," Martha began, taking a deep breath. "First off, I think we all noticed that questions about Green and Charlie didn't bother Kenny until murder was mentioned. Now, whilst I don't think he's dim, I'm not convinced he's clever enough to fake that. Think about his reaction when Millicent Ferguson was mentioned. Sure, he looked a bit bothered about us bringing up a three year old case, but when asked about Charlie he actually relaxed. Surely that's the only way to understand him saying what he actually said. If he'd been anticipating the link he'd have been far too careful to say what he did say ..."

"So you didn't see any suggestion of him having spent three years nurturing a hatred deep enough to kill for?" Jeremy asked.

"No, no I didn't," Martha nodded. "And then, when I think about his reaction re: Green ... Well, I don't believe he had a clue who he was being asked about. And that's crucial. All along we've agreed the location of Green's death points very, very strongly to him having been lured there somehow or other by someone he knew ... I just don't see Kenny as that person."

"Well, for what it's worth," Jeremy smiled. "I agree with you."

"For what it's worth," Rosie giggled. "As in 'I'm just a poor little cake-baking DCS down from the Yard so what's my view worth' ..." she smiled.

"Rosie, that's unfair," Jeremy protested.

"It's OK, I'm only teasing," Rosie smiled still wider. "I can't see an argument with Martha's points ... anyone else?"

"No, no ..." Gerard began. "No, I think she's right as well. But if it wasn't Kenny ..."

"Hey, I still want us to get him for all the rest. The rape, the GBH ..."

"Martha, I think we all do," Rosie assured. "But for now, we need to go where Gerard was pointing: if it wasn't Kenny, who was it?"

"OK, well I did a little research this morning," Martha smiled while producing, as was becoming her signature habit, a scruffy piece of paper.

"The idea was we'd all get a lie in," Rosie smiled.

"I did," Martha insisted. "Unlike you tele addicts, I was asleep by 8pm. Sport is so not my thing!"

"All work ..." Gerard teased.

"Yeah, well, someone's got to keep things going," Martha smiled back. "Anyway, this gun ..."

"Isn't that funny," Jeremy reflected. "I looked that up too ..."

"Oh, OK. Well if you want ..."

"Not a bit of it, tell us what you found."

"Right, well first off: it's old."

"Really?" Rosie pondered.

"SIGs aren't," Martha explained. "They're the number one gun in Switzerland. Which, by the way, has got a lot of guns for a small country, did you know that?"

"No, not at all. I mean, why?" a genuinely surprised Rosie asked.

"Well, this penknife army of theirs ... it's tiny ..."

"So where do all the guns ..."

"The militia. Evidently, all Swiss men under forty are in it. They go off every now and then and play soldier games and stuff, but other than that, they go about whatever business they've got, their guns safe at home in case anyone invades ..."

"Did you get all this too?" Rosie asked of Jeremy.

"Eh, no. All I checked was the gun ..." he replied a little apologetically.

"Yes, well," Martha continued. "So, coming back to that. There are lots of guns locked up in people's houses and most of them are SIGs. But not SIG P210s. That's the key here, I think. This Maidstone unit were very specific about it being this particular model, weren't they Gurmel?"

"They were. Made me repeat it back to them."

"Right. It was last used by the Swiss army in 1975."

"What? How come?" Jo asked.

"Got replaced by a new, better and cheaper model ..."

"The P220," Jeremy put in.

"So you did get this bit then?" Rosie smiled.

"Indeed. Probably from the same place as Martha, so we may need to double-check. I think Wikipedia is reliable, but it isn't exactly an academic, peer-reviewed source ..."

"OK, but assuming what you and Martha have found out is fact, we're looking for a killer possessing an old, what, getting on for forty year-old gun?"

"Could be older, it was the militia issue from 1949 to 1975," Martha read. "But there's another point here - it's valuable. For some reason or other this old P210 is a gun of choice for shooting competitions and that kind of thing ..."

"The Olympics?" Gerard asked jokingly.

"You know what, I never thought of that," Martha admitted a little perturbed. "I was about to say the gun was as rare as hens' teeth. It never occurred to me London might be full of the things right now ..."

"At last," Jeremy burst. "Something I thought of first. I checked. Olympic pistol competitions are for much smaller guns, .22s ... And as far as I could find, SIG don't make them!"

"Phew, idea intact!" Martha grinned girlishly. "Well, so that's it really. Evidently, in what is a quite legal and regulated market, a SIG P210 will cost you about £2,000, maybe more."

"Wow," Gurmel whistled.

"Exactly. And I'm sure I read some report or other a few months back saying there were so many of those plastic Glocks washing around London right now the price is down to about £200 ..."

"Or less," Jeremy confirmed.

"Mmm," Rosie pondered. "So what are the possibilities? One, the killer owns the weapon. Could have got it any number of different ways. Could even have bought it if they're rich enough. But however they got it, they would know it was rare and distinctive ..."

"Which would mean," Gerard continued. "They would know we'd identify it and eventually get round to having this conversation. Meaning, either they absolutely don't care - they think they're safe from any suspicion or discovery ..."

"Or they have used it to make us think it's all about Gallini's Swiss enemies," Jo put in.

"Actually," Rosie nodded. "That is a good point. There are so many odd things about this case that we have to keep asking whether what we're seeing has all been carefully created to get us looking in the wrong places. OK, but what's the second possibility?"

"I suppose it's the one we thought of last night," Gerard suggested. "The killer has been hired by someone else who supplied this rare gun."

"I do agree that is a possibility, maybe even the most plausible one," Martha began. "I even agree the idea we kicked around last night could fit: that whoever the killer is, they decided - or were allowed - to sort out some personal stuff first before killing Gallini. But no matter how we hypothesise this, the point we absolutely must not forget is that at least one of the victims, Ian Green, must have known the killer ... That has to be why the SIM card got changed, to stop us seeing the connection."

"We know all that," Rosie began with a hint of irritation in her voice.

"OK," Martha smiled to ease the tension. "But I do feel that whenever a new idea occurs, we tend to let that point drift out of our thinking ..."

"Mmm, yes, well ..." Rosie mumbled.

"So, I was going to suggest," Martha continued. "Unless anyone else wants the job, that I spend some time today looking again at Green's background. Plus, there's also the link we got yesterday to the mysterious Flipz and Crisz to follow up ..."

"Yes, OK," Rosie began. "No, seriously Martha, you're right, that is a good idea," she smiled. "So, back to the owner of the gun," she continued, businesslike again. "Obviously, a third possibility would be it still belongs to the person it was originally issued to, save the only person that could be true of - if my maths are correct - is Herr Gallini. And for all that we might just about dream up a connection between him and Ian Green - via Green Senior - the evidence is rather unhelpfully not pointing towards suicide!"

"Or ..." Martha began slowly, conscious she was in danger being seen as too-clever-by-half, a criticism she'd borne with barely disguised exasperation since she was about six. "Or, the present owner could have inherited it, been given it by someone who was in the Swiss militia some time between ... whenever it was," she offered while pretending to be unable to find the relevant note.

"1949 to 1975," Jeremy put in helpfully.

"Exactly," Martha smiled while trying desperately not to look smug. "Or he could have stolen it - or borrowed it - of course ..."

"Why do I just know you've got an idea?" Rosie smiled.

"No, not really."

"Not really?" Rosie asked.

"No. But I was thinking, we ought to find out a little more about Mr Cassidy, don't you think? I mean, I don't have the first idea how he could connect to Ian Green, but if Gallini had an old SIG you'd think the Mr and Mrs who ran his house would know ..."

"Why?" Gurmel puzzled.

"The Help always know where everything is," Martha replied with noted confidence. "Besides, seeing as there doesn't seem to be a butler, isn't it bound to be the chauffeur?" she tried to joke.

"Ho hum," Rosie sang.

"But the more general point," Jeremy pondered. "About an old gun staying in a family for generations. That is a bit of a nuisance."

"A nuisance?" Gerard asked.

"Yeah. I mean it doesn't exactly help us narrow the list, does it? Given what Martha has found out about the Swiss militia, there could be a fair number of these guns around, passed on by fathers or uncles or whatever. It's not a poor country. Just because some people will pay a lot for one doesn't mean those with them want to sell."

"Actually, maybe what keeps the price high is the fact no-one needs or wants to sell great-uncle William's favourite gun," Gerard pondered.

"Great-uncle William?" Jo puzzled.

"William Tell. He was Swiss, wasn't he?"

"Oh yeah," Jo smiled. "Do SIG make crossbows too?"

"Maybe that's how they started," Jeremy smiled. "But you'd like to think one of them would get spotted in Customs!"

"Is it easy to get a handgun into the country?" Gurmel asked.

"Not as difficult as it should be," Jeremy replied despondently. "Hence all those Glocks. But you do make a good point ..."

"Really?" Gurmel laughed. "What was it?"

"That we're in danger of overcomplicating things. It's a Swiss gun, but it's over here. For all that it is interesting knowing about the thing's history and stuff, the questions for us are: who would want to bring one here; and why? Actually, in all probability, that's just one question ..." Jeremy mused philosophically.

"It is?" a slightly lost Rosie asked.

"Yes," Martha put in. "Or at least, probably," she smiled. "If the gun was Gallini's, then he must have brought it over thinking it offered some protection ... Which means he must have believed he had something to fear. His murder suggests he was right. The most logical alternative is that it was sent over here with the precise intention of making that murder happen."

"So we discount all the other possibilities - belongs to a gun club, belongs to someone who prefers old and expensive things, got stolen ..." Jo asked.

"Not the stolen point, not that at all," Jeremy suggested. "No, that is something we should check on, maybe ..." he continued while looking at Rosie. "You might ask Mrs Gallini whether there have been any break-ins at their house recently. And also whether her husband kept a gun."

"Yes, you're right, we should ask. Actually, I think we might as well ask Gallini's son and this Mr Battersby about a gun as well. There's no point not telling them we've identified it. So not then asking if there could have been one in the house would seem rather odd," Rosie agreed. "OK, so let's just think about who does what. Jo and I will need to leave soon to see the Gallinis and Battersby, Martha has booked herself a morning going through records, Gerard," she smiled across to her apparently lost-in-thought Sergeant.

"What, yes ma'am," Gerard bluffed.

"You've obviously got something in your mind."

"Yes, just a small thought. Might be quite off-the-wall ..."

"OK," Rosie nodded while trying to recall when, if ever, Gerard had indulged in anything like off-the-wall thinking.

"Mrs Dearmer ..."

"Mrs Dearmer!" Rosie exclaimed with obvious surprise, noting without understanding how Martha seemed to be looking across to Gerard with something like surprised admiration.

"Yeah ... look. I've got no reason to think it was her, but something Jo said yesterday made me think ..."

"Me," Jo put in, sharing Rosie's surprise.

"Yeah. It was just a throw away comment, but you said Mrs Dearmer had a slight accent. Maybe a bit like Mrs Gallini's ..."

"Well, yeah, I did say that. Didn't you think she had an accent, ma'am?"

"Yeah, I suppose ... But Gerard, she's tiny and ..."

"Is there a Mr Dearmer?"

"You know what, I was going to ask exactly the same question," Martha grinned before adding with less honesty. "Then I forgot ..."

"But I still don't see ..." Rosie replied blankly, her eyes narrowed with genuine confusion.

"The name," Jo suggested. "Of course. I mean, first off Halina Dearmer sounds a little un-English. I just thought that maybe she was French or something. But don't you remember what Mrs Gallini said about the Swiss having all sorts of different sounding names, Italian, German ..."

"So the question is - supposing Mr Dearmer is Swiss?"

"Exactly," Gerard smiled.

"Well, I can't say I'm in any way convinced ..." Rosie began.

"Maybe I could just see if there are any obvious records on Mrs Dearmer or any Mr Dearmer," Martha suggested helpfully while all-but laughing with amazement at Gerard - and, apparently, Jo - having the same idea as her. Then again, she thought, maybe that's how good teams work: sometimes challenging each other's thinking but at other times all generating the same thought.

"OK, why not. So, are we done? I'll ring Kenny's solicitor again before I go, make sure he's still on for 2pm ... We'll need to think about how and when we say we're not going to pursue the murder charges ..."

"Make the bastard sweat as long as possible," Gerard suggested.

"Well, I guess we all think that ..." Rosie began. "Look, I was going to suggest you and Gurmel go and see the Cassidys, but really, we need to know before this afternoon whether this Mary Lee will make a statement ..."

"We've enough with the possession figures to resist bail today," Jeremy put in.

"Yes, but we'll have to get him before a judge by Tuesday when there's bound to be a formal application ..."

"Of course," Jeremy agreed. "Look, I spoke to her a bit yesterday, not that means anything in itself but I'd be happy to take a ride up to the hospital and talk to her. At least try to get a feel for her state of mind."

"Thanks, that will help."

"The other thing I do need to do," Jeremy continued. "Is check a few details on Green senior and Brinks Mat. I'm sceptical about that being key here, not least because there have been so many false dawns with that case that I kind of doubt we'll ever really solve it ..." he mused. "But, that is the main reason why I'm here ..."

"Presumably, tomorrow," Martha suggested. "When these city people are back?"

"That's what I was thinking," Jeremy nodded. "So I wouldn't mind a bit of time later," he continued, looking to Rosie. "For us to discuss ideas and possible questions to follow through."

"Yes, of course," Rosie agreed, disarmed and charmed all over again by the non-pushy way DCS Benson went about the task of not bothering to throw his rank around.

"OK, well, so I guess we leave you in charge Martha," Rosie nodded, a frown of self-effacing bemusement narrowing her gaze as she half-recalled the young TDC's explanation for the demise of the old SIG: replaced by a new and better model.

Chapter 32

Rosie felt strangely nervous, uncertain even as she and Jo waited for the receptionist to finish her phone conversation. Maybe it was the sense of history still living in those marble columns and expensively decorated walls. Or maybe it was the let down of knowing she had little of any great worth to tell the younger Herr Gallini. The previous day, when their euphoria on arresting Kenny had been at its highest, she had thought of ringing Mrs Gallini, sharing the good news. She was glad she hadn't.

Perhaps, she pondered, it was a deeper if related ennui. A feeling that everything to do with the case was slowly drifting further and further apart. Like the ever expanding universe extending the already unintelligible concept of infinity to an even more unfathomable extreme.

"Ah yes," the ineffably jolly receptionist smiled. "Herr Gallini asked us to save the Old Card Room. Take the stairs to the first landing and then turn right, it's at the end of the corridor."

The door was open, and as they walked in Mrs Gallini stood and walked across the dark wooden floor to meet them. Even though she wore a pair of flat, plain black shoes, the noiselessness of her walk was almost eerie. "Detective Inspector," she smiled politely. "And Detective Hartley ..."

"Mrs Gallini," Rosie smiled back while accepting the curious formality of a handshake. Maybe it was the presence of her stepson and her husband's secretary, maybe it was just proof of a darker mood, but she looked sadder and more in mourning today in a black skirt, black blouse and dark grey jacket.

"Come, sit down," the woman continued in her gently accented English. "And I'll introduce you," she offered politely while walking slowly towards the waiting group, all four standing with impassive politeness. "You met Petra and Michael, of course ..."

"Of course, hello," Rosie smiled nervously at the two attentively curious children, their big blue eyes staring up at her with a look she could not help but interpret as wanting to know when everything was going to be normal again.

"Hello," Jo echoed.

"Detective Inspector," a tall, almost quintessentially Italian man said while holding his hand out.

"This is Roberto," Marianna Gallini confirmed needlessly. "Stefan's eldest son."

"Herr Gallini," Rosie replied, gently shaking the man's perfectly manicured hand. "Please understand how very sorry we are for your loss and how very determined we are to find your father's murderer."

"Thank you," Roberto Gallini replied with a surprisingly pronounced German accent, while subtly offering his hand to Jo. "Detective," he smiled.

"And this is Hamilton Battersby."

"Detective Inspector, Detective," the rotund, puffy-faced man replied with a pronounced, if hard-to-place, northern English accent delivered with a slightly comical camp lisp.

"Sir," Rosie smiled while wondering at the contrast between the perfectly dressed and controlled Swiss and this slightly slobby looking guy in a dark suit that didn't look as though it quite fitted any longer, with a white shirt which most definitely did not fit around his jowly neck.

"Please, let us all sit," Roberto suggested.

The arrangement the Gallini family had chosen seemed, to Rosie, to be deliberate and revealing. On a two-seater sofa opposite the chairs set for her and Jo, Roberto Gallini sat with young Michael to his right. Marianna sat with Petra on an adjacent sofa. Mr Battersby sat in a chair to Roberto's left. The symbolism was clear: the family's response to tragedy would be calm and ordered, with Roberto as it's new head.

"We have, as you would expect," Rosie began, looking at Roberto, his dark eyes still and clear. "A few questions we need to ask ..."

"Of course," Roberto smiled thinly.

"But first, I thought I should ask if there were any points you wanted to ask me about." Even as she asked this question Rosie was uncertain of its purpose, the idea for it had just popped into her head as she glanced from one disconcertingly attentive Gallini to the next. Their calm and patience were impressive, but maybe also just a little contrived. They must, she had felt intuitively, have some ideas about what happened, if only the usual - and virtually always incorrect - worry about madmen on the loose. They ought also to have questions, surely, about when if at all to return to Hurst Hall.

"No, I don't think so," Roberto replied without bothering to glance at either his step-mother or Hamilton Battersby.

"Why has my father been killed?" Michael asked in perfect, accent-less upper middle-class English.

Rosie smiled sympathetically towards the boy, his blonde hair so perfectly combed, his dark suit so incongruously adult, his guilelessness so chillingly challenging. "That, Michael," she said neutrally, determined not to sound like some patronising aunt. "Is the question we have been asking ourselves for the past two days. So far, we can identify no reason."

"I see," Roberto nodded. "So the questions you need to ask us ..." he posed, not finishing the thought.

"Are whether you can think of any reason, any enemies, any threats, any issues ..."

"Yes, of course. Hamilton and I discussed this when we heard," Roberto replied, unaware, as far as Rosie and Jo could tell, of how pointed was the inference that such matters were not ones he would also have discussed with his father's widow. "We can think of no explanation. Of course we have rivals - in business, maybe in other fields," he suggested. "But we truly did not believe we had enemies. Not enemies who would ..."

"I understand," Rosie said slowly, watching to see whether the straight-backed guy was going to show some sign of emotion, distress even. He didn't. "Can I just ask, what did you have in mind when you said: other fields?"

"Oh nothing specific. Just the other things men do ... sport, politics, endowments ..."

"Did your father have an interest in politics?" Rosie asked.

"No, not really," Roberto smiled. "And I fear my answer now might be misunderstood," he suggested with seemingly genuine concern. "I wasn't really thinking of specific things my father did. More of the kinds of thing the bank does. You know, we sponsor different things. We inevitably get asked for an opinion on matters of policy ..."

"I see," Rosie smiled.

"Good," Roberto nodded with apparent relief.

"But, and I am sorry to keep pressing on this, you can think of no reason to believe any of those contacts, exchanges, rivalries could explain ..."

"No, really, it's just ... that isn't how my country is," Roberto insisted.

"No," Rosie replied thoughtfully. "Mrs Gallini said something similar yesterday ..."

"So Detective Inspector," Hamilton Battersby began.

"Yes Mr Battersby?" Rosie asked sharply.

"If that's ..."

"What, all?" Rosie asked, her eyebrows arched with incredulity. "No Sir, it isn't."

"Oh, oh, I s-see," the man replied with sudden timidity, seeming to shrink before Rosie's dismissive stare.

"Now," Rosie picked up, looking from Roberto to Marianna and back. "I need to ask you both a very specific question and I can see how it could be misunderstood," she smiled considerately. "So, perhaps I should first tell you this: we have identified the gun that was used ... is it OK to talk of this now?" Rosie asked of Marianna, glancing quickly to her children.

"Yes, of course," the woman replied with tuetonic stoicism.

"OK, so the gun used to kill Herr Gallini was a SIG ..."

"Really?" Roberto replied with believable surprise.

"Yes," Rosie continued. "And SIGs are not especially common in this country. But more than that, the precise model of SIG used is, we understand, actually very rare anywhere outside of Switzerland. It was a SIG P210 ..."

"How can you be so sure?" Roberto asked.

"Because that model creates a unique set of grooves on the ..." Rosie stopped in mid-flow, disconcerted by the staring, unblinking eyes of Petra and Michael.

"I understand," Roberto nodded. "And I believe there were others, including a young policeman, which of course saddens us all deeply."

"Indeed. And thank you," Rosie nodded. "You will understand, therefore, that the use of this particular and, we understand, rather old gun ..."

"Sorry, how do you know it was old?" Battersby asked.

"Because it was last manufactured in 1975."

"But, I don't understand ..." Battersby babbled.

"No, but I suspect the Detective Inspector does Hamilton," Roberto suggested to the puzzled looking man, before turning his attention back to Rosie.

"Well, maybe," Rosie smiled. "But we could use a little help. We understand that most men in Switzerland serve in the militia?"

"Yes, it is a very important part of our civic duty," Roberto replied with an ingrained sense of pride.

"Indeed. And it is common practice for members to keep their weapons at home?"

"Yes, but locked away, of course. I too have a SIG, locked in a cabinet ..."

"Of course," Rosie smiled. "But if our understanding is correct, yours will be a later model. I take it your father was once in the militia?"

"Yes," Roberto replied more slowly.

"And if my maths are correct, he would have joined before 1975. So you see, I have to ask: do you know where your father's gun is right now?"

"The answer is No, I'm afraid."

"And is that No, but you have an idea it could be in one of a few places ... Or No, no-one has seen it in a long time?"

"Well, more the latter," Roberto smiled. "You are quite right to assume my father had a pistol and that such a fact was no secret in the house. In the old house, he kept it in a cabinet in his study. But I do remember very well that when we moved, it did go missing. That was of concern, obviously ... I was away at boarding school by this time, then university ..." he recalled. "I really don't know whether it turned up again ..."

"Mrs Gallini, can I ask: did your husband have a gun here, as far as you know?"

"Detective Inspector, you know that would have been illegal," Battersby put in pompously.

"I'm hardly going to worry about that right now, Sir," Rosie replied dismissively. "Mrs Gallini?"

"Not as far as I know, I have never seen him with a gun even though, like Roberto has said, back home it is perfectly common for a man to keep his militia gun into old age."

"Yes, so we understand," Rosie nodded. "So, you can see," she continued, looking back and forth between Marianna and Roberto. "One line of enquiry we have to follow is that the use of this old and rare - at least for England - gun, points to the killer having some kind of connection to your family's life in Switzerland."

"Yes, yes, I see that," Marianna said sadly, her arm now around a suddenly distressed Petra. "Detective Inspector, is there anything else you need to ask of me right now?"

"No, not that I can think of ... Other than, what are your plans for the next few days, are you going to stay here, or go back to Hurst Hall ..."

"No, not back to the house, not yet ..." Marianna sighed. "But in any case, well Roberto was going to talk to you but you will understand, we need to take Stefan ... take his body home," she said quietly, her lip trembling slightly as her incredible resolve began to dissipate.

"Of course," Rosie smiled empathetically. "I can think of no reason why ..." she paused, looking down at the pale and sad-faced Petra. "I'm sure that is right. And if we need to check other things, presumably we'll be able to ring you?"

"Of course," Marianna smiled. "Even in the mountains our telephones work," she said lightly. "Thank you Detective Inspector," she added while motioning for her children to stand. "You have been so very kind."

Rosie watched with admiration the way Marianna gently pulled her children close and then, with equal gentleness, led them from the room.

"Can I add my thanks too, Detective Inspector," Roberto said, crossing his legs and falling into the buttoned back of the sofa, a certain tension visibly lifted from him. "Marianna tells me you and the other officers have all been very attentive, kind and caring."

"Thank you," Rosie smiled. "Although I am very conscious that none of us has yet come close to answering Michael's question."

"No, that is true," Roberto accepted. "And I have to include myself in that criticism. So, I am assuming, now that my stepmother has left us, there are some more questions you would want to ask?"

"There are ..." Rosie began.

"Of course," Roberto continued. "Well, again, Hamilton and I have, as it were, compared our thoughts," he offered with his first mixed-idiom of the interview. "And I feel we can say with almost total certainty that my father's marriage was a good one. Marianna is ... well, you have seen for yourself," he smiled. "My father ... well I think I should tell you before you hear it from someone else, my parents' marriage was not exactly perfect. I believe they did once love each very deeply, perhaps did still when my mother ..."

"It's OK Herr Gallini," Rosie all-but whispered, just a little uncertain where all this was heading.

"Yes, thank you," the man smiled thinly, looking for the first time less than collected or calm. "So, what I'm telling you is I do not believe there are any affairs or indiscretions waiting to be uncovered. I believe, since my father married Marianna, he has lived a happy and faithful life."

"I see, thank you," Rosie accepted. "But of course, you understand I have now to wonder about the time beforehand ..."

"Yes, of course, I ... Well I'm not totally sure about my mother. I want to say nothing could possibly have happened, but I'm not sure ..."

"And your father?"

"There, I'm sorry to say I have no doubts. However, I am telling you all this also because even though I believe there probably are some small little scandals in my father's past, they really are quite a long time back. After my grandfather died and my father took over as head of the family and the bank ... well work became his entire life ..."

"Can I ask, when was that?"

"What, when he took over?"

"Yes."

"Early in 1991. I was at university then, so I guess the change didn't affect me so much. But for Angelina and Marco ..."

"They are your sister and brother?"

"Yes, a little younger than me. Angelina would have been about fourteen when my grandfather died, Marco about ten ... They hardly saw anything of our father for the next few years, while my mother ..."

"Please go on, Herr Gallini," Rosie encouraged considerately.

"My mother is from the south of Switzerland Detective Inspector, the Italian region ..."

"Yes, so I understand."

"Well, to a German that is all the explanation one needs. Italians are wild and wilful and ..."

"But to a half-Italian, half-German?"

"What a very perceptive question," Roberto smiled. "Well, I guess we all love our mothers and I certainly loved mine. She was vivacious and stunningly pretty but ... Well, I have absolutely no doubt Marianna is a ten-times better mother to Petra and Michael then my mother was to my sister and brother ..."

"Your father was lost in work, your mother not around much either. Is that the point?"

"Pretty much! Put like that, it makes us sound like poor little rich kids I suppose ..."

"No, honestly, that was not what I was thinking at all," Rosie insisted reassuringly.

"No, well, I guess I have said more than I expected," Roberto smiled with touching openness. "But the point really was I cannot see anything in the last twenty years of my father's private life that could explain ..."

"Herr Gallini," Rosie began apologetically. "Affairs are never simple things, are they? Who knows how many people they affect ..."

"I suppose that is true ..."

"Now, you said you were sure of your father's infidelities. Could there be a link there, an angry husband who has been waiting for an opportunity ..."

"I ... I just don't see that," Roberto protested. "My father ... he ... I just don't think he would ..."

"What, risk a possible business relationship by sleeping with the wife of another man of his standing, class?"

"Well frankly ... No, Detective Inspector."

"And how about the wife of someone less important, maybe a clerk at the bank?"

"I suspect that may well have happened but ... Look, you do understand, SIGs, they are only issued to Officers ..."

"Actually, No. I didn't properly understand that point. But we're leaping ahead, Herr Gallini. Yes, I am interested in the gun because I can only think of two explanations for it being here in England. The first is it was smuggled over for this very crime. The other is it was here in the possession of someone who had long harboured a grudge against your father. But either way, I'm sorry to have to say it is as likely the gun was stolen from an ex-Officer as it is someone of such rank actually pulled the trigger!"

"Yes, of course, I see the point," a more sullen and defeated Roberto accepted. "All I can say is, I don't actually know the names of any ..."

"None of them?" Rosie asked incredulously.

"N- ... no, no, I don't think so," Roberto replied while, for the first time, avoiding Rosie's gaze.

"Herr Gallini," she began slowly, quietly and carefully. "I have no doubt, no doubt whatsoever that you want to do everything you can to help us find who killed your father. Can I just check one thing: when are you hoping to return to Switzerland?"

"Probably Tuesday, not tomorrow any way."

"OK. So would you please, after we've finished here, think again about your father's past. Perhaps talk to your sister and brother. Perhaps to any other people who might have more knowledge ... more specific knowledge about people he may have upset, be they business rivals or cuckolded husbands ..."

"Cuckolded?"

"Sorry," Rosie smiled. "Your English is so good I perhaps forgot to take care with my choice of word. A cuckold is a very old English word for a man made to look foolish by another man's successful lust for his wife."

"I'm embarrassed," Roberto smiled. "I bet that word is in Shakespeare. My father always insisted we read and understand Shakespeare."

"Always wise advice," Rosie nodded. "But back to my point, please tell me you will give this more thought and let us know of any possible disagreement or slight that could, after all these years, have festered into murder."

"Yes, OK, of course," Roberto agreed.

"So," Battersby asked after a few moments silence. "If there's nothing more."

"Actually Mr Battersby," Rosie smiled without meaning it. "We are not done. There are some questions we need to ask you."

"Me?"

"Yes. Now, I'm taking it from something Herr Gallini said earlier that you are aware that we are investigating a triple murder?"

"Well, yes. Although no-one had been quite so specific ..."

"The first victim will mean nothing to Herr Gallini, but to you? Well, his name was Ian Green ..."

"Should I know that name?"

"He was Gerry Green's son."

"Oh," Hamilton Battersby breathed in obvious surprise, his hand nervously running over his stubbly chin, a finger sliding down between his shirt and neck, loosening the collar a little further. "I ... we hadn't heard that at all ..."

"Who are these people?" Roberto asked.

"We commissioned a builder," Battersby explained. "Some works to the Conservatory and Orangerie ... there was an argument ..."

"Why wasn't I told this?"

"It wasn't a problem, we'd ..."

"Can I ask," Rosie interjected. "The gates to Hurst Hall, they were open on Friday. Was that ..."

"Not sure," Battersby answered quietly. "There was a problem with them when the work was being done. We were waiting for ..."

"So you have no direct reason to think Mr Green or his people deliberately put them out of action?"

"No ... well to be honest, the idea had never occurred ... Why, do you?"

"What," Rosie asked. "Regard Mr Green senior as a suspect?"

"Yes."

"Well, without sounding like some clichéd television detective, I cannot ignore any possibility. But as far as we can tell, there is no obvious reason why Mr Green would have wanted to kill his son ..."

"Sorry?" Battersby asked blankly.

"The gun, Hamilton," Roberto chided. "As the Detective Inspector has already told us, the same gun killed all three victims."

"Exactly," Rosie smiled deciding not to complicate matters with an admission of one missing bullet. "Unless either of you can think of another connection between the Greens and Herr Gallini?"

"What kind of connection are you thinking of, Detective Inspector," Roberto asked.

"Well, the only obvious one would be as investor and banker," Rosie smiled.

"So you think this Mr Green may have some kind of account with us?"

"I have no idea," Rosie replied, still maintaining a wry, questioning smile. "There is a suggestion in Mr Green's past that he may once have been looking for a home for a rather large sum of money. A home outside of this country ..."

"I see," Roberto replied thoughtfully.

"Do you, well I don't," Battersby blustered.

"I don't know how much you know about the way banks in my country operate ..." Roberto began.

"Not very much at all Sir," Rosie accepted. "But the generally understood story here is that they are very ... private. That monies deposited there are beyond scrutiny ..."

"I see," Roberto nodded, his hand cupping his chin, his eyes unblinking in concentration. "Well, some of that is true, which does create a problem. Whilst we do, as required by Swiss law, run some checks on our clients and their money, I cannot say that every account is in the name of its true owner," he explained with carefully crafted allegorical clarity.

"So, just to be clear," Rosie smiled. "You could do a little checking for us, both here and in Zurich. But even if you do not identify an account in the name of G. Green we could not take that as proof he does not have money deposited with you?"

"I am afraid to say that is true."

"Supposing I were to say the 'money' deposited may well have been in the form of gold?"

"Then I can be much more precise," Roberto smiled. "It is not in an account with us, nor with anyone else I would suggest. Gold - provided one has proof of legal ownership - can be stored and we do have suitable facilities in both London and Zurich. But no-one can just open a bank account with a bar of gold."

"Legally, you mean," Rosie pressed.

"Not really. The very concept is illogical. It would be like opening a bank account with a diamond or a work of art. The more obvious thing for someone who has gold - legally, of course - but wants access to currency, is to sell it and invest the cash."

"Do you trade in gold?"

"All banks hold their own gold reserves and there may occasionally be trading, but trust me Detective Inspector, gold is highly regulated and tracked."

"So what if, to think about a purely hypothetical case," Rosie smiled. "Someone manages to get hold of a lot of gold they don't have legal papers for. What do they do, forge some document or other?"

"Wouldn't make any difference, the gold will be stamped. Their only option is to find someone with the ability to melt it down and reproduce it with a new provenance."

"Oh, right," Rosie nodded. "So who could do that?"

"Here?" Roberto smiled. "The Bank of England. In my country, the Schweizerische Nationalbank - or Swiss National Bank. In the US, the Federal Reserve ... You get the idea?"

"Yes, OK. Thank you," Rosie replied thoughtfully.

"Detective Inspector," Roberto added considerately. "Please don't misunderstand me. What you are asking, it has happened. There is no doubt of that. But the process of converting stolen gold into money was never easy. And the change of Government in Libya has now made it all-but impossible ..."

"Libya?"

"Yes."

"All-but?"

"Well, question marks remain about the Russian banking system. But since the sell-off of all state utilities, it is much harder to find a home for a truckload or two of Roubles," Roberto smiled.

"So Rütger's doesn't like accepting Roubles?"

"Honest answer? No. Sterling, Yes. Swiss Francs, Dollars, Yen and Euros, of course. Renminbi ..."

"Eh?"

"Chinese currency, now open to limited trading against the Dollar, so we accept that. Anything else, not unless we have an existing relationship with the client."

"Well, you learn something every day," Rosie smiled. "Sometimes lots of things, thank you."

"My pleasure," Roberto nodded. "And I will check to see if we have an account for this Mr Green. Gerry you said?"

"Yes, but I suppose it would be worth checking under any of the family names. Do you have a record of those, Detective Hartley?" Rosie asked.

"I don't think I do ma'am," Jo replied, quickly thumbing through her notebook. "Could we let you have that later, Sir?" she asked of Roberto.

"Of course, no problem. So, are we finished for now Detective Inspector?"

"I think so ..."

"Could I just check a small detail," Jo interrupted. "Mr Battersby, we were wondering, what exactly is your role?"

We were? Rosie thought, while recognising that Jo's question gave her the chance to observe Gallini and Battersby for a moment.

"I'm afraid, Hamilton," Roberto laughed. "The Detective thinks you take shorthand or something. Mr Battersby is the family's Private Secretary, Privatsekretär in German. A kind-of in-house adviser on matters of law ..."

"I see, so you're a solicitor?"

"No, not quite Detective. I was Company Secretary to the bank here in London, but when Signora Gallini died ..."

"When my mother died we found ... Well, we found that our family affairs had become a little complicated. Lots of property was in my mother's name so we needed to sort that out. So my father asked Hamilton ..."

"I see," Jo smiled. "I know you've been thinking about this question over and over, Sir," she continued. "But was anyone left aggrieved by the sorting out Mr Battersby did?"

"No, truly," Roberto smiled. "It wasn't like that. There was a small estate my mother had inherited from her father. That we gave to her two nephews. There were no other claimants, it was really just a question of ..."

"Tax?"

"Yes," Roberto laughed. "OK. Yes, basically. And since then, we've just kept Hamilton on. Taking care of family investments, that kind of thing."

"I see," Jo nodded.

"When did your father come to live here, Herr Gallini?" Rosie asked.

"About four years ago."

"Why?"

"Why," Roberto repeated. "Well, a few reasons. First, I think he just wanted to get away from Zurich. It is a small town really and he had lived there all ..." he paused a moment, obviously stopping himself saying: 'all his life'. "I think, partly he had tired of hearing people still talking about his 'new' marriage. You know, things like 'married again so soon', or 'she's so young, was just a clerk' ... and so on."

"I see."

"Plus, he said he wanted to avoid the situation he faced when his father died, becoming head of the bank overnight. So, I have been running things at home, but with him here whenever I need advice ..."

"I see, thank you," Rosie nodded, seeing for the first time a genuine frailty in Roberto's resolve. "But, and I'm sorry to press, why here? I believe you have offices elsewhere. New York ..."

"We do. New York, Frankfurt and Hong Kong. To be honest, I'm not sure we ever asked why he decided to come here. Maybe I should ask my stepmother?"

"If you would," Rosie nodded. "Your father's decision to come and live in this country could have been made for any number of reasons. Even so, the fact remains that some connection or other seems to have followed him here."

"Yes, you have made that very plain Detective Inspector ..."

"Sorry ..."

"No, don't be. I do see now, you must be right. Like I said earlier, I will speak to my sister and brother to see if they can think of anything, anything at all from our father's past that could help you."

"Thank you," Rosie said on standing. "And we'll ring through those various names. We'll find our own way out, thank you. And Mr Battersby, thank you also."

Chapter 33

"Hiya," Martha smiled on seeing Gerard and Gurmel return. "Anything?"

"Nah, dead end I'd say," Gerard replied.

"You agree?" Martha asked of Gurmel.

"I just do what the Sergeant says," Gurmel suggested obediently. "But besides the fact the Cassidys do seem very nice, Mrs C was with Mrs Gallini at the school, while Mr C was at the Olympics ..."

"You mean, that's where he *says* he was ..."

"Yeah, well," Gerard smiled, remembering the pernickety lesson the DI had delivered about being precise. "You're right, we didn't ask for his ticket stub ... We kind of thought all the pics he insisted on showing us of the Duke and Duchess of Cambridge and Prince Harry were probably proof enough."

"Eh?"

"Seems he was only a few rows behind them. Must have spent half his time taking pics of the Duchess," Gurmel chuckled.

"I'm surprised their Special Branch team didn't confiscate the camera," Gerard added.

"So, not Mr C then," Martha summarised.

"Nope. So what have you got?" Gerard asked.

"Well, first off, doesn't look like there's a Mr D either. Obviously, there's not much you can check on a Sunday. But she does have a driving licence, in the name of Miss Halina Dearmer ..."

"So what's with the 'Mrs' then, or did we get that wrong?"

"I don't know. I mean, I don't think we got it wrong. I'm sure she gave her name as Mrs Dearmer the first time ..."

"Maybe she refers to herself as Mrs to avoid being thought of as an old spinster," Gerard suggested.

"I wondered that," Martha agreed. "Obviously, none of this totally rules out her having been married and reverted back to her maiden name ..."

"No, I guess ... so you think Dearmer is her maiden name?"

"Yes," Martha said with some certainty. "And the record actually shows no changes of name. Her date of birth is 17 February 1968 and her first provisional licence was issued in April 1987 ... in Harrogate."

"So that accent was Yorkshire!" Gerard laughed. "Oh well. Is that it?"

"Actually Sergeant," Martha smiled proudly. "That is very much not it. Sit down and listen to this. Ian Green was arrested on the afternoon of 13 July 2011, driving a hired van containing twenty boxes of cigarettes. Various brands, but all sourced from Portugal ..."

"Portugal?" Gerard asked, sitting at his desk opposite Martha.

"So the detail on the charge-sheet says."

"Mmm, guess there must be an easy route from there or something," Gerard pondered. "Anyway, twenty boxes? Doesn't sound like a big deal?"

"Must be lots of packets in a box or something," Martha suggested. "His admission was to a charge of attempting to avoid paying tax on forty thousand cigarettes. Anyway, here's the more interesting part. The record shows that although he admitted knowing they were smuggled - he'd evidently driven down to Portsmouth to collect them - at first he claimed to be doing that for a Mark Phillips ..."

"Phillips?" Gerard mused.

"Yeah," Martha giggled a little wistfully. "So, first off Green says he was working for this Phillips. Then he seems to have had second thoughts and withdrew his first statement, making another saying he was acting alone. After that he refused to answer any questions about who he met in Portsmouth, how he knew who to meet, etc, etc."

"So he was got at?"

"What does Phillips sound like?"

"I don't know," Gerard replied blankly. "I think my mum used to have one of their washing machines ..."

"Ho hum," Martha smiled indulgently while reaching for a separate scrap of paper. "Right, Mark Antony Phillips, aged thirty. A few different addresses in Forest Hill. A few spells inside for drug smuggling and dealing ... now," she continued, her voice and look suddenly making Gerard think of a patient but deliberate school teacher. "Try saying Phillips the way you might after a few too many beers ..."

"Feel-lips ..."

"Could be. Try it a little quicker."

"Flipits ..."

"Flipz?" Gurmel suggested.

"Exactly," Martha smiled. "I thought you didn't drink?"

"I don't," a sightly puzzled Gurmel replied.

"Flipz?" Gerard repeated.

"Well, it's a possibility, don't you think?" Martha asked a little uncertainly.

"Well, OK, a possibility," Gerard replied with a look that was not convinced.

"Yeah, exactly," Martha laughed. "So, I thought I'd see if anyone connected to the case remembered anything ..."

"Don't tell me, they're all up at the Olympics," Gerard laughed.

"Yeah well, funny you should say that," Martha replied with obvious disapproval. "Both of our PCSOs who are supposed to cover Penge are. I wanted to talk to them to see if they had ever heard of Flipz and Crisz ..."

"I'm lost," Gurmel confessed.

"Don't worry, stick with me," Martha smiled like an older sister suffering a younger brother's sniffles. "So, that was out. Well, Sergeant Bacon downstairs says we can contact them if we need, but evidently it takes ages to get a message through or something. But, back to where we were. So, I've got the charge sheet and of course it belongs to Lewisham. So I looked up the two arresting officers in the internal directory. Zip. They weren't there. I was thinking they must have quit, but just as a long shot I thought it worth checking to see if they'd just transferred out of the Met. So I rang Lewisham, spoke to the Desk Sergeant, nice man ..."

"You're good on the phone aren't you," Gerard commented with genuine admiration.

"Not really," Martha replied, slightly taken-aback by the distraction. "I actually dislike ringing people out of the blue, but how else you going to find stuff out? Anyway, turns out one of the arresting officers, a PC Gina Michael hasn't left. She's on maternity leave."

"Oh, OK ..."

"And she's not Gina Michael any longer. She's Mrs O'Neill."

"OK, fine. So can we talk to her?" Gerard asked dumbly.

"Gerard," Martha interrupted with a little exasperation. "Doesn't the name O'Neill ring any little bells ..."

"What? ... never!"

"Yep, she's Mrs Inspector O'Neill. And no, I haven't rung yet. But I did get their home number. The baby's evidently only a few weeks old and the Sergeant said this Gina had a hard time of the birth. So, I was thinking we might talk to the Inspector first, you know, seeing as we know him and that ..."

"Yeah, I guess ... thoughtful," Gerard smiled.

"The other officer has evidently left the force, left about six months ago. But have a listen to her name: Eloisa DiMaria - doesn't that sound cool? She's probably a model or something now. The Sergeant did say: good looking girl, with enough politically-incorrect feeling to suggest she was probably seriously stunning," Martha reported teasingly.

"Did she leave a forwarding address?" Gerard asked wryly.

"Have to wait till tomorrow for that," Martha replied. "Seems only Personnel at the Yard know stuff like that. Anyway, so what d'you think?"

"Well, yeah, OK. It's worth following-up. Have you tried Lewisham CID?"

"Yep, twice. No reply ..."

"Olympics?" Gerard suggested again.

"Who knows. The Desk Sergeant didn't say it in so many words, but he did say he knew they were a bit short-handed at present. There are, though, two on duty. Out somewhere or other but he promised to leave a message for them to ring."

"OK, well, might as well try Mrs O'Neill then ... Hey up, the DI's back."

"Hi ma'am," Martha smiled cheeringly while searching for evidence that her earlier pushiness might have caused a little tension.

"Hi, anything?"

"A few things, still checking ... Don't think there's a Mr Dearmer though."

"Oh well, keep thinking Martha. We'll get there in the end," Rosie smiled. "Gerard," she continued. "We need a word about our interview with Kenny, now a good time?"

"Oh, right, well," Gerard replied while watching the clock tick past 12:30.

"Don't worry, I'm on sandwich detail," Jo grinned resignedly on rejoining the team.

"Oh right, in that case," a newly happy Gerard replied. "Anything but egg."

"Oh yes, no egg for me either," Rosie nodded, adding over her shoulder while walking on towards her room. "Nor anything with mayo ..."

"What can I get you?" Jo asked Martha.

"Where are you going?"

"Over to Waitrose. I don't think anywhere else will be open on a Sunday ..."

"Oh good. So not the canteen ..."

"Good Lord no."

"Right, well, no egg ..." Martha laughed. "But other than that, I'm good with most things."

"Gurmel?"

"Well, no egg, no fish, no ..."

"Tell you what," Jo interrupted. "You can come with me."

Martha was just picking the phone up again when Jeremy walked in. "Hi, any good?"

"Honest truth," the DCS replied with a thin, unconfident smile. "Fifty-fifty at best. But really, I think by tomorrow the answer will be: no way ..."

"Oh dear," Martha nodded with acceptant disappointment. "I think there's a better chance with Kylie Smith. But of course, she didn't actually witness anything ..."

"Won't stand up," Jeremy replied plainly. "Anyway, how's your morning been?"

"Well, OK. Still following up some stuff on Green. But seems Gerard and I were both wrong about Mrs Dearmer, or rather I should say Miss. No sign of a husband ..."

"Oh well ..."

"That's what the DI said," Martha smiled.

"Senior officers for you," Jeremy shrugged.

"But, there was one thing for you. Imogen Wilson rang ..."

"She rang you?"

"Yes, I called her on Friday, left a message. But she said you'd tried today?"

"I did, and left a message, with my number," Jeremy smiled ruefully.

"Yeah. I said I'd get you to ring her back."

"OK, thanks. She probably thinks I work for you!"

"Well," Martha grinned, shrugging her shoulders and opening her palms to suggest total innocence.

"Mmm," the DCS nodded. "One day, no doubt. Is the DI in her office?"

"Yep, with Gerard. I think they're discussing the next interview with Kenny."

Martha's phone rang as she watched Jeremy tap gently on the DI's door.

"... really, wow. OK, thank you Sir. Thank you very much," she babbled excitedly while raising her hand to hush Jo and Gurmel, who seemed to be in full-flow with some argument over tuna. "And I really should have asked earlier, Mrs O'Neill, how is she? And the baby, of course ... aw, that's good, that's good ... Give her my love," Martha offered as though she were talking of an old school friend.

"And?" a quizzical Jo asked.

"Oh nothing," Martha smiled, "I think I've just cracked the case, that's all!"

Chapter 34

"Interview commencing at 15:12, Sunday, 5 August 2012. Present: Mr Mark Antony Phillips; Mr Phillips' solicitor, Mr Caswell; Detectives Cunningham and Hartley of Bromley CID; and Detective Sergeant Szabo of Lewisham CID. Mr Phillips," DS Sonja Szabo continued. "You are being held on suspicion of importing 200,000 cigarettes with the intention of avoiding Excise Duty and VAT ..."

"DS Szabo," Caswell interrupted. "I think I made it quite clear yesterday that my client will answer no further questions on this matter. Now, either you ..."

"You did indeed say that," Sonja smiled. "And it is my intention to return to that matter shortly. First though, my colleagues wish to ask your client some questions relating to another matter."

"What other matter?" Phillips asked with somewhat disarming politeness.

"Mr Phillips," Jo asked with just a hint of nervousness in her voice. "Can I ask, do you know an Ian Henry Green."

Martha watched Phillips closely as he answered Jo's opening question. He was, she could not help but notice, a very good-looking and well-groomed guy. Even after an overnight in the cells he looked bright and well-scrubbed, his short fair hair shimmering slightly beneath the harsh lights which also emphasised the delicacy of his tan. His deep blue eyes looked at Jo impassively as he listened to her question, his cupped hands resting untroubled against the desk.

"No," he replied without a trace of emotion.

"I see," Jo continued. "I have to say I find that a little surprising, seeing as we have evidence to the effect that you collect the rent for the flat he lives in on the Apostles' Estate in Penge ..."

"Don't know it ..."

"On Tuesdays, according to the evidence we have."

"Detective Hartley," Caswell interrupted with oily charm. "My client says he does not know what you are talking about."

"That is a pity," Martha put in. "You see, we had hoped we could sort a few things out today, but if that's not possible ... Well, there are a few live cctv cameras covering the walkways into and out of the estate. We could obvious go through the footage for a few Tuesdays past, but that might take a couple of days during which time ... your client will have to stay here."

"On what charge?"

"Sorry," Sonja apologised sweetly. "Didn't I say. My colleagues are working on a murder enquiry ..."

"Murder?" Phillips asked sharply, his cool momentarily threatened.

"A triple murder, in fact," Sonja explained with a disconcerting smile.

"Ian Henry Green was one of the victims," Jo added.

"What? No, no. That can't be right. You sure you got the right ..."

"The identification is definite, Mr Phillips. Ian Henry Green was shot sometime between 7:30 and 8:30am, Thursday last."

"No, I can't ... No ..."

"Mr Phillips, should we perhaps have a word ..." Caswell asked.

"Maybe, in a moment. Look," Phillips began, looking quickly from Sonja to Martha to Jo, concern but no real sense of fear in his eyes. "I do not kill people. I am nothing like that ..."

"At the moment, we are not in a position to decide whether we think you are a suspect or not ..."

"So why this conversation?" Caswell asked sharply.

"Because," Jo replied calmly, meeting the solicitor's stare with a determined look of her own. "We do have reason to believe your client met Mr Green on Tuesday night ... And so far, the only person we know for a fact met Green later than that is the one who killed him ..."

"How do you know that?" Phillips asked.

"What, that you met Ian Green on Tuesday?" Martha asked.

"Yes."

"We are police officers, Mr Phillips," she smiled. "We investigate, we talk to people, we find things out."

"OK ..."

"Mr Phillips, I really ..." Caswell tried to insist.

"It's OK. They've been sniffing round Green since he got out. Before then in fact," Phillips explained. "OK, first thing," he continued, looking directly at Martha now. "I do know Green and I did not kill him. Why would I?"

"The first question we considered," Martha began. "So, we asked around and what seemed to pop up was the suggestion that Mr Green owed you money from before he last went to prison ... Could that be true?"

"Owed me money?" Phillips replied calmly. "For what?"

"Well, there are a couple of possible answers to that," Martha suggested. "But, for what it's worth, I don't think that sounds very likely either ..."

"So, what?" Phillips asked, suddenly puzzled by Martha's disconcertingly enigmatic style.

"So what do I think?" Martha smiled. "Well, like I've already said, until now we have not been able to decide whether to make you are a suspect or not. Your answer to this question should help: what did you need to see Green about on Tuesday night?"

"I ..." Phillips began, his eyes betraying for the first time obvious uncertainty.

"It's OK, I understand your dilemma," Martha nodded sympathetically. "You see, to me the most logical explanation for you meeting Mr Green on Tuesday night wasn't because you wanted to collect something from him ... It was to thank him."

"I'm finding this speculative line of questioning most tiresome," Caswell put in superciliously.

"Then perhaps you'd be better advised to stop interrupting," Martha suggested with disingenuous politeness, backed-up with a piercing stare. "So we can get through it nice and quickly. Now, Mr Phillips," she continued, turning from the open-mouthed lawyer to his client. "I was saying. You owed Ian Green, didn't you? Some of the time he recently served should have been yours, shouldn't it?"

"Hmm," Phillips pondered, raising his hands to his mouth in the manner of a prayer while he considered his options. "Look," he tried. "Is there a way we could have an off-the-record conversation about this?"

"Not with a solicitor present," Sonja ruled.

"No, I understand that ..." Phillips nodded.

"And whilst I'm willing to say I've no interest in reopening the 2011 matter that led to Green's last conviction," she continued. "If there is a connection between him, you and the seizure we made on Friday ..."

"Yes, I understand," Phillips nodded. "OK ..."

"Mr Phillips?" Caswell asked. "Would you rather I left?"

"No," Phillips replied before turning back to look again from Jo to Martha to Sonja. "OK, so you're not interested in what happened last year?"

"No," Sonja nodded reassuringly.

"Right, well in that case," he continued, looking solely at Martha. "You're right. Why on earth would I want to kill him. I owed him. He did, like you said, take the time. So, Yes. I did meet him on Tuesday. It was him that asked to meet, by the way. I would have quite happily said what needed saying next time I called round."

"So why didn't he want that, I mean ... No, hold on," Martha smiled self-deprecatingly. "Tell me first where you met?"

"In the Paper Mill ..."

"Sorry?" Martha asked.

"It's a pub in Sydenham," Sonja explained. "Once had a reputation for drug dealing although the new landlord assures us that's all in the past. You find that now Mr Phillips," she asked. "Not that kind of place anymore?"

"I really had no idea it was ever ..."

"So, is that all he wanted," Martha asked. "A little free supply?"

"Like I said, I don't know ..."

"Do tell me if I've got this wrong, Mr Phillips," Martha smiled. "But haven't you completed terms in prison for both drug smuggling and dealing?"

"I'm a reformed character," Phillips smiled in reply.

"Of course you are," she nodded. "What was I thinking? OK, so what did he want?"

"He ..." Phillips began, choosing his words carefully. "He wanted to know if I knew of any work he might get. You know, a proper job, that sort of thing ..."

"And you were able to put him onto something straight away?"

"No, I just said I'd ask around ..."

"I see," Martha grinned. "OK, so did he say where he was going that night?"

"Er ..." Phillips paused, for the first time unable to offer an instant reply.

"Shall I tell you what I find most interesting about your hesitancy, Mr Phillips," Martha smiled with a hint of victory. "It is that you didn't just say: home, I suppose. That's what most people would have said. Something like that anyway. But you know he didn't go home, don't you?"

"How ..."

"You tell me."

"No, sorry. I've told you all I'm telling."

208

"Really?" Martha smiled. "Well, in that case I think we will have to hold you on suspicion ..."

"What! Why? I've told you ..."

"What you have told us, Mr Phillips, is that you met Ian Green sometime on Tuesday evening. At present, we know of no-one else who saw him before his body was discovered ..."

"His brother ..."

"His brother. Are you saying he told you he was going to his brother's?"

"Yes."

"Which one? I forget their names, but there are two I believe."

"I ... I'm not sure," Phillips replied.

"OK. Well, like I said. We'll hold you on suspicion while we check with them both ..."

"Wednesday," Phillips said quietly.

"Say again?" Martha prompted.

"He was going to stay with his brother. I honestly don't know which one, but it was Wednesday night ..."

"So where was he going Tuesday night?"

"Portsmouth."

"Portsmouth," Martha repeated. "OK, I rather suspect DS Szabo would like to ask how you know that ..."

"No hurry," Sonja offered.

"Thank you," Martha smiled at her new colleague. "So," she continued, looking unthreateningly, almost conspiratorially into Phillips dark-blue eyes. "I'm thinking that right now, you're trying to work out whether you might get away with telling us that Mr Green just kind of said, in passing like, that he was off to Portsmouth for the night after which he was going to pop in and see his brother. Something like that ..."

"Go on," Phillips nodded.

"Go on?" Martha repeated with an obvious trace of sarcasm. "I don't think I need to 'go on'. We both know how stupid such a story would sound ... I don't think you're stupid, Mr Phillips."

"No, OK," Phillips smiled. "He told me on Wednesday afternoon."

"Right, well I think we may be almost done," Martha thought out loud.

"There is one question you might want to consider," Sonja suggested. "As Mr Phillips knows, we raided his garage ..."

"My client has not admitted ownership or control of that garage," Caswell put in.

"No, he hasn't," Sonja accepted. "But I doubt we'll have much trouble proving that ... assuming we have to," she posed while looking straight at Phillips. "Well, we'll see," she continued after getting no immediate response. "Right now, I've got a different question in mind: who do you think tipped us off?"

"How should I know," a suddenly resigned Phillips asked.

"Alright, let's put it a different way. What would you have done if Green had told you he was going to do it. Perhaps he rang you on Wednesday night with some incredible James Bond bullshit about having decided to set you up ..."

"Don't be ridiculous," Phillips snapped.

"Is it ridiculous? It would explain why you killed him ..."

"I did not kill him!" Phillips insisted. "I'm not like that ..."

"People are scared of you, Mr Phillips, aren't they?" Sonja persisted. "More specifically, Ian Green was scared of you, wasn't he? That's why he withdrew the first statement he made ..."

"What statement?"

"Last year. To begin with he named you, said he was working for you. Then he changed his mind ..."

"That was nothing to do with me."

"In one sense, I accept that is true," Sonja agreed. "I did check the records and he saw no-one, made no calls, didn't do anything but sleep between making his first statement and telling us he wanted to change it. Which is my point," she said slowly while holding Phillips' gaze. "He didn't need anyone to come in and tell him life would be better if he just took the time ..."

"I didn't kill him."

"No? You sure? Not even after he rang you and said: Hey loser, now it's your turn?"

"No, no, that's just ridiculous. Totally ridiculous. Look, enough. I've as good as told you: Yes, it's my garage. Yes, I knew those cigarettes had been smuggled ..."

"From Portugal again?" Sonja asked.

"Kind of," Phillips smiled ruefully. "They're from Gibraltar, driven up through Portugal and then across to the ferry from Santander ..."

"Really, OK, that's helpful," Sonja nodded.

"Good. OK, we done?"

"Detective Cunningham?" Sonja asked.

"I think so, for now," Martha nodded. "You'll resist bail?"

"Of course."

"OK, yes," Martha agreed. "Mr Phillips," she continued. "Thank you for your help. We will obviously follow-up with Mr Green's brothers to check on his whereabouts Wednesday night ..."

"Of course," Phillips nodded politely.

"And obviously, if we have further questions we'll be in touch. But that's all for now."

"Sorry, before we finish," Jo put in. "Can I just pick up on something Mr Phillips said earlier ..."

"Of course," Martha nodded.

"You said something like: They've been after Green since he got out," Jo recalled. "Who had?"

"Who?" Phillips all-but laughed. "You lot, of course."

"Police?"

"Of course, who else?"

"So Green told you the police had been round ..."

"No, he didn't need to tell me that. I had one of yours asking after him a couple of weeks ago. Then again last Saturday ... No, Friday, day he came out."

"Not sure," Sonja replied to Martha's quizzical look.

"OK, right, well," Martha mumbled. "Like I said, we ask questions. Anyway, thank you for now."

Chapter 35

"Hello," a gruff, London-accented voice answered.

"Mr Green?"

"Yeah."

"My name is Detective Kandola. Sir, I ..."

"You work for that Russell?"

"Eh, No Sir, I ..."

"Bert Harris?"

"I'm with the team investigating your son's murder, Sir. Led by DI Charlton ..."

"Never heard of him."

"No Sir, he's a she ..."

"What?"

"DI Charlton is a lady, Sir. Now ..."

"Terrific!" Green replied in a way that made it obvious he found the news anything but. "So, you work Sundays then?"

"Until we catch whoever killed your son, Yes Sir," Gurmel replied, hoping that the conversation was about to go more according to plan.

"Yeah, right," a slightly less gruff, but nonetheless obviously sceptical Green replied.

"One of the things we've been trying to do, Sir," Gurmel continued. "Is clarify what your son was doing the few days before he was murdered. We believe we now know where he was to Wednesday afternoon, and have been told that he planned to spend Wednesday night with one of your other sons ..."

"Who told you that?"

"A friend of your son, Sir. So, I was wondering ..."

"How d'you know this friend didn't kill him?"

"We don't. That's why we need to check the information he gave us," Gurmel replied firmly. "So, I was hoping you could let me have contact numbers for your sons, Michael and David I believe ..."

"Can't have been David, he's in Tenerife ..."

"Michael then ..."

"Hold on."

During the full minute he spent listening to silence Gurmel smiled ruefully at the task he'd got. While Jo and Martha had got to go out on their own - which was OK, Martha had done all the research after all - he'd ended up as little more than an usher, shuttling back and forth all afternoon as Kenny met his solicitor, then the solicitor had a private meeting with the DI and Gerard, then another private meeting with Kenny.

Still, the outcome was better than they had dared hope. Meaning, when he told Martha he had to hold the phone away from his ear to avoid deafness from the loud screams, yelps and woo-hoos she and Jo belted out. He'd giggled at the thought of the two of them stuck in traffic, due to some accident on the Catford one-way, jumping around in an unmarked police car like a pair of schoolgirls at a boy-band concert.

His colleagues had been almost as pleased with the outcome of their own afternoon. Whilst they didn't see this Phillips as the killer, they were able to take a little satisfaction in having helped Lewisham solve one of their cases and tidy up an old one. It seemed the threat of a murder charge conjured up confessions like there was no tomorrow.

"Hello," a calmer, more polite voice said.

"Hello, Mr Green?"

"Michael Green, Yes."

"I see. Thank you, did your father say ..."

"He said you're trying to work out where Ian was. Or something like that."

"Yes. Well, specifically, where he was Wednesday night. We've got information saying he stayed with his brother. Was that you?"

"No, I haven't seen him for over a year."

"Oh?" Gurmel replied.

"Sorry, you are ..."

"Detective Kandola."

"Well Detective Kandola, the fact is I didn't really get on with Ian. So I was certainly not going to have him round for tea on ... Wednesday you said?"

"Yes."

"And David's away ..."

"So your father said. Does he have more to do with Ian?" Gurmel asked, instantly regretting the present tense.

"A bit. But I don't see how he could have seen him since he got out."

"Is there any chance Ian had a key to your brother's ..."

"None. Ian was a thief, Detective. No-one would give him a key to a khazi for fear he'd steal the seat."

"Hmm ..."

"I suppose ..."

"Yes?"

"Look, I'll be going past David's on my way home. I'll pop in ..."

"You do have a key?"

"Yes."

"OK, that would be very helpful, thank you. You can reach me on this number any time."

Chapter 36

"Come on then, tell us all about it," Jo begged as she and Martha sat at the table Gurmel had taken in the corner overlooking the park.

"Yes, do, come on," Martha smiled while picking up a menu. Having got a call back from Gurmel to say they were being let off early, she'd suggested they take a little time out, picking a small wine bar round the back of Bromley she knew would be open all afternoon on a Sunday.

"Well, I didn't really see anything," the shy young Sikh apologised, his big hands held in surrender, his big dark eyes staring from Jo to Martha and back, unblinkingly.

"Drinks," a rather bored looking, school-aged waitress asked.

"What kind of lemonade do you have?" Gurmel asked.

"What kind?" the girl asked incredulously. "I dunno, comes off a tap I think ..."

"I see," Gurmel replied disappointedly. "How about tonic water, do you have that in bottles?"

"Eh, I think so. Not sure ..."

"Sparkling water?"

"Bottle?"

"Please."

"Big or small?"

"How big is big?"

"About ... like this," the girl replied, holdings her hands parallel to each other, maybe ten inches apart.

"We'll take a large bottle of that then," Jo put in. "And I'll have a large glass of house white."

"Same," Martha smiled.

"Food?"

"Give us five?"

"Alright," the girl accepted without enthusiasm.

"Gurmel Kandola, you are one fussy man," Jo teased. "I swear, if I hadn't chosen we'd still be in Waitrose picking sandwiches."

"You two known each other long?" Martha asked smilingly.

"Nearly three years, about that. Why?"

"You're like an old married couple," Martha giggled.

"Yeah, well, guess it's all that time we spend together in the car."

"Oh really," Martha smiled with a hint of innuendo.

"Gurmel is the slowest, most careful driver I have ever met. We only live about five miles away, but I swear sometimes it takes an hour!" Jo babbled away.

"That's unfair," Gurmel protested. "Besides, the traffic ..."

"So, you live near each other?" Martha asked.

"Yeah, I live just the other side of West Wickham ..."

"And I live in Shirley," Gurmel completed the sentence. "Meaning I do most of the driving!"

"But you'd never met till here?"

"Nope. How about you? You live round here somewhere, don't you?" Jo asked.

"Yeah, just up the hill. You probably drive past my flat everyday."

"Right. So you from Bromley?"

"No, Fulham."

"Fulham, wow!" Jo all-but gasped. "That's like, cool, isn't it?"

"Maybe, I suppose," Martha replied evasively. "We used to live in Notting Hill, but my parents decided to move after the film came out ..."

"Really, why?"

"Guess they got fed up with tourists knocking at the door looking for Hugh Grant!" she grinned.

"Gosh, wow," a momentarily star-struck Jo gasped. "So what you doing here? You move here when you got the job?"

"Yeah, I did actually," Martha smiled. "My parents said they'd buy me a flat and I couldn't really see the point in looking further away ..."

"So your parents bought you a flat, in central Bromley," Jo said slowly and enviously.

"Er, yeah," Martha said more carefully, a little embarrassed. "I like it here though. Even if I change jobs I think I'll stay, it's easy to get around ... ah look," she burst, relieved. "She's on her way, what we going to eat?"

"How long you been in the Force then?" Gurmel asked Martha as the girl turned away with their order.

"Two and a half years. I applied just as I was finishing Uni. Got accepted but decided to do a bit of travelling first. You?"

"Four years. I was a PCSO in Croydon for a year or so. Then got a PC post here."

"And you Jo?"

"Pretty much the same, save I was a PCSO here first. But you weren't?"

"No," Martha smiled. "I'm ... I'm on this graduate programme thing ..." she allowed somewhat reluctantly.

"Well, why am I not surprised?" Jo giggled.

"What does that mean?" Martha asked a little defensively.

"Nothing ... nothing at all," Jo smiled reassuringly. "Other than that you are just so obviously clever. You'll be running this place soon, you mark my words," she continued while picking up the cold glass of pale white wine. "Anyway, to us. Let's hope we all do alright."

"To us," the three of them sang, clinking glasses.

"OK, come on Gurmel," Jo insisted. "You were going to say ..."

"Well, OK ... oops, sorry," Gurmel said, reaching inside his jacket for his ringing phone while smiling back at his colleagues in a way that suggested no disappointment on his part at all. "Kandola ... Yes Mr Green, thank you for ... really ... he had ... Wow! Left there ... Yes, I see ... coming back, of course ... No, please don't move anything. Can you lock it ... Yes, and leave a note for your brother ... Yes, we'll send someone in the morning just to check the place over. Thank you Mr Green, thank you very much, that is very helpful."

"Well?" Jo and Martha both gasped after what seemed like an interminable moment of silence as Gurmel switched off his phone and returned it to his pocket.

"Looks like Ian Green spent Wednesday night in his brother's Summer House ..."

"How could he be so sure?" Martha asked, nodding towards Gurmel's now hidden phone.

"No attempt to tidy up. The brother in question, David, almost certainly wouldn't have been happy about Ian in effect breaking in to what, by all accounts, is his newly built pride and joy. Something a bit grander than an old wooden shed, I gather. Meaning, so the other brother, Michael, is guessing, Ian must have intended going back after meeting whoever it was he met in the woods."

"Yeah, but I've been to Ian Green's place," Martha recalled. "It was a tip, no sign of the guy being especially house-proud ..."

"He left a small rucksack containing £15,000 behind a chair!"

"Wow!" Jo and Martha whistled in harmony.

"Well, that fits," Jo added.

"Lasagna?" the bored girl sang over Martha's shoulder, making her jump.

"Eh, yeah, that's mine," Jo said.

"Plain chicken and plain rice was yours, wasn't it?" the girl said with a look that suggested total incomprehension.

"Thank you," Gurmel replied.

"And Chicken Caesar Salad," she concluded triumphantly while reaching around Martha to place the bowl down. "Any sauces?"

"What?" Martha asked in surprise.

"Any sauces," the girl repeated. "Peri-peri, mayo ..."

"No, I don't think so," Martha replied while trying her best not to think about the horror that would be a Caesar Salad covered in ketchup.

"Fifteen grand," Jo sighed while breaking a piece of pitta bread. "Did you think there could be that much profit on smuggled cigarettes?" she asked of Martha.

"I honestly had no idea ..." Martha pondered. "I suppose Phillips might have added something for last time?"

"Maybe, I guess ..."

"So," Gurmel began while delicately cutting his chicken into the tiniest of pieces. "Green was doing some kind of smuggling run Tuesday night ...?"

"Same as last time, but a bigger load," Jo nodded.

"Five times bigger," Martha pondered. "I wonder ..."

"What?"

"Probably not important, but I can't imagine Phillips sat around doing nothing while Green was inside."

"No. So what you thinking, he must have other people who make the trip?"

"Yeah, that. But also, how's he got away with it? I mean, where does all the stuff go?"

"I dunno," Jo mumbled around a mouthful of lasagna.

"Do you think there must be something going on with the ..." Gurmel began, his voice becoming more and more of a whisper with every syllable. "... Local ..."

"I don't know. I don't even know how you'd begin to raise such a suspicion ..."

"The DS would know," Gurmel suggested.

"True," Martha nodded. "He's in tomorrow, right?"

"Yes. He said we should all meet at 9am. Go through things and decide who will do what during the morning while he sorts out the Kenny stuff."

"And the DCS and DI are off up town?" Jo clarified.

"So I understand," Gurmel nodded.

"I don't know," Jo sighed dismissively. "I mean, I can't say I know that much about this Brinks Mat thing ... it was like, years ago. Plus, the DI asked that Roberto Gallini about moving hooky gold and sure, you can say: well, he would say that wouldn't he. But basically, it sounds like a no-no ..."

"I can't say I really know what they're hoping to find out ..."

"Didn't the DCS say he wanted us to meet to talk about that?" Jo remembered.

"Oh yeah," Gurmel nodded. "He did. Well, that never happened. Or if it did, it was just the three of them."

"Oh well, while the cats are away ..." Jo giggled before taking another mouthful of lasagna.

"The one thing I have heard a few times about Brinks Mat," Gurmel added thoughtfully. "Is corruption. There were all sorts of suspicions about some of the police involved on the investigation."

The three of them sat in silence for a few moments, eating and thinking.

"Well," Martha said. "Maybe there's nothing like all that with this cigarettes thing, but," she continued looking directly to Jo. "We should have asked Phillips who it was called to ask him about Green."

"Ring that DS Szabo, get her to ask him," Jo suggested.

"Yeah, I suppose ..." Martha replied uncertainly.

"You don't have to tell her we think there's something odd with all these cigarettes flying around. Not least seeing as no-one smokes anymore ..."

"No, of course not," Martha smiled. "Did she say when they got the tip off?"

"No, I don't think she did," Jo thought. "I suppose that could be of interest. I mean, supposing you had your doubts about someone here, but didn't think anyone would take you seriously? Tipping off someone you did trust would be a way ..."

"Would you trust that Sonja Szabo?" Martha asked.

"Actually, Yes. Yes I would," Jo suggested. "She seemed as puzzled by Phillips comment about having had a visit as we are."

"True," Martha agreed taking the final mouthful of her salad.

"Well that makes two of us," Gurmel smiled dimly.

"Jo'll explain," Martha smiled back while looking for her phone. "I'll go and make that call."

"Well?" Jo asked as Martha returned.

"Yeah, said she'd ask him tomorrow. She's on her way home now but back on at ten. Said she'd wondered what he was on about as well. She also said that from memory, the tip off came in mid-morning on Friday ..."

"So after Green had been shot."

"Seems so."

"Hmm," Jo pondered. "Hold on, Miss Happy's coming - we having another drink? Gurmel's driving."

"Why not," Martha smiled.

"Excellent," Jo nodded, answering the girl before she even spoke: "Yep, all good. Two more glasses of this white, thank you. You OK for water?" she asked of Gurmel, who nodded tamely in reply.

"So," Gurmel wondered. "What d'you think we'll get to do tomorrow?"

"Well, I don't know ..." Martha replied uncertainly. "Few things to follow up still ... By the way, what did happen with Kenny?"

"Well, like I said," Gurmel began. "There was lots of tooing and froing, then suddenly the DI said he's going to confess and I was like: wow, to everything?"

"But he has!" Jo burst.

"Not the murders," Gurmel replied fussily.

"Yeah, well. Seeing as we didn't think he did those, that's perhaps not such a great shock!" Jo laughed.

"Yeah, well," Gurmel smiled. "But other than that, yeah. The GBH, the rape of the girl ..."

"Jade," Martha put in a little absent-mindedly.

"Yes. And three others ..."

"You know, it was as good as the threat we might want him for murder that led Phillips to admit the smuggling. There's a pattern there," Jo giggled while helpfully passing her and Martha's empty glasses to the girl who, almost with a smile this time, handed over two fresh.

"DiMaria," Martha mused. "Does that sound anything like Dearmer to you?"

"Not really," Gurmel replied.

"Maybe, a little I suppose," Jo pondered before taking a slow sip of wine. "But ... why?"

"Names," Martha replied enigmatically. "I just think there is something in this case about names ..."

"Really, right, OK ..." Jo nodded like she might to an unintelligible old lady on the bus. "Did you ring through the names of the Greens?' she suddenly asked of Gurmel.

"I did. Spoke to Herr Gallini himself. He sounded nice enough."

"Hmm, yeah, I guess ..." Jo mused thoughtfully.

"He said he'd get back to us tomorrow."

Monday, 6 August 2012

Chapter 37

The team - minus Rosie and Jeremy - met in the DI's room a little after 9am. It was obvious from the off that Gerard was distracted. More focused on the paperwork he had to complete for the Kenny case than he was on Martha, Jo and Gurmel's excitement about the progress they believed they had made. Yes, well - he had observed unenthusiastically as they confirmed Ian Green's movements in the final couple of days of his life - that was all useful, but it didn't of itself help them identify the last person he actually met.

No - Martha had accepted - but there were a few other leads (she'd exaggerated) she, Jo and Gurmel could be getting on with, if he wanted.

And so the three of them had found themselves out in the open plan section with their map, their A1 pad still covered with hopeful Post-It notes, and no real idea what to do with themselves. For a while, Martha even managed a modicum of interest in Jo and Gurmel's discussion of the sheer improbability of Andy Murray's win in the tennis.

But the novelty of that moment soon wore off and she started to think she should go and see if there was any help she could offer Gerard. For all that she still hardly knew him, she sensed he was not the kind of guy who would easily cope with stress. And for all that Kenny had confessed, being appointed Officer in the Case was anything but a cakewalk. Far from it. It was now Gerard's job to make sure there were no cock-ups with the process that might let the guy off through some nonsensical technicality or another.

Then, shortly after 10 o'clock, DS Szabo rang. What she had to say didn't help hugely. All Phillips could remember - or was prepared to say - was that the policewoman who came round asking about Green was one of those who'd searched his garage.

Still, that was enough to justify another phone call.

"Hello."

"Hello, Mrs O'Neill?"

"Speaking," the slightly out-of-it voice replied.

"Hi, I'm Detective Cunningham from Bromley CID. Your husband spoke to you yesterday about ..."

"Yes, about a case."

"Yes. Look, I'm so sorry to trouble you again, you must be so busy with your baby and stuff ..."

"Yes, well, he's just gone to sleep so maybe I've got a moment," came a reply lacking any discernible confidence.

"That's so helpful, thanks. Just a couple of things I'm trying to clear up about this Mark Phillips ..."

"Yes," Mrs O'Neill yawned.

"OK. So we have it that you and a PCSO DiMaria arrested Ian Green in July last year."

"Yes. Actually, I do remember it fairly well," Gina O'Neill said with a hint of enthusiasm. "Simply because it was kind of funny. We'd been walking around there for the best part of three days because there'd been a spate of housebreaking and really, we only started questioning him for something to do!" she laughed.

"Right, well, the job's like that at times, isn't it. In the last couple of day we've cleared up, I don't know, three or four crimes while totally failing to get anywhere with the one we're working on!"

"Yeah," Gina giggled again, before adding more seriously. "Billy says it's murder?"

"Yes, three murders actually," Martha confirmed before wondering whether such news was what a woman worn-out by her new baby really needed. "Anyway, there was a specific question I wanted to ask. There's nothing on the record, but Mark Phillips says you interviewed him at the time?"

"Interviewed? No, not exactly," Gina laughed once more. "When we arrested Green he was parked across the drive to a private garage. That was really why we stopped to talk to him in the first place. Anyway, even though he changed his statement, the DS who'd taken the case decided we should get a warrant and search it ... which we did ..."

"Empty?"

"Completely. Spotless in fact. Cleaner than my house right now!"

"Well, you should get the Inspector on to that," Martha suggested, liking Gina O'Neill more and more.

"I'll tell him you said that. Anyway, Phillips came out of a nearby house asking what we were doing ..."

"So he admitted it was his garage?"

"Oh yeah, no argument. Then again, why wouldn't he? It'd probably cost him £100 to have the place swept!"

"Can you remember who was there, who he talked to apart from you?"

"Yeah, of course. It was just me and Eloisa ..."

"DiMaria?"

"Yes. She was the PCSO for the area."

"I see. You mentioned a DS?"

"Yes, Sergeant Nancy. But she didn't actually come ..."

"Sergeant Nancy? She was CID?"

"At the time. But I guess you met her as part of Billy's TSG?"

"I did, yes," Martha replied thoughtfully, adding quickly: "Seemed very good."

"Yes, she was well thought of. That's why Billy recruited her."

"Of course. Any idea why none of this is on the case file?"

"Not really, that would have been for Zeta ... Guess she didn't see the point seeing as it was a waste of time?"

"I guess," Martha accepted a little reluctantly. "And after that, did you and this Eloisa go back to talk to Phillips at all?"

"No ... well, certainly I didn't. I suppose she might have. Like I said, it was her area ..."

"Forest Hill?"

"Yeah. Not a lot goes on there really. Housebreaking, because just about everyone who lives there is up in town all day. Bit of dealing, not much though ..."

"Sounds perfect," Martha sighed. "Why'd she leave, d'you know?"

"No, not at all. Guess she got bored. She seemed to like the job, but then again, I only ever got the impression that was all she saw it as - a job."

"Any idea what she did before she joined?" Martha asked on instinct.

"No, sorry. I only really spent those few days with her, although I guess we did spend a lot of time talking, nothing else to do! She was nice, a bit shy at times but bright - had been to some College or other. Pretty too ..."

"Yeah, the Duty Sergeant told me yesterday," Martha put in.

"Yeah, I don't doubt. I suspect half the Borough had her as a pin-up. Oh dear, the baby's waking ... Anything else I can help you with Detective?"

"No, you've been a great help, thanks."

Martha mouthed 'coffee' in response to Jo's offer while flicking through the Met's Internal Directory, eventually finding the number she wanted.

"Personnel."

"Hi. My name's Detective Cunningham, I'm with Bromley CID ..."

"Detective ..."

"Yes. The case we're working on right now, well it's a bit complex but an ex-PCSO has popped up a couple of times and we'd like to talk to her ..."

"Ex-?"

"Yes. She was based at Lewisham and seems to have left the Force a few months back ..."

"Lewisham you say?"

"Yes."

"And you're Bromley?"

"Yes, but there is a link between one of the victims and a person known to Lewisham CID."

"Victims?"

"Yes, sorry, didn't I say - we're investigating a triple murder."

"Oh, yes," the voice replied with a vague awakening. "Did I read something about this ..."

"Possibly," Martha accepted, continuing crisply: "So, basically we were hoping you could let us have a last known address for the ex- ..."

"Sorry ..."

"Sorry what?"

"We don't ..."

"Don't what?" a mildly irritated Martha interrupted.

"Personnel information. It's not something we can just ..."

"Sorry, I just said, this is a triple murder investigation. We believe this ex-PCSO may have important information ..."

"Is she a suspect. It would be different if ..."

"No, she's not a suspect. At least, not as yet ..."

"Well then, what you'll need to do is get a senior officer ..."

"What?" Martha barked sharply.

"I'm sorry Detective ..."

"Cunningham."

"Yes. I'm sorry Detective Cunningham, but there are rules about this sort of thing you see. I can't just go ..."

"So you're saying I have to go and interrupt my senior officer and get him to talk to you, yes?"

"Er, No, not exactly. He has to complete Form P ..."

"That's not going to happen," Martha interrupted. "DCS Benson ..."

"DCS?"

"Benson, from Serious Crimes. Right this moment he's in conference with people from the City Police, so if you just let me have your name I'll go and get him out to talk to you ..."

"It's ..." the voice began before trailing off uncertainly. "So, you're working for DCS Benson?"

"He's down here helping out, Yes," Martha replied.

"OK, but look, I'm not supposed to do this you know. It's ... what was the name ..."

"Eloisa DiMaria."

"Hold on, this'll take a minute or so."

Martha looked around the nearly deserted CID floor. Over on the far side, DI Russell was talking to a PC she'd never had much time for, while DCI Harris' door was shut, meaning he was in and asleep. At least Jo and Gurmel seemed happy enough, chatting away down by the tea point.

"Detective Cunningham."

"Uh-huh."

"So you wanted last known address ..."

"Please."

"OK. Well, we only have one: 7 Telson Court, Crest View Drive, Petts Wood ..."

"Petts Wood, well what d'you know," Martha breathed.

"Is that helpful?"

"It certainly could be. Do you have a date of birth, by the way?"

"27 January 1988."

"Thanks. Anything else there I ought to be interested in?"

"Detective, I've already told you, I'm not ..."

"Yes, I know, but if you want I'll tell the DCS you've been very helpful. Might help one day ..."

"No, it's OK," the voice replied. "Actually, there isn't much more here. No previous work history, just says worked abroad ..."

"When did she join?"

"May 2010."

"School, Uni ... ?"

"South Bank, 2007 to 8. Must have dropped out I guess. School before that ... Scadbury College ..."

"Never ..."

"You know it?"

"It's connected. It certainly is connected ..." Martha muttered.

"Happiest days of our lives, eh? School ..."

"What? Yes ..." Martha accepted without thinking. "Thank you. That really has been so helpful."

"You're welcome. Have a good day."

"You too," Martha smiled. As she put the receiver down Jo's police issue mobile rang - or rather, sang with some irritating pop thing - while also buzzing across the top of her desk.

"Detective Hartley's phone ... Er, she's just," Martha hesitated, no longer seeing Jo up at the tea point. "Who is calling? ... Yes, OK, just a moment Sir," she said more excitedly.

Cupping the phone between both hands, Martha stood and all-but ran down the office, spotting Jo about to step out to the landing. "Jo," she called loudly. "Gallini!"

"Detective Hartley ... Yes Sir. Thank you for getting back to me ... Yes, oh, I see, none of them, not even ... OK, well it was worth a try, thank you for ... Yes ... Yes ... when? ... Yes, you did mention that. So, in the Summer of '87. What was her name? ... Magdalena, Magdalena what Sir? ... No, of course, I see. How about other staff from that time, might they ... you don't ... well it might be Sir, it might be ... an Italian name ... if you would Sir, or we could ring if ... OK, no that's very helpful, thanks."

As she ended the call Jo smiled sheepishly at the open-mouthed and news-hungry Gurmel and Martha. "Gotta dash ..." she apologised while walking quickly across the landing towards the ladies.

"Well?" an impatient Martha asked when Jo got back to her desk.

"Sorry, I was bursting," Jo giggled, sitting down and taking a big gulp of coffee. "Well, irritating gap on the name, but his sister remembered that around the same time they were moving house - which is when it seems the father's gun went missing - there was an incident with a young woman they'd had as a kind of nanny for the Summer ..."

"Called Magdalena?"

"Yes, Magdalena something Italian. He said he'd ring his sister and brother again to see if either could remember her last name. Doesn't know where any of the old staff are, he says ..."

"Must be such a problem ..." Gurmel suggested facetiously.

"Exactly," Jo smiled. "Anyway, other news was no news. He says none of the Greens have - or ever had - an account with Rütger's ..."

"Ever?" Gurmel asked. "How can he be so sure?"

"Well," Jo laughed. "What he actually said was they only have records for the last hundred years, but I guessed that was probably enough!"

"Names ..." Martha pondered over her coffee cup. "Magdalena / Halina ... DiMaria / Dearmer ... I don't know ..."

"Who was it said she saw someone with a little brown dog?" Jo asked of Gurmel.

"Hold on," he replied while gazing intently at his computer. "Gloria Gascoigne."

"I don't suppose she's in, is she?"

"I can check," Gurmel suggested while looking a little blankly at Jo. "If you want ..."

"You've seen this Mrs Dearmer's dog," Martha said.

"Yep. It's little and brown. Called Roger ..."

"Could it be? I mean, I did that checking yesterday. Looks like she's from Yorkshire ..."

"According to Gloria, the dog was with a young woman," Gurmel read from his notes on screen. "But Mrs Dearmer is ..."

"No, wait a minute," Martha interrupted, thinking back. "That wasn't quite what she said. She said ... she said: very pretty. That was it. A very pretty girl ..."

"Very pretty?" Jo repeated.

"Exactly," Martha smiled. "Two people now have described this Eloisa DiMaria as pretty ..."

"Let's see if Gloria's in, no harm ..." Jo said, picking up one of the clunky old internal phones.

"Be quicker to go down and check the board," Gurmel suggested. "I'll go."

"So what are you thinking?" Martha asked after a minute's silence.

"Not sure really," Jo smiled. "I mean, first thing is: we're bored! Not only do we not have any new leads, we haven't even got any leaders to blame for it!"

"Yeah, well, guess the second's true," Martha smiled.

"So we might as well run a little more with the pretty girl with the dog ... did they say she was running?"

"No, that was someone else," Martha recalled. "You know," she continued, slightly lost in thought. "I spent some time last night looking up about this Brinks Mat case Benson is so keen on ..."

"And?"

"Well, I'm sure the DCS is a bright guy and everything ..."

"But?" Jo pressed.

"OK, so it was a big thing. A lot of gold that's never been found. But really ... Well, if Green senior had been a part of it, why wasn't he caught?"

"Isn't that the point? Benson probably thinks he's going to put the past to rights. Get whoever it was and make himself Commissioner in the process."

"Yeah, but the gold's gone, hasn't it?" Martha insisted.

"Well, I'd say so," Jo agreed. "Whoever stole it would have just taken whatever cash they could get for it and start spending, don't you think?"

"That's exactly what I think," Martha agreed. "What's more, it kind of looks like that's precisely what they did do. Then they all started to fall out with each other. I read one thing that said money from the robbery had been used to start all sorts of businesses: builders, like Green - which I suppose is Benson's connection. But also car dealers, a few restaurants, a health club ..."

"Oh well, guess they're all living well ..."

"No, that's just the point. Five of those thought to have been in the gang - or maybe it was six, I forget. Anyway, a fair-few, they're all dead. Shot by an ex-mate ... presumably."

"Nice people," Jo smiled wryly. "Ss in: not!"

"Definitely," Martha agreed. "But anyway, you want to know the one thing that I thought just screamed out about the whole affair? Corruption."

"Oh yeah, that's what Gurmel said yesterday, wasn't it?"

"He did. And the stuff I read all as good as says it out loud. Every tip-off seemed to get followed-up a few days too late. Every raid failed. And even the few arrests that were made went wrong, witnesses withdrew, evidence got lost, etc., etc."

"Yeah, well, it was all a long time ago Martha. Things can't still be ..."

"That's just it!" Martha burst. "Something happened again a year or so back. All I could find was an old newspaper article, but it seems this special team at the Yard got a tip off that there was some Brinks Mat gold, together with cash and jewellery, stored in a vault in the City. Anyway, so there was a raid, but what d'you know - they got there too late, again! All they found was a bag containing some grains of gold, which sounds like a bit of a mickey-take to me."

"So what, they took their time so the vault could be cleared?"

"Or they took the stuff for themselves, I suppose. No mention of our DCS in the article, I should say," Martha added.

"No ..." Jo replied thoughtfully. "So, did you talk to that DS Szabo about, you know, wondering how Phillips hadn't got caught before?"

"No, I kind of didn't really know how to. I will talk to Gerard when he's done with the Kenny stuff. But to be honest, I don't see how anything funny with Phillips really connects to our case. Phillips isn't the killer ..."

"No, we're as one on that."

"Nope, she's been given a week off," Gurmel explained.

"Oh well," Martha sighed despondently.

"Tell you what," Jo suggested brightly. "Let's get a camera ..."

"Why?" Gurmel asked.

"Mrs Dearmer said she goes for a walk with her Roger at noon every day. If we get a move on we could park up and take a few pics ..."

"And?"

"Well, first off, we could show them to the others who were with Gloria, see if they think it's the same dog. You never know. And maybe even go and see Gloria, if we think we've got enough ..."

"But we haven't got anything like enough, have we," Martha put in. "I mean, we really don't have any reason at all to suspect this Mrs Dearmer, other than she's got a dog ... and if you really, really strain at it, you can make her name sound half-way Italian ..."

"Sounds good enough to me," Jo smiled. "Plus, I know this will sound jealous, but she's obviously got money without any sign of a job ..."

"Hmm, you sure ..." Gurmel pondered uncertainly.

"Look, we're just going to try and get a photo of the dog."

"We don't let her see us?"

"No, we park a little way off and take a few pics from the car ... You any good at that?"

"OK. How hard can it be?" Gurmel smiled.

"I'll drive," Jo said. "We've only got half an hour! You go and sign out the camera with one of those fancy lens things ... you coming," she suddenly asked of Martha.

"Yeah, why not," Martha replied uncertainly. "Nothing else to do. What have we got to lose?"

"Any chance of getting made proper Detectives, I suppose," Jo smiled.

"Oh yeah, oh well," Martha smiled back, collecting her things.

Chapter 38

"Well?" Jeremy asked as they stepped out of the Financial Services Authority offices onto North Colonnade, the imposing grandeur of Canary Wharf towering over them to their left.

"Honest truth?" Rosie asked, following the seemingly confident DCS into what seemed to be yet another glass and marble office block.

"Of course," he smiled, adding: "this way" while leading them down to a walkway reassuringly signposted for the Docklands Light Railway.

"Waste of time," Rosie replied.

"Oh really. Oh ..."

"Sorry," Rosie smiled while following the DCS' lead and flashing her Warrant Card at the bored looking woman standing by the mechanical gates into the station.

"Yes, well ..." Jeremy mumbled while quickly checking the overhead screen. "That one, platform 2."

It was now a little after 10am. Meaning the rush hour was over. Meaning, the surprisingly clean and undamaged, driverless train was all-but empty, apart from a couple of trendy young guys down the other end of the carriage.

"OK, go on," Jeremy prompted.

"Well, what more's to say?" Rosie asked. "I just don't think we learned anything there."

"I thought the Hong Kong connection was interesting," Jeremy suggested.

"Hardly new though, was it. I mean, Hong Kong has been at the crossroads of west:east and north:south trade for centuries ..."

"But this thing about Russian mafia money being changed into Re-ren ..."

"Renminbi," Rosie completed. "Again, that's not exactly news ..."

"I didn't know it," Jeremy confessed.

"Oh, well ..." Rosie smiled while trying not to look superior. "Even so ..."

"Yes, even so," Jeremy laughed self-deprecatingly. "So, overall, do I get the feeling you're not really buying the whole gold-link idea?"

"We hardly touched on that," Rosie put in.

"Well, Imogen Wilson did say there were rumours about the way a few banks with Hong Kong bases operated ..."

"She did," Rosie accepted. "Or more precisely, she told us that the US Federal Reserve had picked up some rumours. Unless I missed it, she didn't offer any particularly British or European insight, just repeated stuff she'd picked up from the Americans ..."

"That doesn't make it wrong," Jeremy insisted, looking round to see the name of the latest station the train had stopped at.

"Of course it doesn't," Rosie nodded. "But at the same time, we're surely more interested in what happens closer to home. The US have some very specific issues with drug money from the south bouncing across the Pacific and back again ..."

"Sorry?"

"America has a rather long Pacific coast," Rosie smiled patiently. "Hong Kong is actually rather near ..."

"Oh yeah ..."

"Now," Rosie continued, "Europe. I did speak to Herr Gallini yesterday - and before you say anything, I know there is a view that says he may well have plenty to hide. But it still seemed reasonable to get his view on gold laundering ..."

"And his view is?"

"That's it's now nigh-on impossible. A lot has changed in the last fifteen years or so. The thing about gold is the same as art ..."

"Eh?"

"Provenance. If I - Rosemarie Charlton - try to sell a canvass covered with a variety of weird dashes and scrawls, I'll get next to nothing. But if I can produce papers from auction houses and experts saying those dashes and scrawls were put there by Picasso ... bingo, millions."

"And Herr Gallini said that's it with gold ...?"

"He said it is now. Thirty years ago, when the Brinks thing happened, it was easier ... and I checked some of what Gallini said with your favourite source Jeremy ..."

"Which is?"

"Wikipedia!"

"Oh yeah," Jeremy laughed.

"Besides which, I thought it was an open-secret that all the gold got melted down at the time. By that Tony Henneke, who is now inside for killing some boy on the M25?"

"Well, that was the assumption ..."

"So surely then, the link, if there is one, isn't about gold but money? And no doubt a long string of investments ... Gallini did agree to search for any accounts in the name of Green, by the way."

"There won't be any," Jeremy stated with certainty.

"No, I thought that too ... is this our stop?"

"It is," Jeremy nodded.

Rosie was like a bug-eyed child following Jeremy out of Bank station, up Prince's Street, along Lothbury and then through a warren of pedestrian alleys. She wasn't sure she'd ever been in the City of London before. Maybe once on some school trip or something, but it was not a place she knew at all. Meaning the business of it, the variety in the architecture, the oddity of the road and alley names all added up to a small adventure. She was rather disappointed when - it seemed quite suddenly - they arrived from a narrow twitten between two tall, modern glass buildings to face the Victorian splendour of City Police Headquarters.

The discussion with Superintendent John Carney had, to begin with, been just as tedious as the earlier meeting with

Imogen Wilson. Though the two people were polar opposites in terms of accent and mannerism, they were twins in self-importance and the art of sounding like they were saying something extremely profound and important, whilst actually saying nothing of interest to any but the wilfully gullible.

The problem, Rosie feared for the first twenty minutes of so, seemed to be that DCS Benson was as gullibly impressionable as she was bored. It wasn't just that Carney made every titbit of knowledge or information sound like he and he alone were the first to find it and see its importance, it was the theatricality with which he brushed aside any enquiry about evidence to support the speculation he was passing off as fact. She was, therefore, just starting to nod off when Benson said, almost as an aside:

"OK, so let's talk about DCI Harris."

"Well, the truth is Jeremy ..." John Carney replied carefully, his eyes noticeably flicking towards Rosie.

"It's OK, we're together on this," Jeremy smiled back while watching a once-again bug-eyed Rosie pouring herself another cup of the City Police's awful coffee.

"Hmm," John breathed with an uncertain look on his face. "Well, truth is, this gambling club thing. It's not exactly a high priority ..."

"Funny money?"

"Sure, that was the suspicion. But we've not found anything to back that up ..."

"No new whispers about secure stores, pathways out ... Dublin, Reykjavik ..."

"No, they're both trying to rebuild confidence and all that shit ... Have you spoken to the FSA?"

"Yeah. They seem to know nothing other than what the US tells them," Jeremy replied, casting a rueful smile back to Rosie.

"Situation normal," John nodded while watching Rosie staring unblinkingly at him over her coffee cup. "Do you want me to order some fresh?"

"Eh, actually," Rosie smiled. "Yes. If you would."

"It won't be any better. Just hotter."

"Oh well, hotter would still be good," Rosie replied.

As Superintendent Carney slipped out to find someone to get more coffee, Rosie glared quickly at Jeremy: "Something I should know?"

"A few things," Jeremy smiled. "Just stick with it and I'll fill in the gaps once we're through ... So," he continued as their host closed the door again and walked back towards his seat. "Let's just make sure we're all on the same page. We've got a triple murder out in Chislehurst that seems to link Gerry Green - who popped up years ago in connection with Brinks Mat - and the head of a smallish Swiss bank once thought to have a route, via Tripoli and Islamabad, for laundering gold ..."

"Yeah, we got that. My Sergeant checked with our MI6 link," John nodded thoughtfully. "This Rütger's is believed to be part of a small group of banks knowingly cleaning-up money, alongside legitimate transfers of US aid to Tunisia, Iraq, Afghanistan and Pakistan."

"But?"

"But there's nothing to suggest Sterling's involved, or even Euros. Mostly Roubles through Hong Kong and drug-dollars through New York."

"So you're not aware of any specific interest in this Stefan Gallini?"

"No, sorry Jeremy, nothing."

"OK," he sighed thoughtfully. "Can we just go back over the Farringdon Securities thing ..."

"Remind me," Rosie smiled with contrived nonchalance. "Farringdon Securities?"

"It was set up in the mid-nineteenth century," John explained. "Then suddenly, twenty years or so back, there was a wholesale change in the Board of Directors. Just about every one of the new lot seemed to appear on at least one list of those thought to have been connected to Brinks Mat ..."

"So what, you thought they were going to use this ... this ... Is it a bank?"

"No, well not as such. In simple terms, it's just a big old building with fantastic security and loads of safety deposit boxes tucked away in an underground vault."

"So what was the attraction?"

"Legally, it isn't in London at all ..."

"Eh? So where is it?" a puzzled Rosie asked.

"In Jersey," John smiled. "Look, no point asking me much more because I don't really understand half of this stuff. But the bottom line is, anything stored in Farringdon Securities is beyond the Bank of England's scrutiny. Meaning beyond us too."

"Wow," Rosie whistled.

"But," Jeremy put in. "To cut a rather complicated story short, between us - City and the Met - we got the idea of a link between this Farringdon Securities and an unlicensed gambling club. Known as the Ludgate, it seemed to pop up around the City from time to time ..."

"And what, this club was a front for laundering money?" Rosie asked.

"Kind of, not serious millions though ..."

"It was more the kind of place where medium-scale dealers, smugglers, fraudsters, could change up any money they thought was traceable, have a good night out, lose a little, pay the House fees and then go home with a briefcase of nice, clean folding," John explained.

"Hold on," Rosie began pensively. "I've heard of this Farringdon place, haven't I?"

"Probably," John smiled thinly. "Eighteen months ago, we raided it. We'd managed to get a couple of under-covers inside the gambling club. Made a few contacts and got together enough evidence to convince the Duke of Normandy to let us ..."

"Duke of Normandy?"

"Yeah," John laughed. "That's what they call the Queen in Jersey ..."

"No way!"

"Something to do with the 13th century ... don't ask! But the point is, like I said, this Farringdon Securities is legally in Jersey, so we had to get the Head of the Jersey States, aka the Queen, to agree ..."

"It failed, didn't it," Rosie recalled. "But the press ... that's right, the story was all about Brinks Mat. Why didn't I remember that before ..."

"Don't worry about it," Jeremy smiled. "It was all a fuck up from first to last. Then, somehow, some half washed-up hack on the Mail got told the story that all we'd found was a bag of gold dust ..."

"Got told by whom?" Rosie asked.

"That's one of two vital questions we've not been able to answer," John sighed. "First, who leaked news of the impending raid. Second, who put around the Brinks Mat line."

"And is that why we're here?" Rosie asked of Jeremy. "Something to do with my boss?"

"You're boss? Phew," John whistled. "I didn't realise that. You've obviously cleared all this ..." he asked of Jeremy.

"Something like that," Jeremy replied ambiguously, not actually answering either question. "So, let me just make sure I've got this straight, John, then we'll leave you to get on. As far as you know, this unlicensed gambling club is still popping up, but for all that it might be cleaning dirty money, it's small-scale?"

"Yep."

"And is the connection to Farringdon Securities still live?"

"I would think so, but we'll never get the go-ahead to raid again ..."

"No," Jeremy pondered. "Which makes you wonder whether we were just being played along from the out ..."

"That's my guess," John nodded. "Not only did we come out looking like the same bumbling fools who failed to nail the Brinks thing first time around, this little off-shoot of theirs is now untouchable ..."

"But didn't I read the Directors all changed again, after the raid?"

"They did, Yes. So your man Green's no longer on the list. In fact, the Director list is exclusively Jersey-based now ..."

"But what's your guess about the Ludgate Club?"

"Well, I am sure some of the old Farringdon guys were behind it. They saw a niche - I mean, people like Green, their only profit these days comes from cash-in-hand, which equals VAT fraud ..."

"And his son seems to have been on the fringes of cigarette running ..."

"Exactly, another crowd with cash to sell. They're not stupid, they know we've got millions of traceable floating around ..."

"Yeah, OK. But, last question. I know nothing's been done officially, but has Harris been picked up at all in the last six months or so?"

"Not as far as I know Jeremy, and truly, I think I would know. So, either he's stopped going or someone's been making sure he's south of the river before he passes out dead drunk. You heard anything?"

"Nope, nothing. OK, always a pleasure John," Jeremy said, standing up to shake Carney's hand.

"Likewise. And lovely to meet you DI Charlton."

Chapter 39

Having giggled guiltily through their five minutes of secret surveillance - all without authorisation - Martha suggested they go and look at where Eloisa DiMaria lived.

"So, do we knock?" Gurmel asked as they pulled up just past a somewhat incongruously located small block of flats.

Telson Court was a typically unlovely 1970s build. Three storey, flat roofed, square, grey and cheaply built. Yet it sat halfway down a pleasant road of neat and stylish semi-detached, owner-occupied houses. The area was not as desirable as Mrs Dearmer's street or those near her. It was, no doubt, dismissed by some as being on the wrong side of the railway tracks. But it was nice enough all the same. And to be fair, for all that the block looked in need of some care and attention, there was an air of calm about it - no broken windows, wind-borne trash or burned out scooters.

"You know, this is only a short walk from the car park where we found Ian Green's car. And Kenny's, of course," Gurmel added, looking around.

"This must be council, right?" Martha asked.

"Guess so, or housing association," Jo replied. "Which is basically the same thing."

"So how could a twenty-something get a place like this, legitimately?"

"Good question," Gurmel agreed. "I mean, I doubt this is like the Marsfield where half the flats are run by crooks."

"No," Jo nodded. "Unless she grew up here. Maybe she lives here with her parents?"

"Hmm," Martha mused. "Did I mention that this Eloisa DiMaria went to the same school as the Gallini children, Scadbury College ...?"

"No ..." Jo breathed. "Can't be cheap ..."

"You wouldn't think so," Martha agreed.

"Any idea how much?" Gurmel asked.

"Er, well ..." Martha began. "Around £4,000 a term ..."

"£4,000 a term!" Jo whistled.

"Could be more," Martha added. "Although it's not exactly a top end school. Then again, could be less if she was bright. But however much it is, you would not think ..."

"I agree," Jo nodded. "You wouldn't think someone living here could afford any kind of private school ... Come on, let's go and knock."

"And ask what?" Martha pondered.

"I don't know," Jo smiled. "You'll think of something!"

The three of them stood outside number 7, which was on the top floor, for a minute or so, ringing the bell, knocking the knocker and ringing the bell again. Apart from themselves, they heard nothing.

"Hello," a cheerful looking old woman in a garishly bright housecoat smiled, as they made their way down the functional concrete stairs.

"Hello," Martha smiled.

"Looking for someone?"

"Yes, as it happens," Martha nodded, now standing a couple of feet from the woman who stood rather proudly on a large mat outside her front door. "We're from the police, we were looking for ..."

"Moved out I think, haven't seem them for a while ..."

"DiMaria, Eloisa DiMaria," Martha said, completing, so she thought, the sentence.

"Who?" the old woman asked, leaning her head to one side in a gesture typical of the hard-of-hearing.

"Eloisa DiMaria," Martha said more loudly.

"I heard you the first time," the woman replied sharply. "I said who? Never heard of Louisa-what-you-said."

"We have this address as the last known ..." Jo put in sweetly. "Eloisa DiMaria, she was a police officer too ..."

"Nah, sorry, you must have the wrong place. Watkins, that was their name. Mother and daughter. Nice enough ..."

"How old were they, would you say?" Martha asked.

"Eh ... girl was quite young, mother older I suppose."

"Yes, that would make sense," Jo smiled indulgently. "But the girl, was she still at school for example?"

"No, not at school."

"So," Martha asked. "Would you say she was as old as me, for example."

"I don't know, how old are you?"

"Twenty-three."

"Really. My, you don't look it. Still, that's what they say isn't ..." the woman mumbled.

"So the girl," Martha insisted. "Would you say she looked older than me, or younger?"

"About the same I'd say."

"Good, fine," Jo smiled. "That's very helpful. Watkins you say?"

"Yes, Mrs Watkins."

"Tell me," Gurmel put in. "My guess is you've lived here quite a while?"

"Twenty-five years, longer than she's been alive," she giggled while nodding at Martha.

"Never! Well, I'm certainly not going to ask how old *you* are because I know I won't believe the answer ..."

"Seventy-nine."

"No way!" Gurmel smiled broadly. "So, you know everyone here? I mean, there are only, what, nine flats?"

"Yes and Yes," the old woman smiled.

"So how long did Mrs Watkins and her daughter live here?"

"Oh, about six years, could be seven. No more than that. Came from ... now where was it she said they came from? Mottingham, I think," the woman recalled proudly.

"I see. And what was the daughter's name?"

"Elizabeth. Pretty girl, like your friend here," the woman smiled conspiratorially at Gurmel while nodding towards Martha.

"That pretty!" Gurmel replied, nodding as if impressed while watching Martha blush.

"Yeah," the old woman said while looking Martha up and down. "I'd say."

"Well, thank you Mrs ..."

"Hopkins, and you're welcome. I live at number 4," the woman added helpfully, seemingly unaware of the large number 4 next to her right elbow.

"Would you happen to know the names of all the other tenants?"

"Of course," the woman replied breezily before asking. "Eh, but why do you need to know?"

"Oh, just to keep things tidy," Gurmel smiled, sensing in Mrs Hopkins an unreconstructed cleanaholic.

"Oh, OK then."

While Gurmel stayed to collect the names, making a note also of the housing association's office address and telephone, Jo and Martha walked down to the street and waited.

"Well?" Jo asked once they were all together again.

"Well, first thing to say is I think Mrs Hopkins is a very observant lady ..."

"Don't you dare start with that stuff, Gurmel Kandola ..." Martha hissed.

"As if I would," he replied. "My wife would kill me ..."

"You married?"

"Yep, sorry," Gurmel giggled teasingly, drawing a weak punch to his arm for his trouble. "Ouch! Anyway, all I was saying is, I think what she said is probably reliable. We can check with the housing association of course, but I bet they'll confirm that the tenant is a Mrs Watkins ..."

"Hmm," Jo pondered. "Well, I also think Mrs Hopkins likes to keep up with what goes on ..."

"But," Martha prodded.

"Well, first off, for all that I cannot think of any reason why she might have done this, we don't know for a fact that Mrs Watkins was the woman's real name. Could have been anything ..."

"No, that is true," Gurmel accepted.

"I think we should ring the Housing people," Martha suggested. "I mean, there are a few things that seem odd, not least the implication that what looks like a fairly desirable piece of social housing is empty."

"Oh yeah," Jo agreed, looking back to the block and then up and down the tree-lined road. "Of course," she continued thoughtfully. "All Mrs Hopkins said was she hadn't seen them in a while ..."

"I asked her about that again while I was collecting all these names," Gurmel put in. "This time she said several months, which is hardly any more precise but still long enough, you'd think, for the landlords to want to move someone new in ..."

"Come on, let's go to the school," Martha suggested. "You can ring on the way," she smiled to Gurmel.

Gurmel was still battling patiently with some jobsworth clerk as they pulled into the extensive and well-maintained grounds of Scadbury College.

"Well, you can see where the money goes," Jo whistled while gazing along the broad façade of the elegant collection of stylishly modern buildings. "Guess we park in here," she assumed, following a beautifully drawn sign pointing towards a totally empty Visitors' Car Park.

"Of course," Martha sighed. "Holidays. I wonder if there'll be anyone here ..."

"Other than gardeners, you mean," Jo said, pointing across to three guys busying away on some intricate looking pruning.

"Indeed."

"I'll stay and try to sort this," Gurmel suggested while pointing to his phone with a mixture of resolute determination and pessimistic despair.

On first glance, the large reception area was more upmarket office than suburban school, although Martha noticed the functional combination of heavy-duty, non-slip flooring (in a marble effect, of course) and thick rubber footplates to the various doors off the corridor ahead.

"Hello, can I help you," a well-dressed woman asked on suddenly appearing from a door behind the reception desk.

"Yes, I hope so," Martha began. "My name is Detective Cunningham, this is Detective Hartley. We're, er ... is there somewhere we could talk. Perhaps with the Principal or ..."

"The Principal isn't here this week. None of the teaching staff are ..."

"No, of course," Martha smiled sympathetically. "I realise it's holiday time, but wasn't there something here last week?"

"Yes, the Nursery only finished on Friday and we also had some other activities for the Junior School ... Sorry, what is this about?"

"Can I just ask first, your role?"

"I'm Mrs Fairley. I'm the School Secretary."

"No holiday for you then," Jo smiled.

"Next week. This week there are a few things to do, but the main thing really is following up on those from next year's intake who haven't sent in their Fee Plan ... Well that and handing out A-level results on Thursday ..."

"I remember it well," Martha smiled. "Totally nerve-shredding."

"Yes, well I'm sure there'll be some surprises and a few tears. But anyway ..."

"Yes," Martha accepted. "Is there somewhere we could at least sit?"

"Yes, OK," Mrs Fairley accepted, her face betraying a hint of irritation.

The Secretary's office was like those in most schools: four desks crammed into a space barely big enough for two, surrounded by filing cabinets, bookcases and cupboards one would have to move a chair or wastepaper basket or some other impediment to open.

"This is Miss Knight," Mrs Fairley nodded to a mousey looking woman in her early twenties.

"Look," Martha began, sitting with Jo on the edge of the desk next to the Secretary's. "The first thing I need to be sure of is this: Did you know, I mean is the school aware of the murder of the father of ..."

"Murder," an instantly nervous Miss Knight gasped behind Martha.

"Father?" Mrs Fairley asked.

"Yes. We're investigating ... Well, we're investigating a rather complex matter," Martha tried to explain, looking back and forth between the two women. "But one victim is a Mr Gallini. Herr Gallini actually, he has two children ..."

"Oh my god," Miss Knight cried.

"Is this what I heard on the radio the other day?" Mrs Fairley asked.

"Probably," Jo confirmed. "But the name hasn't yet been released to the press ..."

"No ..." the Secretary accepted blankly.

"Do you know the children?" Jo asked.

"I don't think so," Mrs Fairley replied. "Do you Gill?"

"Not to look at, but I know the name."

"Oh yes, I know the name ..." Mrs Fairley echoed before looking back to Martha. "We know all the names in here," she smiled, nodding around the room.

"Then you are exactly the people we need," Martha smiled. "As I said, this is proving to be a complex matter, but there is someone we'd like to talk to who we believe was once a pupil here ..."

"A Scadbury pupil?" Mrs Fairley asked with obvious shock, not to say incomprehension.

"Yes, but that doesn't mean what I think you're imagining," Martha said reassuringly. "Just, like I said, someone we'd like to talk to ... Save they don't seem to live any longer at the address we have. So, I was hoping ..."

"You were hoping I'd do something you probably know I ought not," Mrs Fairley suggested.

"Well, maybe," Martha nodded. "But this is a murder investigation and we're talking about an ex-pupil. Someone who is twenty-four now, so there are no child protection issues ..."

"I understand Detective," Mrs Fairley smiled knowingly. "And I have no doubt Mrs Barrington-Hawkes ..."

"Is that the Principal?" Jo asked, trying to hide her mirth at the St Trinianesque name.

"It is. And she wouldn't want us to be all silly about this, I'm sure," Mrs Fairley suggested. "So, go on."

Between them Gill Knight and Mrs Fairley checked two large, clothbound books, a filing cabinet labelled 'Archive' and a card index stored inside one of the hardly accessible cupboards.

"Sorry, no record at all, I'm afraid," Mrs Fairley declared with an obvious sigh of relief.

"Any joy?" Gurmel asked as Jo and Martha got back to the car.

"No," Martha replied pensively. "They say they have no record of Eloisa DiMaria as a pupil ..."

"Didn't you believe them?" Jo asked with surprise.

"Oh yeah," Martha nodded. "But that doesn't mean it isn't odd. I mean, surely the Met take up references? All the more so, I would have thought seeing as, from what Personnel told me, Ms DiMaria had no previous work record ..."

"Oh yeah, I see," Jo accepted.

"Well, the rent is still being paid on 7 Telson Court," Gurmel reported.

"Really?" Jo asked in surprise.

"Seemingly so. Took ages to get past all sorts of 'we really can't tell you' till I got put onto a Mr Anderson, who is the manager, or something like that. Anyway, he was most concerned about police interest, etc., etc. ... And then even more concerned about the possibility that 'something might have happened' ..."

"You know, I did think that," Jo insisted. "But given we were on dodgy ground even going there, I couldn't see how we could justify getting someone to open up."

"Well, worry not. I said we'd meet Mr Anderson there ... in about ten minutes, actually," Gurmel smiled on checking his watch.

Chapter 40

The bells of St Paul's were peeling frantically to confirm it was exactly midday, as Jeremy and Rosie walked into the ultramodern and elegant café on Paternoster Square. They sat at a table against the far wall, ordered a cafetière of some ridiculously expensive coffee, to go with their even more ludicrously priced sandwiches, and watched quietly for a few minutes as the place filled up.

"OK," Rosie sighed after, she thought, displaying her best moody brooding for nearly fifteen minutes, including the walk down from Wood Street. "Have I been dragged into some internal affairs thing?"

"Internal Affairs?" Jeremy smiled "That's a bit CSI isn't it?"

"OK, so what should I call it?" Rosie asked, still not feeling exactly good-natured.

"Look," he began more earnestly. "Before you go getting the wrong end of anything, my interest, the Yard's interest come to that, is in the possibility of a link between your case ..."

"My case?" Rosie laughed petulantly.

"Yes Detective Inspector," Jeremy replied sharply. "I really don't think you can doubt that. Not once have I tried to act like I think I should lead this investigation ..."

"So why are we up here?"

"We are here Rosie because your Detective Cunningham ..."

"You are surely not going to try and blame her," Rosie replied defensively.

"Blame her!? On the contrary, you have yourself a potentially very talented detective, very talented," Jeremy repeated. "She contacted me because she saw a possible connection to some form of organised crime ..."

"But didn't I just learn that she was wrong?"

"Where on earth did you hear that?" Jeremy asked with a look of puzzled amazement on his face. "Her interest was sparked by a possible Brinks Mat connection and it remains possible that something to do with that is lurking in the background ..."

"Does it? But I thought you and Superintendent Carney ..."

"Ruled out a contemporary gold link, Rosie. That doesn't mean these murders might not have something to do with issues or relationships between Brinks' *people* ..." he nodded knowingly, while sitting back as the waiter arrived with their coffee, sandwiches and an unordered but very welcome jug of iced water.

"OK, let's start again," Rosie offered with a conciliatory smile while accepting a tall glass of cold water. "So, what is your best guess on the connection between these murders?" she asked, before munching into her mozzarella and tomato ciabatta.

"Hmm, well ..." he pondered, picking up a couple of vegetable crisps. "Mmm, these are nice ... Anyway, I do think your Martha is right to keep on seeing Ian Green as the key ..."

"I agree," Rosie nodded. "But at the same time, there has then to be a link to Gallini."

"Agreed also," Jeremy accepted, before adding quietly. "And the young PC?"

"I really do fear the choice was purely random, just to create chaos," Rosie sighed before taking another bite.

"Which makes our killer very cold and calculating," Jeremy considered before starting in on his chicken salad bap.

"And that tends to point to something organised ... Is that what you're thinking?"

"Well," Jeremy pondered before taking another bite, chewing slowly and deliberately for several seconds. "That was the obvious thought on Friday. I mean, I can see one possibility: that the murder of young Green was meant to send some kind of message to his father ..."

"A message related to this gambling club for example?"

"That was what I had in mind when I came down, Yes. That was why I thought we needed to talk to John ..."

"And this business with DCI Harris? Which I'm still expecting some explanation of, by the way," Rosie smiled before taking another large bite of her ciabatta.

"Yes, well," Jeremy nodded, putting his bap down and pouring two cups of coffee, taking a couple of sips of his own before continuing. "First off, Yes. I am going to be talking to your boss - we just call it Disciplinary by the way," he smiled. "You don't need to be involved ..."

"OK. Not that I'm bothered."

"You don't like him?"

"I wouldn't quite put it that way. I mean, I hardly know him ..."

"He's your squad leader ..."

"I've been in this post for just over three years, during which time I've had two review interviews. Each lasting a couple of minutes. Both telling me what a great job I've done ..."

"Well, there you go," Jeremy laughed.

"Exactly! He's never asked me a single question about any case. He's no different with DI Russell, so at least I know it's not a girl thing!" Rosie smiled.

"Yeah, well," Jeremy replied more seriously. "This isn't just about him being lazy."

"OK, so what is it about?"

"A few things," Jeremy said, popping the last of his bap in his mouth before taking time to refill their waters and coffees.

Rosie sat in silence, playing with the crumbs of the vegetable crisps left in the bowl for a moment before picking up her cup and breathing in the wonderfully aromatic scent of what was truly lovely coffee.

"Right, well the most obvious thing - and the one that will justify his suspension ..."

"You're going to suspend him?" a genuinely surprised Rosie replied.

"Yes, Detective Inspector. It does happen! And I'll threaten him with losing his pension to try and get more out of him ... But whether we would ..." he tailed off for a moment, taking another sip of coffee. "Better than John's, eh?"

"Immeasurably."

"Anyway, so you're thinking: What more is there ...?"

Rosie nodded.

"OK. Most of the recent background you got. From the surveillance John's people put in, we have evidence that Harris went to this Ludgate Club at least three times ..."

"Really?" Rosie said slowly.

"Yes. I wondered whether that was clear. This club, by the way, it's not all about crooks. Far from it, actually. There are plenty of young - and not so young - people in the city with money to lose. So this thing is quite classy ..."

"So why unlicensed?"

"Lots of reasons, but the most obvious being to keep it very discreet. Entry is strictly by invitation only."

"So why would a Detective Chief Inspector ..."

"Exactly, DI Charlton. Of itself, the fact that he got invited is suspicious. And that he accepted, a disciplinary offence."

"I see. So you're going to interview him, see if there's more?"

"That's the idea."

"What about Jeffrey?"

"Yes, well ..."

"Good Lord, you don't think he's involved?" Rosie gasped incredulously.

"What, No!" Jeremy laughed. "General view is he's limited but straight. But ..." he paused, his eyes betraying the sudden realisation that he had not bothered to check for any whispers about Jeffrey's relationships around the Borough. "You like him, you close?"

"Eh? No! When he told me you were coming I told him to fuck off ... No, actually, I think I told him to get the fuck out of my office," Rosie admitted.

"You didn't want help?"

"I didn't want to be pushed aside like some silly little girl," she replied. "But hey, it's OK, you haven't been like that. In fact, seeing as I'm going to need a new job after all this I've been on my best behaviour with you. Really," she smiled coquettishly before finishing her coffee.

"Is that so," Jeremy replied as if far from convinced. "You want anything else, dessert of some kind?"

"Well, more coffee would be good ... And I bet they've got something chocolaty on the menu."

More coffee ordered, together with two slices of chocolate cheesecake, they settled back into the conversation.

"There is one other thing you ought to know about Harris," Jeremy began. "I said that whilst I doubt these murders have anything directly to do with Brinks Mat gold there could still be a connection. That is Harris. There is no question he knows Gerry Green. He was a DS on the first investigation, which lasted for about three years, by the way ..."

"Really. And how come you know all this?"

"My first job as a DCS was to complete an evidence review of the whole case. There had been a couple before, but the new Commissioner felt they'd been weak. Possibly deliberately so ..."

"Superintendent Mitchell said he'd always thought there had to have been something seriously funny about the whole thing ..."

"Yeah, well he's not wrong. What's he like, by the way?"

"Why you asking?"

"It's OK, I'm not here checking up on the whole of Bromley Borough. I don't know him at all, but I thought he seemed like a pretty smart and decent guy ..."

"That's my view too."

"Yeah," Jeremy grinned. "AC-Ops said the same."

"Not that you're checking up on us!" Rosie laughed

"Ah, here we are," Jeremy smiled, rescued by the waitress delivering their fresh coffee and desserts. "So," he continued while looking approvingly at his slice of richly chocolaty cheesecake. "Whilst we'd never be able to prove anything, Harris' name popped up a few times, close to a failed raid here, a botched arrest there ... and one of those was of Gerald Arthur Green."

"I see," Rosie nodded meaningfully, teasing her fork into her own slice.

"Now, all that's in the distant past. But something odd happened a week or so back. Your DI Russell rang for info on Green. Which was all routine and proper, he'd taken on the thing with Battersby. The very next day, Harris rang, fishing for what we'd told Russell!"

"Hmm ..." Rosie thought for a moment, her mouth full. "That's weird."

"Yeah," Jeremy laughed, breaking off a piece with his fork. "Interesting, suspicious and baffling - so I guess weird covers it," he nodded before emptying the fork into his mouth.

"So Harris was, what, looking out for Green?" Rosie asked, licking chocolate from her lips before taking another mouthful.

"Well, that's a possibility," Jeremy agreed, another piece of cake poised ready. "Or it could just be that he'd heard some talk around the office about Russell, Green and the Yard and thought he ought to find out what all the fuss was about."

"Yeah," Rosie began after a pause devoted to cake eating. "Because for all this stuff against Harris is interesting, isn't there a danger it's distracting us?" she pondered, playing with the last piece on her plate.

"Go on," Jeremy encouraged, finishing his dessert and pouring out some fresh, hot coffee.

"Well, we're all agreed - although Martha thinks we keep on forgetting," Rosie smiled while arching her eyebrows. "That Ian Green must have known his killer. No other explanation works for why he would have agreed to a meet in such an out of the way place ..."

"Agreed," Jeremy nodded, sipping his coffee.

"So, obviously enough, we thought we'd be looking for possible enemies. Then we got Charlie, then Gallini ... And then up popped this thing between Green senior and Gallini ..."

"And?"

"And suddenly we forgot that Gerry Green had lost a son and started to look for a fit between the evidence we had and stuff to do with the man's past."

"Yes," Jeremy nodded once more. "I do think that is fair. But equally, I think it is also fair to say we've all begun to rethink that simple idea of Gerry Green bad: ergo, killer ..."

"Ergo?" Rosie smiled, popping the last piece of cheesecake into her mouth.

"Latin," Jeremy smiled with knowing needlessness.

"Oh, I know what it is ..."

"Just surprised to hear it from a Yard DCS?"

"Maybe," Rosie smirked. "Maybe ... but back to the point ..."

"Which, like I said, is a fair one. We have perhaps not paid enough attention to Gerry Green as a victim of crime.

Perhaps every bit a victim as Gallini's family ... Although when I say 'we', I don't think I speak for your Martha ..."

"You like her, don't you?" Rosie grinned.

"Like I said before, I think she has great potential," Jeremy replied with due seriousness. "Not least, because she just never stops thinking ..."

"I agree," Rosie nodded, breathing deep on her coffee's rich aroma. "So where have we got to?"

"Well, not quite full circle," Jeremy smiled. "There's one other player ..."

"Who?"

"Battersby."

"Him?"

"Yes. Two thoughts," Jeremy began. "First off, like you said, up popped a link between Gallini and Green senior and off we went ... Save, that wasn't the link, was it?"

"No, of course," Rosie nodded, "Green's row was with Battersby ... In fact, we don't actually know whether he ever met Stefan Gallini ..."

"Exactly so," Jeremy agreed. "Meaning, we don't even know who gave that building work to Green. Or why."

"No Indeed ... all Battersby said about it, when I spoke to him yesterday, was 'we' ... That was it: we commissioned a builder ..."

"Commissioned?" Jeremy laughed. "Is he really that pompous?"

"Oh yeah," Rosie confirmed, refilling her cup and taking a long, slow, thoughtful sip. "You said two thoughts?"

"Did you check for a record?"

"Shit," Rosie smiled apologetically.

"No worries. Almost nothing, not even a speeding fine ... Save ..."

"Go on."

"A Formal Caution for Importuning. Thirty odd years ago, but worth knowing ..."

"Hmm ... he did seem a bit camp ..."

"There you go then!" Jeremy suggested with a wry smile.

"So, what does all that add up to?" Rosie asked a little dimly.

"I'm not sure it adds up to anything, as such. I mean, it's all very circumstantial ... But blackmail's hardly an uncommon motive ..."

"So you think Battersby's a suspect?"

"Of course!" Jeremy laughed over his cup. "We'll get nowhere if we don't start suspecting people!"

"But," Rosie replied, her face betraying surprise bordering on incredulity. "I just don't see how Battersby could have a motive for killing his own boss?"

"No, me neither. And the fact the same gun was used on Ian Green and Gallini makes any complicated idea of some kind of tit-for-tat unworkable. But let's just go back to the idea these murders are about getting at Gerry Green. You wouldn't need to be that clever to assume the killing of the man's son and someone he'd had a major row with would get us jumping to all sorts of conclusions, now would you?"

"No ... But didn't we just say we're not sure he'd had a row with Gallini anyway?"

"Indeed, but how do we know Gallini was the intended victim?"

"Wow, I truly had never thought ..." Rosie smiled, impressed.

"Yeah, well, it's just a set of thoughts," Jeremy nodded a little shyly. "And frankly, given the history of various Brinks Mat suspects, you have to say the more likely scenario - assuming Green's fallen out of favour with someone or other - is that they just shoot him. Why complicate things ..."

"Unless ..." Rosie pondered. "Let's forget for a moment we're not falling for it. Supposing we did. Supposing we stumble over something else that points to Green and we make enough of a case to put him away for it ..."

"Go on ..."

"That would be exactly what you'd want if your issue with Green is all about time ... Time he should have served. Maybe time someone else got when it should have been his?"

"Now that, Detective Inspector," Jeremy smiled. "Does sound like a motive."

"Hmm," Rosie pondered. "A motive ... and the argument set-up the opportunity ... and you're obviously thinking the link could be Harris ..."

"It's a possible, don't you think? Let's assume he's run up some serious debt at this club. Maybe one he's already tried to get Gerry Green to help him out with, but got nowhere ... Then someone else chats him. A little time passes and suddenly, like you said, an opportunity seems to arise ..."

"... and the Swiss gun? That's just to make us work at it?"

"Maybe. Or maybe it's just coincidence. I'm not running away with this," Jeremy held his head to one side to emphasise his reassurance. "Not least because it still seems too complicated for the kind of people who might have decided to get at Green ... But there is one possible reason which I hadn't thought of until your point about time ..."

"Which is?"

"Earlier, you mentioned Tony Henneke, aka The Smelter. He's got an appeal pending that could see him released in a year or so. We don't want that. Equally, on my guess is, not too many of his Brinks Mat friends will want it either. It's bound to destabilise things. He'll expect a share of whatever money is tucked away in Jersey ..."

"Looked after by this Farringdon Securities?"

"Seems a fair guess to me," Jeremy nodded.

"Being the same people behind this gambling club. What sort of money might Harris owe?"

"According to John's people, the club is fairly strict. Minimum deposit of £50,000, maximum credit £100,000. Probably not a lot to some members, but to Harris ..."

"You know," Rosie thought sadly. "The more I think about it - no matter what idea we play with - the killing of PC Scales ... it doesn't make sense. Gallini's killer must have been really jumpy knowing there were so many police around ..."

"Well, supposing that was part of the message to Green, something like: and don't think your friends in the police can protect you on this one?"

"Hmm, you know," Rosie nodded pensively. "In a sick way, that does fit ... I mean, apart from anything else, it suggests the reason why we can't find any specific motive for wanting Scales killed is that there isn't one. So sad ..."

"Totally," Jeremy nodded while raising his hand to catch a waiter's eye. "And for what it's worth, I find it hard to believe Harris could have known that was planned ..."

"Me neither. He may have been crooked and lazy, but it beggar's belief that he would collude in that ..."

"All of which means, I need to talk to him. And we need to talk to Gerry Green ..." Jeremy concluded, picking up the bill. "Am I getting this?"

"That's very kind," Rosie smiled.

Chapter 41

"Yes. Trevor Anderson of the Bromley Trust," the tall, thin and unfashionably moustached man replied to Gurmel's simple enquiry. "Detective Kandola?"

"Yes. And my colleagues are Detectives Cunningham and Hartley. Have you been up yet?"

"No, I thought ..." the Trust's man began, a hint of timidity obvious in what was left unsaid.

"OK, shall we go then?" Gurmel suggested breezily.

Number 7 was tidy, well-ordered but, from the thin layer of dust covering most surfaces, not lived in for a few months or so. In the kitchen, the fridge and freezer were both empty, their shelves pulled out to stop the doors closing. The cupboards, however, still contained a variety pots, pans and crockery. Two drawers were full of assorted cutlery and utensils. The larder - though containing very little - did still hold a few tins of soup, tomatoes and fruits in syrup. The beds were unmade, but with blankets neatly piled on each. While the wardrobes and chests of drawers in both bedrooms still contained some, mostly winter, clothes, giving a general impression of an orderly leaving with some intention of return.

The lounge seemed to confirm this impression. There were no carpet marks or shadows on the walls to suggest any furniture had been taken. Yet the old fashioned sideboard carried not a single photograph or trinket, while the settee and armchairs were each covered by plain, white sheets.

"OK, so what can you tell us about your tenant, Mr Anderson," Gurmel asked.

"Yes, well," the guy began evasively. "As I said earlier, when we spoke ..."

"Yes Sir," Gurmel smiled. "I know, this is all very difficult. But it is also very important. My colleagues and I are investigating murder, Mr Anderson. And someone of interest to us once gave this as her address. Save her name wasn't Watkins, but DiMaria, Eloisa DiMaria ..."

"But I said, we don't know that name ..."

"Exactly. Now one possibility is this place had been sub-let. Do you know when you or any of your staff last actually spoke to your tenant, this Mrs Watkins?"

"Not off the top ..."

"Have you ever seen her or spoken to her?"

"I don't think so, not personally. But ..."

"Yes, go on Sir," Gurmel encouraged, while Martha and Jo sat down on the sheet-covered sofa to watch, instantly sending a cloudburst of dust up into the air.

"... it just looks like she's just gone away," Anderson mused while watching the dust dance and float in the sunlight coming in from the far window.

"It does, Sir," Gurmel agreed. "And the fact the rent is still being paid could suggest she has every intention of coming back ..."

"Exactly, so ..."

"But you don't actually know that, do you Sir?"

"Well, no ..."

"Indeed, all we can say we know for sure is that this place has been very carefully cleared. We may think Mrs Watkins did that herself, but we don't know that for a fact. Do we?"

"Well, No. I guess ..." Anderson replied, suddenly looking round as if expecting to discover some previously hidden indication of something truly dreadful having happened in one of his flats.

"And that, for us," Gurmel continued calmly, while nodding to Jo and Martha for emphasis. "Is a problem. Not least because it doesn't look to me like she's going to walk back in any moment, having only popped down to Morrisons. We need to talk to Mrs Watkins rather urgently, assuming that ever was her name ..."

"Oh, but we do make checks you know," Anderson insisted while pulling a thin file from an envelope.

"Good," Gurmel smiled. "So, if you could just share with us what you know, we'd be most grateful."

"OK," Anderson agreed resignedly. "Tenant was Mrs Kathleen Watkins. Moved here in November 2004 with her daughter, Elizabeth, who was sixteen at the time ..."

"Any idea why they came here?"

"Yes, they were previously in another of our properties which we de-peopled ..."

"De-peopled?" Gurmel laughed.

"Yes, means moved people elsewhere so we could modernise ... oh yes, sorry," Anderson blushed. "Bit of jargon ..."

"So where were they before?"

"26 Fairacre, Court Farm Road, Mottingham ..."

"OK, thank you," Gurmel smiled, writing the information down.

"And how long had they been there?"

"Let me see," Anderson replied while flicking through some pages. "Ah, OK. Mr and Mrs Watkins first became our tenants in 1995. Actually, that would have been with Bromley Council," Anderson put in with a nerdy flourish. "Bromley Trust wasn't created until 1998 ... Oh dear, oh I see ..."

"What Sir?" Gurmel pressed.

"Mrs Watkins became sole tenant in 1997, Mr Watkins having died ... hmm," Anderson pondered thoughtfully. "Well, it's not crystal clear why, but my guess would be this was simply to reduce the rent. Shortly after Mrs Watkins became the sole tenant, we moved her and her daughter from a house on one side of the estate into the flat in Fairacre ... Then, like I said, we moved them here in 2004 ..."

"Is there anything else?" Gurmel probed.

"Not really. We've written to her each year asking for confirmation her daughter still lives with her ..."

"Is that because you'd move her again if her daughter wasn't living with her any more?"

"Yes," Anderson smiled thinly. "So, as you might guess, each time she's replied saying she is!"

"And I asked when she was last actually seen or spoken to?"

"There are a few different entries recording phone calls, that's quite common," Anderson confirmed.

"So, she's been renting from you since 1995," Gurmel summarised from his notes. "And she's been a good tenant?"

"Yes. Never been a problem payer. Had the odd complaint about windows and plumbing, but who hasn't. No, I'd say she's been a very good tenant."

"A rather exceptional one indeed," Gurmel smiled. "To carry on paying rent while not even living here ..."

"Mr Anderson," Martha put in. "We know that on some estates subletting is rife. Maybe you even have that problem with some of your other blocks?"

"It happens," Anderson agreed.

"And I doubt you really have the staff to go round checking - I mean, so long as the rent keeps coming in?"

"Well, yes, that is true. But ..."

"But a place like this?" Martha prodded.

"Places like this do kind of police themselves, if you'll pardon the expression. Usually, as soon as anyone even hints they might be leaving we'll get a call from one of the others trying to put in a word for a friend or relative ..."

"But that hasn't happened here?" Martha asked. "We spoke to one of the others earlier and she said she hadn't seen Mrs Watkins for a while. A few months ..."

"Actually, it has happened," Anderson blushed. "I've got three notes here saying we've had calls ..."

"I see," Martha smiled. "But maybe that's my point. You'd had calls, but weren't able to follow them up."

"No, I see that."

"What do you do when you do identify someone subletting?"

"Oh, we evict, every time," Anderson replied with certainty. "And ban the original tenant. In fact, their name goes on a list shared with other housing associations across the country ..."

"I see, so there are penalties ..."

"Yes, of course."

"So, all things considered, you'd think it fairly unlikely Mrs Watkins was keeping the place on with the idea of subletting?"

"I would."

"How about just passing it over to her daughter?"

"That could happen," Anderson accepted. "I mean, in all honesty someone could get away with that for quite a while ... But Mrs Watkins would have to find somewhere else for herself. And anywhere she tried would almost certainly make a few checks and find her registered with us."

"But not if she gave a different name?"

"No, but she'd have to have some proof of previous address and that kind of thing. It's not easy just inventing a new identity, Detective."

"Is it not?" Martha replied sceptically. "OK, thank you Mr Anderson, that's been helpful. We'll leave you to get on with whatever you need to do ..."

"Oh, I'm just going to lock up," Anderson replied nervously, as though he feared being left in the place alone lest an irate Mrs Watkins come back and find him.

"Can I ask," Jo smiled while Anderson searched for the right key. "Do you allow tenants to have dogs?"

"No. You'll no doubt find plenty on some of our estates, but here ..."

"The place pretty much polices itself?"

"Yes," Anderson smiled, slipping the keys into the envelope.

As they walked down they saw Mrs Hopkins standing outside her flat again. Martha, Gurmel and Mr Anderson all offered a friendly greeting, Jo fell back a few paces.

"Well?" Martha asked as Jo met them again outside the block, Anderson having already driven off.

"First off, she just said dogs aren't allowed, in a way that made me think she would definitely complain if one moved in. However, she did then say she knew Mrs Watkins looked after a little dog for a friend now and then - and she couldn't see any harm it."

"Hmm," Martha sighed. "Is that a connection, d'you think?"

"Why don't we show her the pics of Roger and Mrs Dearmer," Gurmel asked.

"Why not?" Martha smiled.

Back, a few minutes later, on their now familiar spot outside on the pavement, they pondered what to make of Mrs Hopkins' confident insistence that Roger wasn't the dog she'd sometimes seen Mrs W with - 'though he is a cutie isn't he ...' - and that Mrs Dearmer had never visited the block any time she'd been there.

"Well, basically," Gurmel considered, breaking a long period of dispiriting silence. "We can't take that as proof Mrs W did not know Mrs Dearmer, or Roger the dog ..."

"True though that is," Martha nodded. "Our report back to the DI would have been far more impressive if she'd said: oh yeah, that's Mrs Watkins' sister Magdalena ...!"

"She said there was another ..." Jo said, slowly and thoughtfully.

"Who, Mrs Hopkins?" Gurmel asked.

"No, Mrs Dearmer. When the DI and I saw her she said ..." Jo continued while replaying the visit in her head. "Yes, that's right, Roger is a Brindle Cairn ..."

"Brindle?" Gurmel asked.

"Means brown," Martha put in.

"Yeah, basically," Jo nodded. "And Mrs Dearmer said she also regularly sees a guy with a Westie ..."

"West Highland White Terrier," Martha said for Gurmel. "Clue's in the name! One of my aunts has got one. Dotes on her ..."

"And apart from the colour, they are very similar to Cairns," Jo continued. "But ... Yes, that was it. She also said she sometimes sees a lady with a Wheaten Cairn ..."

"Wheaten also being brown?" Gurmel asked.

"Well, No, not quite," Jo accepted. "Well, not dark brown anyway. But the point here is Gloria's description ..."

"That is right," Martha agreed enthusiastically. "She said brown and we've - well, I've ..." she smiled self-critically. "I've been assuming dark brown ..."

"Whereas Gloria may well have meant light brown," Jo beamed as though she wanted to add QED, like an eleven year old solving their first equation.

"OK, so let's go and ask her," Gurmel suggested.

"Who, Gloria?" Martha asked hesitantly.

"I was thinking maybe Mrs Dearmer first. See if she can add any other information?" Gurmel replied teasingly.

"What a good idea," Jo smiled, "I was thinking exactly the same!"

Chapter 42

As they walked the short distance to Cannon Street station, Rosie tried Gerard's, Martha's and even her own office number.

"Guess they're busy," she suggested to Jeremy sheepishly. "Anyway, my car's at Sidcup ..."

"That where you live?"

"Yes, why. D'you know it?"

"I do indeed. It's where I grew up! Small world ... Ah, there we are: platform 8."

"Yep, two minutes, that was lucky. So, you a grammar school boy then?" Rosie asked. "Supposed to be very good I'm told, son of one of my neighbours goes there ..."

"Me, no," Jeremy laughed. "Big comprehensive up on Avery Hill, although I think they were going to close it down ..."

"Oh, really," Rosie replied like you might to someone who admitted enjoying daytime television.

"And you?"

"Yes, as it happens. Tonbridge."

"Might have guessed!" Jeremy laughed as they settled down in the largely empty train.

As Rosie drove into the wide driveway of Hurst Hall, a couple of SOCOs were collecting cones, rolling up tape and generally packing up. Over by the sheds a large truck was doing something or other with Green's skip.

"Hello Detective Inspector," a voice called from the porch.

"Oh, hello," Rosie replied, seeing Siân Roberts walking down towards them. "Nearly didn't recognise you without a white space suit."

"Yeah, fetching aren't they," the bright-eyed, tousled haired woman smiled.

"So, you just finishing up?"

"Yes. We sent you an interim report this morning ..."

"Oh, OK. Thank you. Haven't been in the office yet."

"No, well, of course, you must be so busy," Siân replied considerately. "Anyway, just bringing the skip back ..."

"Oh yes, wow," Jeremy exclaimed, impressed like a small child watching big machinery in action.

"What's he like?" Siân asked as the two of them watched the DCS walking over to the guy returning the large, full skip to its place.

"Well," Rosie laughed conspiratorially, the way women do when taking pity on men's foibles. "He's not that bad, really! So, the skip. Anything?"

"Lots of rubbish!" Siân laughed. "But No, No gun. Sorry."

"It is what it is Siân," Rosie smiled. "Seen much of the family?"

"Yeah, there have been a few comings and goings, although I think I saw Mrs Gallini and the children leave again about an hour ago."

"We're actually wanting a word with Mr Battersby."

"Oh yeah, podgy guy. He's been fussing around most of the morning. Worried we might damage a fountain or something."

"So, as far as you know, he's in then?"

"Yeah, think so. And the final report will be with you later."

"Anything in it that isn't in the interim?"

"Eh, No," Siân smiled.

"OK," Rosie smiled back, stepping towards the front door.

By the time the door was opened by the diminutive, ruddy and irrepressibly cheerful Mrs Cassidy, Jeremy had rejoined Rosie, though his interest still seemed to be located over his shoulder in the shape of the large, hydraulic-powered truck now lifting its stabilisers and getting ready to leave.

"Hello, I'm Detective Inspector Charlton, this is Detective Chief Superintendent Benson. We need a word with Mr Battersby, is he around?"

"I'm sure he is," Alice Cassidy sang in her sweet, Irish brogue. "Come yourselves in and I'll find him for you."

Rosie and Jeremy waited in the high ceilinged hallway, idly looking at the collection of family photographs that covered the long wall from the door to the staircase, some in snow, some in the height of summer, all one way or another highlighting the energy and health of Herr Gallini's second wife and their children.

"Detective Inspector," Hamilton Battersby said on appearing from a door seemingly hidden beneath the stairs. "And ..."

"Detective Chief Superintendent Benson," Jeremy smiled, shaking hands.

Battersby was dressed almost identically to the day before, in an ill-fitting suit, white shirt that wouldn't fasten around his jowly neck, narrow dark-red tie and slightly scuffed black shoes. His thinning dark hair, flecked with grey, looked in need of a wash and comb. His face in need of a close shave. And his complexion in need of some sun.

"Sir, there are a couple of things we want to clarify. Is there somewhere we can sit?" Rosie asked.

"Of course, let's go in here," Battersby suggested, opening the door to a long, narrow room that obviously now functioned as a library, but which at the same time felt like an oversized cupboard. "There are some chairs down the end," he offered, pointing to the ornately arched French doors.

"What a curious room," Rosie remarked, looking back along a space that was higher than it was wide.

"Yes. We think it was once some kind of garden room," Battersby explained. "This long wall here was probably all windows and doors onto the terrace, save that then got built over with the Orangerie."

"Ah, well, how very apposite," Rosie smiled. "Because one of our questions relates to that: how did you come to hire Green & Sons?"

"How?" Battersby replied, a hint of detachment in his voice. "Well ..." he began with annoying slowness. "Herr and Frau Gallini had been talking about making some changes. Then they put together some rough sketches to show what they wanted to do and then we called Green & Sons to take a look and provide a quotation."

"I see," Rosie smiled patiently while wondering why the Gallinis put such trust in someone who seemed so boringly unimpressive. She had kind of forgiven him his lack of spark or charm when compared to the naturally outward - if maybe also a little oleaginous - Roberto Gallini. Now, with no comparator but himself, Battersby seemed even more lacklustre. "But why Green & Sons?"

"Oh, I'm not sure really."

"OK, so who else did you ask to quote?"

"No-one else, Detective Inspector."

Rosie felt she was in danger of wanting to throttle the guy. For all that he was obviously designed for discretion, not given to being garrulous, his diffidence was becoming irritating. "Mr Battersby, why do I feel you are being evasive?"

"I ... I don't know ..."

"Then I'll tell you. Yesterday, I asked you and Roberto Gallini if you were aware of any connection between the Greens and Herr Gallini ..." Rosie paused for effect. "And you didn't reply ..."

"But Roberto, he ..."

"He did indeed engage with the question, Mr Battersby. In a way you are not! Now, why did you go to Green & Sons and them only. Whose idea was that?"

"Detective Inspector, I really don't see ..."

"Mr Battersby," Jeremy put in. "In the early 1980s you accepted a Formal Caution for soliciting homosexual sex I believe ..."

"What possible connection can that have, Detective Chief Superintendent," Battersby all-but shouted back.

"I have no idea Sir," Jeremy smiled cruelly. "Any more than I know why I suddenly find myself suspicious as to why you won't help my colleague with a perfectly simple question."

"I just don't see ..."

"And I don't care whether you see the significance or not, Sir!" Jeremy interrupted sharply. "Although if I'm honest, I really doubt that you don't. So, either you or Herr Gallini asked Green & Sons first because you had some reason, a recommendation maybe, to think they'd be good for the job. Now, why don't you want us to know which?"

"Because I don't think there is - or was - any kind of connection, as the Detective Inspector put it. Maybe Herr Gallini just saw them working elsewhere, or something like that ..."

"So, let me just be very clear here Mr Battersby," Rosie said with deliberate slowness. "You are saying that when it came to seeking a builder, Herr Gallini told you to give Green & Sons a call?"

"Yes. I mean I cannot remember the precise words," Battersby replied, sliding his finger down between his shirt collar and neck as though relieving an itch. "But it was something like that ..."

"Something like that. Well, let's see if we can be more precise. Did he also say something like: And don't call anyone else?"

"No ..."

"So why didn't you call in another couple of firms. What was it Roberto Gallini said of your role ... you take care of family investments, is that right?"

"It is."

"Well, I may not be an expert on these matters, Mr Battersby, but I think it is commonly accepted that one should always get at least two quotes for any major expenditure ..."

"Yes, but Herr Gallini had suggested them and they seemed to understand very quickly what needed doing ..."

"Did you get a written quotation?"

"Oh yes."

"I see. So what went wrong?"

"Sorry, what do you mean?" Battersby asked.

"From the statements we have on file, Mr Battersby, it is clear that a moment was reached where you and Mr Green believed different instructions had been given," Rosie suggested with delicate precision while remembering some of the more colourful description in Green's statement.

"Yes, well that is one way of putting it," Battersby replied with a little animated feeling, his face an angry grimace.

"But how come? I mean, you told us there were sketches and a written quotation. So how could a misunderstanding arise?"

"There were some changes ..."

"To the original, what does one call it. Specification?"

"Yes. Not that major really ..."

"You thought," Rosie put in.

"Yes, well ... but initially Green himself said they weren't a problem ..."

"Which is builder speak for: sure, we can do that," Jeremy suggested. "Not quite the same as we can do it for no extra cost, is it?"

"Well, no, but even so ..."

"When Green told you, what was it, a couple of weeks later ..." Rosie asked.

"Something that like," Battersby nodded sadly.

"When he told you how much extra, you were shocked. Is that a fair way of putting it?"

"Well, yes," Battersby smiled, suddenly seeing Rosie as a friend. "Exactly so. It was unreasonable. I mean, it was almost double the original quote. I couldn't ..."

"Couldn't what, Sir. See how you were going to explain this sudden escalation in cost to Herr Gallini?"

"Well certainly, that was one concern. But I also thought Green was, you know, trying it on ..."

"According to your statement - and his, I believe," Jeremy put in. "Mr Green made a number of rather coarse references to your sexuality. Is that right?"

"Detective Chief Superintendent, this is the second time ..."

"Surely, you are not going to tell me you don't see the relevance this time, Mr Battersby. Mr Green's abuse of you was, amongst other nasty things, acutely homophobic ..."

"Yes, well, some people are still ..."

"How did he know?"

"Wh-what?"

"How did Gerry Green know you are homosexual, Mr Battersby?"

"B-b ... but I don't know that he did *know*," Battersby replied reasonably enough. "I just thought he was the kind of man who would make that ... that kind of remark. To anger, to intimidate ... He was most unpleasant, Detective Chief Superintendent. Most unpleasant indeed," he sighed sadly.

Jeremy and Rosie sat in silence for a few moments, each feeling suddenly guilty and regretful.

"OK," Rosie began again. "So, you are saying hiring Green & Sons was a mistake, nothing more. You had no especial reason to want to give him the work ... Although you assume Herr Gallini had formed the view that they might be worth using for no better reason than he'd seen them doing work nearby. He assumed they would be the kind of people to take care of their reputation, especially in an area like this."

"Yes Detective Inspector," Battersby smiled shyly. "Actually, that puts it better than I could have, but it was along those lines. Basically, we had no reason to think they were anything but a decent firm."

"We ... or just you, Sir?" Jeremy pressed.

"I don't understand."

"Nothing you have said says Herr Gallini did not have some past - distant or recent - connection with Green. Only that you are unaware of any. Isn't that the case?"

"Well, I suppose ..." Battersby sighed with a look of defeat, like he believed that, despite all his best efforts he had failed to protect his former boss from a hint of unintentional complicity in his own murder.

"OK, well thank you Mr Battersby. I think that's all for now," Rosie said while casting a checking glance at Jeremy.

"Now?"

"Yes Sir. Other questions may arise as the investigation unfolds, we'll see ... Will you be going to Switzerland tomorrow with the family."

"Yes. I mean, assuming ..." Battersby asked like a small child seeking reassurance.

"Like I said before, we do not want to get in the way. When are you leaving?"

"Oh, the flight's quite late in the afternoon."

"OK, well, like I said. Thank you for now."

"Oh, just one other thing," Jeremy said neutrally while standing. "Detective Chief Inspector Harris, you know him of course ..."

"Do I?" a slightly startled Battersby replied.

"Yes, I thought ... Wasn't there some reference to him in your statement about Green?"

"Was there, I ... I don't recall ..."

"Really?" Jeremy smiled. "Oh dear, I must have that wrong. So sorry."

"OK, thank you," Battersby smiled thinly.

Chapter 43

Martha had found the short interview Jo conducted with Mrs Dearmer quietly amusing. First, the woman was utterly charming. Second, how anyone could mistake her educated, upper-class but unmistakeable Yorkshire accent for anything else was beyond her. Third, Roger was clearly one very spoilt - if also undeniably cute - dog. He was indeed the very image of Martha's understanding of a Brindle Cairn.

Insofar as Mrs D had managed to keep focused on Jo's questions, her answers were unspecific but not totally vague. No, she was not sure where the lady with the Wheaten Cairn lived, but believed it was probably 'further round', possibly in 'Great Thrift'. Not least because, when she thought about it she had seen the woman as often in 'Jubilee Park' as in 'the Woods'. Yes, she believed she had seen the dog with other people once or twice, but really could not remember anything about them. Of the woman herself, she was 'well into her sixties, if not older'. Of the dog, he was 'no bairn, never really seemed to run much'. And when it was suggested that perhaps the lady mostly walked earlier in the morning, Mrs D initially looked completely perplexed before answering 'well I wouldn't know'. Finally, when asked directly if she knew of a Mrs Watkins or a Miss DiMaria, she replied No and No.

It was getting on for 3 o'clock when they got back to the car. For a moment, they stood looking at each other, their eyes betraying an uncertainty about how they were going to explain the value and product of the now three hours they had spent chasing the merest slither of an idea.

"I'm starving," Jo had finally said to break the spell.

"Me too," Gurmel had nodded while fishing for his phone.

"And me," Martha agreed, a hint of despondency in her manner. "There's a nice enough coffee bar round by the station. Probably get something in there ..."

"Oh Yes, I see now ..." Gurmel said to no-one in particular.

"See what?" Jo asked.

"Let's drive up this way," he suggested, pointing up Birchwood Road beyond the narrow alley to the caged-in bridge.

"Where does that lead?" Martha asked.

"Well, according to Google maps, to Great Thrift, which is a road ..."

"I knew that," Jo lied.

"From which you can take an alley and a different bridge across to something called Jubilee Park ..."

"Hold on, I knew I had heard of that," Jo said. "The Hotel the Gallinis are in ..."

"Er, yeah. There's a Hotel way over on the far side ..." Gurmel confirmed, scrolling his finger over the screen. "But over here ... Right," he continued more certainly. "Over the bridge, just past the entrance to the park and you're into the car park where we found Green's car. One way out of that puts you in the middle of the shops where we thought we had a sighting of Green. Take the other way and you're in Crest View Drive. It all fits."

"Shit," Jo cooed.

"Fuck," Martha breathed.

"Martha!" Jo cried. "I never thought ..."

"Sorry," Martha blushed. "But do you think ..."

"Well," Jo smiled. "Like Gurmel said, it all fits."

"OK," Martha began, rubbing her wet finger across her plate to pick up the remaining almond flakes and dust of icing sugar. The three of them sat at the same table in the same Costa Coffee that Martha and Gerard had used on Thursday. "So, what doesn't fit?"

"Well ..." Gurmel considered before licking his own fingers. "You know, I could eat another of those ..."

"Me too," Jo smiled.

Given all that happened since the discovery of Ian Green's body, Martha found it oddly comforting to be back in an unchanged space. Not only did the two staff seem every bit as bored as those she'd met four days previous, she felt sure the only other person in there - a thin, elderly man reading a fat paperback - had also been there last time.

"You think it funny no-one has rung us, tried to find out what we're up to?" she asked.

"Well, Gerard's probably up with the CPS by now," Jo thought while looking at her watch. "Oh, maybe not, it's past three-thirty. They'll all have gone home! Anyway, if they want us, they'll ring. So I'm having another almond croissant, you Gurmel?"

"Yep."

"Yesterday you were Mr Fussy ..." Martha chided.

"That was with meat. Sweet things are totally different for an Indian guy."

"Are they?" Martha smiled before turning to Jo who was already on her feet. "Can I just get another black coffee." Looking back to Gurmel she continued: "You know, I think I read somewhere that the people of India eat more sweet cakes and biscuits than just about anyone else?"

"Hmm, not sure about that," Gurmel pondered. "I went to Istanbul a couple of years ago and they had things even I found too sweet!"

"Did they ... best we don't share that with Jo then or she'll be gone in a flash," Martha suggested, sweeping up the last of the cake that had been lunch.

"Here we are," Jo breezed, handing Martha a small cup of steaming hot coffee while balancing two plates on her other arm.

"Hey, that's clever," Martha smiled.

"I used to work Saturdays in a café while at school," Jo replied proudly while putting her and Gurmel's plates down. "I figured we'd be alright for coffee," she added, nodding to the giant lattes she and he were still only halfway through.

"Right, come on," Martha bullied. "What doesn't fit?"

"Well ..." Gurmel began again. "I suppose the first question the DI would ask is why would someone called Elizabeth Watkins join the police as Eloisa DiMaria?"

"Yeah," Jo agreed with a mouthful of croissant.

"And the obvious answers don't seem to work ..." Gurmel pondered.

"Go on," Martha encouraged.

"Well: marriage - nothing we heard suggested Elizabeth Watkins married someone called DiMaria. Divorce - Mrs Watkins is a widow ..."

"Supposing Mr Watkins wasn't the father ..." Jo put in.

"I wondered something similar," Martha nodded. "And maybe the girl wasn't told until ..."

"Until she was eighteen, that would explain why she didn't appear on the school record," Jo completed the thought.

"It would," Martha nodded. "No point ringing the school now. I'm sure Mrs Fairley will have gone home. No Principal around and all that ..."

"But you're thinking we need to check to see if they have a record of Elizabeth Watkins?" Gurmel asked.

"Exactly ... and Personnel also said she'd spent a year at South Bank University, so we ought to check for both names there ..." Martha thought, making notes on the back of a napkin.

"Hold on," Jo ordered. "Earlier on we were assuming Personnel must have got a reference from the school ..."

"Assuming, Yes," Martha agreed. "But we need to check, so I'll add that to the list. What else?"

"Well, I suppose there is a chance they are not one and the same person," Gurmel put in. "I mean, maybe she once stayed with the Watkins ..."

"But the school thing ..." Jo asked.

"I suppose it's possible Eloisa DiMaria is some kind of relation and for whatever reason - maybe just because it looked posher - put Scadbury College down as her old school and got lucky, no reference was taken up," Martha considered. "All of which just points back to the need for another call to Personnel."

"Photo!" Gurmel suddenly burst.

"Sorry?" Jo and Martha asked in unison.

"There must be a photo on file somewhere of Eloisa DiMaria ..."

"Yes, of course there must," Jo agreed. "So we get that and show it to those who were in the woods on Friday."

"Definitely," Martha agreed, adding the thought to her list.

"Yeah, but ..." Jo sighed with sudden despondency. "None of this is going to make any sense to the DI unless we can connect one or both of Eloisa DiMaria and Mrs Kathleen Watkins to Stefan Gallini."

Chapter 44

"Detective Chief Inspector Harris," Jeremy smiled, having opened the door a nanosecond after knocking.

"And you are?"

"Detective Chief Superintendent Benson, Serious Crimes. May I come in?"

"As you please," Harris replied gruffly, pointing to a rather uncomfortable looking chair in front of his desk.

"Thank you," Jeremy smiled even more broadly, closing the door carefully behind him before walking to the chair, sitting down and casually leaning back while crossing his legs.

"So, what can I do for you," Harris asked. "Something about this banker business?"

"Sort of. Tell me about Gerry Green, the botched raid on Farringdon Securities, and the 100 grand you owe this gambling club that pops up around the City once a month ..."

"Do what!"

"Any order will do," Jeremy suggested while picking an imaginary piece of fluff off his trousers.

"Listen, I don't know who the fuck you think you are but ..."

"I just told you who I am," Jeremy interrupted sharply. "And I also told you what I want. Now, if you're going to try and piss-ball around, let's get straight to the crunch. When we've finished talking, I'm going to suspend you from duty. The only question I haven't decided on yet is whether that will be on pay, pending further enquiries. Or with fuck all ..."

"What," Harris shouted, pushing his chair over as he stood. "What fucking right, what fucking right do you ... where's Jeffrey ..."

As Martha, Gurmel and Jo walked into the CID section the words Sit The Fuck Down boomed out through the door of DCI Harris' office. On instinct, they looked across to Gerard, who was back in his familiar desk. Benson, he mouthed. Elsewhere on the floor three faces from DI Russell's team, plus a couple from the Burglary Team now assembling in the far corner, were each turned to Harris' door, like it held some mystical, religious draw.

"What's going on," Jo asked in a husky whisper as she, Martha and Gurmel quickly took their seats around Gerard.

"I'm not totally sure. The DI and Benson got back just a few moments after I'd finished with the CPS ..."

"How did it all go?" Martha asked considerately.

"Yeah, fine. All OK. All good, in fact," Gerard smiled proudly.

"Good. Well done you," Martha nodded in praise.

"Yeah, yeah," Jo said dismissively. "All very good, but what's this all about," she insisted, nodding back to the sound of Harris shouting again.

"All the DI said ..."

"She in there too?"

"No, just Harris and Benson. All the DI said was, it ..." Gerard nodded towards Harris' office. "It is connected, but at the same time is something the DCS had to take care of alone."

"You think it's Disciplinary?" Gurmel asked.

"As I guess, I'd say yeah," Gerard nodded.

"Which must mean there's a connection between Harris and ... What's Benson been most interested in?"

"This Brinks Mat affair," Jo suggested.

"Exactly. Fucking hell," Gurmel whistled.

"Yeah, well, look. Best idea, is save the speculation," Gerard advised. "The DI said she wants a catch-up meeting once Benson's through, which if nothing else suggests he'll be in it, which must mean we'll get told something. I was about to ring you anyway, find out what you've been up to. Found anything?"

"Nah, not really," Martha replied lightly. "Mostly we've just been having a bit of a laugh, nothing much else to do ..."

"Too true," Jo nodded. "Not much point us hanging around for this catch-up. Can't we go, pick things up in the morning ..."

"Eh? Er, well, the DI did seem to want ..." Gerard began.

"Oh, alright then. We'll hang around. Who wants a coffee?"

"Me for sure," Martha nodded. "I'll help."

"Me too," Gurmel said, getting up.

"You want us to get you one, Sergeant?" Martha asked.

"Eh, Yes. OK, thanks," Gerard replied, suddenly finding himself alone like Billy-No-Mates again.

Chapter 45

The debrief got going a little after five-thirty, by which time the shouting in DCI Harris' office had given way to an eerie quiet enveloping the whole CID section.

It had been a few minutes before 5pm when DCS Benson had walked out of that office - closing the door with some deliberation - and strolled along to the DI. He was in with her though for no more than a minute, before returning to Harris. A few minutes later, Superintendent Mitchell arrived, going briefly into the DI before the two of them went down to Harris, entering without knocking. No sooner were they inside than Mitchell and Harris left, saying nothing to any of those around.

One of the officers with the Burglary Team who Gurmel knew said he'd seen Mitchell and Harris on the stairs. Again, nothing was said but it had seemed that the Superintendent was all-but leading the DCI down, a firm grip on his arm. So, the rumour spread like wildfire that DCI Harris - some said looking tearful - had been escorted from the station.

When they assembled in Rosie's room it was, to start, as though nothing had happened. Two fresh pots of coffee were on her desk, the right number of chairs were spread around, the right number of cups at the ready.

"Oh, do we need the boards?" Gurmel asked, looking back into the section.

"Perhaps not," Rosie smiled. "I'm sure we've lots to add, but that can wait. So," she said, looking along the line of expectant faces. "You are going to want to know," she continued, nodding in the general direction of DCI Harris' office. "What all that was about."

"Yeah," Jo admitted, perhaps a little too enthusiastically.

"Yes, well," Rosie replied ruefully. "There are a few things that simply cannot be spoken about just yet. Although I don't doubt rumour will soon fill the gap," she accepted. "But Superintendent Mitchell and the DCS," she continued, this time nodding to Jeremy sitting next to her. "Have agreed that you and you alone need to know a few things, because they are relevant to this case ..."

Gerard, Gurmel, Jo and Martha all sat in total silence, their unblinking eyes gazing with some incredulity from Rosie to Jeremy and back again.

"... in other words," Rosie added. "What you are about to hear you must discuss with no-one but yourselves. Obviously, you will get asked questions, to which you must just say Jeremy and I said we couldn't discuss it ... That's ambiguous enough not to be an outright lie," she smiled. "OK?"

"Yes ma'am," four attentive voices replied harmoniously.

"OK. So, before Jeremy starts, let's do two things. First, well done Gerard, the Kenny papers are all with the CPS and, touch wood, that case will sail along. So well done you," Rosie smiled appreciatively while clapping her hands a couple of times.

A general round of well-dones rang happily around the room.

"And second, let's pour the coffee ..."

With calm and practiced precision, Jeremy explained that, whilst he was not about to rule out a more direct connection to the old Brinks Mat case, his interest since Martha's first call had been in a possible connection between Ian Green's murder and his father's involvement with Farringdon Securities and an exclusive gambling club known as Ludgate.

A joint Met / City Police investigation of nearly two years earlier had found that DCI Harris was a fairly regular club attender, and loser. Having admitted that much - including one incidence of having passed on information in return for the waiving of an early debt - Harris was now suspended pending dismissal. He had insisted, however, that his more recent losses were manageable from his own resources, and that he had not entered into any arrangement to relieve those losses in return for police action or inaction.

"So," Gerard had begun, assuming Jeremy's pause was for questions. "Despite the denial, one concern would be that DCI ... I mean, ex-DCI ..."

"He has already been stripped of rank, Gerard," Jeremy confirmed. "So Harris will do fine."

"Yes, OK. So one concern would be that he has been compromised again by having Green - or one of his associates - pay off or waive his debt?"

"Yes, definitely. And just for the avoidance of doubt in this room, I am going to assign two of my team to what will now be a Disciplinary Investigation of Harris' actions, etc. It is not my intention to involve you. Or indeed, anyone from this station unless they pop up as connections. But obviously, I do expect you to tell either Rosie or me if you hear of anything in the course of your work that could be relevant ..."

"Of course Sir, definitely," Gerard nodded. "But coming back to our case, one thing I'm still not clear on ..."

"Just the one thing?" Rosie asked lightly. "Then you're way ahead of me!"

"Yes, well, one of the things ..." Gerard smiled before asking with serious purpose: "How does any of this helps us? I mean, if this isn't actually about Brinks Mat gold, what's the link to Gallini?"

"That, as someone clever wrote," Jeremy nodded. "Is the question. And the honest answer is, I don't know. That said, whilst we've learned that it would be nigh-on impossible to sell stolen gold now, someone helped that gang get rid of theirs all those years back ... So why not a Swiss banker?"

"But ..." Gerard pondered out loud. "What you're saying is these murders are more likely to have something to do with what the Brinks guys have been up to since?"

"Basically, Yes."

"And, what ... you think Harris might have got caught up in some issue between them?"

"Possibly," Jeremy replied thoughtfully. "As in, once again, I'm not sure. That is why, for now, Rosie and I have agreed we'll take a different tack, one that assumes the motive has something to do with Gerry Green. Could be because of his past or, perhaps more likely, because of something to do with the Farringdon Securities / Ludgate Club thing …"

"So," Rosie took over. "The DCS and I plan to interview Mr Green tomorrow, during which we'll put to him the thought that, like it or not, he may very well be the reason these murders have been committed, even though the link to Stefan Gallini is hardly clear …"

"Ma'am, just on that and the link to Harris," Gurmel put in. "I spoke to Green yesterday …"

"Did you, why?"

"We," Martha put in. "Got told Ian Green was going to see his brother on Wednesday …"

"But as we didn't know which brother, I rang Green senior," Gurmel continued.

"OK," Rosie nodded.

"Yes, and in fact got to talk to one of his other sons, who helped us a lot. But on Harris. The point I thought you'd want to know is that Green asked me if I worked for Bert Harris."

"Did he?" Jeremy asked interestedly. "And how did you understand that at the time?"

"Well, I'm not sure," Gurmel considered. "He actually asked first if I worked for DI Russell, so I was thinking he thought I was ringing about the Battersby affair. But then he asked about Harris and I suppose I was thinking it was all a grade thing, like he wasn't up for talking to a mere Detective … but maybe that was me being too sensitive," he smiled.

"Well, maybe," Jeremy nodded. "But obviously, one thought now is that he unintentionally gave away a hint of some kind of expectation …"

"But …" Gurmel hesitated. "What does that say for DI Russell?"

"Hmm," Jeremy pondered.

"Actually," Rosie put in. "I don't think there's anything odd in that part. DI Russell broke the news of Ian Green's death."

"Did he?" Jeremy asked. "I hadn't picked that up ..."

"He went round on his way home on Friday. We were just all so frazzled ..." she continued. "But the reference to Harris, well that certainly supports the idea of a link between them," she pondered. "Yes, well done Gurmel, connecting threads. That's what we do ..."

"Agree with that," Jeremy nodded.

"So," Rosie continued. "The DCS and I will work more on that tomorrow. But tell me, what have you been up to?" she smiled at her three TDCs.

"Yes, well ..." Martha began, looking enquiringly along the line and getting encouraging nods from Gurmel and Jo. "Well, besides helping Lewisham get a confession from a cigarette smuggler, we have ... maybe Gerard has already told you this?" she asked, her confidence needing a boost.

"No," Gerard answered. "Didn't get the chance."

"Oh, right, OK," Martha continued.

With a calm assurance, she explained how they had clarified Ian Green's movements on the Tuesday night through to Thursday morning, learning that he had earned himself £15,000 in the process. She then went on to explain how Phillips' throwaway remark had sparked an interest in Eloisa DiMaria, an interest that had developed as the story had become more complicated, to the point that she and the others felt they needed at the very least to nail down whether Eloisa DiMaria and Elizabeth Watkins were the same person. And alongside that, see if there was any way of establishing whether the dog Kathleen Watkins was believed to look after on occasions was the other Cairn terrier Mrs Dearmer had mentioned, the implication being it could also be the dog Gloria Gascoigne had seen being walked by a young woman.

"The cute little brown dog," Gerard repeated just above a whisper. "I knew this was all about dogs," he huffed.

"Yes," Rosie smiled indulgently.

"Was this an early theory or something?" Jeremy asked.

"Theory exaggerates it," Rosie replied. "But we did spend a bit of time wondering what kind of person fits in a woodland. Then, there was this specific mention of a dog walker by the PCSO closest to Charlie Scales ... I mean closest to where," she tried to correct herself before pausing: "No, I was right first time."

"Eh?"

"PCSO Gascoigne and PC Scales were in a relationship ... she found him."

"Oh dear," Jeremy sighed.

"Yes," Rosie agreed sadly. "But, because of that little theory we do just need to be very clear about what we have here ... And please, don't get me wrong," she smiled at the little team. "What you've been up to sounds like very good work ..."

"Thank you ma'am," Martha, Jo and Gurmel said with obvious pride, glancing wide-eyed at each other.

"I agree totally," Jeremy nodded. "It may turn out to add up to nothing ... I'm sorry," he laughed, looking at the crush suddenly erasing the young TDCs' smiles. "But it does happen. Maybe you're close to something very important. But even if not, you have followed the evidence. That's what really matters ..."

"Yes," Rosie agreed with a little more circumspection. "But can I just be clear: when did you first make the dog connection?"

"Well, I suppose that was me," Jo accepted hesitantly. "The thing is though ... Well, I think this is relevant anyway. The reason I thought of it to begin with is not the same as the reason we now think it could be significant. At the start, we were kind of fixed on the possible similarities between DiMaria and Dearmer as names. I suppose you think that silly ..." she trailed off.

"Detective," Jeremy replied seriously. "No, is the simple answer. To do well in this job you have to be able to look at facts and ideas from a number of different points of view. So word games, off-the-wall connections, they can all be useful. The thing we have then to guard against is allowing an idea to become an obsession, to become something we invest so much in we get dragged into wanting to prove it right ..."

"But that's my point," Jo replied insistently. "We actually proved ourselves wrong on the names thing. The evidence didn't lead to Mrs Dearmer at all ... but something she said did then connect ..."

"Of course ..." Rosie nodded. "Not Brindle, lady I see has a Wheaten ..."

"Exactly ma'am," Jo smiled.

"So the thing is," Martha began. "We started all this looking for someone who Ian Green knew, someone who - somehow or other - could have got him to those woods. Eloisa DiMaria seems to tick that box. More than that, from what we've heard she went looking for him ... And she's supposed to be very good looking while he's spent the last nine months in prison ..."

"Yes, I see ..." Rosie nodded. "I see the point ... OK, well it's definitely worth more effort. So, I think we let you three carry on making enquiries in the morning. Which means you'll have to come with us, Gerard," Rosie apologised. "Sorry!"

"Crosses I have to bear."

"Ma'am, Jeremy ..." Martha began slowly. "There was one other thing we just wanted to mention. It's nothing directly to do with our case, but ..."

"OK, go on."

"How could someone get away with releasing hundreds of thousands of smuggled cigarettes into a small area without the police noticing?"

"Well, I ... eh?" Rosie replied, puzzled.

"Something about this Lewisham case?" Jeremy checked.

"Uh-huh. Look, I've just realised there was one point of detail I didn't make clear. The colleague who helped us identify Eloisa DiMaria as the officer who recently went to see Mark Phillips is Inspector O'Neill's wife ..."

"Well I'll be," Rosie said.

"I meant to mention it, ma'am," Gerard apologised.

"Yes, not that there's anything in the least odd to do with what she told us," Martha continued. "On the contrary, she was very, very helpful. But one thing she told me simply does not appear in the official record at all. Evidently, there was a raid of Phillips' garage just after the time of Ian Green's arrest. The garage had been swept clean."

"Suggesting a tip off?" Jeremy asked.

"Well, that's one possibility. And of itself, it may not be that compelling - Phillips would have already known of Green's arrest. But the thing I cannot get my head around is this. All the evidence suggests Phillips has been running smuggled cigarettes for a while, two years, maybe more. Presumably, he can only be selling them on to local pubs and shops and stuff ... So why has no-one noticed?"

"Well, there could be any number of reasons ..." Rosie began. "Not a high crime area, so not a massive presence. Generally speaking, it feels like a victimless crime, unless you happen to work for Customs ..."

"Indeed, but there are other possibilities," Jeremy pondered. "Leave it with me, I'll ask my team to do some digging. There is an on-going file on cigarette smuggling, so there may be some linkages to be made. You mentioned Mrs O'Neill and obviously this Eloisa DiMaria, did you get names of any other officers involved?"

"Yes," Martha replied quietly. "That was the other thing. At the time the lead CID officer was Sergeant Zeta Nancy ..."

"Of TSG?" Rosie asked.

"Now, but not then. Not when Ian Green was arrested anyway."

"Gosh," Rosie sighed. "Look, well done Martha," she added. "In fact, well done all three of you. Truly splendid work."

"Totally agree," Jeremy nodded. "Makes me wonder whether we need turn in at all tomorrow, Detective Inspector?"

"Well, a day off sounds good ..." Rosie smiled.

"Oh, but before we forget. We should mention Mr Battersby."

"Yes," Rosie nodded. "On our way back, the DCS and I went to see Mr Battersby, the Family Secretary, basically to try and find out why they'd given their work to Green & Sons in the first place. And ... well, the bottom line is, I'm not sure we absolutely did. Battersby is one very uptight man, but the most likely explanation seems to be no more than that Gallini had seen the Greens working locally so assumed they were OK ..."

"Taking care of family investments, that kind of thing ..." Jo remembered.

"Sorry, what was that?" Jeremy asked.

"Oh, probably nothing. I asked what Battersby did ... Well, I just thought it weird to have a bloke around calling himself the Secretary ..."

"But you're right," Rosie nodded thoughtfully. "That is exactly how Roberto Gallini described Battersby's role. I actually remembered that myself, earlier ..."

"Money," Jeremy sighed. "What stronger motive is there?"

"Yes, but even so, it's not an obvious fit, is it?" Gerard argued. "I mean, unless he stands to inherit a lot, his motive can only be, what ...? To cover up that his hands have been in the till ...?"

"Could be," Gurmel suggested. "Herr Gallini catches him out ..."

"But that wouldn't explain the sheer elaboration of this case ..."

"Unless ..." Gurmel began. "What if Battersby knows Green ... Yes, supposing Harris wasn't the only one owing Green's club. Supposing Battersby did too ..."

"What, and the work was a way of paying him back with Gallini's money?" Gerard asked.

"Well, there is some kind of logic there ..." Gurmel pondered. "But I suppose it only really works if we complicate the motivation. Murder of Ian Green is telling Gerry Green to back off. Murder of Gallini is meant somehow or other to implicate ..."

"You know," Jeremy put in. "I almost had this kind of thought myself ... and I mean only almost, nothing like as clear as you are drawing it out. I actually asked Battersby if he knew Harris, but it was just a random thing because I had Harris in my head ..."

"But what if they do know each other?" Gerard asked. "Holy fuck."

"Yes, well, let's not run ahead of ourselves. All we have right now is reason to dig a little deeper into this Hamilton Battersby ..." Rosie considered.

"Didn't he say he'd previously been Rütger's Company Secretary?" Jo asked.

"He did."

"Hmm," Jeremy mused. "Well there's no harm in asking colleagues in the City Police and FSA to check on him. I'll do that."

"OK," Rosie nodded. "So, anything else? No ...? Right, well TDCs," she called like a schoolmistress at assembly. "You'll have the best part of the morning, I think, to work through some further enquiries on Eloisa DiMaria, etc."

"Yes ma'am."

"Gerard, let's you, Jeremy and I meet up at 9am. We'll just find out where Green is and go and see him there. No reason to drag him in ... yet."

"OK."

"Right, well I think we're done for the day."

Tuesday, 7 August 2012

Chapter 46

The CID section was much busier than usual. Just about everyone on DI Russell's team was at their desks by 8:30, and their furtive whispering and even more furtive sideways glances suggested they were discussing how much Gerard, Gurmel, Jo and Martha might know. And even more importantly, how best to go about getting them to tell.

By 9am, even DI Clarke's team were in, and they'd not been seen much for the past month since joining with Croydon on an investigation focused on illegal immigration and people trafficking.

By the time Rosie and Jeremy dragged Gerard away, the only empty desks were those of the Burglary Team, who not unreasonably were at home tucked up in bed.

Jo was first to face any kind of questioning, from the DS she'd first been assigned to before getting moved to Rosie's team. "Hi Jo."

"Hiya Maggie," Jo smiled while making the team coffees.

"Exciting stuff, eh?"

"What is?" Jo replied blankly.

"Well I was going to say Olympics," Maggie giggled. "Unless you've anything more interesting you want to talk about?"

"No, quite happy to talk about the Women's Omnium," Jo smiled. "Seems like quite an interesting idea, and that Laura Trott, well ..."

"Women's what?"

"It's a bike race, Maggie. Happens today. I thought you'd know that!" Jo laughed, turning away with two coffees and a tea on a small tray.

But for cheek and directness, Steve Collins and John Connelly couldn't be beat. Walking across what for uniform officers was alien ground, they called out: "Hey guys," before getting even halfway to where Martha, Jo and Gurmel sat.

"Hello," Gurmel replied warily as the two PCs perched themselves on Gerard's now empty desk.

"Just saw your DI leaving with the DCS," Steve said.

"Aw, that's a shame. I'm sure if they'd noticed they would have stopped for a coffee," Jo smiled.

"Yeah, course," John smiled. "Me and him are like that," he claimed, his fingers wrapped together. "In fact, we did catch a quick word: I said, what about this Harris business. He said, can't stop right now Jonny boy," he grinned, staring directly at Martha now. "But go and see Detective Cunningham, she'll explain ..."

"Is that it?" Martha laughed dismissively. "No attempt at bribery. No big bar of chocolate. No flowers? No promise of a posh night out with the two of you for exclusive company. Not even a bit of flattery: go and have a word with that drop-dead-gorgeous Detective Cunningham ..."

"Oh yeah, course. That's exactly what he said," John insisted.

"Did he?" Martha laughed.

"Thing is guys," Gurmel smiled. "Even if we knew anything, we obviously wouldn't be able to share it with ... uniform," he said with distaste, like a Lord of the Manor might refer to a passing labourer.

"But seeing as we don't know what you're talking about ..." Jo smiled.

"It's probably just as well you didn't waste your money on Toblerone and tulips," Martha concluded.

Chapter 47

Whilst a little offish on the phone, Gerry Green had agreed to a discussion at home. His house was in many ways typical of a builder. Originally a rather attractive looking Art Deco cube, it now boasted three extensions, each with a different finish and style making for an overall effect that was confused, if not totally risible.

Any passer-by might wonder what on earth possessed the local Council to grant planning permission for such architectural violence. But such a passer-by would be rather missing the point: people like Gerry Green didn't bother themselves with civic niceties such as consent. Quite what the neighbours, in what was actually a very nice and quiet road, made of Green wasn't too hard to guess: they probably tut-tutted endlessly to each other while keeping out of the man's way whenever they could.

The man himself was large - a little over six feet and broad with it - and smartly dressed, in black trousers and a rather expensive looking polo shirt in pale blue. His hair was jet-black - far too completely so to be natural - and neatly combed. His big, round face was also just a little too deeply tanned, suggesting sun bed topping up those Dubai weekends. Yet this further suggestion of vanity served only to emphasise the cragginess of his features: a bulbous and slightly bent nose, plus a mosaic of lines etched around his mouth and eyes.

"Mr Green?"

"Course," the gravelly voice replied while holding out a large hand, the wrist to which carried a gold Rolex.

"Detective Sergeant McAvoy," Gerard replied, accepting the handshake. "And this is Detective Inspector Charlton and Detective Chief Superintendent Benson."

Green arched his eyebrows in recognition of Jeremy's rank, though he said nothing as he politely shook his hand after simply nodding at Rosie - the idea of shaking a woman's hand not being one he was able to understand, let alone bother with.

"OK. Well, come in."

"Trains an interest of yours, Mr Green?" Gerard asked, looking around at the drawings of various steam locomotives hung around the rather impressive study.

"What?" Green asked, sitting himself in a large, dark-red leather chair while gesturing for Gerard, Rosie and Jeremy to use either of the matching two-seater chesterfields. "Oh no, got them from a house I was doing. People was gonna throw 'em out but I thought they'd work in here. Never really looked at them though!" he laughed. "Look, you want tea or something?"

"Coffee, it you wouldn't mind," Rosie asked.

"Be instant."

"Instant's fine," she smiled untruthfully.

"Same, if that's OK," Jeremy said.

"Me too," Gerard added.

"Oh well, that's easy enough. Hold on."

Green returned a few minutes later with a tray carrying four non-matching mugs of coffee, a bowl of sugar, a bottle of unopened milk and one spoon.

"If my wife had been around she'd probably have made you a fancy pot full ..."

"She away, Sir?" Rosie asked on instinct.

"Gone to stay with her sister for a few days. Upset like. Well, you'd understand," Green suggested to and of Rosie.

"Of course. Please tell her we are doing everything we can to try and identify who killed your son Mr Green."

"Yeah, well ... Yeah," Green mumbled without any obvious sign of emotion.

"One of your other sons, Michael, he was very helpful. We now know where Ian was the night before he was murdered ..."

"Dossing in David's garden, I understand," Green completed with some obvious disapproval.

"Yes, indeed. Having apparently earned himself a sizeable amount of money the day before."

"Dumb fucker."

"Yes, well. I guess we think that too, frankly," Rosie nodded. "Having just got out for the same thing. But, having chased down a few leads, we don't think your son's murder is linked to his involvement in cigarette smuggling. Or at least, not directly."

"What does that mean?"

"It means that whilst the person Ian was working for is in custody, charged with smuggling - well, tax evasion to be exact - we are not anticipating further charges. Obviously, that could change if new evidence emerges ..."

"So who did do it then?"

"That's why we're here, Mr Green. We're hoping you might have information that might help us ..."

"Well I don't fucking know who killed him."

"No Sir. And I'm sure if you did, you would tell us. But it's possible you may, when you think back, be able to help us identify people who might have wanted to kill Ian. Possibly people who might have wanted to do that to send some kind of message or warning to you?"

"Me? What the fuck ..."

"Perhaps you could begin by telling us a little more about this dispute you had with Mr Battersby at Hurst Hall."

"How is that relevant," Green asked carefully.

"To be frank, I don't know at the moment whether it is or not," Rosie replied. "Oh, but of course, you may be unaware that the day after Ian was killed, Mr Battersby's employer was also murdered. At Hurst Hall in fact."

"Eh yeah. Well, No," Green corrected himself, picking up his mug and taking a slow sip before continuing. "I mean, I did hear something had happened there, it was on the radio wasn't it? Yeah," he answered himself. "But ... are you saying the two killings are connected?" Green asked with sudden calm.

303

"Yes Sir. No doubt about that whatsoever ... Same gun."

"But that's ... I mean, that just doesn't ..."

"What, Sir?" Rosie asked. "Make sense?"

"Yeah, exactly that. I mean, how can that make sense ... Unless there's some loony wandering around with a gun ..."

"Happens in America, doesn't happen here," she suggested. "So, what do you think the connection is?"

"What, me?" Green asked, his washed-out grey eyes suddenly gazing intently at Rosie. "Why you asking me?" he added, his voice losing its gruff certainty.

"Because it seems to us that the obvious connection is you."

"Now hold on ..."

"Sorry Mr Green," Rosie smiled. "I fear you may have misunderstood. I'm not saying I think you are consciously the connection. That you actually played some kind of a part ..." she paused, watching Green's reaction. "What I am saying is: it seems possible that, somehow or other, these murders are about you."

"No, no, can't possibly be," Green claimed without total conviction. "No, you must be wrong. Well wrong. Can't be ..."

"Well, we'll see. Now, if you would, we have a few different possibilities we want to discuss, simply to see if you can identify anything that might give us a lead. So, back to Mr Battersby, you and he had an argument ..."

"Yeah, well, I've accepted the fucking Caution," Green said with obvious displeasure.

"Indeed you have. One question I just wanted to clarify: how did you know Mr Battersby is gay?"

"What, you kidding me?"

"No Sir, I'm asking you."

"Huh!" Green sighed diffidently. "You spoken to him?"

"Yes."

"Well, there you go ..."

"Eh, No, Sir. That doesn't explain it. Or at least, it doesn't explain the certainty with which you called him a ... oh now let me make sure I get this quite right," Rosie said with apparently earnest concern for accuracy, taking an open folder from Gerard.

"Ah yes, here we are, you said ... I should say, by the way," she smiled, looking directly into Green's now suspicious eyes. "That this is from Mr Battersby's statement, but you didn't deny saying it when you were interviewed ..." she paused a moment before continuing, pronouncing every word from Battersby's statement with plumy precision.

"So, you said: you better get yourself some fucking good protection you queer prick, you hear me? I want that fucking money and if I don't get it I'll hurt like you wouldn't fucking believe, you cocksucker ..."

"So Mr Green," Rosie asked with a cold, hard, unblinking stare. "How did you *know* he was homosexual?"

"Look, I really don't ..."

"Mr Green," she put in sharply. "I did not read that stuff out for pleasure. I read it because it very plainly suggests that you weren't speculating on Mr Battersby's sexuality, you were sure of it. So I ask again, how did you know?"

"Look, I didn't *know* as you put it. Not in any certain way. I lost my rag, I admit I lost my rag big time. But you're making out I called him that because I knew something, when all I was doing was trying to scare the fat shitbag ..."

"Mr Green," Rosie replied patiently. "As far as I know, an ability to pull a trigger is not an exclusively heterosexual thing."

"No way, you don't think!?" Green all-but gasped.

"Now obviously," Jeremy took over. "We had a bit of a chat about all this before coming to see you. And, if I'm honest, I have to say I think it a little, how to put it ... extreme. Yes, a little extreme to imagine a man would shoot another man's son just for being abused over his sexuality ..."

"Yeah, exactly ..."

305

"Which is why I'm thinking there has to be more to it. What money were you referring to?"

"The money he owed me, of course."

"Yes, but owed you from where?"

"The job. Where the fuck else?"

"Yesterday, Mr Green, I had to interview Detective Chief Inspector Harris ..."

"Do what?"

"Or, to be more accurate, former Detective Chief Inspector Harris. He has been stripped of rank and suspended pending dismissal ..."

"So?" Green shrugged his shoulders in an effort to express a total absence of any concern. He failed. His movement was too staccato, his eyes too open, his lips too tightly shut.

"You have known Harris a long time, haven't you?"

"Known," Green laughed. "What, as in been nicked by him ..."

"Well it's funny you should say that," Jeremy smiled. "Or perhaps a little foolish, seeing as that's the one thing that has never happened, isn't it. Not once were you arrested by Harris ..."

"What I meant was he's been ..." Green blustered.

"Mr Green. Let's just get some stuff out of the way. I'm not, today, interested in events way back in the distant past. What I am interested in is what I understand is commonly referred to as the Ludgate Club ..."

"I ... I don't know what ..." Green began.

"Mr Green," Jeremy continued with chilling patience. "You know I know that isn't true. It's not going to do much for Harris now, but he has been of some help ..."

"No, No ... I don't ..."

"Now what don't you believe, Sir? Do you not believe he would have admitted passing a tip-off about the intended raid of Farringdon Securities eighteen months ago? Is that what you don't believe ..."

Jeremy, Rosie and Gerard all gazed coldly and impassively at the now restless but defiant looking Green.

"OK, your time's up," Green said standing.

"Sergeant," Rosie said calmly.

"Gerald Arthur Green, I am arresting you on suspicion of conspiracy to murder ..."

"You're fucking what?" Green shouted.

"Arresting you, Sir," Jeremy confirmed. "You don't want to talk here, that's fine by us. We'll take you in, you chat with your solicitor, we'll get you a copy of Harris' statement and carry on from there. OK?"

"No it's not OK," Green replied. "It is very much not fucking OK. Look, I've lost a son, murdered by some fucking loony and all you wanna do is fuck me about over something to do with some bent copper. It ain't my fucking problem," he insisted forcibly while actually sitting down rather meekly.

"Thank you for that," Jeremy replied sarcastically. "Now, as I was saying, we know Harris tipped you off about the raid and we know why - you waived the £100,000 he then owed this Ludgate Club ..."

"He says ..."

"Indeed, that is true, Mr Green. He says. And if you're thinking a disgraced former DCI won't make the most compelling witness in Court, I would have to agree with you. But before you relax too much, ask yourself this: how well will you come across? Not to beat about the bush, Mr Green, you do have some anger management issues, don't you?"

"Anger management ... oh yeah, very funny," Green sneered.

"Not that hilarious, really," Jeremy continued. "You see, besides your behaviour today - which a good barrister might suggest is due to the grief you're suffering for the loss of a son ..."

"Yeah, exactly ..."

"Not that you seem to have been that close. You didn't see him after he came out, did you?"

"So what?"

"Nothing really. Just that I don't really think the grief trip holds up at all. In fact, I'm not even sure you're that bothered Ian is dead ..."

"Of course I'm fucking bothered, he was my son ..."

"Yeah, well ..." Jeremy mused. "But he wasn't much use, was he? I mean, you didn't want him in your firm and I'd be willing to guess you never once took him to this Ludgate Club of yours ..."

"It ain't my club, it's ..."

"It's?"

"Look," Green said with sudden resignation. "What has all this shit got to do with Battersby?"

"Well, I know you already know the answer to that Mr Green," Jeremy smiled. "But I agree, time we stopped dancing around ... Battersby owed the club money too, didn't he?"

"This a trap?"

"No, No it isn't. I'm not going to deny that colleagues in the City Police are interested in this club, and indeed its connection to Farringdon Securities ... And in case you're thinking otherwise," Jeremy smiled. "I don't mind in least your friends knowing that. Although, then again, I'd be shocked if they didn't already. So, we clear, this isn't about the how, it's about the what: how much did he owe?"

"I don't know."

"Is that: I don't know, but I could probably find out? Or another pretence about not knowing what I'm talking about?"

"This isn't a trap?"

"Mr Green, you're not new to this, are you? Have we administered a caution?"

"No ..."

"So nothing you say can be used ..."

"I don't know how much he owes and I'm not going to find out ... But Yes, I believe he does owe a bit. Probably 100k ..."

"Because that's the maximum the club allows?"

"Yes. But like I've been saying," Green continued, leaning forward again, more animated. "For all that you've made the link, I don't get it ... oh, wait a mo ..."

"Go on."

"No, No. You've been too fucking clever for your own good. You think that poof and me had a deal so he could pay off his debt as part of the contract?"

"It did occur to me, Yes," Jeremy nodded.

"Nah, I didn't own Battersby's debt. Harris', yeah, OK. I did buy up that one. But I hardly knew Battersby, maybe seen him there a couple of times tops ..."

"But can I just be clear, he approached you about the work?"

"Yeah, kind of ..."

"At this club?"

"Yeah, OK. But not him. Someone else said they knew he was looking to have some work done, lived near me, that kind of thing ..."

"And you said?"

"I said tell him to give me a ring. What's wrong with that?"

"And he did ..."

"Yeah, and I went round, looked at these prissy drawings he had ..."

"When he rang, did he make the connection with the club?"

"No, but how could he. I don't think I even knew his name then ..."

"But you recognised him when you got there?"

"Yeah, sure ..."

"Hmm," Jeremy pondered, looking at Rosie and Gerard. "What do you think?"

"A difference of expectations?" Rosie wondered.

"Indeed," Jeremy nodded. "Indeed. Look, Mr Green," he continued. "I think that will be all for now. Thank you ..."

"You still thinking it's him?" Green asked.

"I'm still thinking it's possible, but that is strictly between us. I don't want any stupid vigilante crap going on, you hear?"

"Of course," Green smiled. "As if I'd know how."

"I'm serious. This is still very circumstantial ... but maybe someone with serious money worries would shoot another man's son just for being called a cocksucker ..." Jeremy continued while looking at Green more considerately. "I said earlier that I doubted you ever took Ian to the Ludgate Club. Was I wrong?"

"Yeah," Green smiled. "But only the once. He supplied a few boxes of cigarettes for the smoking room," he laughed before adding: "Like you said, no caution!"

Chapter 48

Harris inspired interruptions apart, the early part of the morning dragged. Well, not for Gurmel. With ease - though he would have argued: charm - he got through to a very helpful individual at South Bank University who confirmed that an Eloisa DiMaria had been accepted onto a degree course in Art, Design & Media Studies, starting Autumn 2007. She dropped out before the end of her first year. Yes, the University could also say her prior education had been in the independent sector. But No, the name of the school was not recorded on their system and it would take quite a while to find the original files. Yes, when asked, they confirmed that date of birth they held for Miss DiMaria was 27 January 1988; and they had no flags or notes to suggest she had applied to any UK Higher Education institution since.

Jo, having tried Scadbury College by phone for the best part of half an hour, decided to drive over there, thinking that what with it being holiday time Mrs Fairley and her assistant might simply unplug the switchboard. Yes, she accepted, Gurmel's info pretty much tidied things up anyway, but they might as well be certain.

Martha was tempted to go with her, save she had no choice but to wait by the internal phone for a call back from Personnel. Having gone through the same rigmarole as the day before with someone new, the woman at the other end had reluctantly agreed to dig the file out again, save that she couldn't do it for half an hour or so because of a meeting. Martha would have exploded, but for the fact the woman took her initial stunned silence as consent and hung up.

It was nearly 10:15 when the phone rang.

"Detective Cunningham."

"Ah Detective," the sweet and unhurried voice replied. "Personnel. Sorry it's been a while. Now, you wanted to know who provided the school reference, did I understand that correctly?"

"Yes, is there a name?"

"There is ... Mrs K. Watkins ..."

"QED ..."

"Is that helpful?" the voice asked.

"Very helpful indeed, thank you so much," Martha breathed happily. "Oh, just one more thing, the person I spoke to yesterday said there isn't very much background on Miss DiMaria's original application ..."

"Eh, no, just school and a year at South Bank ..."

"Yes, we've confirmed the South Bank point. But I was wondering: I'm sure I had to give three or even four referees. What happens in a case like this ..."

"We ask for a personal referee or two ..."

"And?"

"Hold on ... Yes, here we are. We got a reference from a Dr Maura Nichols of Heatherside, Little Thrift, Petts Wood ..."

"And that definitely refers to Eloisa DiMaria?"

"Oh yes, it's very clearly presented ... Perhaps her GP or something?"

"Yes, perhaps. Well, look, that's been ..." Martha trailed off while trying to work out why Gurmel was waving his arms furiously, making some odd pressing gesture with finger and thumb. "Oh yes, sorry, I almost forgot," she suddenly burst. "A photograph. Could you e-mail me a photo of Miss DiMaria?"

"Well, not really, we don't have ..."

"I thought you had to enclose a photo when applying?"

"Oh yes, but that's not electronic is it? Her last station may have ..."

"Could you scan in the one you have got then. This really is very important."

"Oh well, yes, I see ... OK then. Is that all?"

"Yes, I promise," Martha laughed. "Thank you so much."

Martha daydreamed and pondered for the couple of minutes it took for the e-mail with the scanned in photo to arrive. When she opened it she understood why people

could not stop themselves describing Eloisa DiMaria /
Elizabeth Watkins as pretty. The picture quality wasn't great,
but even so the girl had huge and haunting eyes, a cute
button nose, high cheek bones and a pouting mouth that
somehow made her look naïve yet vampish at the same
time. Could someone like that be a killer? Did the fact that
she knew enough about police ways and reactions explain
the sequence of murders?

"Personnel."

"Hi, it's Detective Cunningham again ..."

"I've just sent the photo ..."

"Yes, I know, thank you, it's here. Look, I know I said that
was all, but actually, there is something rather suspicious
about those references ..."

"I know I read the information out correctly," came a quick
and defensive reply.

"I'm sure you did, but I think ... Well, look, could you scan
them over to me d'you think. Ms DiMaria is now a suspect
..."

"Really, in a murder case?"

"Yes, 'fraid so ..."

"No problem. I'll do it now."

Martha had no sooner put the phone down than it rang.

"Detective Cunningham ..."

"Martha, it's Jo ..."

"And?" Martha asked, a combination of intuition and logic
having already guessed what Jo had to say.

"OK, yep, Elizabeth Watkins was a pupil here from
September 1996 through to 2006. And guess what else ..."

"Her mother works there," Martha replied matter-of-factly.

"How did you know ..."

"The reference the Met got was signed Mrs K. Watkins
..."

"Really ..." Jo said slowly. "But there's something else ... Something's not quite fitting. Did I say Mrs Watkins left?"

"No," Martha replied interestedly.

"Evidently it's a common thing. Pay is poor, but staff gets a place half-price. Meaning as soon as the kid finishes they leave too ..."

"So she left in 2006?"

"Yeah, that's what I was told ..."

"But Eloisa DiMaria didn't join the Met until 2010 ..." Martha thought.

"That was what was bothering me," Jo agreed.

"Look, wait there. I've just asked Personnel for copies of the references. The other is from a GP in this Thrift place ..."

"This is all just too coincidental," Jo suggested.

"Isn't it just. Yeah, wait there Jo. We'll come over and check this stuff out."

"No time for those," Martha said to Gurmel as he returned with yet more coffee. "Things to do. We're off to the school ..." she smiled while hurriedly opening the latest files from Personnel and hitting print. "By the way, that Trevor guy from the Housing people. Did he say the Watkins started renting in 1996?"

"Eh, hold on," Gurmel replied, flicking open his notebook. "No, 1995."

"1995," Martha repeated while collecting her things. "No month or anything?"

"No."

"And we never asked why they started renting, did we? You know where they'd been before?"

"No, why?"

"I'm not sure," Martha pondered, collecting the papers from the printer. "Just a feeling it might be relevant. Come on, I'll drive, you can ring Trevor on the way."

Chapter 49

As they pulled into Manor Park, Rosie saw the unmistakeable figure of Hamilton Battersby heading towards Hurst Hall, a newspaper tucked under one arm, a lightly filled bag of shopping swinging alongside him as he walked. Gerard parked up a few yards further on to allow Rosie time to get out.

"Good morning Mr Battersby."

"Good morning, Detective Inspector," Battersby replied suspiciously.

"I'm glad we caught you. We just need another word," Rosie smiled.

"Really, well, OK," Battersby replied, nodding along the road.

"Actually, here will be fine," Rosie insisted as Gerard and Jeremy joined her by the side of the car.

"Well, it's hardly ..."

"Just a couple of questions, Sir. First, forgive me. I must have got the wrong impression. But I thought you said yesterday that you contacted Green & Sons because Herr Gallini suggested them?"

"Yes," Battersby replied, more suspicious still now.

"Oh," Rosie replied with exaggerated surprise. "You did say that. Why ... when that isn't true?"

"I beg your pardon," Battersby said without conviction.

"That wasn't the case, was it? You rang Mr Green because someone you met at the Ludgate Club told you he was a builder ... didn't you?"

"I don't know ..." Battersby tried, before continuing: "How did you ..."

"We investigate, we talk to people, we find things out ... that's what we do, Sir."

"Oh god ..."

"Hmm," Rosie considered. "I'm not sure whether that answers my next question. Let's see. So when did Herr Gallini find out about the money you owe?"

"What? No, no ... No, that didn't happen ..."

"What didn't happen, Sir? Are you saying Herr Gallini never found out that you owe this Ludgate Club, what is it, £100,000?"

"Not quite," Battersby replied sadly, carefully putting his small bag of shopping on the floor while gathering his thoughts.

"Not quite," Rosie repeated. "But the rest of the question, Sir. When did Herr Gallini find out you hoped to clear some of that debt through this deal with Green ..."

"What? He didn't. I mean, there wasn't any deal ..."

"No, so we understand," Rosie interrupted. "Green wasn't interested, was he. Just wanted to get all he could for the work you'd actually asked him to do. So, how did he put it, Mr Battersby ... Pay up or your boss gets to hear where the rest of his money goes?"

"Not quite that," Battersby accepted sadly.

"But along those lines," Rosie nodded empathetically. "Far from agreeing to help you sort out this gambling debt, he wanted to make you pay extra for the Orangerie project, is that about it?"

"Yes, I suppose," Battersby sighed. "Hideous man ..."

"And so, when that all got too out of control, what? You just said: No ... is that it?"

"Yes, of course. What else could I do? I mean, I couldn't ..."

"Couldn't what, Sir?" Rosie asked after allowing a moment's pause.

"Couldn't possibly agree to pay what he was asking. The work just wasn't worth that," Battersby replied hurriedly, earnestly.

"No, but then again. Would anyone have noticed? I mean, your job is to take care of family investments ..."

"Yes, but the bill. It would have looked ... Well, preposterous compared to the quote ..."

"But you could have hidden all of that, couldn't you Mr Battersby? I mean, that was what you were hoping to do when you commissioned Green & Sons in the first place ... Wasn't it?"

"No!" Battersby cried before guiltily looking down to his feet, reaching down to fiddle with his shopping bag, nervously pushing his newspaper tighter beneath his arm.

"But it was, wasn't it?" Rosie insisted. "You as good as admitted that a moment ago. You rang Green because you knew that he had some influence in this Ludgate Club. Maybe you'd heard that he'd sorted out the debts of one or two other people ... DCI Harris, for example ..."

"Who?"

"We mentioned him to you yesterday Sir," Jeremy reminded. "Detective Chief Inspector Harris ... He was also a regular at the Ludgate Club."

"Was he, I'm sorry, I really don't know ..."

"But you did know Green had influence, didn't you?" Rosie pressed.

"Yes, in a way I suppose ..."

"So that's my point," Rosie smiled with controlled triumphalism. "You thought that if you gave the job to Green, he'd maybe help you out. Sort things ..."

"I suppose ..."

"You suppose. So how do you suppose that was going to happen, Mr Battersby? Other than by you slipping some extra cash inside payment for the work Green & Sons were doing ..."

"Yes, OK," Battersby accepted sadly. "But it didn't happen. That's what I've been telling you. It didn't happen ..."

"We know that," Rosie nodded. "We know that very well. What we're not sure of is how you then dealt with the situation ..."

"What situation?"

"The situation," Gerard took over. "Being something like this: you had a £100,000 gambling debt that needed paying, along with some thug of a builder trying to rush you for twice the figure you'd told Herr Gallini the work would cost. The situation being, Sir, that you had some serious and pressing money concerns that you simply couldn't tell your boss about ... That's the situation the Detective Inspector means."

"Well, yes ... But I was dealing with Green ..."

"Why couldn't you tell Herr Gallini?" Jeremy asked. "I mean, you'd worked for him for a long time. First for the bank I understand. And then, more recently, for the family. He trusted you. Surely, if you'd explained everything, admitted to being a total fool he would have ..."

Battersby just looked blankly at Jeremy, then Gerard, then Rosie, his eyes carrying the sadness of a proud - maybe too proud - man. A man who simply could not ask for, let alone expect, understanding. A man who, like so many vain men before him, had found himself out of his depth, unable to function easily in a world where weakness is seen as an opportunity.

The instant decision challenge for Rosie was to weigh up where such weakness could lead a man.

"Mr Battersby, I think I see your problem ..." Jeremy nodded.

"Yes," Rosie continued. "It wasn't so much these most recent events that worried you ..." she speculated. "As what had happened in the past."

"Eh?"

"The other times you'd used your position to sort out the odd financial embarrassment here, unfortunate piece of bad luck there ..."

"No ... No ..." Battersby tried to insist, nervously fiddling with his newspaper again.

"Maybe you were worried Herr Gallini had already noticed the odd discrepancy here, unexpectedly high invoice there ... Or maybe you knew he had?"

"Detective Inspector, I really don't ... I mean, I don't think it's fair for you ..." Battersby blustered.

"You are right, of course, Sir. Here is not the place. Sergeant."

"Mr Hamilton Battersby," Gerard began. "I am arresting you on suspicion of the murder of Herr Stefan Gallini ..."

"No," Battersby cried.

"... you do not have to say anything, but it may harm your defence if you do not mention, when questioned, something which you later rely on in court. Anything you do say may be given in evidence ... do you understand?"

"No ..."

"Would you like me to repeat the caution?"

"What? No, I understand that but ..."

"Thank you Sir," Gerard nodded.

"Then, if you'll just get in the car," Rosie suggested, picking up Battersby's shopping for him. "We'll take you to Bromley where we can talk further. Until then, I would advise you to say nothing more."

Chapter 50

It took Mrs Fairley but a moment to spot it. 'Wrong paper', she'd said handing Martha back the copy of the College's reference for Eloisa DiMaria. The Scadbury College header bore the name of Mrs Barrington-Hawkes' predecessor, the more simplistically named Mrs Edwards, who had retired in 2006.

She did remember Lena (as she referred to her) Watkins rather well. Whilst her main duties were all about providing pastoral support to the pupils, she also helped out with some of the more mundane admin tasks, such as sending out brochures and fee requests. Couldn't let her do much more than that though, Mrs Fairley laughed, her spelling was atrocious! And yes, she'd nodded when pressed, Lena did have an accent: Welsh, I thought, though she'd never asked.

The daughter - such a very pretty girl - by contrast was bright enough, by all accounts, but not as clever as she thought she was. She'd been eight or nine when she first started, Mrs Fairley thought, before finding the girl's record. Ah well, I never realised, she'd then said while reading the file. Evidently, Elizabeth had previously attended a primary school in Mottingham which had been closed down since for being so awful, before which she'd been educated at home. That, Mrs Fairley concluded, explained why the girl had taken time to settle, although in truth: she never really did seem to make that many friends.

When asked again to consider the apparently forged reference, Mrs Fairley seemed puzzled by the very concept. I mean, if she'd told us Elizabeth had changed her name we could have reflected that, she'd said with seemingly genuine disappointment.

To Martha and Jo, as they discussed the matter on their way back to the car park, one question dominated: why would anyone feel the need to be so secretive about a change of name? Sure, it might not be an everyday thing for the vast majority of people, but there were possible explanations, not least the one they'd considered yesterday. Maybe the mother had planned years back to tell her daughter, once she turned eighteen, about something she had been too young really to take in when it happened. And that was the point: like Mrs Fairley had said, if asked, with a sensible explanation, they would have been happy to confirm Elizabeth's school record as Eloisa's.

So why didn't Mrs Watkins want to do that? What risk did she see in it?

Presumably, if she'd had anything specific in mind back in 2006, it would have been her daughter's possible university applications. Mrs Fairley could find no record of Elizabeth applying while still at school, nor of any institution having contacted them since. All of which suggested Mrs Watkins' first use of that headed notepaper was tucked away somewhere in the Elephant & Castle. All of which, in turn, equalled planning.

And finally, they'd wondered whether the first of the two gap years was at all significant. Did the girl go off to work abroad - as she'd put on her Met application - as Elizabeth, returning as Eloisa?

Gurmel's news both added to and clouded their understanding. Mr Watkins had, it seemed, grown up on the very Mottingham estate Bromley Council then housed him and his family on, in November 1995. When pressed for anything in the file that might indicate where they were before that, Trevor Anderson finally offered: Well, I don't know if this is significant, but his declared income was a pension from the International Red Cross.

"Where's that then?" Jo had asked.

"Geneva," Martha and Gurmel had replied in unison.

Heatherside, though built in the same Tudor-Bethan style as Mrs Dearmer's house, was both larger and less attractive. Tucked at the end of the small close, it was less than fifty yards from the alley that led to the bridge that led to the car park where Ian Green's car had been found.

"Well, like we said," Gurmel said, looking around. "It all fits ..."

"Save this close seems to be called Little Thrift. Mrs Dearmer said Great Thrift," Jo pooh-poohed.

"Oh yeah," Gurmel smiled. "Oh well, might as well leave it then ..." he suggested, making to get back in the car.

"So, what do we reckon?" Martha asked as they reached the front door, a discreet brass plaque just below the bell confirming Dr M. A. G. Nichols, MB, ChB/BS, nMRCGP. "The family GP?"

There was no answer the first time, even though the sound of the bell could be clearly heard outside. There was no answer the second time, either, nor, Jo noted, any sound of a dog. They thought they heard some noise inside after the third ring but, after a further few moments of eerie inactivity, they started to walk away. They were almost at the end of the drive when a thin voice asked:

"Yes?"

"Dr Nichols?" Martha asked, turning and starting back up towards the house.

"Yes, but I'm not able to accept new patients," the obviously tall but stooping woman explained.

"That's not why we're here," Martha smiled on reaching the front door again. "I am Detective Cunningham, my colleagues are Detectives Hartley and Kandola. We need to ask you a couple of questions about someone we think may have been a patient ..."

"Oh, but I cannot possibly tell you anything about a patient," Dr Nichols insisted sternly, straightening her thin body by way of emphasis.

"Not questions about their medical history," Martha smiled. "In fact, our first question is really about you ..."

"Me?"

"Yes, we need to ask about a character reference you provided ..."

"A character reference? Oh No. Never! I do passports and all of that rigmarole, but not ..."

"I do have a copy," Martha continued. "It was a reference, you see, for someone who wanted to join the Police Force ..."

"Really?"

"Yes. Would it be better if we just came in for a moment? Perhaps you could just sit down and take a look ..."

"Oh, alright," Dr Nichols agreed grumpily, leading them into a large room which no doubt once had a much grander purpose, but was now obviously just a waiting room. Carefully, she sat herself down in one of the more comfortable chairs and gestured for Martha, Jo and Gurmel to sit opposite, even though opposite meant some ten feet away.

"Do you have identification or something," she asked, her bright, inquisitive eyes now examining them one after the other.

"Of course," Martha smiled.

"OK, OK," Dr Nichols nodded at the trilogy of Warrant Cards held up for her, even though there was no possibility she could read anything from them. "Tell me again, what is it you want?"

"I have here," Martha began. "A copy of a reference, in your name, for a Miss Eloisa DiMaria. It's quite detailed ..." she observed, standing up.

"Sorry Detective, can't be mine. I know all my patients."

"Perhaps you could just take a look," Martha insisted, now standing by Dr Nichols' side.

"What for, I've just told you," the woman replied irritably. "I don't have a patient by that name. Never have ..."

"Is this your signature?"

"What, how do I know. I haven't got my glasses ..."

"They are on a chain around your neck, Madam."

"Are they? Oh, so they are ... hmm ..."

"So, is that your signature?"

"It does look like it, that I cannot deny ... But I really don't understand," the woman replied, looking up at Martha with almost childlike innocence.

"How about Kathleen Watkins and her daughter Elizabeth?"

"What about them?"

"Are they patients of yours?"

"Yes, of course ..."

"Why: of course?"

"What?" Dr Nichols asked, seemingly confused again. "Because they've been with me for years. But what has this," she continued, shaking the reference dismissively. "Got to do with Mrs Watkins?"

"Well now," Martha smiled, sitting down next to Dr Nichols. "Let's see if we can clear up the mystery ... Tell me about Mrs Watkins ..."

"Why, she's my Housekeeper. You just missed her, in fact ..."

"Off to walk the dog?"

"How did you know that?"

"Intuition," Martha smiled. "And Elizabeth?"

"She's gone away somewhere. Not sure when Lena said she'll be back. Perhaps you can ask her yourself ..."

"Hopefully we can," Martha nodded while offering Dr Nichols the rather hazy photo of Eloisa DiMaria. "Is this Elizabeth?"

"Why yes, of course. But how ..."

It was forty-five minutes before Martha heard the front door open, followed by the telltale sound of a dog shaking. During that time Dr Nichols filled in most of the gaps.

Mrs Watkins and her daughter registered in 2004, having just moved into the area. They weren't especially regular callers, but Mrs Watkins knew the then receptionist - they lived near each other, I believe, Dr Nichols had recalled. So, on her old receptionist's recommendation - Mrs Murphy, Margaret, such a dear - Lena stood in for a week here and there: She was always free during school holidays, sometimes Elizabeth helped too ... then they went away somewhere ...

When pressed, Dr Nichols did believe they went to visit some relatives abroad for six months or so, during which time Margaret Murphy started to get ill. I was quite frantic for a while, had to use these dreadful temps, she recalled with displeasure. But then Lena came back and Margaret retired.

More recently, Dr Nichols' own health had started to falter. She had cut down her surgeries and passed about half her patient list to a colleague nearby, but kept Lena on full-time to help organise the house: Making sure the cleaner didn't skimp, doing all that internet shopping doo-dah, that sort of thing ... oh, and walking Rosie of course.

Rosie - Jo, Gurmel and Martha guessed, obviously enough - was Dr Nichols' dog, though the name still amused them childishly. But the connection to the DI also, intuitively, made them all consider the likely consequences of what they sensed they would soon be doing. Nodding to Gurmel to continue engaging Dr Nichols, Martha and Jo grabbed a quick word, following which Jo excused herself to make the call.

It was about a couple of years ago, Dr Nichols thought, when she'd first muted the idea that she might retire, but keep Lena on as a Housekeeper, perhaps staying over some of the time. She still hadn't found the courage, as she put it, to retire completely: I've been doing it for so long, she smiled thinly. But even so, because of the difficulty she found with stairs, she had moved her bedroom down, letting Lena take over the whole of the upstairs: it just seemed natural, it's such a big old house.

"Lena's been living here more or less all the time for a year now, I suppose," Dr Nichols summarised. "And Elizabeth for the past few months - she lost her job, the poor dear. But she is so lovely, so pretty ... Ah, but here's Lena now ..."

"Hello, who are you?" the slightly podgy, dark-haired woman asked of Jo, as she closed the door.

"I'm Detective Hartley," Jo replied, getting up from the old and battered - but very comfortable - leather chair she'd been sat in, waiting. "Would you be Mrs Watkins?"

"Yes," the woman replied slowly, nervously and maybe also just a little resignedly. "What's this about?"

"You know what? I rather think you already know."

"What? No, sorry. Look ..." Mrs Watkins spoke quickly now, taking off her jacket, kicking off her muddy boots, reaching for a towel on a hook behind the door and bending down to clean the paws of the light-brown, dark-eyed, waggy-tailed dog at her feet.

"Rosie, I believe," Jo smiled.

"Yes, how did you know ..."

"Oh, Dr Nichols told us her name. But we've been looking for her for a few days now ... Ah, this is one of my colleagues, Detective Cunningham ..."

"Mrs Watkins," Martha smiled.

"Yes, look, I've got things to do," she insisted. "Dr Nichols ... I have to prepare lunch and then there's the correspondence ..."

"Where's Eloisa, Mrs Watkins?"

"Sorry?" the woman replied, a startled look on her face.

"Your daughter, Eloisa DiMaria ..."

"She's ..." she began hesitantly before continuing with a sudden tone of defiance. "She's gone."

"Ah, there you are dear," Dr Nichols said from the entrance to the waiting room, Gurmel by her side. "These are police officers. They need you to help them with some references or something or other ..." she smiled.

"Indeed we do," Gurmel agreed, gently taking the elderly doctor's arm. "And we will need Mrs Watkins to come with us ..."

"What!" Mrs Watkins gasped, being momentarily silenced by Martha's piercing stare.

"But we'll get someone to help sort out your lunch for you. So where's the kitchen, down here?" Gurmel asked, pointing down the long and poorly lit hallway.

"Well, yes. But I'm not sure I ..."

"Let's just go down then, shall we," Gurmel suggested patiently, while leading the increasingly confused woman with a firm hand, turning halfway down to call: "Come on Rosie."

"Now Mrs Watkins ... Lena," Martha continued, watching the sweetly enthusiastic little dog trot after Gurmel like she'd known him all her life. "I asked you where Eloisa is. You said gone ... Gone where?"

"I ... I'm not sure. I ..."

"In this country? Or abroad?"

"I ... Look, why are you asking after her?" Lena Watkins replied with renewed defiance.

"Lena," Jo put in. "We've already been through this. You know why we need to talk to her ... Don't you?" she asked firmly, after a deliberate pause.

"No, no, I'm not ... I mean, I can't help you. I ..."

"What Lena?" Martha asked. "Won't? Is that what you're really saying. You won't help us?"

"I ... I can't ..."

"Well, in that case ..." Martha began, nodding to Jo.

"Mrs Kathleen Watkins," Jo said slowly and sternly. "I am arresting you on suspicion of conspiracy to murder Herr Stefan Gallini ..."

"Oh No," Lena sighed.

"... you do not have to say anything, but it may harm your defence if you do not mention, when questioned, something which you later rely on in court. Anything you do say may be given in evidence ... do you understand?"

327

"Yes."

"Then perhaps, if you could put your shoes back on ..."

"I can't wear those," Lena replied, nodding down to her muddy walking boots. "I'll get some clean ..." she said, starting to walk towards the stairs.

"OK, we'll go together," Jo insisted.

As Jo followed Lena Watkins upstairs, Martha stepped outside just as Tilly Cowdrey from Family Liaison was parking up. Having listened attentively to Martha's summary - which added up to saying Dr Nichols was going to be without her live-in carer for at least the rest of the day, and quite possibly a lot longer than that - Tilly explained that while she and Stella Reeves could provide some support for maybe a couple of days, it would make sense to arrange for the local Social Services Department to carry out an Assessment of Need. In reply to Martha's worried assumption that would take months, Tilly had smiled confidently, insisting: Not for me it won't.

As Jo was leading Lena out to her car, Gurmel and Martha agreed he would stay behind for half-an-hour or so. Partly, because the elderly doctor seemed comfortable with him around, so him staying should ease the handover to Tilly. But mostly, so he could take a quick look around. And, given the camera was still in the car they'd used, they both thought a photo of Rosie could be useful.

Chapter 51

"Interview commencing at 12:37, Tuesday, 7 August 2012. Present Detective Inspector Charlton and Detective Sergeant McAvoy. Your full name please, Sir," Gerard asked.

"Hamilton Aloysius Battersby."

"And your address and date of birth please."

"Hurst Hall, Manor Park, Chislehurst; 16 May 1957."

"Thank you. And having understood your rights, you have elected not to call for a solicitor to be present at this time, is that correct?"

"Yes Detective Sergeant."

"OK. So, Mr Battersby, we arrested you at 11:25 on suspicion of the murder of Herr Stefan Gallini ..."

"Which I deny ..."

"Indeed, Sir. And I believe, from a comment you made after your arrest, that you believe you can prove that, at the time of Herr Gallini's murder, you were out of the country."

"Exactly so, Detective Sergeant. Amongst others, Herr Gallini's eldest son Roberto can verify that."

"Indeed. And we will, of course, check that. But for now, let's assume we accept that ..."

"Then, what's this about," Battersby asked. "Why am I here?"

"Because Sir, unless we have misunderstood the timings, you didn't leave for Switzerland until around 6am on Friday, 3 August. Is that correct?"

"Yes, the taxi was booked for six. My flight was 7:45 from London City. So, I must ask again, why am I still here?"

"Ian Henry Green," Gerard replied.

"Who ... Oh yes," Battersby nodded neutrally.

"Now, as I believe you know," Gerard continued. "Ian Green, son of Gerry Green, was shot on the morning of

Thursday, 2 August about - at a rough guess - half a mile from Hurst Hall. Can you tell us what you were doing that morning between 8am and 12noon please ..."

"Sorry, wh-why?"

"Because Sir, we would like to know," Gerard replied calmly.

"But this is preposterous. I have no idea who this Ian Green is ... Well, sorry, no, that's not quite right," Battersby stumbled.

"Go on," Gerard encouraged.

"Look, I recall the Detective Inspector saying ..." Battersby continued, looking imploringly at Rosie for a moment before turning back to Gerard. "Saying that Mr Green's son had also been shot ... I'm not sure whether you told me his name?" he asked, looking to Rosie again.

"I believe I did, Sir."

"Yes, well, there you are," Battersby nodded to Gerard. "Yes, I had heard Ian Green's name and that he too had been shot."

"Thank you. Now, perhaps you would tell us where you first met Ian Green."

"First met? I ... have I ever met him? Did he work on the house ..."

"No Sir, he did not work on the Hurst Hall project. He was in prison at the time."

"Well then, I really do not see, Detective Sergeant ..."

"Perhaps I can help then," Gerard smiled. "You met Ian Green at the Ludgate Club ..."

"I did? ... But how, you just said he's been in prison ..."

"Yes, came out a couple of weeks ago after serving nine months. Before that, you would have seen him and his father at the Ludgate Club."

"Well, I may have done," Battersby replied, more lightly and confidently than before. "But I can honestly say I didn't notice. I only became aware of who Gerry Green was, what, a few months back. I told you that earlier ..."

"OK," Rosie interrupted. "I think we'll take a break at this point ..."

"Does that mean I am free to leave, Detective Inspector?"

"No Sir, it does not. It means you will return to the cells while we verify - or not - your claim to have been out of the country when Herr Gallini was killed."

"And this Ian Green?"

"We may well have further questions to ask about him in due course. Thank you for now, Mr Battersby. Interview suspended at ... 12:49."

Chapter 52

Martha and Jo spent half an hour or so talking to Lena Watkins - as she confirmed she preferred to be known - sitting in the car, parked beneath Bromley Police Station. They both knew the risk: little, if anything, they found out would be admissible as evidence. But then again, they weren't after evidence as such, just information and an understanding of the background to what, on the face of it, seemed like a chillingly cold and calculated crime. Having then spent a further twenty minutes with the Duty Sergeant, booking Mrs Watkins in, they got back to the CID section only moments before Gurmel.

"Well?" Jo asked as the three of them reached their desks.

"OK, first off, no sign of a gun, nor anything else obviously useful. Then again, I've no idea what half the books in Eloisa's bedroom are about. Lots in French, but also a few in German and Italian ..."

"Isn't that just the Swiss all over?"

"I guess, except she grew up in Mottingham, hardly Einstein country! Anyway, I managed to find Erica Johnson and John Connelly in the canteen. John says he thinks he and Steve did see someone with a dog like Rosie when they were chasing after the weird guy, but on a different path. So he can't say he really saw the walker, although he's sure it was a woman. Erica was a bit more certain, although again she couldn't really say she recognised Eloisa from the photo."

"OK, so it's still a bit circumstantial as far as Eloisa is concerned," Martha nodded. "But Lena Watkins has admitted to being Magdalena DiMaria, one time nanny to the Gallinis ..."

"Really, then that's it. Surely?"

"I think so," Jo agreed.

"Well, like we keep saying," Martha nodded. "It all fits ... Save, so far Lena has admitted nothing ..."

"True," Jo agreed. "But the fact that she outright won't tell us where Eloisa is does kind of suggest she knows more."

"But that's the whole point now, isn't it," Gurmel suggested. "Finding Eloisa ..."

"Indeed. And actually, from the few things we did get out of Lena, we can't be 100% sure she's done!"

"Really? Shit!"

"Hello strangers," Gerard called on leaving Rosie's office.

"Hiya," Martha, Jo and Gurmel chimed.

"Any joy?" Gurmel added.

"Well, we arrested Hamilton Battersby," Gerard replied nonchalantly.

"What?" Jo asked.

"What for?" Gurmel added.

"Suspicion of murdering Gallini."

"But," Martha put in quizzically. "Battersby wasn't here. I mean, he was in Switzerland," she added, completely puzzled.

"Yeah, that has turned out to be a bit unhelpful," Gerard smiled.

"Eh?"

"Well, simple story is, he does have a motive ... But," Gerard continued after a thoughtful pause. "Opportunity does seem to be lacking ..."

"And means?" Martha pressed.

"Not too sure on that either!"

"Well, there you go," Gurmel laughed to Jo and Martha. "You leave them on their own for a few hours ..."

"Yeah, yeah," Gerard accepted. "So, what about you?"

"We've arrested Mrs Kathleen Watkins," Martha smiled. "Mother of Eloisa DiMaria, on suspicion of conspiracy to murder ..."

"Where, I mean how?" Gerard put in urgently.

"Petts Wood and we followed the evidence," Martha smiled. "But ... there are some issues. How's the DI?"

"Eh, well OK. Obviously a bit pissed we got it wrong on Battersby. She's going to go and see Roberto Gallini again, just to get him to confirm the Switzerland thing. But really, we need to talk to her about what you've got. She was about to grab a sandwich. Hold on, I'll go and see."

With Jeremy off on some (ex-DCI) Harris business, it was the original team once again.

Rosie was challenging and occasionally sceptical. The evidence the team had was either circumstantial, speculative or inadmissible. Yes, Eloisa DiMaria fitted the - rather vague - description of someone seen at the time of Charlie Scales' murder. As did the dog. And Yes, they had identified a connection between the girl's mother and Stefan Gallini.

But whilst Martha's idea for a motive had logic to it, they had no actual facts to support it. Moreover, no weapon had been found - which, the DI suggested critically and grumpily, was just as well seeing as Gurmel's search had been illegal anyway. Similarly, the reactions they had drawn from Lena Watkins might be incriminating of her daughter, but they could only be taken as hearsay.

Sure, the girl did have a known connection to Ian Green. Moreover, her time as a PCSO would have given her enough inside knowledge on police operations to have predicted the likely response to the murders of Ian Green, and then PC Scales. Yet, such knowledge - together with the unquestioned opportunity - still stacked low against the magnitude of the crime. There has always to be a balance between the crime and the motive, Rosie had insisted forcibly.

Yes, of course, Martha had accepted, before then challenging the innate assumption in the DI's argument that such balance was for them to weigh. Surely, the point was: people see things differently. For us, killing Green and Charlie solely as plot devices to get to Gallini feels totally heinous. But, to her, rejection might feel equally wicked.

So, in the end, Rosie accepted that they had to suspect Eloisa DiMaria.

After a quick chat with Superintendent Mitchell, it was agreed that he, Gerard and Gurmel would go over to Lewisham Police Station and get all the info they could about Eloisa. Any known friends and possible hiding places. Meanwhile, Rosie, Jo and Martha would go and see Roberto Gallini.

Chapter 53

"Herr Gallini, thank you for finding the time to talk to us again. I don't think you've met Detective Cunningham before."

"Detective," Roberto smiled charmingly, if also just a little too lasciviously.

"Detective Hartley you have met."

"Of course, Detective," Roberto nodded. "Shall we sit down. I have asked for some coffee."

They had met in the same Card Room used on Sunday. Roberto took the same two-seater sofa, though this time sitting where his stepbrother had. Rosie and Jo took the same chairs as before, Martha sat on the other sofa adjacent to Roberto.

The room seemed somehow larger to Rosie, although that could have been, she thought, because of Petra and Michael's absence. Their attention to every move and every word had been - innocently and unknowingly, of course - quite stifling. The children's absence, together perhaps with Marianna's as well, seemed also to have lifted from Roberto any - self-imposed or otherwise - need to overact the role of family head. Whilst he remained studiedly polite and, perhaps as a direct result, obsequious, there was more of a hint today to suggest not all of his charm was false.

"Herr Gallini, Roberto," Rosie smiled. "There are two matters we need to discuss, although the first need not take long."

"As you need Detective Inspector, although as I said, we are taking the 17:10 home ..."

"Indeed ..." Rosie replied noncommittally.

"Ah, coffee."

They waited while the waitress poured four cups from the large pot.

"OK," Rosie continued. "The first thing I need to tell you is we arrested Mr Battersby this morning ..."

"What!" Roberto gasped, half choking on a mouthful of coffee. "Why?"

"Well, maybe it's best if I just check a detail first. Can you confirm that he was with you in Zurich, from around midday on Friday, 3 August?"

"Eh? Yes, of course ... I believe he was in the city earlier than that but ... Sorry, why are you asking me this?"

"Very simply because that is enough for us now to release him."

"But I still don't understand. Why was he arrested?"

"Yes ..." Rosie sighed thoughtfully before taking a sip of coffee to extend the pause. "I trust, when I explain, you will understand that whilst I did need to give this some thought, I feel I truly have no choice but to answer that question fully ..."

"I'm sorry, I'm really not following ..."

"You may recall that last time when we spoke we touched on the problems Mr Battersby encountered with a local builder, a Mr Green?"

"Yes, I do. You said this man's son had also been shot."

"Indeed. I also asked whether either of you - you or Mr Battersby - were aware of any connection between Mr Green and your father."

"Yes. And we were not."

"No. We have since, however, established a very specific link between Mr Green and Mr Battersby ..."

"A link, what link?"

"A link that we had to investigate because it could have been a motive for murder ..."

"What!" Roberto asked with a hint of anger.

"A link that also appeared to connect Mr Battersby to Mr Green's son ..."

"Oh my god."

"Yes. But the first thing to say is, we no longer have any reason to suspect Mr Battersby of any involvement in either murder. He will therefore be released ..."

"But, Detective Inspector? Do I sense a but?"

"You do Sir, you do. Mr Battersby owes an unlicensed gambling club a sum just short of £100,000 ..."

"No..."

"... Mr Green has influence at this club and it seems Mr Battersby awarded the contract to Green & Sons in hope of being able to settle his debt inside payment for the work."

"Hamilton did this?" Roberto sighed, more sorrowfully than angrily now.

"Yes. And I'm afraid it seems highly likely that this is not the first time he has had to use such a device to settle a gambling debt ... Not, I ought to add, with Mr Green. He is many things, but on this occasion it seems he did nothing to encourage Mr Battersby ..."

"Oh dear ..." Roberto smiled thinly and disappointedly. "OK Detective Inspector, I now understand your rather cryptic remarks to begin with," he laughed kindly. "I take it there will be no charges in this matter unless we wish to bring them?"

"Yes, Roberto, that is correct. We will only speak again about this if you ask."

"OK, thank you. Obviously I need to think about all of this ... You say he will be released, this afternoon?"

"Yes, of course. Was he due to fly with you?"

"Yes, yes he was. Well, like I said," Roberto continued, regaining his business-like poise with impressive ease. "I will deal with this. Now, you said there were two matters?"

"Yes," Rosie smiled back before looking to Martha. "Detective Cunningham."

"Thank you ma'am. Herr Gallini ..."

"Please, Roberto," the man sang with intentionally seductive Italian charm while obviously trying to work out the significance in the change of dynamic.

"Roberto," Martha replied with a sweet faux-smitten smile. "Could I just ask you to look at this photograph a moment," she continued, handing over the now slightly dog-eared print out. "You'll forgive the poor quality ..."

"Should I know this girl?"

"Well now, that's a rather complicated question," Martha replied opaquely. "I think there are, indeed, good reasons why you *should*, but equally I very much doubt you have ever met her. Her name is Eloisa DiMaria ..." she paused a moment, watching Roberto Gallini with an unblinking stare. "Now, maybe I'm wrong, but I thought I detected just a glimmer of recognition there Roberto?"

"I ... the name ..."

"Yes Roberto, the name," Martha agreed, using the man's own name in an increasingly controlling way. "Yesterday, when you spoke to my colleague Detective Hartley here, you said you would talk to your sister and brother to see if they could recall the last name of the young woman who was working for your family when you believe your father's gun went missing ..."

"Yes, yes ..."

"Yes, yes, what, Roberto?"

"My brother thought it was just a pet name. How you say, a nickname ..."

"Let me guess: Mary Magdalene?"

"How ..."

"Well, it wasn't exactly hard," Martha smiled.

"No?" Roberto replied, a surprised, puzzled look on his face. "Well, anyway, Angelina said No, she thought that it was indeed Magdalena's proper name ..."

"As in: Magdalena DiMaria?"

339

"Yes," Roberto replied with obviously thoughtful and impressed comprehension.

"I see. So obviously there must have been a very good reason why you didn't ring and tell us this. What was it?"

"I'm sorry Detective?" Roberto replied, trying to imply indignation in an attempt to regain control of the discussion.

"Why didn't you ring Detective Hartley to tell us you had remembered the name? That the girl who worked for the family in ... 1987, I believe," Martha put in after a carefully placed pause. "Was called Magdalena DiMaria?"

"Well, I'm not sure the way you put that Detective is entirely fair. I would have told you, of course, but ..."

"Yes," Martha encouraged.

"Well, apart from anything else," Roberto began with a little animation. "When my sister, brother and I spoke again, we thought ... Well, we thought this whole business about the gun getting lost ... You remember," he continued while looking straight to Rosie as if for support. "You were interested in the fact my father's service revolver went missing."

"Indeed we were," Rosie nodded.

"Well, Angelina, Marco and I, we spoke about that again. And we really are sure it must have just got lost as part of the house move. It doesn't seem possible that someone like Magdalena could have taken it ... Or even would have. Apart from anything else, her family, they were from the same town as my mother ... So you see ..." he concluded, his voice trailing off uncertainly.

"Actually Roberto, No, I don't see," Rosie replied dismissively. "Detective Cunningham hasn't asked you about the gun. She asked you about the name ..."

"Yes, OK ... I'm sorry. I suppose I should have rung sooner ..."

"That photograph, Roberto," Martha continued. "Is of Magdalena's daughter, Eloisa ..."

"Her daughter?"

"Yes. Like I said, it's not a great print and the picture itself is a couple of years old. But, for what it's worth, she and I are very similar in age ..."

"Really, well you look very young to me," Roberto smiled, once more just a little too intently.

"Well, I think I'll take that as a compliment. I mean, in our teens we all want to look and act older than we are, don't we? Then, in a blink, time flies by and suddenly twenties are about to become thirties ..."

"Truly, Detective Cunningham," Roberto cried theatrically. "I shall simply not believe you if you try to tell me you are thirty ..."

"No," Martha smiled. "I was born in 1988. August, as it happens. I have a birthday coming up ..." she paused. "I see you doing the maths. I'm twenty-three, Roberto. Eloisa, though, is already twenty-four. She was born 27 January 1988 ..."

"I see ..."

"What do you see, Roberto?"

"Nothing in particular, Detective," Roberto replied with unconvincing nonchalance.

"Hmm," Martha mused doubtfully. "Well, let's just do some more maths. A girl born late January 1988 would have been conceived, when ... Sometime in April 1987 I make it. You?"

"Yes, I suppose."

"Why did your father dismiss Magdalena?"

"I ... I'm really not sure. I mean, it happened while I was away ..."

"OK, take a guess."

"No ..." Roberto replied quietly, slumping back in the sofa before suddenly sitting back up, trying to recover control. "No, Detective, you cannot possibly know what you are implying ..." he continued, offering Martha back the photograph of Eloisa.

"We arrested Magdalena DiMaria a couple of hours ago."

"You arrested her, but how? Is she here?"

"Yes. She has lived in this country since 1995, under a different name I might add. So, for most of her life Eloisa has also lived here, obviously enough ..."

"I see ... But why have you arrested her?"

"Because we had grounds for believing she knew that Eloisa murdered your father."

"The daughter did!" Roberto cried with genuine shock, looking again at the picture. "But ... but why?"

"Because she thought he was also her father."

Roberto stared back at Martha, his body motionless, his eyes open and unblinking, his mouth poised as if to say something but no words were getting out.

"Now I, of course, never met your father," Martha continued. "But I have seen a photograph of him. Sure, it was recently taken and he may have looked different as a younger man. But even so, that girl looks nothing like him ... does she?"

"No, no I guess not ..."

"How old would you have been in April 1987, Roberto?"

"In April that year I would have been fifteen ... my birthday is in May."

"But, like I said earlier, in our teens we maybe try to make out we're older than we really are ... Magdalena was eighteen at the time."

"Yes," Roberto replied wistfully, his eyes drawn to the picture of Eloisa once more.

"So, although, as I understand it, you would have been away at boarding school during term times. During the holidays ... Well, I can imagine you wanting to spend time with Magdalena ..."

"I ... I really had no idea," Roberto all-but whispered, his eyes and thoughts momentarily fixed on the photograph of his daughter. "But Detective," he burst with sudden anguish.

"You said a moment ago that you believe this Eloisa murdered my father ..."

"Yes ..."

"So ... So, are you saying that Magdalena ... That she did, after all, take my father's old SIG?"

"No Roberto, I am not saying that. I cannot say for sure she didn't, but it seems there is a far more likely explanation. I'm not sure how much you knew about Magdalena, her background I mean?"

"Well, like I said, I know she came from the same town in Ticino as my mother's family. But from quite a poor family herself, I believe ..."

"Her mother was from Geneva ..."

"Really? I didn't know that ..."

"Yes, from a more middle-class family. I believe you explained before that a SIG such as the one we're concerned with would have been an officer's revolver?"

"Yes, I did say that," Roberto nodded. "Although I fear I made myself look a bit pompous at the time," he accepted, looking to Rosie.

"It was relevant information Roberto," Rosie smiled, waving away his apology.

"Indeed," Martha continued. "Because whilst we are not 100% certain of this, it seems highly probable that Magdalena's uncle would have been a militia officer ... And he would be of a similar age to your father ..."

"And, Detective?" Roberto prompted.

"Well, a few things. First, Magdalena has already told us that she went to stay with her uncle Guillaume after your father dismissed her. That is where she had the baby ..."

Roberto looked sadly down to the photograph of his daughter again, a pained expression furrowing his brow.

"Geneva is also where she met the man she married. An Englishman, working for the International Red Cross. He, it seems, was much older than her. In fact, he became eligible for some kind of pension late in 1994. But not a very generous one. So, partly for financial reasons, but also because England was his home, the family moved here the following year. Sadly, he died a couple of years later ..."

"How sad ..."

"Indeed, of course. Quite why Magdalena did not return to Switzerland, I'm afraid I haven't really understood. It may be that she simply isn't sure herself. No doubt there were for her issues of pride - not wanting to be a burden again to this uncle. It seems also she had decided to bring Eloisa up as an English girl, one believing that the only man she'd ever had around to call Dad was indeed her father. But the consequence is that mother and daughter had to get by on not very much money - the Red Cross pension did not continue ..."

"If only she'd ..."

"Yes, well, there may yet be time for 'if onlys' Roberto, but now we come to the crux of the reality. After Eloisa finished school she and her mother went to Geneva. They stayed there with this uncle for about six months and, for part of the stay Magdalena's mother - Eloisa's grandmother, whom she had never met by the way - was there also. For whatever reason - Magdalena is a little vague on this - during this time Eloisa was told that the man she'd been brought up to believe was her father wasn't ..."

"Not anything more?"

"No, or at least Magdalena told us she did not say anything more. But even the little that was said had quite an impact on the girl. From then on, she insisted on being known by the name she had originally been given - Eloisa DiMaria. Not the one she'd been brought up with. And it's possible that would have been that ..."

"But?"

"Magdalena and Eloisa went back to Geneva for Christmas last year. Magdalena insists that she neither encouraged nor welcomed this, but it seems the uncle decided to tell the girl the whole truth. There is a reason. By chance, Magdalena had learned that your father was now living barely a mile from her. She'd mentioned this to the uncle ..."

"So you think all of this created a real sense of hatred?"

"Seems so. I might mention that at the time, Eloisa was working for the Metropolitan Police ..."

"Good Lord," Roberto cried.

"Indeed," Martha smiled thinly. "Although, but for that fact I doubt we would have ever made the necessary connections. Anyway, she was only in a support grade. Twice she failed to make it to Constable. On the second occasion she resigned and this time went to Geneva alone, for about a month, returning here a few weeks ago. You probably won't know this, Roberto, but your father dismissed Magdalena on August 3rd, 1987 ..."

"That's ... the same date?"

"Indeed it is."

"But ..." Roberto pondered thoughtfully. "Why did she think my father was also hers?"

"Well, again we cannot be 100% sure of this right now, but on the basis of what Magdalena has told us we have no reason to believe she or her uncle did anything to encourage Eloisa towards what is, of course, a truly tragic crime ..."

"Indeed," Roberto nodded sadly, his eyes drifting from the photograph back to Martha. "I assure you, Detective, I have not forgotten the other lives ..."

"Of course not," Martha smiled acceptingly. "But the key to what we might perhaps think of as Eloisa's mistake would appear to lie in the fact that Magdalena never told anyone who fathered the child ... The uncle must have just assumed ..."

"Oh dear ... oh dear god ... And Magdalena, you said she knows what Eloisa has done?"

"She does now," Martha nodded. "That said, I do not believe she knew in advance. Even so, for all that she has told us many things - Detective Hartley and I spent some time talking to her earlier - she has so far refused to provide any information that might help us find her daughter ..."

"I suppose, even *in extremis* a mother will try to protect her child ..." Roberto considered philosophically.

"I guess ... But in doing so, she may very well be putting you at some risk, Roberto ..."

"Me? How ...?"

"Magdalena told us that when she realised what Eloisa had done she told her she was wrong ..."

"Wrong?" Roberto repeated, already understanding the point.

"Yes, and the way she said it ... Well, Detective Hartley and I both believe what she meant was she'd as good as told Eloisa she'd killed the wrong man. We tried to press her to say more, but she just kept repeating the same phrase: I told her she was wrong. For what it's worth, we have no reason to believe she has actually named you as the father. Nor, indeed, that she knows you are in the country ..."

"But you're thinking, the uncle ... It's maybe not so very hard to work out?"

"Exactly," Martha smiled empathetically.

"Which brings us to a question," Rosie put in. "Whether Magdalena would tell you any more than she has told Detectives Cunningham and Hartley ..."

"Yes, I see. Of course ..." Roberto accepted.

"It's a somewhat irregular idea," Rosie continued. "And one that carries various risks ... But for all that she has reason to feel a good deal of anger towards your late father, Magdalena has not shown any sign of hating you. Isn't that so Martha?"

"Yes ma'am ..."

"Martha, what a lovely name," Roberto smiled.

"Thank you. I like it!" Martha confirmed girlishly, unintentionally offering a self-confident and emotionally stable contrast to the image Roberto could not help but hold of a daughter he, thirty minutes earlier, knew nothing of. "So, like the Detective Inspector says, Magdalena has not given the impression of blaming you for very much at all. Indeed, she seems always to have assumed - rightly, we can now see - that your father never told you ..."

"Oh No, please," Roberto sighed, looking once again at the photograph.

"Yes, I'm afraid it seems your father always knew. Magdalena plucked up the courage to tell him she was pregnant with your child and he ..."

"Oh dear, how ... Of course I will talk to her, of course. I'll ..." he continued, talking quickly while making to stand. "I'll need to make a few arrangements, Marianna and the children can go as planned. I'll get a later flight or ..."

"The last flight today leaves at 19:10," Rosie put in helpfully.

"Thank you Detective Inspector, you seem to think of everything," Roberto smiled admiringly. "So, perhaps if you can give me a few minutes ... then we'll ... thank you, thank you again for the consideration you have shown in dealing with this ..." he continued while walking out of the room, his mind lost in a cocktail of obvious but painful thoughts.

Chapter 54

Martha threw her jacket into the bedroom as she walked down towards the kitchen, almost finding the chair by the tall chest of drawers. It was 9:30pm and, like each of the five days before, she felt physically drained. The backs of her calves felt tight, her shoulders tense and her neck a little stiff. She touched her toes five times thinking she needed to stretch her back, remembering on the first how much she'd always disliked PE.

For all that she felt weary in body, she was anything but tired mentally. On the contrary, her mind was full of scenes and snippets from the six days she'd spent being a detective for real.

Mechanically, she prepared a sandwich for toasting: cutting and buttering the bread; slicing the cheese and tomato; fitting the bits together; grinding on plenty of black pepper; then sliding the thing under a now red-glowing grill. She drank a small glass of coconut milk while washing and cutting up some celery, digging out a twee little porcelain dish she'd found in a junk shop in Cambridge. Although chipped, it had a lovely leaf pattern and, coolest of all, a little recess for the crushed salt.

She poured herself a large glass of red wine, turned the half-done sandwich over and then took the celery and wine into the lounge, switching on the radio as she headed back to the kitchen. Taking a plate from the wall cupboard she cut the now ready sandwich in half, put the used knife and oven tray in the sink, switched off the grill and headed for her favourite chair.

All this without thinking of anything but the investigation and the now on-going hunt for Eloisa DiMaria.

The day had been both amazingly exciting and deeply frustrating. For all that they had solved the case, there was simply no telling how long it might now take to find Eloisa.

They had, of course, to assume she still had possession of the gun. But for all the possibility that she might use it against Roberto had to be taken as real (were she to learn and/or admit to herself the truth) the chances of her discovering where her true father was seemed slight. Put another way, they - most specifically, Rosie and Roberto - truly believed Magdalena would tell them if her daughter made any contact. Quite how the girl might respond to an attempted arrest, however, was obviously hard to predict.

During the day Gurmel, Gerard and the Superintendent had spent several hours with colleagues at Lewisham.

Gerard had been full of praise for Lewisham's new DCI, a guy called Phil Snell who Gurmel had briefly met during his time at Croydon where Snell had been a DI. With Sonja Szabo - who they all thought they could trust given her understanding of the Phillips interview - they had reviewed activity in Forest Hill during Eloisa's time there, and in particular anything that could connect to cigarette smuggling. A few half-thoughts and could-be ideas did pop up and the four of them took a ride around the area.

The Superintendent and his counterpart - an evidently highly-committed but also highly-strung woman called Gill Adey - spoke to a number of those who had worked with and managed Eloisa during her two years as PCSO. Interestingly, she'd been mentored by three different PCs, the main reason being - said her Sergeant, Patricia Reynolds - that she complained about the first two seemingly spending half their time trying to ask her out.

This general idea of someone uneasy with the attention her beauty brought was given a different gloss by a couple of women who'd been in her joining group, both of whom were now PCs. They said that right from Day 1 in training Eloisa had always seemed irritated when forced to be the centre of attention, yet at the same time got quite sullen whenever she felt she was being left out of something or other.

No-one was aware of Eloisa having any especially close friends in the borough.

The reports from her two failed interviews to make Constable were almost identical in recording that, whilst the core of her answers was sound, too often she drifted into over-intense, almost obsessive elaboration. The panels had both worried whether she would be capable of handling a number of competing priorities.

Almost as an after-thought - inspired by an aside from the scratch-CID team, who had thought to take a quick look at Phillips' seemingly empty place - the two Superintendents went looking for Sergeant Nancy, learning to Adey's evident surprise that she'd been granted a week's leave despite the Olympics' moratorium.

O'Neill explained that the leave - to attend her sister's wedding in Latvia - had been booked for well over a year. Apparently, the entire extended Nancy family were travelling - literally by trains, boats and planes - to the country the grandparents fled at the end of the war. In the circumstances, O'Neill had insisted, he really didn't feel he had any choice.

As to Eloisa, he had obviously learned of the direct connection with the Phillips case from his wife. He did also recall Zeta suggesting Eloisa DiMaria as a possible for a support post they'd had, dependent though on her making Constable. Beyond any lose work connection though, he'd never heard of Zeta and Eloisa being friends and in any case he would swear on anything that his Sergeant would have nothing but contempt for someone capable of killing another officer.

One possibility did suggest itself though. The fact that Zeta's week away had been such common knowledge for so long amongst colleagues meant there was a chance that Eloisa had noted it also. For all their training, police officers were as liable to leave a spare key under a favourite plant pot as anyone else. Given that the flat was not very far from Phillips' place, O'Neill offered to deploy a two-man team - one armed - through the night to look for any sign of life in either.

Closer to home, Superintendent Mitchell decided, on the back of a conversation about possible places Eloisa might find a bolt-hole, that a patrol around the Mottingham estate where the Watkins' had previously lived made sense. He also decided - as a precaution, without gainsaying the idea that the chances were slim of Eloisa now knowing both who and where her real father was - to place a guard at Roberto Gallini's Hotel, once it became clear he would be staying another night.

As Martha finished her sandwich the 10pm news began. Feeling, if anything even more awake and alert, she took her plate and dish to the kitchen, returning with the bottle to refill her glass.

Inevitably, the news announcer could not wait to get onto the Olympics. Evidently Chris Hoy and Laura Trott - who Martha had at least now heard of - had both won yet more gold on their bicycles. Meanwhile, two previously unheard of brother's had come first and third in some ridiculously heroic event of running, swimming and bike riding. While someone else she'd never heard of had made bronze at the high jump. But, interestingly - for Martha, at least - the British team had won the Dressage event at Greenwich, one of the few things she would happily have gone to watch had leave not been cancelled.

As she sipped her wine the newsreader moved onto a story about the Church of England selling its shares in News International, evidently because of the phone hacking thing. Confusingly, having not given the story her full attention Martha was left unsure what their problem really was. There didn't seem to be any suggestion that the Archbishop of Canterbury's phone had been tapped. Although maybe that was the problem: perhaps journalists' disinterest in the Church's thoughts on the latest celebrity sex-scandal was a metaphor for fading significance?

The next item was more disheartening, delivered now in a hushed and sorrowful tone. Kent Council had been fined - or something like that - for refusing to find a home for a sixteen year old boy thrown out by his mentally ill mother. The background was a sad list of bad-breaks and worse choices, all of which left the kid a thief and a drug-addict, living in a tent somewhere outside Dover.

Taking another sip of wine Martha reflected on the luck of life. But for a callous, unsympathetic decision - which for all anyone would ever know, Stefan Gallini may often have regretted - Eloisa DiMaria would have grown up in privileged circumstances, going to one of her country's best schools, followed by a top university somewhere in Europe or the US.

For sure, Magdalena had worked as hard as she could to make things good for her daughter. But Scadbury College was hardly a first rank school, as was perhaps borne out by the fact the girl then signed up for Art, Design & Media Studies at the South Bank University. Presumably she choose one of England's weakest institutions simply to be near home. But, if she'd been a serious prospect at anything important then King's or UCL would have snapped her up in no time. Then again, someone serious would have lasted more than a year wherever she went.

Of course, to Kylie Smith the life Eloisa had lived would look like unimaginable privilege. It was curious - Martha thought without actually worrying whether it really was statistically odd - that she, Eloisa and Kylie should be pretty much the same age. In another lifetime they might have all gone to the same school, the same drama classes, the same riding school, the same any number of other things. They might have been three best-friends - loyal to each other yet fiercely competitive, each determined to get the best grades, the best clothes, the best part in the school play, the best university place, the best boyfriend, etc.

Instead, Kylie had seemingly been destined from a young age to make a living selling herself. That was achingly sad. She may not have been blessed with Eloisa's stunning looks, but there was still a prettiness about her. She was also sharp and caring in her own hard-shelled way. In fact, in many ways her life - as crappy as she might see it - could be seen by others as infinitely better than Eloisa's. Because, for all that she might feel she'd already thrown much of it away, something in her background, in the way she'd grown up, in the values - or whatever she might call them - that guided her had at least stopped her throwing away any chance of a different future.

And what about Candy and Jade Lee, who was going to put something good into their lives? Maureen Freeman might try, but she hardly had a reservoir full of happy experiences to draw on for inspiration. Likewise their mother. Likewise Kylie. And, in all probability, any other well-meaning soul living on that soulless and soul-destroying estate.

Compared to them, what did Eloisa have to complain about?

But of course, we only know what we know. And having seen the incredibly gentle and respectful way Roberto and Lena had greeted each other, Martha could not stop herself wondering whether the two of them - ridiculously young though there were at the time - could have made a go of it together. With all the support a rich and well-connected family could offer or buy, surely they could have?

In that context, Stefan Gallini had a lot to answer for.

Having left Roberto and Lena alone for a while, the DI spoke to them both together - with Martha just a silent witness this time. It took Rosie less than a minute to conclude that Lena really did not know where her daughter could be. She knew of no close friends, nor did she think the girl had either the money or the intention of leaving for Switzerland. So, Mrs Kathleen Watkins was formally charged with harbouring an offender and released on bail which Roberto guaranteed.

Taking a long, slow sip of the now perfectly-warmed wine, Martha pondered the vagaries of her job. She still wasn't really sure why she'd decided to join the police. It was hardly a common career choice for a Paulinas. The alumnae of her famous (to say nothing of expensively exclusive) school included writers and doctors, actresses and musicians, as well as the odd politician, journalist and sportswoman. But as far she knew, no-one else had sought to make it as a detective.

Insofar as any answer seemed to work - well, other than some hint of rebellion: refusing to join her father's advertising company or follow her mother and sister into teaching - it had always been the appeal of being a Maigret, Marlowe or Poirot.

Sure, it was all a bit romantic and she'd never been stupid enough to think the job would not be gory and dispiriting some of the time, frustrating and disappointing lots of the time. But to be given the responsibility of examining some unwanted and unacceptable event, collecting and sifting evidence to work out who made it happen and why, that had always looked like something worth doing.

And now? Well, albeit after just one case, she could see that, in the real world, evidence was fickle. It was like a breadcrumb trail mice had got at. It shifted about, it said different things to different people. It even said different things at different times to the same person. For sure, when she'd first tracked through the connection Superintendent Mitchell had made to Gerry Green, the possibility that the whole affair was linked to another, more organised, crime had seemed plausible. Then, the more the DCS and DI had become obsessed with old gold and modern gambling, the more sceptical she had become.

In the end, the facts had proved her right. Yet actually, the evidence Jeremy and Rosie put together did make a pretty compelling case for arresting Hamilton Battersby. And it turned out that funny little man was guilty of being both weak and dishonest, so in a way they did achieve some good. But supposing Battersby hadn't had such an obvious alibi? Would the case against him have run on and on, notwithstanding his admission to being a fool but denial of a being a killer?

And what about luck? How can you stay sane knowing that the difference between success and failure depends on luck. For all that it had been straightforward diligence that had got her to Phillips, on another day that throwaway comment of his about recent police interest in Ian Green simply wouldn't have been made. Or if made, not spotted. Or if spotted, it's significance simply not grasped.

Machiavelli regarded fortune as a woman in need of dominance. Well, setting aside the old political-fixer's chauvinism, what if one day you get out of bed too fed-up to make your own luck? What happens then?

Was that what happened for Charlie; he forgot to make his own luck? If she needed one reason to stay, to give the best of herself to such a fickle and frustrating job, then it was Charlie Scales. She knew that if and when she told her mother she'd worked on a case involving the killing of a police officer she'd face daily pleading, backed-up by tears, for her to quit. But the fear of being killed trying to save decent people from the likes of Ryan Kenny was really no great fear to her at all. The fear of not catching someone who would kill someone like Charlie, apparently for no better reason than to create a diversion, that was truly scary.

Wednesday, 8 August 2012

Chapter 55

Having all been at their desks for at least a quarter of an hour, the team plus Superintendent Mitchell met in Rosie's office just after 8am.

The reports from the various patrols in Forest Hill and Mottingham were disappointing, if hardly surprising. Similarly, news from Roberto Gallini's Hotel was no news.

After a morale-boosting little talk about how impressed he was by the detective work that had got them to where they were now, Mitchell had observed wryly that finding Eloisa DiMaria was going to be nigh-on impossible without some better intelligence on possible friends, favourite places, etc. So, that was what he wanted Rosie and the team to focus on.

Meanwhile, he and Superintendent Adey had agreed - although he admitted this was largely because they had no better idea! - they would each deploy some people in both Forest Hill and Mottingham, looking around, asking around, showing Eloisa's photo around. He wasn't exactly hopeful, but then again, he'd be foolish not to at least give it a go.

In answer to Gerard's question about an international arrest warrant, he said he and DCS Benson had caught a quick word on that last night, with the DCS offering to go into the Yard to sort it out before coming back down to Bromley later in the day.

Once Mitchell had gone, they'd spent a fruitless half hour trying to work out where to start, in the end all but giving up. For all that Rosie wanted to emphasise her agreement with the Superintendent's call for fresh intelligence, in the end she more or less suggested that until better ideas turned up it might make sense for Gerard and Gurmel to go over to Forest Hill and see what the Lewisham team found, seeing as they were now known to colleagues there. Similarly, she thought she might take a ride out to Mottingham.

Which left Martha and Jo with the chauffeuring job. Roberto Gallini's flight was leaving at 10:05 and the DI thought it would be worthwhile them taking him, if only to see if he had any further reflections following his meeting Magdalena.

The trip over to London City Airport was easy and pleasant enough, but for all that he was unfailingly attentive it was obvious that Roberto Gallini had a mind-full of difficult and conflicting thoughts which, in all decency, Martha and Jo didn't feel they had any right to disturb. So, having parked in the short-stay, walked into the terminal building with him as a courtesy, they said their thanks and headed back to the car.

"Happiest days of our lives ..." Martha mumbled after a few minutes silence.

"Sorry?" Jo asked while trying to find the right exit from the somewhat confusing car park.

"School. Someone said that to me the other day: happiest days of our lives ..."

"Yeah, well," Jo sneered. "Can't say I agree. I hated school."

"You hated it? Really?"

"Well, maybe hate's a bit strong. But I certainly wasn't hanging around any longer than I had to," Jo smiled, content now that she was on the road back to the Woolwich Ferry. "No doubt you loved it?"

"Hmm," Martha pondered. "No, I think I'm with you inasmuch as I don't think extremes really get it. I didn't love it, but I certainly didn't hate it either. There were things I liked, people I liked ... And things I didn't ..."

"And people you didn't?"

"Yeah, sure," Martha giggled. "Miss Stephenson, took English. Harridan of a woman."

"I suppose it must make a difference which school," Jo pondered.

"You think? I don't know, I mean you only know what you know. You might have hated my school, I might have loved yours ..."

"Trust me," Jo laughed. "You would very much not have loved mine! Anyway, what's the point?"

"If you had to, could you find your way around your old school? Right now, even in the dark?"

"Martha Cunningham, you are a genius," Jo cried.

"You think?" Martha asked, just a little touched by shyness.

"No wonder you went ... Where is it you went?"

"Cambridge you mean?"

"Yes ..." Jo sighed admiringly if just a tad jealously: "Genius, total genius."

Chapter 56

To say the least, Rosie was highly sceptical of Martha's latest little theory. For all that she accepted Jo's point that it was no less plausible than the ill-focused and so far totally result-free patrolling of streets in Forest Hill and Mottingham, the fact they'd already wasted a good deal of officer time on speculative action justified more circumspection.

Gerard was equally dubious, although that seemed to owe most to his own total disaffection with every minute of his own schooldays, meaning he could not imagine anyone - even a triple murderess with few other options - voluntarily going back.

By the time, just after 3pm, they all - Superintendent Mitchell and the DCS included - poured into the room for yet another debrief, a combination of frustration, tiredness and the recognition that Martha had been right before made Rosie at least open the idea up.

To Martha's uncontrollable delight, Jeremy and the Superintendent were instantly on her side, reasoning that if Eloisa had simply been unable or unwilling to get herself out of the country, it was certainly plausible that she would seek to hide in a place very close to home. Rational, because she might well think the police would assume she'd get as far away from the scene of her crimes as possible. Indeed, as a former officer it was actually very likely she would make that assumption. Rightly, given the initial scepticism shown to Martha's idea!

And more than that, she would have known that apart from a few administrative staff and gardeners, the place would be as good as empty for the next few weeks.

Yes, the more you think about it, Rosie had finally accepted, it actually does make sense. A kind of in-plain-sight hiding place.

And so a plan was made. Given the time, Martha and Jo were released to make contact with Mrs Fairley. Obviously it was touch and go whether she'd still be at the school, so they rushed down to the car pool, Martha then ringing on her mobile while Jo broke as many traffic rules as she needed to get out of a busy Bromley centre. They did indeed get to the school too late but, after wandering around in aimless anger they found a small plaque by the main gates with an 'in case of emergency' number. That connected to the School Caretaker - who lived five minutes away - and yes, of course, he replied breezily, he had a number for the Secretary.

While Martha and Jo cleared the idea of action with Mrs Fairley - who decided she'd just have to agree all this herself seeing as she doubted Mrs Barrington-Hawkes would have her phone turned on in the deepest Languedoc - Superintendent Mitchell sorted out a small team of six uniform plus two armed officers.

After some simple thinking, the discussion had concluded that the most obvious strategy was a visit to the school at twilight. If their thinking was correct, Eloisa DiMaria would have no reason not to put on some kind of light - the school was completely cut off from any outside observation.

Time seemed to drag desultorily. Having had a decent briefing with the uniform team, including the by-now serial volunteers of Wilco Wilkins, Steve Collins and John Connelly, everyone was given a couple of hours free-time. The plan was to leave for Scadbury College at 9pm. But what can you do with such time?

Having rejected, out of lethargy, a variety of suggestions, Jo, Martha and Gurmel accepted Gerard's idea of a walk over to the large Weatherspoons where at least they could get a sandwich and half-decent coffee.

Although not one of them was going to admit it, they were nervous. Maybe each in a different way, yet inevitably all in the same way: for all that they could guess at some of the uncertainties, anger and jealousies that may have driven Eloisa DiMaria, the fact remained she had killed one (anonymous to her) police officer, so presumably she would kill another if she thought she had to.

As a refuge from such dispiriting thoughts, they let their conversation drift into the comfort of intra-office gossip. Gerard said he understood Jeffrey had been back all day, but didn't leave his room. More intriguingly still, DCS Benson had evidently spent something like an hour and a half with him. Much longer - so had reasoned Jeffrey's secretary - than might have been needed to explain the Harris business.

After much evidence-free debate they concluded that Jeffrey was too confused by self-importance to be a crook like Harris. A conclusion that inevitably led them to wondering about when he might just fade away into retirement.

Then, led mercilessly by Jo, the three TDCs teased and bullied their Sergeant into an admission that, yes, of course, if Rosie became DCI then he'd hope, you know, but there were others …

Like who!? Jo had burst, never that Maggie Pugh! She's as hopeless as they come … Nah, you're a shoe-in. And for brains, you should get them to make our girl here Sergeant, she'd smiled seriously while nodding to Martha.

Jo!, Martha had exclaimed, embarrassed and shy. Oh don't worry, Gurmel had suggested resignedly, I doubt there's anyone here with the imagination for that.

By 8:30pm they were in the Main Briefing Room, collecting vests, radios and other equipment.

Having picked up a set of remarkably well-labelled keys from the Caretaker, the entire team, led by Superintendent Mitchell, walked down the tree-lined driveway into the school. Making use of various trees, bushes and the odd outbuilding, they worked their way around to the side of the main building.

So far, they had not caught any sign or sight of life in the school.

The rear of the school was more complex than the front, with bits of building poking out in all sorts of unhelpful directions. So, after a very quick chat they decided on two things. First, the need for local knowledge - with Gerard dispatched to persuade the Caretaker to join them. Second, to split into four groups: one, to be led by Sergeant Wilkins, would go back and watch the front of the school; the other three - led by the Superintendent, Rosie and Jeremy - would fan around behind the rear.

It was a little after 10pm when, with hope fading faster than the summer light, Gurmel spotted it, a dim glow in a small window on the second floor. Relishing his moment, the Caretaker spent a theatrical couple of minutes calculating the best way to ensure not just quiet entry into the building, but also the guarding of all possible exits from what he knew instantly to be the Languages Suite.

At 10:15, with the gentlest of taps on the door the Caretaker identified, Rosie said: "Eloisa, this is the Police. If you still have the gun please put it down. Otherwise we will have to shoot you when we enter ..."

There was no reply.

Reprising their Marsfield roles, Steve Collins and John Connelly took the shields with Bromley's most experience marksman, Bobby Ford, tucked in behind. Rosie tried the handle, finding it unlocked. With slow determination she twisted the knob and pushed the door open, letting Steve and John take one long stride into what was a large room with an assortment of tables and chairs, bookcases and cupboards.

"Hello," the mesmerisingly pretty young woman sat calmly by the window smiled.

"Eloisa DiMaria," Jo said quietly as she and Martha walked slowly between Steve and John, crossing the room confidently. "I am arresting you on suspicion of the murders of Ian Green, Charles Scales and Stefan Gallini. You do not have to say anything, but it may harm your defence if you do not mention, when questioned, something which you later rely on in court. Anything you do say may be given in evidence ... do you understand?"

"Yes."

Chapter 57

"Interview commencing 23:11, Wednesday, 8 August 2012. Present Detectives Hartley and Cunningham. Your full name please."

"Eloisa Ānaïs DiMaria."

"And your date of birth and address please," Martha asked.

"27 January 1988. 7 Telson Court, Crest View Drive, Petts Wood."

"Thank you. You have been arrested on suspicion of murdering Ian Henry Green, Constable Charles Renwick Scales and Stefan Mathias Josep Gallini. Bearing in mind your rights, which you have said you understand, is there anything you want to say in this matter."

"No," Eloisa replied, sitting up straight and calm, her eyes looking slowly from Martha to Jo and back again.

"Oh well," Martha shrugged before turning to face Jo, picking up on an old conversation. "So really, I was like you. I mean, everyone was getting one at college. Carrying it around like the latest proof of how important they were ..."

"You know, that's my impression of Cambridge as a whole. Full of snobby people - no offence," she smiled. "Wanting the world to know how clever they are."

"Well they *are* clever," Martha insisted. "But you're right. Far too many are also just so convinced that their college or their family or their ambitions are simply *the* best. Then again, there's only one thing worse than showing everyone how well you're doing and that's having them know you're not exactly on the up. I cried for a week during my first year because I didn't get an invite to the Rowing Club Ball ... so embarrassing!"

"Must have been. Lucky for us you pulled through," Jo smiled.

"Thank you," Martha nodded with theatrical humility. "So anyway, I resisted. I couldn't see the point. Or more to the point, I couldn't see anything it could do with it that I couldn't do on my little laptop ..."

Jo and Martha each, from the corner of their eyes, watched Eloisa, judging by the nanosecond the girl's mood and, in particular, her willingness to accept being ignored, being left out.

"That's how I see it now," Jo replied.

"Yes, because it's true ... But," Martha smiled. "The thing is, if you just want to browse or read a book or look something up, it's just so much quicker. And, let's be honest, it does look so cool ..."

"What are you talking about?" Eloisa interrupted irritably.

"The iPad," Martha replied. "Do you have one?"

"Yeah, of course ..."

"See, there you go," Martha smiled to Jo, as in: I rest my case. "Your father's got the iPad mini," she continued to Eloisa. "I do think they are neat ..."

"My father?"

"Yes, he was using it earlier to check that his flight was leaving on time ..."

"What are you talking about," she snapped.

"I just told you," Martha replied. "The iPad mini. Your father has one. Funky red cover too ..."

"Look, I don't know what kind of stupid childish game you think you're playing, but if you've nothing else to say to me then ... Why then, you'll have to let me go, won't you!" Eloisa insisted defiantly.

"Eloisa," Martha began patiently. "Let's just get one thing very clear. You are not going to be released. On the contrary, you will be charged, tried and - I have no doubt - sent to prison for quite a time. Prison is not going to be very much fun for you, either. It's not just the guards who dislike those who kill police officers, it's the prisoners themselves. Add into that the fact that you were once in the police ... Well, like I said. It's going to be difficult for you ..."

"You think I care?"

"No, I doubt you do. I would imagine you thought you would get away with it, but you're not stupid ..."

"I'm not, I never was. I don't know why ..."

"Yeah, yeah," Martha interrupted dismissively. "You don't know why you didn't make Constable. Well, if it's any consolation, we don't either. Then again, that's got nothing to do with the point I was making. I was thinking you must have known there was a risk you'd get caught. So, given that, I accept what you just said. You don't care it's all going to be hideous for you."

"Yeah, well ..." Eloisa replied, a little sadly now.

"But what I'm not clear on is this: how does it feel knowing that it was all for nothing? That you got it so wrong?"

"What ... what do you mean?"

"Look, for someone who thinks she's not stupid you are being incredibly dim. Who did I just say has an iPad mini?"

"Nah, you're just playing some sick game," Eloisa snarled. "I don't have a father."

"No Eloisa, that is not true," Martha replied kindly, sympathetically. "You killed the wrong Gallini. You now no longer have a grandfather. But your father, he is very much alive ..."

"Look, you're just trying to mess with me. Fuck my head about. That kind of shit ..."

"No Eloisa. No we're not. Tomorrow, if you want, you can talk to your mother. She will confirm what I'm saying. She met with your father yesterday. Today, he's gone home to Switzerland to bury his father - your grandfather - but he'll be back in a few days. Whether you want to see ..." Martha pondered, watching the first tear falling from the girl's eyes. "Well, we'll see, we'll see ..."

"No, no," Eloisa replied, her lips pursed, her throat trying to swallow back the tears, her eyes blinking like a scared rabbit caught in the headlights of a runaway truck called Despair.

"Yes, I'm afraid Yes," Martha whispered. "Eloisa, it really is none of my business why you decided it was reasonable and necessary to murder the man you believed was your father. Maybe, even though Stefan Gallini wasn't that, you can still justify to yourself what you did because of the way he treated your mother. He did dismiss her. Threw her out of his house knowing she was pregnant with his son's child ... his grandchild."

"He knew that?"

"Yes," Martha nodded. "And when you do talk to your mother, please don't try to blame her for not telling you these things. She tried to bring you up innocent of the trauma she had to live through. Equally, I don't think you can blame your uncle - who obviously knew most of the truth - for then guessing wrong on the one point of fact your mother chose to keep secret to herself. Because the only person who deserves blame for the deaths of Ian Green, Charlie Scales and Stefan Gallini is you ... Isn't it, Eloisa?"

"Yes," Eloisa sighed, gentle trickles of tears rolling down either side of her cute nose, skiing off her pouting lips to fall, moments later, onto the unlovely cream formica of the table top.

"Thank you for that," Martha nodded.

"What ..." Eloisa sniffled. "What's my father's name?"

"Roberto. And for what it's worth, I have no doubt at all that until I told him yesterday, he had no idea of you. None whatsoever ..."

"I see, OK. Thank you."

"Where's the gun?"

"Behind some books in my room at Dr Nichols' ..."

"OK, we'll get it. And your old uniform?"

"In a bag on top of the wardrobe."

"The gun, it belongs to your uncle Guillaume?"

"Uh-huh," Eloisa nodded, her eyes betraying a now troubled mind. "The Constable ... Scales you said?"

"Yes?"

"You knew him, I guess ..."

"Yes Eloisa. He was a friend to Detective Hartley and me."

"I see ... I ... I don't know what to say ..."

"Best say nothing then," Martha replied stony-faced, tears forming in the corners of her eyes.

Epilogue

Chapter 58

The Thursday had been anticlimactic in some ways, ineffably sad in most ways.

Having not got away from the station until after 1am, Martha and Jo had been given the morning off to sleep and rest. Inevitably, though, neither could do much of either. Given she'd had to drive, Jo picked Martha up on the way in, the two of them walking onto the CID floor just before noon to be greeted by beaming, congratulatory smiles from Gerard and Gurmel, plus a small bunch of tulips and a bar of Toblerone left on each of their desks.

"Steve and John brought them up," Gurmel explained, needlessly really as both Jo and Martha were already reading the small, carefully written labels.

"From Terry and Gloria also," Jo nodded, her words choking in her mouth.

"Yeah, they said," Gurmel smiled sweetly. "John's spoke to them both. They just wanted to say thanks ..."

"But ..." Martha began, stopping as DI Russell suddenly appeared.

"I just wanted to say, well done," the tall, always worried looking DI said. "From what I hear," he continued, looking from Martha to Jo and back again. "Exceptional work, very well done."

"Thank you Sir," Jo replied, a little, for her, shyly.

"Yes, but it wasn't as though it was just us," Martha protested. "Gerard, Gurmel ..."

"Martha, trust me," Gerard smiled. "I would never have solved this case ..."

"And I just take the photos," Gurmel suggested, his big, brown eyes shining with self-deprecating good nature.

"Like I said," Ray Russell repeated before leaving. "Exceptional work, well done."

Martha re-read the little card attached to the tulips. "Did Gloria write these, d'you think?" she asked of no-one in particular.

"Not sure," Gurmel answered.

"Well, 'with love from Terry, Steve, John and Gloria' doesn't sound like a guy thing," she giggled.

"I haven't seen her," Gurmel pondered. "In fact, I'm pretty sure they said Terry would be back next week, but not Gloria ..."

"Maybe she dictated it ..." Jo suggested, her bottom lip still trembling. "Aw, that's so lovely ... even if I can't say I feel like I especially deserve it. All I do is the driving," she giggled, walking round to give Martha a girly hug. "And make the coffee. Who wants what?"

The team spent the best part of an hour chatting slowly and contentedly about the previous six days, sharing out the chocolate, drinking their way through two rounds of coffees and, without making a big deal of it, listing out what needed to be done now.

Yet throughout the conversation, Martha could not stop herself thinking about all the lives the whole affair had affected. All the victims. And, for all that she felt as sad as everyone else for the pitiless, needless and so totally undeserved death of Charlie Scales, she was finding it increasingly difficult to hate Eloisa DiMaria. She hated what the girl had done, but at the same time she felt she too was a victim.

Not a victim like Lorrietta, Marjoria and Geri Scales. Nor like Marianna, Petra and Michael Gaulter-Gallini. Nor like the Greens. Or Roberto Gallini and his sister and brother. Nor indeed like the Cassidys, whose futures seemed now dependent on where Marianna decided to bring up her fatherless children. Nor even like Lena Watkins, who would now have to live the rest of her life knowing she had failed in the single ambition she had devoted herself to for virtually all her adult life: ensuring a happy and contented life for her only child.

Yet Eloisa DiMaria was also a victim. A victim of her own flawed and callous reasoning. A victim no doubt of some inflated sense of her own worth and purpose. But a victim also of one single act of thoughtless unkindness, committed before she was even born. For all that the cause and effect was complex - with plenty of crossroads along the way, at any one of which fate could have taken a different turn and so found a different outcome - Stefan Gallini's selfishness began the trail that led to Charlie Scales' death.

How little any of us know of the harm we cause.

Given her maudlin state of mind, Martha was miffed for no more than a nanosecond when the DI announced that Jo would be the Officer in the Case. Miffed for less time, therefore, than it took for Rosie to explain that she'd agreed some leave with the Superintendent, meaning Martha could take a long weekend.

It was an offer she was certainly not going to argue about. For nearly two months she'd been badgered by three college friends to join them on a little trip to Seville, turning them down again and again because all police leave had been cancelled. So, not wanting to miss a moment, she'd dug her iPhone from the bottom of her bag and walked out to the landing to make the call. As she finished she notice a text pop in. 'Well done. Let me know if ever you want a job at the Yard. Jeremy'.

How did he get my personal number, she wondered as she walked back to her desk, guessing the answer in Jo's childish grin.

The weekend in Seville was wonderful, glorious. The perfect tonic. The three friends were those she'd spent most time with at Cambridge yet, for one reason or another, the four of them had never managed to be all together for more than moments since. And so they spent their time chatting and laughing, reminiscing and gossiping while: visiting Alcazar, the Giralda, Casa Lebrija and the many museums; walking in the footsteps of Carmen and Don Juan, finding great tapas down every street; dozing in the shade or fooling around the pool in the late afternoon sun; before heading out into the still warm night to eat, drink and dance embarrassingly poor Flamenco.

Back at her desk the following Tuesday, Martha found herself alone. Gerard, Jo and Gurmel were all on leave. The morning was boring beyond belief. No-one to talk to and, worse still, a pile of unclosed files plonked on her desk by an unsmiling and seemingly rather tense DI. Have a look, see if you think there's anything more we could do, was all the advice or instruction she got.

The afternoon was totally different. The rumours had evidently been bubbling for a few days, so Erica Johnson had told her. Bang on 3pm, Rosie and Ray Russell had suddenly appeared on the section and led everyone who was there down to the Main Briefing Room, which was already full with various uniform colleagues plus, unusually, a goodly part of the traffic team.

Sat up front were Chief Superintendent Jeffrey, Superintendent Mitchell and, somewhat incongruously Martha thought, DCS Benson.

Jeremy was at his charming, witty and self-effacing best, explaining for those who didn't know him that he'd recently been in the borough on work-experience, following DI Charlton's team around. That got Rosie and Martha a round of applause, applause which undoubtedly also thanked this suave - but OK-really - Yard guy for getting rid of DCI Harris for them.

Then the announcement was made. Jeffrey was retiring: after serving the people of London with commitment and distinction for thirty-five years … And so on. The new Borough Commander was to be Chief Superintendent Mitchell, an announcement that brought huge cheers, whistling and a general atmosphere of such celebration Martha could not help but feel momentarily sorry for the obviously confused, if too dim to be crest-fallen, Jeffrey.

After it was all done, Jeremy stopped and had a chat with Rosie and Martha, touching on the case only to say both AC-Ops and the Commissioner had asked him to pass on their thanks and congratulations for excellent work. As he left he'd smiled knowingly at Martha, asking: did you get my text?

"What was all that about?" Rosie had asked nosily.

"Said if ever I wanted a job at the Yard ..." Martha had begun.

"Martha, your immediate future is here," the DI had insisted firmly as the two of them got back to the section.

"OK," Martha smiled. "I was only answering your question. And what about your future?"

"Not sure yet," was all the answer she was giving.

Gurmel was back on the Wednesday, and, after taking in the news about their new Borough Commander and the apparently on-going absence of news about who was going to replace Harris - and, now of course, take up the Super's old post - he jumped at the chance to get out.

Being in no especial rush, Martha had happily let Gurmel drive. It was a drizzly, miserable morning which made the miserableness of the Marsfield estate all the more crushing. The place itself was at least quiet: no boys on bikes, no Rumanians on guard, no anything at all frankly.

The door to 17 Tarn was opened promptly by a surprised and surprisingly friendly Kylie Smith. "Good Lord, Martha Cunningham ..."

"I'm flattered you remembered my name."

"Listen lady," Kylie smiled, while ushering them inside. "What you said to me ... Well, you were right. People's gotta stand up. And anyhows, you got him. That means something. You wanna coffee?"

Martha and Gurmel stayed for three-quarters of an hour, gently and subtly finding out all they wanted about the health and well-being of Maureen, Mary, Candy and Jade. But also and more importantly, the state of things now Kenny was off the scene. An uneasy truce seemed to be prevailing between the mysterious Mikey and the Rumanians. Some young guy called Dan was doing deliveries and collecting, but as far as Kylie understood it, the profit from Tarn was being shared.

As she listened Martha kept on fighting back the urge to offer to do something for Kylie, get her off that estate, find her a job. Something. Anything. She was, the more she watched and listened, someone worth investing in. Her accent was nothing like those of her college friends, whilst in so many ways her life experiences were probably beyond their comprehension. Yet there was so much about her that would have just fitted in so well during the weekend in Seville. Indeed, Martha was willing to bet, there was every chance Kylie was a much better dancer than any of them, and probably no less interested in gardens, oranges and dark-red wine. One day, she promised herself, I'm going to do something good for her.

Her reason for wanting to talk again to Lena Watkins was far less altruistic; selfish more like. The case was as good as done. Eloisa had confessed (including an admission to having forged her own references, using paper her mother had kept for scrap). There were therefore no charges for Lena to face. And Jo and Gerard had done an excellent job sorting out the paperwork.

Yet something still did not quite fit. Something in the theory that had led them to Eloisa felt, if not actually wrong, then incomplete.

Lena Watkins seemed genuinely pleased to see them, which was really rather sad. Yes, she'd seen her daughter a couple of times. Yes, also, she'd spoken to Roberto by telephone … and also her uncle, who was terribly upset, of course. Yes, at least for now she thought she would stay in England, not least because Dr Nichols needed someone to look after her …

The way that thought tailed off as good as admitted: and I don't really have anything else left to do with my life.

The missing piece, when it did just drift out during their conversation, took Martha back to her previous reflections on the uncertainties of the detective's craft.

She is already missing her running, Lena had said of her daughter.

Two gentle questions later and Martha saw that they had, on that fateful Friday, been closer to catching Eloisa than they had realised. The girl didn't walk the dog, couldn't stand the thing evidently. She ran. Always had. But perhaps more so than ever since returning the last time from Geneva.

That was the other activity, of course, that was so common in woods and open spaces that no-one even thinks to mention it. All those dog walkers they'd talked to only spoke of other dog walkers because ... Well, partly because they spent most of their time looking out for familiar human and canine faces. But also, because the questions they answered were asked by people who'd already decided their suspect was another dog walker.

It probably was nothing more than Eloisa's good looks that put Charlie off guard, but that was enough. It didn't really matter that three - supposedly trained to observe - officers had mistakenly seen the person running in sunglasses and a hoodie as a man. Steve Collins and John Connelly might, if they'd maybe been allowed to set off just a few moments earlier, have caught their 'weird guy' before she had a chance to commit the murder she'd already wasted two lives trying to set up.

Indeed, come to that, if only the three of them - Rosie, Gerard and Martha - had crossed that bridge a little later or a little more slowly, Eloisa DiMaria would have run into the back of them.

But that, of course, had been her cruel genius. It wasn't just hiding out in her old school that deserved an 'in plain sight' label, each step in her coldly calculated crime had been the same. A girl so local that no-one was going to take any notice of her and some guy walking down the street that Thursday morning. An oft-seen - to the point of not being seen at all - jogger in the woods on the Friday morning. And then, most calculating of all, just another anonymous policewoman walking down Manor Park amidst a flurry of curious but no doubt important activity.

Why didn't she just go after Gallini, why the callous use of Green and Charlie? It was pointless asking the question because it seemed unlikely Eloisa would really be able to put an answer into words. Yet Martha could not help thinking that the girl's rejection for Constable played a small, albeit subliminal part. Rejected by her grandfather, rejected by the police. Somehow, those disappointments had driven a reasonably intelligent girl into a madness no-one could or would ever forgive.

Chapter 59

For no better reason than a cussed fit of laziness, Martha was last in on the Thursday. It was the 16th of August, her last day as a twenty-three year old. What the hell, she'd thought as she lingered through her breakfast, rebel!

When she got there, just after 9:30am, the place was abuzz with speculation once more. Moments earlier, DIs Charlton and Russell had been called to Borough Commander Mitchell's office: must be about the DCI post, his secretary had told everyone.

It was an hour later when the team were called into Rosie's office to be told they weren't her team any longer. She'd been promoted to DCI. Yes, she was very happy, very proud, a little sad also for Ray, who was a good colleague (sub-text, so I think I can handle him) ... and so on. But the truth was written in her eyes: she was one ambitious lady who was pleased others had seen she was exactly the right person for the job.

"Now, if the rest of you will excuse me," she smiled. "I need a word with Gerard ..."

"Yes!" Jo had rasped as they walked back to their desks, making some silly finger in the air salute she'd seen a runner perform at the Olympics. "He gets DI, we all get to be made proper Detectives. Perfect."

"Sounds good to me," Martha agreed. "I mean, I'm not worrying about this probation thing, but even so ..."

"It would be nice to get it out the way," Gurmel completed.

"Exactly. D'you reckon they'll let all three of us stay together, you know, as Gerard's team?" Martha pondered.

"Can't be sure, can you," Jo replied a little pensively. "I mean, you should be OK, you were here first so that's only fair. But me and Gurmel ... Well, Russell's alright but even so, I can't say I fancy working with that Maggie Pugh again ..."

"Agreed," Gurmel nodded. "And this trafficking investigation DI Clarke's people are on doesn't sound very nice …"

"No, but …" Martha began. "Maybe, if it came to it, I could do that. I mean, don't you worry what's going on in that other block up on the Marsfield?"

"With the Rumanians … well, yeah, I suppose … Oh, hold on, here he comes," Gurmel whispered. "Act busy."

"OK team," Gerard breezed lightly. "Martha, you're next …"

"Me? Really, what for?"

"Mine is not and all that … DCI Charlton just asked me to ask you to pop in," he replied, holding his hands open to indicate powerlessness.

"Hi Martha, take a seat."

"OK ma'am, thanks," Martha smiled a little suspiciously.

As she sat she noticed the lace to one of her new pixie boots - black, soft ruffled leather, with a purple edge to the sole - was loose. So, she leaned down to retie it, fiddling a moment then with the narrow-bottoms to her otherwise baggy grey trousers before sitting back up, straightening the sleeves to her short black bolero jacket, another Seville purchase.

"You OK?" Rosie asked indulgently.

"Yeah, of course. Er … Det … hmm," Martha pouted a moment, hoping for a clue as to whether he was indeed now a DI. None came. "Gerard said you wanted to see me about something?"

"That is very true. I have here your Personnel File …"

"Really, what for?" Martha asked, even more suspicious now.

"Oh well, there are times when it has to be got out …" Rosie replied a little evasively while flicking through the thin, manilla folder. "Not a great photo …"

"Yeah, well. I was about to go off travelling, so it seemed a good idea. Guess you only find out short hair doesn't suit you after you've had it cut," Martha smiled ruefully while trying to see what it was the DCI was reading.

"So, it says here you went to St Paul's Girls School, then Newnham College, Cambridge ..."

"Er, yes ... And?"

"And that you got a First in something called the Classical Tripos ..."

"Yes," Martha nodded slowly, totally clueless as to where all this was going.

"... going to be difficult for you ..."

"Sorry ma'am?"

"I was just remembering something you said when interviewing Eloisa DiMaria. That was a truly exceptional interview. You know that, I suppose?"

"Know it ... er, well, I'm not sure. We just ..."

"I spoke to Jo about it, while you were away. Guess I should have thought to ask you, but I forgot. Anyway, she said you had the idea of ignoring DiMaria after hearing that feedback from her Initial Training ..."

"Yes ..."

"Not many people would have thought of that Martha," Rosie smiled. "I certainly wouldn't have ... But now I know why everyone thinks you're so clever," she continued, waving the folder playfully. "It's because you are! Yet that's my point. I rather suspect that when more people find out about your background ... Well," she sighed concernedly.

"But, sorry ma'am. I'm obviously being anything but clever here, so tell me: why would anyone be interested?"

"Who knows?" Rosie replied without answering.

"Sorry?"

"Who, out there I mean. Who knows that you went to what I believe is the best girl's school in the country and then took Classics under probably the only classicist most of us have ever heard of. And only then because of her comically unkempt appearance on television ..."

"She's ..." Martha began to object.

"Please Martha," Rosie insisted, holding her hand up to stop Martha's protest. "Just think for a moment. Who knows those things?"

"Well, no-one really ... Jo and Gurmel know I went to Cambridge. Not sure about Gerard ..."

"He didn't ..."

"So you told him?" Martha asked, pulling an irritated face. "Why?"

"Because, Martha," Rosie replied slowly. "Some people are going to be very, very jealous in ..." she looked theatrically at her watch. "Well, about now actually. Not Gerard, I hasten to add. Nor Jo or Gurmel. No, they all seem to be pretty much in awe of you ..."

"Ma'am, are you winding me up? Is this some kind of pre-birthday piss take ..."

"Martha, what would Professor Beard say about one of her best using such language?"

"Oh trust me," Martha laughed. "She uses far, far worse ..."

"In Latin and Greek, no doubt?"

"Oh yeah, of course!"

"Well I wouldn't know, but she looks like an OK lady on the telly. So I'd be willing to guess that if she knew what Gerard has just told Jo and Gurmel, she would be every bit as proud as they are ... And indeed, as I am ... Detective Inspector Cunningham."

"Sorry?" Martha said after some five seconds of stunned silence.

"Right, so here's the problem," Rosie began seriously, closing the file and leaning forwards across her desk, her eyes fixing Martha's. "Unless you are going to do something stupid like resign, you are going to walk back out there the youngest Detective Inspector, as far as Jeremy can tell ..."

"Jeremy?"

"Yes, I'll come back to him. But right here, like I just said, in a moment you will find lots of people wanting to say how truly wonderful they think it is that this crusty, chauvinistic, patronising, pedantic and, at times, downright infuriating organisation has decided to do something so thoroughly modern and sensible ... That is, promote you to lead one of the CID teams in my squad ..."

"You ... I mean ... No, you cannot ..." Martha gasped, finding it hard to concentrate. "Are you honestly telling me I just got promoted to DI?"

"Yes."

"Wow," she sighed, suddenly grasping the enormity of the moment. "Wow ..."

"And I'm also telling you that there will already be some out there, maybe on DI Russell's team, maybe DI Clarke's, or just elsewhere around the place ..."

"Does everyone know?"

"Yes, people like to know things Martha. So, while you've been in here, team leaders have been announcing my and your promotions. Mine might not be such a surprise. Yours ... well, let's be serious, it will be a shock. A huge shock, in fact. Not that you need be bothered about that. You are being promoted in this rather exceptional way because a few of us see in you someone with exceptional potential - that's me, Chief Superintendent Mitchell and DCS Benson and, through him of course, the Commissioner ..."

"But I've never met him ..."

"No, but you will in the next day or two. The point is, of course senior people think good things about you. As if they'd risk promoting you if they didn't. But others ... well I believe I can already here someone out there moaning about 'that posh little rich girl with friends in high places ...' And whether you like it or not Martha, soon enough someone will find out how much it costs to send someone to your old school ..."

"And that's not going to be much fun?" Martha smiled knowingly, remembering the intention she had when using that phrase with Eloisa. "Yeah, well, like I'm bothered," she continued confidently before pondering. "But all this, how could you ... I mean, you've only just found out about your promotion, haven't you?"

"Not quite, I was told last night. But you're right to assume it has taken more than a few hours to clear yours ..."

"So?"

"So you were going to be made DI today regardless of what happened to me. I'm just so pleased I did get the job of telling you," Rosie smiled. "Quite how I'm going to get on managing you, well we'll see," she giggled. "But I'm looking forward to it. Now, we'll need to do boring things like look at caseloads and all that later - there are a few changes I need to make between you, Ray and Steve Clarke's responsibilities ..."

"But you said Gerard knows ..."

"Yes. And for all he said he's hoping one day he'll make DI ... Well, as I'm sure he's dying to tell you himself, he totally thinks we've made the right choice and hopes you'll agree to him being your Sergeant ..."

"Jeez, that's going to be a bit odd ..."

"Yeah, well, I think you might as well get used to that Martha. I suspect we'll all end up calling you ma'am!"

"Oh yeah, as if ... And Jo and Gurmel?"

"Gerard's just ended their probation. That's your team, DS McAvoy and Detectives Hartley and Kandola ... So, as I'm not hearing you say you're going to resign, there are some people outside waiting. Oh, by the way, happy birthday for tomorrow ..."

"Thanks ... for everything ma'am."

"Rosie. From now on, it's Rosie."

"Woo-hoo," Jo as good as screamed as Martha walked out of Rosie's old office (soon to be hers) bounding down from her desk like a Fresher on the first day of Rag Week. "Woo-woo the fucking hoo," she sang, grabbing Martha in an agonisingly tight hug and spinning her round before more carefully placing her back on the ground, kissing her excitedly on both cheeks.

Next up were DIs Russell and Clarke, each quite obviously awestruck yet also genuinely delighted for her, politely shaking her hand while assuring her of their support should she need it.

Gurmel then placed his huge hands on her narrow shoulders and kissed her on the forehead, no words were - or needed to be - said.

Gerard, shy and awkward, just stood and smiled. "Don't worry, you deserve it far more than me, ma'am ..."

"Gerard McAvoy, don't you dare start with that ma'am crap," Martha burst.

"B-but, I can't not ..."

"Listen, you want to stay on my team? Learn!" she smiled before hugging him, then looking on benignly as the crimson blush flushed across his face.

As they got back to their bank of desks Jo's phone rang.

"Yes, this is Detective Hartley. Yes, that's right, I am ... Yes ... well it was, it's now DI Cunningham," she continued, smiling across to Martha. "What? ... Really?" she then gasped, her brow furrowed, her mood darkened. "When? ... So, you think what? ... I see, OK ... yeah, later then. Yes, fine, I'll tell her. Thanks."

"Well?"

"Well, Detective Inspector Cunningham," Jo began, pursing her lips while taking in what she's just heard. "That was Bexley. Gerry Green's been found dead. Hung himself, apparently!"

"What the fuck?" Gerard gasped.

"What the fuck indeed," Gurmel agreed.

"They thought we'd want to know, having seen his name connected to our case," Jo explained. "And suggested we talk later. Looks like suicide, but in the circumstances ..."

"Who's their DI?" Martha asked.

"Some guy called Lewis ... I said he could ring you later, that OK?"

"Of course, no worries. Right, I think it must be my turn to get the coffees," Martha suggested unaffectedly. "Who wants what?"

* * *

Continued in The Chislehurst Connection ...

The Chislehurst Connection
(The 2nd Cunningham File)

"Hiya," Erica smiled. "The Duchess not around?"

"Got some gig up at, oh ... what's that place called?" Gerard asked of Jo, apparently in earnest.

"Sandringham."

"That's the one. Whole family's there evidently ..."

"Of course. What was I thinking!"

"So, guess you'll have to make do with us!" Gerard apologised. "You have a good day yesterday?"

"Yeah, not bad, tell you the truth. Went to the boyfriend's parents. They're alright, till they get tipsy! Anyway, guess you want the story?"

"Please," Gerard and Jo replied, like children being offered jelly.

"Right, well, it's not much. You'll want to talk to the woman, Mrs Beatrice Lane, she ... Well, at first, she wouldn't say anything. Then she babbled away like there was no tomorrow. She does seem both scared and worried, so I think there may well be something serious to it. What she says is her husband, Denny, got a call just before 3am. She says it obviously worried him - she was only half awake but he seemed agitated, kept looking out the window ... Then he said he had to go to the garage ..."

"This garage?" Gerard asked, pointing to the double wooden doors a little way down the side of the house.

"No, over in Bexley. Seems Mr Lane has got some valeting place over there ..."

"OK," he nodded, a quizzical look on his face.

"He's a car cleaner ... at three in the morning?" Jo pondered.

"Quite!" Erica nodded. "So, I pressed her a little on what she thought he might have to go there for. She said she assumed the alarm must have gone off ... Evidently he had trouble with it a couple of months back ..."

"You checked that?" Gerard asked, a little too sharply.

"Hold on!" Erica chided. "No, is the answer. But I assumed, once you'd got all this, you would want to talk to Bexley. But this is the rest, as far as I got it. So, he goes out, a little after three. Half an hour later he rings her. Tells her she's to do nothing till he gets home. Don't answer the door. Don't ring anyone. Talk to no-one ... She said he sounded serious, like he was really worried, but wouldn't say anything more. So, she lay awake the rest of the night, waiting, fretting. She tried his phone a little after five, but it went straight to voicemail. At that time she looked out the front and saw this silver van parked opposite. Frankly, it could have been nothing," Erica observed, shaking her head slightly. "But I guess she was in a state. Anyway, the neighbours also saw a silver van leave at six-thirty ..."

"Ah yes," Gerard said, his face now a study in concentration and thought. "Trainspotter said it was a neighbour that called?"

"A Mr Wilkinson, lives here," Erica explained, pointing to the adjacent house.

"Why? Why'd he call?"

"Well, first off, I would say they don't seem like nosey fusspots or anything. He says he knocked for Mr Lane at nine as arranged - they were going to take their boys and a ball to the Rec, over there somewhere," she said, waving her arm vaguely in the direction of the shops. "Thought it odd he got no reply. Then thought he heard one of the Lane children sobbing. Then Mrs Lane trying to quieten the boy ... But still no answer."

"Well, if nothing else," Jo nodded. "You have to say he deserves some thanks ..."

"Agreed," Gerard accepted. "In fact, we must do that before we go ... so," he continued, looking to Erica. "What happened when you got here? Mrs Lane just open the door?"

"Well, No. We went next door first anyway, seeing as they made the call ..."

"Of course ..."

"And they both, Mr and Mrs Wilkinson, came with us here. We rang a couple of times, got no answer. Then, without a word to us, he leaned down and talked to Mrs Lane through the letterbox. Must have guessed she was in the hall. She opened the door and burst out crying. Mrs Wilkinson was great ... guess she needs thanking also."

"OK. So, what sort of a state is Mrs Lane in now?"

"Well, anxious still. But since she calmed down she's started to ask what we're going to do. Mary's with her ..."

"And the Wilkinsons?"

"They're still in. The lady stayed with Mrs Lane for a bit, then took the children in with her. There was a bit of noise out in the garden a moment back, so I guess they're being entertained."

"OK ... so what d'you think?" Gerard asked of Jo.

"What do I think!" Jo laughed. "How do I know ... But, on the face of it, she does seem to have some reason to be worried ... hmm," she paused, looking at Erica. "No hint of a marriage problem? For all we know, he went off to see some other Mrs Christmas and fell asleep ..."

"Guess you can never be sure ..." Erica thought. "Just ... well, the worry did seem real enough."

"And she has opened up to you," Jo nodded in thought. "Maybe best ..." she continued, looking to Gerard now. "If Erica and I go in and talk to her. A woman's touch?"

"Yeah, feels right to me too," Gerard nodded. "I'll go talk to the Wilkinsons. You say they also saw this van?"

"Yeah. When Mrs Lane mentioned it I sent Mary over to check. Evidently, Mrs Wilkinson was up doing something or other and opened the downstairs curtains just before the thing pulled away. She said she thought it odd. Didn't recognise it as one that's usually around here ..."

"OK. Sorted. You two go talk to Mrs Lane. I'll knock for the Wilkinsons ..."

"Presumably we want the address of this garage?" Jo checked.

"Yeah. Unless you get a sense of anything else, I guess we take a ride over there ... Better also get the make and registration of Mr Lane's car, we might as well put a search out on that."

Half an hour later they headed off towards the address in Bexley village. With Jo driving, Gerard rang the local station at Sidcup, getting through to a grumpy sounding Sergeant Brown. No, they'd had no report of an alarm going off at Lane's Valeting Services over night. Nor of anything else in the area.

"Has some fancy cars there, mind," Brown mumbled with a tad more enthusiasm.

"So, you know it?"

"Not to use. Happy cleaning my own car, thank you very much. It's by Carr's. Went there in, what, April I suppose. With the wife. Wanted a new patio. Waste of money that was, rained all summer-long, save for the bloody Olympics ..." the obviously habitually grumpy Brown continued.

"And Carr's is?"

"Big old gravel works. Pretty much worn out now. But they're good for stones, paving, that kind of thing. Not that you'd really want to give him your money ..."

"No, right," Gerard agreed to quieten the guy down. "So, we're on our way over there. Got a report Mr Lane is missing. May be suspicious ..."

"Bet you're going to say you want one of us to meet you there ...?"

"No, we ..."

"I'll get a car along," the guy announced with unexpected good humour. "You be long?"

"About fifteen ..."

"Blimey. Alright, leave it with me. McCoy you said ..."

"McAvoy ..."

"Right."

"Well, it's more than I was expecting," Jo commented as she pulled onto the shiny black forecourt of a rather imposing gun-metal grey warehouse.

"Yeah, me too ..." Gerard agreed.

Out of the car, they slowly took in the full 360. The road this far had been properly made, passing between a church and its vicarage on one side, a cemetery on the other. Tree-lined, clean and calm. Then suddenly, all that ended.

Beyond the tall and wide metal building that was Lane's Valeting Services, there stretched a vast moonscape, hemmed in - in the distance and all sides - by high escarpments, being the confirmation that what they were looking at was once a significant hill, or series of hills.

"The Sergeant at Sidcup said it was a big, old gravel works ..."

"Really?" Jo replied, her eyes gazing off to the left, seeing a train running along the edge of the quarry face. "Well, I guess big covers it ..."

"I really had no idea this place was here ..."

"So, what are those buildings?" Jo asked, pointing a way up a dirt track to what looked like an old house, with a few big sheds alongside.

"Carr's ..."

"Cars?"

"Oh, No, sorry," Gerard laughed. "I didn't spot that when he told me. But he said there was a yard beyond this ..." he recalled, pointing momentarily to Lane's. "Sells patio stones or something. Called Carr's ... Man, this is a bleak place," he added, his eyes scanning the area, from the elevated train line on the one side, to the far distance with its scattering of electricity pylons and then over to the right till his gaze fell back on Lane's. "OK, so let's take a look."

"No sign of Lane's van," Jo observed.

"Not much sign of anything!" Gerard mused as they walked towards the wide shutters in the middle of the building, there not being any obvious door - or even window.

"Aha, help's arrived," Jo suggested, nodding to the approaching patrol car.

"Detective Sergeant McCoy?" the portly, slightly florid Constable asked, hitching up his trousers as he got himself out of the car.

"McAvoy ..."

"Indeed ..."

"Gerard ..." Gerard offered, as friendly as a man can be when faced with complete indifference to the intricacies of his family name. "And this is Detective Hartley ..."

"Jo ..."

"Indeed," the guy nodded in mid-waddle. "I'm Constable Morris," he added, with a priggish formality that put Jo and Gerard in mind of their own Sergeant Tyler. "OK, so, you want to take a look, right?"

"Well, yes. Seems the owner, a Mr Lane ... obviously enough!" Gerrard laughed self-consciously while quickly glancing up to the bold, blue letters that spelt out the company name. "Seems he got called out last night. Wife thought it had to be an alarm problem ..."

"Nope ..."

"No, your Sergeant said. Which adds to the suspicion. A little while after leaving home, Mr Lane rang his wife, apparently in some agitation. Told her not to talk to anyone ..."

"But she did."

"A concerned neighbour ... but the place looks all locked up?"

"We'll see ..." Morris said, in something of a breathless gasp, the effort of waddling while fishing in the pocket of his coat for something or other seemingly all a bit too much.

"OK, there's an entrance round the far side ..." he added, nodding to the right corner of the building while shaking a small bunch of keys musically.

"Oh, right. You hold a set ..." Gerard said, unnecessarily.

"Only recently. There was some problem with the alarm a few months back, like you said. They keep some pretty valuable cars here ..."

"Keep them?" Jo asked.

"Yeah," Morris nodded as they reached a solid-looking steel door painted exactly the same shade of grey as the rest of the building. "Mostly, I think it's just stuff they're working on. But he also keeps a few for some people, hence all the security ..." he continued happily, nodding up to the little cluster of cameras peering each and every way around the corner of the building. "Typical," he sighed as last of three keys fitted the topmost lock.

Two more locks later and they were in, with which a shrill, piercing alarm went off.

"Hold on," Morris shouted over the din while finding a piece of card in another pocket. "Got the numbers here," he added, waving the note as he disappeared into the dark interior.

Seconds later the place was aglow with bright, white florescent light. Jo and Gerard stayed by the open door, watching as Morris made his way down to a desk pushed up against the metal wall and, reading from the card, punched a set of numbers into a small consul, the yellowy-orange flashing lights of which changed to a calming green the instant the shrill siren stopped.

"That works then," Jo laughed, her ears still ringing. "And that," she added, pointing across the clean, empty floor to the gleaming black VW parked on the far side, its nose barely a foot from the shutters. "Looks like it could be Lane's van,"

"You've been here before," Gerard noted more than asked of Morris as all three of them walked across to the van.

"Just the once, one of those alarm call-outs. A couple or three months back ..."

"But you knew about the cars ...?" Gerard asked, looking around a space that must have been something like fifty feet by thirty, empty save for scattered equipment and the black Transporter.

"Yep, this is it," Jo nodded, checking the registration.

"Being kept, you mean?" Morris replied. "Yeah, there were definitely a few on that last call-out and the Sergeant said, just now like, that there were a couple of old Ferraris being stored here when he came up. Kind of hoped to see them," he grinned disappointedly, his eyes pretty much following Gerard's own scanning of the place.

"No-one in the cab," Jo called from the far-side of the van to Gerard and Morris. "Which is locked ..."

"You gloved?" Gerard asked hurriedly.

"What you take me for?" the unseen Jo huffed.

"OK, come and try the back," he asked, before turning back to Morris. "So, you think it odd the place is empty?"

"Who knows? It's Christmas, guess anyone with a fancy car wants it at home or wherever to take for a ride ..."

"Maybe?" Gerard mused. "Thing is, we've had this other case going for a while now. Basically, details an insurer held on a number of expensive cars went missing, many of which have since been nicked ... Oh shit," he gasped as Jo opened the back door to the van.

Bound, gagged and lifeless lay the figure of a stocky guy in a grey tracksuit and garish green and blue trainers.

"That fit the description?" Gerard asked of Jo.

"Yep ..."

"Yeah," Morris agreed, unclipping a flashlight from his belt. "Pretty sure that's Lane," he nodded, the thin beam of light making the man's face look deathly pale.

"There's a pulse," Jo confirmed, leaning across the body, two fingers pressed gently against the neck. "But he feels pretty cold ..."

"OK, let's get an ambulance ..."

After carefully releasing Lane's binds and gag - conscious that they ran the risk of contaminating possible evidence traces - Gerard rang Erica Johnson. She and Mary Holmes had just left the Lanes'. Rather need you to go back, Gerard had explained. Mrs Lane needed to be told that they'd found her husband, seemingly drugged but otherwise apparently unharmed. She also needed to be asked if she knew where they could find information on any cars that might have been in the warehouse overnight.

Meanwhile, Constable Morris had checked with Sergeant Brown: No, they had never held any details of cars stored at Lane's, just knew that he often had a few there overnight. Separately, Brown had said he'd have no problem if Gerard wanted Bromley's SOCOs to take the van.

The Bexley Sergeant's selfless generosity meant, of course, that Gerard had to ring the always gracious Richard Bartholomew, head of Bromley's SOCO team, catching the guy in a moment of ungraciousness as he set off for a family lunch at Chapter One. Well, Gerard had accepted, there probably wasn't much to lose in having the van collected the following day.

As a long-shot, Jo had thumbed through her notebook and found numbers for both Kent Quinton & Patrick Driscoll, the insurance guys: getting no further than voicemail for either.

The three of them then kicked their heels for another twenty minutes or so, wandering the floor, noting out of boredom how clean the unguarded mechanism for the large lift at the far end was. No doubt the thing had a few uses, one of which was obviously to connect to a robust looking platform on which Morris recalled seeing a couple of cars on his previous visit.

Beneath that there were a few separated spaces: a small kitchen; a surprisingly neat and clean washroom; an office with one rather cluttered desk and two locked filing cabinets; and a storeroom with 5 litre bottles of various car-cleaning products neatly stacked on metal shelves. With Morris offering to make them a plain, black instant - no sign of any milk - Jo and Gerard had flicked through the lists, old receipts and cryptic notes on the office desk, none of which made any sense.

With the long-awaited sound of a siren in the distance, Gerard's phone rang. As was to be expected, Mrs Lane was now relieved and anxious at one and the same contradictory moment. Even so, Erica had managed to get two names and a telephone number out of her. Evidently Lane had a Cory Carpenter working pretty much full-time; and a Josh Blackett on Fridays, which was usually an especially busy day. Josh was a student though and, as far as Mrs Lane knew, he'd gone home to somewhere in the Midlands for the holidays.

The paramedics' first thought was, like Gerard's, that Lane had been drugged, probably with some kind of benzodiazepine to judge by the faint banana-like hint in the guy's shallow breath. Certainly, they could find no obvious wounds or contusions. Should be OK to talk the following day, they'd suggested - although depending on the specific drug used, he might stay drowsy and confused for a couple of days.

All of which at least left Gerard feeling less anxious about leaving their one piece of evidence unexamined till the morning. Having then managed to get no further than voicemail on the number Erica had given him for Cory Carpenter, he, Jo and Morris agreed they'd best lock up. Which the by now very bored Constable did with commendable pace and care, resetting the alarm and then all three locks to the door.

"So, what's your guess?" Jo asked as they followed Morris past the church, the Constable indicating right towards the village centre, she left, out towards the North Cray Road.

"What's my guess ..." Gerard pondered, looking out the window at the neat row of Victorian cottages. "Hey, hold on," he suddenly burst as Jo was about to shoot straight across the mini roundabout. "Hang a left ..."

"Er, why?" she asked, obeying.

"Just want to check something ... Well, I'll be," Gerard cooed a minute or so later as they topped the hill and pulled to a halt in the semi-circular entrance to a neat little estate, its selection of Art-Deco villas glistening in the drizzle. "This is where Gerry Green lives ... or lived."

"Really ..." Jo replied, making clear - without in any way meaning to - her total mystification as to the significance of the point. "Er, and?"

"And ... well, and nothing, I suppose!" Gerard laughed. "It just occurred to me, as we were driving out, that the houses on this side ..." he continued, pointing to those on the left. "Must kind of back on to that quarry."

"What a shame," Jo nodded, thinking that when the obviously expensive places were built they probably stood atop rolling countryside. Now they looked down on grey despoliation.

"Yeah ..."

"You don't think there's a connection?"

"Well, I could give it one of those grave never-say-never speeches the DCI is so fond of, but one thing's for sure: Green senior didn't do it!"

"Did Bexley ever clear that up?"

"As far as I know, it just got left as suicide. I mean, he hung himself ..."

"But, why?"

"Because someone had found out he was a poof!"

"But some people must have known that anyway," Jo protested, not without some logic. "Why'd he get outed? I thought that Bexley DI was interested in that question. Spoke to Martha a couple of times ..."

"Guess there wasn't enough to think it anything but sad. I mean, he obviously had his past, but he didn't seem that awful when we met him. But … well, poor guy: first his son gets killed for the same nothing reason as Charlie Scales; then someone outs him … Guess he'd had enough … come on," Gerard suggested.

"OK …" Jo nodded, pensively. "Go on then," she continued after doing a U-turn and heading back down the hill. "You were giving me your guess."

"My guess? Well, I think you've probably already made the most obvious connection. I bet a torn paper hat that there were a couple of cars there insured by Q&D …"

"A torn paper hat!?" Jo laughed.

"Yeah. Well I'm not letting you have my cracker prize from yesterday, best present I got! A policeman cannot have too many plastic magnifying glasses!"

"Is that a fact," Jo replied wryly, slowing down as she approached the mini roundabout at the village end once again. "But, if you think there's been a theft …"

"Well, don't you?"

"Like you said, seems likely. But if it's likely …" she continued, accelerating as the narrow lane became the North Cray Road dual-carriageway. "Shouldn't we have asked around a bit, see if anyone saw anything?"

"Ask who, that place was like the edge of the world …"

"The vicarage?"

"Oh yeah …"

"That little row of twee cottages … There must, surely, have been a bit noise. I dunno, trucks or something to take cars away?"

"You're right, of course you are," Gerard accepted without argument. "Guess … well, who's got a clear head on Boxing Day!?"

Five minutes later, after a minor detour to get off and then across the dual-carriageway, Jo parked up outside the rather modest sized, stone-built, Gothic-styled house. Both the church and its vicarage had been built to look old. But the perfection of the stonework, together with the neat red-tiled roofs, said very late nineteenth century. Probably same time as the cottages on the High Street. Probably all related, somehow or other.

However, as deserted as the quarry works - and, indeed, Lane's - had been, so was the vicarage and its locked up church. Presumably, after his big day yesterday, god's representative in this small parish had decide on a rest cure somewhere else.

"Oh well, we tried," Jo grinned disappointedly.

"We did. And I've just realised I forgot something else," Gerard acknowledged. "Lane's place had cameras ..."

"Oh shit, course it did," Jo agreed. "Mind you, I didn't see a computer or anything looking like a recorder ..."

"I doubt they're dummies though, that wouldn't make sense. If Lane had told his insurers ... I wonder who this is?" he mused on seeing a dirty, scruffy, silver saloon pass by, its obviously broken exhaust spewing dark clouds of something noxious into the damp, chilled air. "Let's go see."

The car was parked on Lane's forecourt, at the corner nearest the side entrance.

"Shut," Jo observed needlessly as she and Gerard got to the plain, grey-metal door.

"And silent," Gerard said, equally unnecessarily while stepping back to look for any other possibilities as to where the driver might have gone.

"Wait or knock?"

"Er, well ..." Gerard dithered.

"Knock then," Jo decided, hitting the door with a gloved fist while shouting as loud as she could: Police. "Well?" she asked after a few moments.

"Knock harder!" Gerrard smiled, his mind quite randomly picturing the caricature Englishman abroad: if they don't understand you first time, shout. So, taking over from Jo, he rapped with drum-like sharpness on the door three times before bellowing. Seconds later the sound of a lock being turned replied. "See!" he laughed.

The guy that opened the door looked genuinely shocked, his slightly odd shaped eyes - one big, round and wide open, the other seeming to peer through a narrow slit - flicking from Jo to Gerard and back.

"Police," Gerard said conversationally while holding open his Warrant Card. "Can I ask who you are?"

"I ... Cory Carpenter. I work here," the still startled guy replied.

"Oh, right," Gerard smiled. "I'm Detective Sergeant McAvoy, I left you a message ...?"

"Really?"

"You didn't get it?" Gerard asked, a little challengingly.

"No ..."

"So, why you here?"

"Lainey called ..."

"Lane? Mr Denny Lane?"

"No, his sister, Elaine ..."

"His sister's called Elaine Lane?" Jo asked, a rueful giggle in her voice.

"Yeah. Well, No. Not now," Cory corrected himself. "She's Carpenter now."

"As in, you're Carpenter?" Gerard asked, a look of confusion now frowning his brow.

"Yeah. She married my brother ..."

"Ah, I see. And why did she call you?"

"Said something had happened. To Denny. Down here. Said Bea'd been on. In a state ..." the guy babbled in staccato half-sentences.

"Right, OK ..." Gerard nodded sympathetically. "Look, I think we need to come in. We need to talk to you."

Cory Carpenter was a sweet, shy and essentially dim guy. Added to which, the poor boy obviously had something wrong with a hip or leg, meaning he walked with the kind of painfully lopsided gait usually reserved for butlers in comic horror films, or jailers in a Dickens novel. Save he was too young for either role, being no more than early twenties.

As Gerard explained the little they knew, so Cory's mismatched eyes seemed to grow duller and duller. Dull with disbelief. Not - Gerard and Jo both thought - with anything suggesting either real fear or suspicious knowledge. For all that he came across as totally and honestly worried for his boss, friend and brother-in-law, he did not give off anything to suggest any insight at all into what had happened.

With a nerdish, enthusiastic, breathless rush he listed the cars left in the garage on Christmas Eve: a Bentley Continental GT; a Porsche GT3 RS; and an Aston Martin DB9. Plus two Ferraris they kept permanently up on the platform for Freddie Carr: a 1971 365 GTB/4 Daytona; and a 1985 Testarossa.

When not talking about cars, Cory's speech was slow, and his thinking slower still. Meaning he often corrected himself midway through a point. He so obviously - like a child eager to please a favourite aunt and uncle - wanted to be helpful, but:

Only he and Denny knew which cars were left, Josh having finished up on Friday. Apart from their owners, Jo had suggested, to which he nodded without seeing any necessity to the point.

No, they'd never had a theft before.

No, he wasn't aware Denny'd had any threats or anything like that - another question which he answered while showing mystification at its asking.

On the practical stuff of facts, Cory was pretty much useless. When asked for contact details for the cars' owners, all he could say was Denny kept lots of stuff locked away in the office, but he didn't know where the keys were. How about Freddie Carr, Gerard had pressed - but he's just up there, Cory had replied, pointing through the walls towards the vastness of the used up quarry.

How about the cctv, Jo had asked. Oh yeah, Denny sometimes does things with that on his iPad, the guy answered.

With the feeling that further questions would be an abuse of poor Cory's guileless complaisance, Gerard gently turned the conversation to next steps. We'll need to come and collect Denny's van tomorrow, can you be here to let us in?

The vagueness of Cory's nod spurred Jo into checking they'd got the right telephone number for him. They had - when he pulled his phone from the pocket of his jacket, together with a half-eaten chocolate bar and a couple of screwed up strips of chewing gum still in their foil - the voicemail waiting message was clear on the screen.

"So, 9am OK then," Jo had pressed, obviously unsure as to when the SOCO team would actually arrive.

"Oh, yeah. That's when we open up anyway," Cory had offered.

"Well, actually," Gerard tried to explain as simply as possible. "We'll need you to keep the place closed till we've got the van, and just checked for any other useful evidence ..."

"But, Denny ..."

"Mr Lane won't be working tomorrow, Cory," he said, as gently and considerately as he could, watching the guy's one good eye looking back at him with confusion and some distress.

"But ..."

"Tell you what," Jo took over. "Let's lock everything up now and then perhaps you might want to talk to your sister-in-law ..."

"She said she was going over for the kids ..."

"Mr Lane's children?"

"Yeah ..."

"Of course. Well, I suspect Mrs Lane will want to go and see her husband in hospital ..."

"Denny's in hospital?"

Jo sighed, sympathetically but with a hint of exasperation. Had the guy just not followed? "I'm afraid so, Cory. Queen Mary's, I believe. But I'm sure Elaine will know. So, let's lock up here now, nothing more we can do till tomorrow …"

And so, with the cares of the world now pressing on the young guy's shoulders, he set to resetting the alarm - something he seemed to be able to do with unthinking, mechanical ease. And then, as fast as he could, to limping to the door.

Once he'd turned the key in the final lock, Jo suggested. "Tell you what, Cory. Why don't we take the keys, keep them safe for you. Save you any worry. You just meet us here at nine in the morning, yeah?"

"OK," the guy accepted, without any hint of doubt as to any sense of rightness in the idea.

"Poor sod," Gerard sighed as they watched Cory Carpenter get in his car, a blank look on his face now.

"Yeah. Guess it took a while to sink in, bless him," Jo agreed, getting in their car.

"Fancy getting some lunch?" Gerard asked, looking at his watch. It was 1.30pm.

"Sure … didn't think much of that pub by the little roundabout though …"

"No. There are a couple of better pubs in the village itself, I think."

As they drove back past the vicarage Jo noticed a car in the drive. "That wasn't there before," she suggested, stopping.

"No, you're right," Gerard nodded, looking back over his shoulder to the old but, by the looks of it, well cared for silver Porsche Boxster.

"Let's try again," Jo decided for them both, switching off the engine.

"Yes?" the instantly smiley, welcoming man asked in a voice that rivalled Martha's for upper class refinement. He was probably in his sixties, but with boyish features and floppy grey hair, cut with boy-band foppishness. His clothes - black shirt, white dog collar, dark grey trousers - left no doubt as to his profession; although his bright red - and seemingly new - slippers did add a certain rebelliousness to the look.

"We're sorry to trouble you. My name is Detective Hartley, this is Detective Sergeant McAvoy. We're from Bromley CID."

"Bromley?"

"Yes. It's … well, it's a little tangled, but it concerns the car place just down here …" Jo tried, pointing out rightwards in the vague direction of Lane's place.

"Dennis' place?"

"So, you know Mr Lane?"

"Why, of course. Why ever would I not?"

"Indeed," Jo nodded. "Can I ask, were you here last night?"

"No, I stayed the night with my daughter over in Wilmington …"

"I see," Jo sighed, not quite hiding a certain dispiritedness.

"But, Detective. What has happened?"

"Could we come in a moment?"

"Yes," the vicar replied, like the answer was so obvious as to make the question otiose. "I'm Robert Cunningham, by the way."

"Cunningham?" Jo repeated, this time failing to mask surprise.

"Yes?" Robert asked rather than answered, while closing the door behind the three of them. "Come through here," he offered, leading them across the square hall to a small study that looked out to the side of the church.

"It's just that our boss," Jo giggled slightly. "Her name is Cunningham."

"Her? A lady detective ... what would she be?" Robert asked enthusiastically, obviously a devotee of crime fiction.

"Detective Inspector."

"A lady Detective Inspector. I'm sure Agatha would have approved."

"Agatha?" Jo asked, thinking the guy was bound to say Christie.

"My wife. Well, my now departed wife ..."

"Oh dear, I am sorry ..."

"Oh, don't be, Detective, don't be. Was five, no, six years ago and ... Well, in this job you do rather have to believe it's all for the best. That she's happy up there waiting ..."

"Of course," Jo nodded, accepting the invitation, delivered with a simple, open-palmed gesture, to sit on the old leather sofa opposite the winged armchair Robert was sitting himself in.

"Now, am I to worry about young Dennis?"

"Dennis?"

"You said something has happened, I believe?"

"Oh yes. Sorry, we've not actually met Mr Lane. But he's been referred to always as Denny ..."

"You haven't met him? Well, I don't think many people work Boxing Day, police people and clergymen excepted!"

"What I mean, Sir," Jo explained, her mind now focused, her voice calm. "Is this. We came here earlier, and found Mr Lane tied up and unconscious ..."

"Oh no!"

"We think, I mean, the paramedics were pretty certain, he will be OK. He didn't appear injured as such, just drugged."

"Oh dear," Robert sighed, leaning forward in his chair, his elbows resting on his knees, his rounded chin resting in his cupped hands. "But ... how? Why?"

"Well, we need to do a little more work, and hopefully talk to Mr Lane tomorrow. But ..."

"Of course, the cars!"

"Indeed, I'm afraid ..."

"Alfred will be totally beside himself."

"Alfred?"

"Mr Carr. I take it that's what you were about to say. Someone has beaten poor Dennis around the head to steal Alfred's lovely cars ...!?"

"Eh, well, Yes. Actually, we believe there were five cars taken in total. But Yes, we have been told Mr Carr kept two rather old cars there ..."

"I think he'd prefer you said vintage," Robert smiled without losing the look of genuine sadness from his eyes.

"Of course," Jo nodded. "And I should just say, Mr Lane does not appear to have been seriously harmed. Not bumped on the head ..."

"Oh Yes, sorry. You did say," Robert nodded thoughtfully, sitting back in his chair again. "And you asked if I was here last night, so I take it that is when you think it all happened?"

"It is."

"I see. Well, like I said, No. I went to my daughter's after the midday service. Came back around six for Evensong and got away again at ... hmm, a little after eight. I'm not precise on the time ..."

"No worries. We're fairly certain it happened in the small hours, between around three-thirty and six-thirty ..."

"I see ... and Mrs Lane, the children?"

"The children, we understand, are now with Mr Lane's sister - we spoke to Cory ..."

"So you told Cory. Poor lad. How did he ... I mean, did he ...?"

"He seemed shocked, Sir. Perhaps not at first, but in the end I think he understood ..."

"Poor lad."

"You seem to know them a bit then Sir?" Gerard asked.

"Well, that's a vicar's job, Detective Sergeant," Robert grinned. "But ... well, I guess I'm a frustrated boy racer. Can't resist the chance to look at a nice sports job."

"Then it is my duty to warn you," Gerard began, with a generous smile all over his face. "To take great care in that car of yours. I take it the Porsche ...?"

"Ah Yes. My little indulgence! I bought that after Agatha ... well, you understand. Dennis keeps it looking nice for me ... I do hope he gets better quickly," the vicar wished out loud. "Oh dear, that must have sounded a bit selfish!" he laughed.

"I perfectly understand, Sir ..."

"How did Alfred take the news then?" Robert asked a little gravely.

"Well, actually, we've only just found out about the actual cars ... Just met Cory a few moments back. But he ..."

"So, he doesn't know yet?"

"Mr Carpenter didn't have a telephone number or anything. That's something we were going to look up later ..."

"He only lives up there," the vicar interrupted.

"Up where, Sir? Not the quarry ...?"

"No, don't be daft. Although it is just the other side. Hill Crest ..."

"Hill Crest?"

"Yes, just out of the village, left up towards Dartford Heath."

"Actually, I do know it," Gerard nodded.

"I see ... Er, sorry," the vicar suddenly asked. "Did you say you're from Bromley?"

"Yes, Sir. We are. Local police were here earlier. But Mr Lane lives in our borough ..."

"I see. But you obviously know the area."

"Well, I cycle a bit Sir ... But, as it happens, I actually had occasion to visit Hill Crest a few months back."

"So, you should be able to find it easily enough. Let me take off my Christmas present," Robert offered, jumping from his chair while nodding down to the slippers. "And I'll come with you. Alfred will be very upset. Might help you if I'm on hand ..."

Printed in Great Britain
by Amazon